More Like Enemigas

More Like Enemigas

STEPHANIE HOPE

ISBN-13: 978-1-335-52609-0

More Like Enemigas

For questions and comments about the quality of this book, please contact us at CustomerService@Harlequin.com.

Carina Press
22 Adelaide St. West, 41st Floor
Toronto, Ontario M5H 4E3, Canada
www.Harlequin.com

HarperCollins Publishers
Macken House, 39/40 Mayor Street Upper,
Dublin 1, D01 C9W8, Ireland
www.HarperCollins.com

Printed in U.S.A.

1 2 3 4 5 6 7 8 9 10 HDC 28 27 26 25

To my husband, James, and my daughter, Selena.

Chapter One

Come in. We're Open.

I turn the sign to face the street, alerting anyone passing by that La Mariposa restaurant is here and ready to welcome guests. I twist the lock and turn on the neon "OPEN" sign. The light buzzes slightly before shutting off completely. I tap it a few times, but the bulb continues to flicker. *Useless junk.* I grab it and shake it furiously, capturing the attention of the prep cook, José, who is undoubtedly side-eyeing me while he takes out the premade sandwiches. The sign finally beams a solid blue hue. I pair the Bluetooth speaker with my phone to play the only playlist my mother approved. It's a cringy combination of songs from Celia Cruz, Elvis Crespo, and some other artists that were most certainly the hits during her youth. If I have to listen to "Suavemente" one more time, I may just drown myself in the fish tank by the door. It would be a lovely welcome. Maybe it'll even bring more customers to the restaurant.

"Hi, welcome to La Mariposa! Oh, the dead woman in the tank? It's for ambiance. Enjoy the croquetas!" I guess having the news talk about a local Hispanic woman who drowned in her late father's restaurant is not the PR I need. Not all press is good press.

I've been listening to this playlist long enough to drown it out, but every so often, I can still hear the faint sounds of Celia Cruz crescendoing into my eardrums.

"Not today, Celia," I groan as I put large glass bottles filled with water on each table.

I pull my dark curly hair back into a ponytail. A few pieces fall in the front and frame my face. I tie my apron a little bit tighter around my crisp, white button-down shirt and get to work straightening the forks next to a few plates, then refolding a few napkins until they look identical to the others, and, finally, switching out a cup I swear has hard water stains. Everything looks perfect. As usual.

I walk over to the tall counter at the back. This is where the orders are taken and where I typically spend a ten-hour shift handling the customers and paperwork and occasionally heading to the kitchen to help prep. That is, if I haven't already stayed overnight the night before to give the kitchen staff a head start by peeling all the vegetables, chopping the potatoes, and relabeling all of the containers. Some would say I'm a bit of a perfectionist. Is it so wrong to want things to look a certain way? Several staff members have complained that I never leave them any work to do. One quit because they didn't see a purpose for them to work here when I did everything for them, but I couldn't help it. If I leave them to their own accord, they'll probably peel the vegetables with the wrong peeler. Or cut the potatoes lengthwise. Or worse, mislabel something and cause chaos during the lunch rush. The last thing I need is someone ordering a cheese croqueta and getting ham. No, it's just better if I do it. I get peace of mind knowing it'll be correct, and it'll spare me endless complaints from my mother that something wasn't up to *her* standards. Mariposa not being happy about something? Imagine that.

My phone buzzes on the counter next to me. I hesitate, wondering what it's about. Sighing, I pick it up and scan the message. It's from a girl I've gone on a few dates with.

Genesis: Hey Isa, thanks for dinner last night. I had a great time, but I don't think this is going to work out. You seem really focused on your business, which is great, but I don't know if there's space for someone else in your life. I admire your dedication, but I need more time together. Wish you the best though.

I stare at the screen for a moment. Why does this always happen? Every single time, the same script, just a different face. It's either I'm too busy, too obsessed with work, or too unavailable. The truth is, they're right. I always find myself more comfortable here, at the restaurant, than I ever do with someone else. Even when I'm on a date, I'm thinking about what needs to get done. I come up with excuses—"just a few emails," "need to check on inventory"—anything to avoid getting too close.

Maybe I just don't want to be close to anyone. Or maybe I'm scared of what happens when I do.

I let out a breath and lock my phone, dropping it back on the counter, where it belongs. The weight of the message lingers, but I push it away.

"Morning, Isa."

I look up from my phone to see Faye sauntering in with an orange-colored iced coffee in their hand.

"Uh, what is that thing?"

Faye looks down at the science experiment the barista concocted and laughs.

"It's a pumpkin spice latte."

"It's still summer." I chuckle, knowing full well it's the end of summer, meaning it's basically fall.

"Listen, it's September. Kids are back in school, and I'm ready for pumpkin-flavored everything," Faye says.

They take a long, exaggerated sip of their drink and sigh deeply. "Tastes like heaven."

I roll my eyes and smile.

"Hey, cute bag. Is that new?" Faye walks behind the counter and grabs their apron.

I watch as they fix their eyeliner in the small mirror they pull out of their bag. They play with their pixie cut, ensuring that each strand is neatly placed on the top of their head. I look down at my black Coach bag hanging off one of the shelves behind the counter.

"Thanks! Yeah, it is." I grab my bag and slowly push it out of sight. "Could you prepare the pastelitos?"

"Oh, you mean the ones you already prepared last night?" They laugh and fill the display case with the guava and cream cheese pastries I left out on the counter.

Faye is one of my recent hires, and adding them to the staff is truly the best decision I have made for the business. They are younger than me, around twenty, meaning they're still full of hope and ambition. They're much taller too; some would even describe them as "lanky." Every day, they show up in their straight-leg '90s vintage jeans, a teeny band tee they cropped just enough to barely expose a sliver of their pale stomach when they reach up, and their reliable pair of black Doc Martens. I used to detest their attire—not because I cared, but because my mother had a ton of complaints about how it didn't fit the restaurant. Her constant comments seeped into my head, even though I secretly admire how Faye never seems to care. But, like clockwork, every day, my mother would come in and complain that Faye's style was too "grunge." It didn't go with the image she has continuously tried to put out for the world since I was little. One of refinement. One that didn't make us look like a typical poor Cuban family with a tiny restaurant where we barely make ends meet. Since they are one of the most reliable employees I have had the pleasure of working with, I managed to convince my mother to drop the issue. They are never late, always work hard, and, most importantly, never judge me for my perfectionism. I like them.

"Thanks for always being so understanding," I say.

"What do you mean?"

Faye continues strategically placing the pastries so they lean slightly on each other. It just looks prettier than if you put them together randomly. They get it.

"I know I can be such a pain in the ass as a boss," I groan.

"You? A pain in the ass?" Faye replies sarcastically.

"Shut up. I know I like things done a certain way and to look a certain way, and I know that it bothers some people—"

I pause momentarily to see José side-eyeing me again while peeling a stack of potatoes.

"—okay, nearly every employee here, but you've always put up with it. Even when I change how you stack the cups or fold the napkins, I just really appreciate it."

"Hey, listen. I get it. This was your father's restaurant. It may not be a Michelin-star experience, but it's important to you. I see how important the details are to you and your mom—I mean, mostly her." Faye laughs.

"Much to my dismay," I admit.

"But let's be honest. This is a way better gig than when I worked at that dental office next door. The sound of the drilling alone was going to be my demise. No, really, I would have ended up on the news in a freak accident with the drill stuck inside my ear or something. So, really, don't worry about me. I went to culinary school for a reason. To be around food. And here I am."

They make a pastelito dance in front of my face and laugh before placing it with the rest of them.

Nestled in Union City, New Jersey, La Mariposa sits on a quiet, unassuming block, surrounded by tall, brick buildings that have been there for decades. The kind of place where fire escapes line the windows and faded murals tell the stories of the neighborhood. The leaves are just starting to change, painting the sidewalks in golds and oranges, a reminder that autumn is creeping in. It's got that '90s Brooklyn vibe, but without the hustle of Manhattan. Instead, there's a sense of familiarity here; it's a place where everyone knows your name and you can't walk down the street without running into someone from your childhood. Union City isn't glamorous, but it's home. It's full of families like ours, immigrants who built their lives from scratch, just like my father did with this café. It's small, but it's ours, and it's been a part of this neighborhood for as long as I can remember.

La Mariposa is one of those hole-in-the-wall places where you never stop talking about it once you find it. You tell everyone about that fabulous Cuban café and bakery that had pastries so good, you wonder how you've lived your entire life without eating them. Not to toot our own horn, but I know we are great. My father created these recipes. Some, I think, even came from his mother.

I remember helping at the restaurant when I was ten, even though it was totally illegal, and my father pulled out what he called "El Libro Sagrado," the sacred book, in the morning, and I knew we were about to eat something out of this world. In there, along with other useless doodles and notes, were handwritten recipes older than I was, and you could barely make out what they said, thanks to his undeniable chicken scratch. My father could, though. Not that it mattered since he never let me see it up close. He said it held too many secrets I wasn't old enough to understand. That one day, I would, but after his passing three years ago, my mother took it and boxed it up along with the rest of his things. I haven't seen it since. Even if I wanted to take the book, I wouldn't be able to get it open since he had a lock on it, because of course he did. My father was notorious for three things: his killer food, his obsession with

Sherlock Holmes—since it was the first movie he saw dubbed when he arrived in the States—and his using said obsession to practically torture me with puzzles my entire life.

Before his death, he emailed me PDF versions of several of his recipes while I was at college so I'd feel closer to home. And now, I run the restaurant that houses all of these recipes for the public to enjoy. The format of the restaurant is simple: you walk to the counter, place your order, and we bring it to wherever you choose to sit. If it's takeout, even better.

I hear the rumbling sounds of a truck just outside the store. It's Sunday, so that must be Carlos with the delivery. Late, of course. He knows exactly how to irritate me. I rush to the door to prop it open since he insists on using the front door instead of the back.

"It's faster this way," he'll argue.

I used to argue back, but my mother waved me off and said it was okay. So, I guess, now I just let him through the front door, much to my annoyance.

"Hey, Carlos, you're late again, I see," I say between clenched teeth.

"I just like to keep you on your toes, Isa," he says, winking.

"Do you need help? I can grab those extra boxes in the—shit."

"Hey, it may be old, but I wouldn't call my truck shit."

"Sorry, no. Not you," I whisper.

Carlos looks over to where my eyes have fixated to see a tall man in a light grey suit walking towards the restaurant. Not just any man, but Gabriel, the owner of the building that houses the restaurant—and my father's longtime friend.

"Who's that acere?"

"Our landlord." I swallow, but my throat is dry. "Is it okay if Faye helps you instead?"

I run inside in a panic and grab my bag. I never let anyone help with the food order, but if I have to, Faye is the only person I trust to do it right. It pains me to ask, but I must keep the landlord outside the restaurant.

"Faye! Can you help Carlos with the inventory today? I have to go…deal with something."

"Really?" Faye pipes up excitedly. "Hell yes!"

We both rush toward the door, but I cut ahead.

"Here's Faye—bye," I say as I scurry toward the landlord, stopping him from heading any closer.

"Hola, Isa. How are you doing today?"

"I'm great, Gabriel. Thanks for asking. So"—I rock on my toes back and forth, feeling antsy—"what brings you to La Mariposa? Here for lunch?"

"As much as I love Roberto's media noches, I'm actually here on business."

"Oh, is that so?" I try to act as blissfully unaware as possible, but I know exactly why he's here. I've been anxiously waiting for this day for months. I brace myself for the dreaded words. The ones I know are coming.

"Your last check bounced, mija. So that's three months now that you haven't paid rent."

"I know, I know. I'm sorry. Here, let me write you another check—I promise it won't bounce this time!" I quickly reach into my bag and pull out my wallet, slowly unzipping it, trying to hold back tears.

"Isa—" He pauses for a moment. "Maybe if you stopped spending money on designer bags and wallets, you'd have money for the rent."

I stiffen, my fingers tightening around my Marc Jacobs wallet. "It's not like that. I… I had money saved—my father's life insurance. It kept us going for a while, but…" My voice trails off as the weight of it all hits me. The money is running out, just like everything else.

I hand over the check. "This should be fine."

"Mija, I'm sorry. I don't mean to be harsh. You know how

much your father meant to me. He was my best friend. You're like a daughter to me. It hurts me to see you struggling to keep the restaurant afloat. I've been putting off coming by to tell you this, but it's been three months. I have mortgages and utility bills I have to pay myself."

"I know, I get it. I'm sorry. If you can just give me a couple more months, I promise—"

"I have someone interested in opening up a burger shop here. They have six months' rent to give me up front," he says softly.

Gabriel really was my father's best friend. He basically helped raise me—like a wacky uncle who always had pockets full of candy to share with me. Whenever he came over, he'd help around the restaurant and just crack jokes with my father for hours. Now he's just an old landlord to me, his grey strands shining through his dark beard and hair. He's just someone who collects our money and leaves.

"I see," I say dryly.

"I can give you one more month to catch up. That's the best I can do, mija. I hate to be this guy, but I'm losing money here too."

"No, I get it. I do. I'm sorry I put you in this weird spot. I'll have the money in a month. Don't worry."

How I'm going to make up three months of rent in one month is beyond me. I can already picture myself putting the "For Rent" sign on the door and losing everything my father built. But I can't give up my father's restaurant so easily. It's all I have left of him.

"Well, I have to get back and open up so we can make some money for you." I turn to walk back to the restaurant, feeling completely defeated.

"Wait, Isa," Gabriel exclaims.

I turn around, watching him pull a white envelope from his suit's inner pocket.

"This is going to sound crazy, but I have something for you. From your father."

"Wait, what?"

I walk back toward him, and he hands me the envelope. It's sealed, and the outside is blank except for my name written dead center: Isabella.

"What is this?" I ask.

"I have no idea. I never opened it. Before your father passed—you know, when he started to get really sick—he gave this to me. Told me to give it to you when I felt you needed it the most."

I nod, feeling the weight of it. Everyone rallied around the restaurant at first, helping out, keeping it alive. But as time passed, people moved on, and then it was just me trying to hold everything together with the little bit of life insurance money we received.

"I figured it was maybe money or a hidden will with a trust fund or something. I'm hoping it is. Something to help get you and your mother back on your feet. I know it's been tough since his death, mija. You've always struggled, but not like this. I hate to see it."

I barely make out the words he says as I'm completely fixated on my name written in pen on the envelope. My father wrote it. I rub the pen marks to feel the indent of each letter.

"Thanks, Gabriel. I'm going to go now," I say in a daze.

My heart pounds loudly in my chest. It's been a while since I found another puzzle from my father. The last one was over six months ago—a simple necklace hanging off it. Now I wear it around my neck, hoping to figure out what exactly it's supposed to open. Maybe the answer is in this envelope.

I tear it open and take out the letter.

Chapter Two

"*Isabellaaaaa,*" Maria shouts in a sing-songy voice as she parades herself around the store like it is her own personal runway. "Que tal, cuz?"

"Oh God," I groan as I stare absentmindedly at the letter. "What do you want?"

"Is that how you speak to your favorite cousin? Honestly, I'm hurt."

"Shut up." I scoff, folding the letter and putting it away. I notice Maria eye it for a moment. She's absolutely going to ask me about it later. *Chismosa.*

Maria is my favorite cousin, but I wouldn't tell her that—it would go straight to her head. She occasionally works at the restaurant, bussing tables and handling phone orders, but she mostly just takes photos and posts them to our social media accounts. It's the one thing I have allowed someone else to do for me, mostly because I seem to repel followers. I tried to create a TikTok once, and I'm pretty sure I got negative views because of how bad it was. Our accounts aren't super successful, and she isn't the best at marketing, but it's the only thing we can afford right now. Hell, her services are free, and I can barely afford that.

Carlos walks up to the counter and hands over the invoice for me to sign. I look at the total, muffle a whimper, and sign the bottom. I hand it over for him to sign. Then, I rip off the top sheet and keep the yellow copy.

"See you at the end of the week? Check out the email I sent you for the new items we will add to the menu, including pumpkin. We must get these, okay? I'm training the cooks on how to make empanadas de calabaza."

"Isabella, don't you ever get a break?"

I'm taken aback by the sudden existential question.

Maria snorts. "Carlos, please."

"Excuse me?" I ask.

"You're always working, Isa. You practically run this store, and you don't even own it. When are you going to find some time for yourself?"

I hear Faye giggle in the back as they put away the new inventory behind the old one. I glance behind me and see José's smirk, which he wipes away when our gazes meet.

"Myself?" I scoff. "And do what?"

"See friends? Date? Get married? Live your life? Aren't you almost thirty?"

"Twenty-five, actually. And date? I just went on a date yesterday!"

"Didn't you say it was awful because she said the word 'like' too much?" Maria chimes in.

"Regardless, I *date*. Sometimes. Once a year," I continue. "Besides, I like my job—no, I *love* my job. Why do I need to do anything else? Also, who will be here to warmly greet you and make sure you give us a discount on our next order because of the broken eggs?"

Carlos shakes his head, folds the copy of the sheet into his pocket, and heads out the door.

"See you later, Carlos," I shout, and he noncommittally waves me away as he disappears from view.

"Isabella Valdes? Dating someone seriously? Could you even imagine?" Maria teases.

"I barely have time to shower and feed my cat before rushing here in the morning," I say. "I don't have the capacity in my schedule to be in a relationship."

"Well, you could if you'd delegate some more tasks to me," Faye suggests with an exaggerated grin plastered across their face. "Or José, of course."

I glance over at José. *El ratoncito*, I call him, because that's exactly how he acts. A quiet mouse scurrying around, avoiding any conflict with my mother or me. He side-eyes me once again, and I wink. His eyes widen, and his cheeks begin to flush. I can't help but laugh.

"Faye, I want to. You know I do. I just—"

"I know, I know," Faye puts their hands up in surrender. "One day."

Even if I did have spare time, dating never goes well. I always get the same reviews: workaholic, perfectionist, and even materialistic.

Besides, dating is the least of my problems these days. My biggest problem is that I have been hiding a secret from everyone in the restaurant. Even my mother. It's easy to do when I am the only one that looks at the monthly and yearly revenue reports. I am the one who deals with the accountant every tax season—the one who pays the bills and orders the food.

The restaurant is failing.

I've tried for the past three years to save it. I put an ad out in the weekly paper. I created discounts and specials. Once, I ordered a big sign that was supposed to say, "DELICIOUS CUBAN FOOD," with an arrow pointing toward the restaurant. I planned to hold it on the sidewalk near the busy intersection in the corner for a few hours and wave it around back and forth. However, when I finally received it, it read, "DELICIOUS CUBAN FOOT" in bold red font. I still considered waving it just to attract attention and then parading my bare foot throughout the restaurant. Surely, people would be curious about what made my foot so delicious. Perhaps the chipped red nail polish I applied two months ago that doesn't seem to give up? Or maybe the blisters on my pinky toes from standing for over ten hours every day in the vintage Prada loafers I snagged for $10 at a thrift shop? Despite my efforts, here we are, almost in the negative for August. Shit.

I lied. Someone does know. Only one person other than my landlord, actually. Mostly because I, quite literally, could not contain the stress in my body. I felt like I would burst any second, so I opted to tell my most trusted cousin, Maria.

"Are you even on the schedule today? I have enough on my plate," I say, but I already know she isn't because I make it, and I have never once made a mistake. She's clearly here to ask about my dating life, or because she feels terrible the restaurant isn't doing well. It's not uncommon for Hispanic kids to feel the guilt of helping their family and doing everything they can to fix whatever issues there are. She's been spending more time in the restaurant than ever, taking photos and videos of everything.

"Nope—just dropping by to take some pics."

She pulls out her phone and starts to film a video of the restaurant, panning full circle. She slows down as she films the murals my father painted on opposite walls. One is of a desert and a man in the distance walking toward a blazing sun. The other is a woman wearing a colorful embroidered dress holding a huge basket filled to the brim with maíz. They lay peacefully on top of the light orange walls we sponge-painted together with a darker hue of orange to create a clay-like pattern. My mother absolutely hates it. She says it's gaudy, tacky, cheesy, and every other synonym of the word. She wants to change it to a more elegant, modern style. The only reason I've been able to convince her to keep it is that it's the last thing we have that my father did. I can still see him on every crack in the plaster from nailing family photos up. Sure, it looks like the inside of a maraca, but it's got character. It has him.

"Wave to the camera," Maria instructs as she slowly pans toward the counter.

Oh, God. I wave weakly and bare my teeth into what I think is a smile. Faye runs behind me and waves both their arms up dramatically.

"Isabella, you look constipated. Can you look more natural?"

"I'm trying!" I bare my teeth wider now, undoubtedly looking as if a large mythical snake has petrified me.

"Okay, I'll just cut that part out. This is why *I'm* the face of social media here," Maria says as she flips her hair off her shoulder. She is definitely a good face to have for our accounts. Her darker olive skin tone, complimented by her honey hair, makes her nothing short of an absolute knockout. Mix that with her perfect smile and undeniable curves, and you have the ideal spokesperson to garner attention from the Jersey audience. Maria puts her phone down and grabs my bag.

"Cute bag." Maria grins. Except it's not a typical grin. I recognize this one.

"Shut your face." I put my palm over her mouth.

"What? I didn't say anything. It's cute! I love Coach. Or this one is called, what, Poach?" She snorts.

"Do you want to die? I can make it happen."

"Isa, when will you learn you don't have to buy these fake designer things to impress people? This is why you can't find love. You're lying to yourself. The real Isa is just as cool, if not cooler than this one." She shakes my bag in front of my face.

I sigh. "There is no real Isa."

She looks up at me.

"Sadly, I've been replaced with a bunch of technological parts. I'm a poor android now, Maria. Save yourself," I say in a robotic voice.

"Pendeja. Even as a cyborg, you're lame and poor." Maria throws my bag at me, but I catch it before it slams into my face.

"Why don't we ever have arroz con leche? It's my favorite," she says, changing the subject as she looks into the dessert case.

"Because life doesn't revolve around you. Also, you know my mother's rule. She hates it and won't let us sell it." I roll my eyes.

Maria reaches for a Malta in the small cooler on the end of the counter. Nothing beats the carbonated malt beverage.

"That'll be $1.25," I state with my hand outstretched.

"Put it on my tab." Maria winks and takes another swig.

"You don't have a tab. We don't do tabs here," I complain. "A buck twenty-five."

"Jeez, are we doing that badly?" She sighs and pulls out two dollar bills. "Keep the change."

"Maria!" I look behind me frantically to make sure no one hears her.

"Relax, Isa. No one can hear me," she whispers.

"Still. Don't say things like that. You'll get into the habit and say it at the wrong time. No one is supposed to know about this. No one. Especially not my mother. You know better. And"—I point my finger directly between her eyes, making her go cross-eyed—"you pinky swore."

"Have you considered..." Maria pauses momentarily, looking serious. Suddenly, I'm concerned. She looks around to make sure no one is listening. I inch closer to her. "...selling feet pics on the internet?"

"I'm going to slap you. Be serious."

"I am being serious! People make a ton of money exploiting their little piggies. Maybe this is your calling. I always knew you'd be destined for greatness."

"I fucking hate you. Just promise you won't say anything to anyone."

"You got it, Isa. Mum's the word. Anyways, there is a reason

I came in today besides showing off my beautiful face. I have chisme," she says with a grin.

"You? Have gossip? What a surprise," I retort. "You know, whenever you tell me your chisme, it makes me wonder why the hell I'd tell you my biggest secret."

"That's easy. Because you love me, and I'm amazing. It's not that hard to understand. Plus, we have a pact, remember?"

She did a pinky promise, and that means something. Or it did when we were eight and she peed the bed, and I had to promise not to tell our other cousins so she wouldn't appear lame. To this day, no one knows that she peed on the bed. No, they think it was me. So *I* now have to live with that embarrassment every holiday when our families get together. But we promised, and I would never break that. I just have to hope she feels the same way. Still, it feels like a ticking bomb.

"This is good news, though. So you know our cousin Sofia?"

"Uh, maybe? We have, like, ninety cousins. I have no doubt I have a cousin named Sofia somewhere in New Jersey."

"Wow, you're really gonna play dumb? She's Tía Rosita's daughter. We used to play together when we were younger. You were obsessed with hanging out with her and her best friend. You had the joint quinceañera? Remember when Val—"

"Sh, sh," I say, putting my hand to her mouth. "We don't talk about that. What about her? Did she die?"

"Isa, no." Maria gasps jokingly. "She's getting married to some rich guy. Didn't you get the invitation?"

"No idea what you're talking about. Plus, I'm busy." I groan and turn back to my phone to clear out my emails.

I did get the invitation. It sits on top of the stack of rent-increase notifications, overdue credit card bills, and student loan statements I've been avoiding.

"Okay, I know you did because she told me she sent them to us. Are you just going to ignore it?"

"What do you expect me to do? I have a restaurant to run, and you know my mother. Oh, is that a customer coming in?"

Maria turns around to see a tall man walking toward the door. Whenever we have a customer, I feel like we're one step closer to getting out of the red for the month. Just as I genuinely believe he will step inside, he turns and heads down the strip to the dry cleaners.

"Whomp whomp," Maria taunts. "Time to get the 'closed for good' sign ready."

"Get out," I say, turning around to refill the straw container and keep myself busy.

"Isabella, let me finish! This is important."

I sigh loudly, turn around, and raise my eyebrows to signal her to continue with this boring tale of family members I don't care about.

"Sofia is getting married to some guy who comes from a rich family. I mean, good for her, right? Go Sofia. Couldn't be us, am I right?" She snorts.

"Maria!"

"Anyways, get this. Her husband is a restauranteur and investor."

She pauses. I stare at her, waiting for her to continue, getting increasingly impatient. I can't understand why she can't ever get to the point in her stories.

"*Annnd?*" I say, exasperated at this point.

"Stupid, he's an investor. You could go to her wedding, impress her fiancé with a snazzy business plan, maybe even cook him a few meals to try from El Libro Sagrado, and win an investment."

"First, I can't get into my father's book. It's locked. Second of all, why the hell would I do that?" I laugh, though the thought of my father and his letter sits heavily in the back of my mind, its mystery nagging at me even as I try to focus on Maria. What was in that letter? And why did he leave it for me now?

"To save the restaurant, pendeja," she whispers.

"Maria, how exactly do you think this will save the restaurant?" I whisper back, realizing Faye is in the kitchen prepping some bread for the lunch rush, the only time of day we see an influx of customers in the store.

I stack a few menus to put in front of the register. All the baked goods are ready to be sold to a good home. José has already given me his silent nod of approval. La Mariposa is ready for business.

"Okay, so I was talking to our Tía Maritza, and she heard from our cousin Felipe, who heard from Alessandro that Sofia's fiancé mentioned to Sofia that he wants to invest in a Latin restaurant. Apparently, his family owns a few different restaurants throughout New Jersey and New York, and he wanted to branch out independently. This could be your chance to save La Mariposa. I already spoke to Sofia about it, and she's thrilled to have you come and to help you with the opportunity."

I pause, narrowing my eyes. "Wait. Why would Sofia even care about helping me? We haven't really talked in years."

Maria rolls her eyes, exasperated. "Come on, Isa. Just because you two lost touch doesn't mean she's completely forgotten about you. You guys were close growing up, remember? Every family party, every movie night. You were practically inseparable until—well, you know. Don't overthink it. You two used to be like sisters. Trust me, she wants to help."

"So, what? I show him a business plan, cook some meals, and he invests in the restaurant. That's it?"

"Basically." Maria shrugs. "You just need to wow him with the dishes and speak highly of the restaurant. It'll be so easy, and you come back a hero. De nada, prima."

I feel a flutter of hope inside my gut. Is this my saving grace? The exact opportunity I need to save the restaurant secretly, and no one is the wiser? My mother would continue believing I never fuck anything up. That we still live the life she thinks we do—the one in which the restaurant is still thriving and my father didn't leave us too soon. Maybe I could even buy her out and keep the restaurant under my own name. The excitement builds up inside my chest.

"That doesn't sound so bad. Just pop in the day of, borrow the kitchen for a minute, show him the plan, and then leave a hero."

"Well, so?" Maria chuckles nervously.

"Oh, God… I'm scared to ask," I groan.

"You know Sofia—she's so extra! And she's marrying rich, so what more can you expect from her, right?"

"Spit it out."

"Okay." She sighs. "It's kind of a week-long thing at the summer camp she used to go to every year as a kid. Her only requirement is that you have to go for the six days. It's a few hours away, in the Berkshires."

She blurts everything out so quickly that I have to sit for a second to process everything. I grew up with Sofia, and if there's one thing I won't ever forget, it is how unbelievably jealous I was that she got to go to summer camp every single year. After watching the movie *The Parent Trap* an obscene number of times, I wanted nothing more than to go to camp and find my long-lost twin sister who lived in a fancy home in London, and we would get to switch places. She would get to live in a cramped apartment in New Jersey, in $10 shoes, and I would get to live a life of luxury, owning real designer things. I always thought about how impressed everyone would be that Isabella made it.

One summer, I desperately begged my mother to let me go with my cousin, but she couldn't afford it. I told her I could talk to Tía and see if she could pay for me since she had offered before, but she shut down that notion immediately. It's been a long time since I thought about summer camp, and the opportunity to finally go isn't lost on me.

"So I'd be gone for a whole week?"

Maria nods slowly, anticipating my next move.

"My mother probably won't be invited to the wedding, right?"

"Um, estas loca? Did you forget the drama between Rosita and Mariposa? It's practically an urban legend at this point," Maria recalls.

I didn't forget. If our life were a telenovela, this would be the mystery we'd be trying to solve. When we were fifteen, something happened between Tía Rosita and my mother at our joint quinceañera. No one ever knew what it was, but whatever happened caused chaos when my mother forced both sides of the family to choose between her and Rosita. I guess Maria found a way to stay in touch with Sofia since her mother wasn't directly involved. On the other hand, I wasn't allowed to even think about them. This fact alone will mean that convincing my mother to watch the restaurant while I'm gone will be damn near impossible.

"Yeah, no. I'm not doing that," I decide.

"What? Isa, why not? This is a great opportunity."

"I can't just leave the restaurant for an entire week for something that isn't definite. Who is going to run the restaurant while I'm gone? What am I supposed to tell my mom? 'I'm going to the wedding of the family you hate'? 'The one you envied my entire childhood because they made more money than we could ever'? 'The one you had too much pride to contact when my father died'? Not to mention that this place will fall apart without me. I can't. Thank you for thinking of me, but I just can't."

The thought of leaving the restaurant in someone else's hands makes my palms sweaty. How would they know how to open it properly? And I'm supposed to be gone for six days, hours away, at some random summer-camp-themed wedding for a cousin I haven't seen in ten years? It's just not possible. Still, I feel like this could be precisely what I need, and I can't shake the feeling that it would solve all my problems. But, no, I can't.

"Oof, well then, you're gonna love this next piece of chisme I have for you," she chuckles.

"What more could you possibly have to say?" I moan.

"Well, I already told Sofia you'd do it, and it starts tomorrow."

Chapter Three

The lunch rush came and went with only a few stragglers left behind, which means my mother will be showing up any minute now. She loves to make her entrance as if the rush was a success thanks to her. Almost like a celebrity appearance. The restaurant always looks like it's been raided after lunch. It's our only real rush these days—mornings are dead, and evenings are barely better. Once the lunch crowd clears, it feels as if we're just waiting for the lights to go off for good. No wonder we're struggling to stay afloat. The display case under the counter that holds all of our pastries is practically empty. Faye restocks the cooler with Maltas, Jupina pineapple soda, and the usual Coke products. José is baking to refill the pastry case. Maria is tidying the dining room, picking up dirty dishes and readjusting the chairs to their proper tables. This is always the best part of the day for me. There is something so satisfying about taking something in complete disarray and organizing it, with everything in its place. It's sweet, angelic music to my perfectionist ears.

"Thanks for the meal, Isa! Always delicious," a customer shouts as they leave the building.

I wave back, but they can't see me. I watch the cars peel out of the parking lot onto the highway, my gaze drifting aimlessly—until I spot my mother approaching from across the street. My stomach tightens as she walks toward the restaurant, her expression unreadable, but knowing her, there's something on her mind.

My throat clenches as I watch my mother approach through the front door, and I still haven't digested the news Maria shared with me earlier. I remember seeing the invitation from Sofia in my inbox and feeling excited before promptly remembering I wouldn't be able to go. My mother would have a stroke at the idea of me attending.

"You're a grown-ass woman, pendeja. Just tell her you're going to the wedding," Maria remarks.

"It's not that easy. You know her." I roll my eyes. "I need a better strategy than that."

I feel like I need an entire month to prepare to say anything to my mother. Mentally, emotionally, hell, even physically. Even a written speech I proofread several times and practiced in front of a mirror. Maybe I should learn how to squeeze out a tear or two like the dramatic actresses I watch in telenovelas.

I never know how she is going to react. She's like a ticking time bomb, patiently waiting for me to make the one mistake that confirms her suspicions about me. That, despite her best efforts to ensure I was always presentable and did everything right, I'm not actually perfect, and "where did she go wrong?" Even now, at twenty-five, a quarter of my life has already been lived, and I'm scared to talk to my mommy. Whenever I know she's about to show up, I clam up like I did something wrong. It's the guilt. The undying chronic guilt. Luckily, by this point in our relationship, I have learned the usual steps to ensure a good conversation with Mariposa. One, stay interested in whatever she says. Two, remember she won't ask about your life. She doesn't care. Three, be assured that our talks are always short and, well, not so sweet.

"Hola, Lucia!" My mother calls out to one of our regulars, still finishing her lunch. Lucia always lingers a little longer, hoping to chat—or gossip—with my mother as if they'd known each other forever, even though she is just a customer.

I feel the hairs on the back of my neck immediately prickle at the sound of her voice. I swallow what feels like a huge lump, causing discomfort in my chest. I cough to settle it down. Looking up, I notice my mother heading toward another customer finishing lunch.

"Mari! It's been so long! You look great."

My mother spins slowly, showing off her flowy, undeniably too-expensive dress.

"¿Verdad? It's new."

"Well, it's fabulous. And this bag!"

She leans in to look at the bag closer, making me sweat slightly. It's a Prada bag I got for my mother a couple of years ago. I spent all summer scraping up the little bit of extra money from my paycheck here to get it for her. So now she parades around town with it.

"Gracias. My daughter got it for me—one of the only good things she's gotten for me, verdad?" She laughs, but her words sting. They always do.

"Don't you mean *Frauda*?" Maria whispers in my ear.

I snap my head around and glare at her.

"You shut your trap, or I'll feed you to the goldfish."

It's not surprising that Maria can effortlessly identify a fake. Fashion is her passion. Despite spending all my money, I still couldn't afford the real deal. I found this bag in one of those online secondhand stores. I should have known it was a fake when it was only $150. I just hope no one else notices as easily. At least my mother didn't grow up around expensive things and can't possibly tell the difference.

"Are you going to Sofia's wedding? I saw Rosita post about it on Facebook. I'm glad we stayed friends online before we stopped working together at the firm so I could stay on top of the chisme," Lucia says, smirking.

"Oh, I didn't hear anything of it."

My mother flips her hair slowly behind her head. Her attempt at acting smooth and cavalier. Inside, I'm sure she's fuming. She hates when anyone brings up Rosita's name.

"Bueno, I can't wait to see the photos. It's supposed to be a whole week's event, and only thirty people were invited. It feels very exclusive, verdad? Like a celebrity wedding. It makes me want to crash it."

"Si," my mother replies dryly. "Well, I'll let you get back to your food. I need to get to work."

She turns around abruptly and starts heading in my direction. *Shit.* I nudge Maria to walk away.

"Hola, Tía!" Maria says as she's about to walk away.

"Maria! You are looking gorgeous these days."

"Oh, gracias, Tía." She does an awkward curtsy and tries to shuffle away.

"You'll have to tell me your secrets for your body. I need to get on that diet immediately." She laughs.

"It's just genetics, mostly, I think." Maria shrugs, shifting from side to side.

"Maybe you can teach Isabella a few things. So she can quit those Maltas and get rid of this," she says as she pinches my lower stomach tightly, making me wince.

"Mami!"

"Ay, I'm just kidding, mija. But you do need to eat healthier. No es bueno. You should care more about your figure and how you present yourself," she mumbles as she rummages through her purse, looking for a compact mirror to double-check that she has no lipstick on her teeth.

I glance over at Maria, who is side-eyeing us while she pretends to clean a table. She is such a little shit.

"How was the rush today, mija?" She walks around the store

with her hands clasped behind her back, inspecting the restaurant. This is comparably worse than when the actual health inspector visits.

"Great! Super busy, as usual." I grit my teeth into a smile. She looks up at me momentarily, fixated on my strange grin, and then returns to her daily inspection. I can already feel the walls of my casual facade crumbling. If there is anything I can't be, it's calm and collected. She knows something is up.

"Que bueno, mija," she says flatly.

I wish I could read minds.

I follow behind her trail like a small bird trying not to lose sight of its mother. She pauses and turns around, causing me to bump into her.

"Cafecito?"

I nod and scamper into the kitchen to pour her some Cuban coffee, which consists of an obscene amount of sugar and espresso. It's truly delicious. As I walk back to the table where my mother has taken up residence, I see Maria through my peripheral, giving me two thumbs up. I turn to her and give her one middle finger up so she'll stop hovering. I don't need a cheerleader right now; I need a miracle worker. I need Walter Mercado to predict how this conversation will go so I can brace myself.

"So"—I put down her coffee and sit across from her—"you've heard about Sofia's wedding."

"Claro, mija. How could I not? Everyone I know hasn't shut up once about it on social media. Your cousin Yolanda is a bridesmaid and has already posted photos from the venue. I can't believe her fiancé bought ese maldito summer camp for her. And they expect only thirty people to show up? What about the rest of the family? It's just like them. Trying to show off how much money they have and how popular they always were."

I watch as she lifts the coffee to her nose, taking a few whiffs. Not because she wants to embrace the delicacy of Cuban coffee but because she wants to judge how I made it. I see her nose crinkle slightly before she takes a sip. It's not good enough for Mariposa, but it'll do—which is basically the tagline for my entire existence for her.

"Yeah, so crazy," I encourage. "It's, like, a whole week-long thing, too." I move cautiously as I gauge her temperament.

"I don't even believe it. Who has the time to attend a wedding for an entire week? And they expect the whole family to stay there the entire time? It's all for show, mija. That's what they're always about."

"Yeah, who has the time?" I repeat awkwardly. "Certainly not us."

"You'll do better than that when you get married, verdad? No week-long circus. Just something elegant and tasteful. For me, por favor. You just need to find yourself a good spouse. When are you going to do that, mija?"

"Mami, when do I have the time? I have to run the store, and need I remind you that every single relationship I've had, you had something to say about."

I pause, thinking about my string of failed dates. But if I am being honest with myself, it wasn't just Mami's constant nagging that ended them—it was me. I could never make enough time, never give them what they needed, because the restaurant always came first. I was always putting out fires at work, too distracted to focus on anyone else. And then, when things got rough in the relationships, I'd start seeing everything that was wrong with them, as if my mother's voice had crawled into my head and pointed out all their flaws. I started blaming them for why things weren't working out—too needy, not serious enough, didn't understand the pressure I was under. But the truth was, I wasn't honest with myself about how much I'd pulled away. I couldn't commit. Not when the restaurant was on the brink of collapse.

It was easier to say they were the problem than admit I wasn't even trying. And now? The idea of letting someone in again feels impossible. But still...part of me wonders what it would be like to stop running, to finally find someone who could see past all the mess I made and want to stick around anyway. But there's no time for that. No time for anything except keeping this place alive.

"That's because no one is good enough for my perfect daughter. You used to always listen to your mama, you know." She squeezes my cheeks with the palm of her hands. "Just promise me you won't have a wedding like that."

I sense a hint of resentment in her words. As if my being single is inconveniencing her when really, it's the only thing keeping this restaurant afloat. If I started dating someone right now, she'd try and get me to break it off so that I would be here to watch the place. It's what she always does. She'll say they're taking up too much of my time or don't make enough money. That I need someone more independent so I can spend more time in the restaurant.

"Sure, Mom," I say halfheartedly.

As if a wedding is anywhere on the horizon for me.

"So, about the wedding..."

I look at my mother, but she's sipping her coffee slowly, her face expressionless. I subtly glance over at Maria, who's hiding behind the counter now, pretending to take phone orders. She nods and fans her hand toward me to urge me to continue. I sigh deeply.

"I think I should go," I blurt recklessly.

She chokes on her last sip of coffee.

"Why would you do that, Isabella?"

The way she says my name instantly turns me into a small child on the verge of tears. No, I must be strong. *Stand your ground, Isa. The future of the restaurant depends on it.*

"Well, her fiancé is an investor, and I thought it would be

a great way to expand the restaurant by showing him a business plan. All I'd need is to make a few dishes. We could end up making more money. It would be good exposure and—"

Suddenly, a hand is in front of my mouth, covering my next word.

"Absolutely not. We don't need their money."

Yes, we do.

"And we certainly don't need their exposure."

Yes, we certainly do.

"Mami, if this is about you and Tía, I—"

Her hand reaches back toward my mouth.

"Ch, ch, ch, ch, we don't talk about that," she says, shushing me.

"But no one even knows what happened between you two," I state, pushing her hand away softly.

"And it's going to stay like that. They're toxic. You are not going to their wedding, mija. Especially to beg for money. End of discussion." She stands up, grabs her bag quickly, and rushes out the door.

I sit there for a moment, in shock about what just happened. Surprised? No. Shocked. Definitely. Mariposa would never let her pride falter. Begging them for money would be a cardinal sin to her.

"Well, shit," Maria croaks. "What now?"

"Don't worry. I'm going over tonight to help her make dinner. I have to go to this wedding. It's my last chance to save my father's restaurant. I have one final trick up my sleeve."

"Okay, prima, but it better be a good one."

I head down the street toward my mother's apartment building, which is about twice the size of mine. She's rented there for thirty years—my entire life and then some. When you think of people who live in the city, the true locals, my mother would be one of them. She notices every time someone new moves into the building or when someone leaves. She's been around through the neighborhood's gentrification and watched as so many businesses had to close shop.

When I was younger, I remember my father saying that he wanted to open a restaurant for me and my mother that could stand the test of time. One that wouldn't be affected by the economy or the neighborhood shifting. One that could withstand it all. La Mariposa closing is absolutely not an option. It's his legacy. It was supposed to be mine.

I stand in front of her building. The five stories are mocking me, daring me to enter. I have half a mind to just walk over to the Dunkin Donuts in the corner, eat my weight in munchkins, and just go to the wedding. But I can't. I grip my coat pocket, feeling my father's letter burning a hole through the fabric. What if it's something I'm not ready to hear? Something that changes everything? I've carried it with me all day, but the thought of opening it feels too final, too emotional. Part of me isn't ready to face whatever my father left for me in his final words. I walk up to the door and let myself in through the main lobby. I consider using the elevator but decide the stairs are a better option. I'll get some movement in and have a bit more time to figure out exactly how I will convince her to let me go. I really only have one thing—the secret weapon. I'm not sure if it will work, and I have never had to use it before, but it's my only option.

The closer I get to her door, the more pungent the smell of seasoned black beans becomes. It's almost intoxicating. I can already picture myself chowing down on a massive plate of rice and beans, maybe even with plantains on the side for good measure. Finally, I reach the front door, just a mere few inches away from the peephole. I take a deep breath, already dreading this visit just like every other visit, and let myself in.

"Hola, Mami!" I try to sound enthusiastic and like we didn't have a weird tiff at the restaurant earlier.

"Hola, mija." She sounds fine. The tone of her voice doesn't indicate that she's still upset. This is a good sign. If I want to get to this wedding, I must approach it lightly. Strategically.

Years of practice have taught me that I should be doing something the second I step inside her house. Whether it's cleaning or cooking, I need to be helping in some way. I can't walk into my mother's house and relax. That's just not allowed here. God forbid I ask her if she wants help. That's like committing a cardinal sin. She'd argue that I shouldn't have to ask her if she needed help. I should just "pick up a broom and start sweeping."

Even when my father was alive, when I wasn't at the restaurant bothering him, I just helped her around the house, even though she constantly left it spotless. This has led me to always be on edge when I come over. It's one of the reasons I was so excited to get my own place. For peace and quiet. The lack of guilt if I just want to spend the entire day on the couch binge-watching trash TV.

My mother is standing above the stove, methodically stirring the black beans. There's a moment of silence between us.

"Did you visit Papi today?" I ask casually as I rush to the kitchen to cut the plantains to prepare them for frying.

"Si, claro, mija. I always do." She doesn't look up from the stove.

Something tells me she knows I'm still hung up on the wedding.

"I brought him the flowers you picked out."

My father passed away three years ago from cancer. I was in college studying business when I got the call from my mother that he was placed in hospice. I planned to get my degree and help him run the restaurant with all my new knowledge. His death was difficult for me. It still is. It's like he's still around me, especially at La Mariposa. My mother changed a lot. She had always been demanding, overbearing, and tightly wound. Now she's worse—she's bitter, too.

Growing up, he was the breadwinner, and my mother stayed home to raise me. She relied on him financially, but most importantly, they seemed inseparable. Every night, like clockwork, he'd bring my mother a candy bar and a bouquet of flowers he'd pick up on his way. He would tell her he chose that one with his heart and then kiss her forehead. She'd complain that it wasn't one of the nicer candy bars that come with gold wrapping and taste of hazelnut. I'd giggle at their back-and-forth while I stole her candy bar. I was lucky to have grown up with him my entire childhood. Losing him at a younger age would have probably been even more devastating. We were a dynamic duo. Now it's just my mother and me. Two broken women trying to move on.

"I miss him."

"Me too, mija." My mother continues stirring, not even bothering to connect with me.

"Do you ever wonder if Tía Rosita misses him too?"

She stops stirring. I take a gulp. I'm skating on thin ice.

"No, I never wonder that, because I don't care if she does. Where were they when Roberto died?"

"Mami, maybe they wanted to be there. You haven't exactly been the most welcoming family member."

I start handing her the plantains as she fries them in bunches of five.

"Isa, please. Do you really think they cared about us? They had their amazing life, and we were always struggling. If only your father had chosen a different career, we would have been in a much better place."

I knew she started to resent him a lot when she realized later that owning a restaurant wasn't the money-maker she'd envisioned. I'm not saying my mother is a gold digger, but she has always wanted to present herself like we were more successful than we were. To always be perfect. Nothing can go wrong in her eyes, so they can't go wrong in mine, either.

"Then why don't you just sign over the restaurant to me? Then you wouldn't even have to deal with it, and I can handle everything?" I ask, almost pleading.

She plates the plantains and adds more to the frying pan.

"Because it's all I have left of Roberto. It's how we make our money, mija. Right now, it's working—everything coming in, we manage just fine. But if you took over…well, things might be different. You'd be making decisions, taking a salary, and there wouldn't be as much left over for me. How else would I be able to live here? I'm just thinking about how we can keep everything balanced the way it is."

"Mami, you bought this place and no longer have a mortgage. I'm the only one using my paycheck for rent. You'll be fine. And you could still visit every so often."

Hopefully, not too often. Her giving up the title to me would mean I wouldn't feel tethered to her anymore. I could run the restaurant the way I want. I'd be free.

I shift between my legs, exhausted after running the restaurant the entire day.

I don't dare appear tired in front of my mother, though. I wouldn't hear the end of her rant about how tired she is, because I'm just not allowed to feel exhausted compared to her.

She grabs two plates and begins to serve the both of us, ignoring my plea—I knew better than to bring it up again. I remember when it used to be three plates. I'm sure she does too. I look down at the dish, the perfectly cooked steaming pile of rice with black beans poured over on top. Several plantains sit comfortably on the side, a garnish I can't wait to shove into my mouth. I slowly chew on my food, thinking of how to unleash the secret weapon. The be-all and end-all. The "Can Only Use Once" card. It's now or never. And by never, I mean the restaurant will inevitably close, and I will have single-handedly ruined my mother's life and my father's legacy and be forever known as the World's Worst Daughter.

"Mami, I'm going to the wedding," I state. "It's what Papi would have wanted for me."

She slams her fork on the table, causing me to jump.

"Isabella, how dare you! What do you know about what your father would have wanted?"

"Mami, he loved Sofia, and we all had a good relationship growing up. Did you think I'd forget? I'm sure he'd at least consider going to her wedding if he was alive right now. Whether you like it or not, we're all still family. Not to mention, I'd finally be able to go to that summer camp. The one *you* would never let me attend. I deserve at least that much."

I watch her face closely, analyzing every muscle movement to determine how this conversation may go. I swear I can see a twinkle of sadness shining through. This is the moment. I take a deep breath.

"Also, attending this wedding will be a great way to show the family how well we're doing. I mean, look at you." I use my fork to point at her outfit. "You look amazing. And that Prada bag? Don't you want the family to know you've made it? Rosita? Nosy Maritza, who would definitely tell the rest of the extended family. Alessandro? They'd all be very impressed with us. We have a thriving restaurant. And then I could make them feel bad for never coming to Papi's funeral. They will see you in a different light. No more 'poor Valdes family.' Don't you think we deserve this? And I won't even bring up the business plan. They don't have to know."

I can't believe I just lied so much to my mother. I'm using her worst trait against her for my own personal gain. I'm literally a monster. I'll have to add this to my "things to talk to my therapist about" list.

"Claro, mija," she says softly, digesting every word I say.

I can almost see the gears turning in her head. Her face lights up more at the thought of doing something petty against my aunt than letting me go because I want to.

"It's for a whole week?" She groans. "How could a wedding be so long?"

I pick up my plate and walk to the garbage can to scrape off the last few grains of rice left behind. I open the fridge and take out the flan for dessert.

"Well, it's a whole thing. The invitation is a bit vague, but it mentions a bridal brunch, the rehearsal dinner, a bridal shower—you know, wedding stuff." I shrug, placing the plate in the sink.

"Well, who will watch the restaurant, then?"

How could she not even consider herself as an option to run it?

"Faye will," I suddenly decide.

My skin tingles at the sirens blaring outside the window briefly. Probably the ambulance coming to take me to the morgue when my mother quickly realizes I'm lying to her about this whole idea.

"I can't trust that jovencita to run *my* restaurant alone. So I'll have to do it. Well, I'll help them. I'll supervise."

Suddenly, I feel panic wash over me. It didn't even occur until she offered to watch the place. Giving up control of the restaurant for an entire week is not ideal in any situation for me, but especially in one where my mother may discover that the business is doing poorly, and I have been keeping it from her for an entire year. I feel regretful about even bringing up this conversation. I should have nipped it when Maria suggested it and forgotten about the wedding. But I'm too deep in it now. There's only one way to go. Sofia knows I'm supposed to show up. Her fiancé is expecting to be wowed. And then there's the book…

I haven't even seen it yet—hell, it's still locked—but I can't help hoping that by the time the wedding rolls around, I'll have it in my hands. If I can just get it open, I could finally discover recipes I've never seen before. It could be exactly what the restaurant needs. Not to mention, Gabriel is waiting for the money. I need this. I'm counting on it, even if I'm not entirely sure how it'll all come together.

"No, Mami. Faye will run it. I'll have them call me every day and I'll leave them detailed to-do lists and procedures. You can stop by like usual, but they can handle it. So you don't need to…do anything. Besides, you already do so much." I can only hope I don't sound suspicious in any way.

"Esta bien, mija. Fine. Go to the wedding and impress the hell out of everyone. Then take a photo of Rosita's face when she finally realizes we've done it. We don't need her. Then I'll frame it and put it on my wall."

"Great! So it's settled then," I say happily.

The letter throbs against my skin, reminding me of my second task.

After dinner, I help her clean up and put away the leftover food. As she's getting everything set up for me to take home, I excuse myself to the bathroom. Walking toward the bathroom at the end of the hallway, as I do every time I visit my mother, I look at each family photo she has hung on the walls, trying to resurface memories of my father. I stare at one of myself as a tiny baby being held by my mother and my father, who is hugging us both from behind. Another one is of my parents at their wedding; my mother has a huge belly. It reminds me of those typical shotgun weddings my Tía Maritza would gossip about. My mother assured me it wasn't one, though. And I believed her—she's not the type of person to plan something so scandalous and potentially damaging to her image.

I keep strolling down the aisle, gazing at every photo until I see the one I wish she'd just take down and burn.

"Mami, why do you keep this freaking photo up?" I grab it off the wall and show it to her. She squints her eyes, unbothered to come any closer.

"What do you mean, mija? It's your quinceañera. Why wouldn't I have it up?"

"Okay, but did you have to choose this photo?" I point to the image of me in an obnoxiously poofy blue dress with a huge rip down the front, layers of tulle spilling out and my big calves showing underneath. My face is red and tear-streaked from crying, and I look as if I've just run a marathon. How could she even think this was worth displaying? Next to me are two other teenage girls. One is Sofia in her beautiful pink dress, looking absolutely ethereal. Even her crown sparkles through the photograph. On my other side is the culprit who mutilated my gaudy dress: Valentina Garcia. Her eyes pierce through me still, sending a shock down my spine.

She shrugs, a smile creeping onto her face. "Because it's real. You're my daughter. Not everything has to be perfect."

"Mami, I look ridiculous."

"You look cute! And it was the only photo I was able to get before—"

"What? Before you and Rosita had this random fight in silence and I never saw them again? I still don't know why you can't just tell me the big secret. Your only daughter," I reply coldly.

She doesn't reply, but I didn't expect her to.

As I approach the bathroom door, I hesitate for a moment. I look to my right and see my mother's bedroom door slightly ajar. I look toward the kitchen, but she's busy washing the dishes, her back completely turned away. This is my only chance. The last thing I need for the trip.

I slither into her bedroom, barely moving the door, and tiptoe toward her nightstand. I quietly open each drawer and shuffle through—just a few painkillers and magazines. I reach my hands in between the mattress and box spring and slide them to the end, then repeat on the other side. Nothing. I head toward her dresser and begin rummaging through each drawer, making sure not to make it look like anything was moved. I silently open her closet and start rifling through the boxes on the floor. At the far back is a box labeled “Roberto’s.” *Bingo.* I reach inside, shuffling through knickknacks, a pair of binoculars, and a few mystery books until I feel a leather-bound journal in my hand. I pull it out.

There it is. The book. The sacred book that houses all of my father’s secrets and recipes I can only vaguely remember the taste of. I reach into my pocket to pull out the letter.

You’ll find what you’re looking for in my journal. You have the key.

So this is it. I’m officially going to Sofia’s wedding. I’m not sure if I will be able to pull this off, but there are a few things I need to do. One, ensure my mother doesn’t discover the restaurant troubles or the missing book while I’m gone. Two, I need to impress everyone, secure that investment, and save the restaurant. And three, I must figure out what my father wants me to find in this book.

Chapter Four

"Everything is going to be fine. Right?"

I'm clutching the steering wheel so hard my knuckles have turned white. I keep my eyes fixed on the open highway ahead, preparing for the exit that's quickly approaching. The wedding week has officially started, and I spent two hours this morning extensively training Faye on all of the procedures, from opening the restaurant to closing it. They probably didn't need all the training, but I just want to ensure everything runs perfectly while I'm gone. This is all happening so quickly. The buzzing in my head is almost distracting.

"It's going to be *fiiine*." Maria sips her caramel iced latte in utter bliss. "You don't think Faye can handle it?"

"No, I'm sure they'll be fine. They basically know how to do everything."

"Then it sounds like you're trying to convince yourself. I don't know why you don't let them run more of the store so you can have free time to, I don't know, date someone and get a life. But, hey, look at that tree! It's changing colors."

Maria points quickly at a maple tree whose leaves have a tint of orange on one section. It went by so fast that I almost missed it, which is how I feel most of the season when I'm stuck inside the restaurant.

"I'm just terrified they're going to open the wrong report and accidentally find out that I've been lying to everyone about the restaurant doing well," I finally say.

"Look, I get it—you've been trying to keep things together. But even if they do see the truth, you're doing the best you can. No one can blame you for that."

I shake my head. "They'll think I've failed. What if they realize how bad things really are?"

"You've got José there to help out for the whole week, and he's loyal. He won't let anything slip. I really don't predict anything going wrong."

"Famous last words," I groan.

I look at the road signs as they pass by. Lee is about thirty minutes away, and that's our final destination. I try to focus on the gorgeous landscape of evergreen trees mixed in with birch and maple, creating a beautiful tunnel through the highway. The trees on either side are mostly green, but here and there, I can see flashes of red, gold, and orange as the leaves turn for the fall foliage. Sweeping rock walls tower over the right side of the car. Large, lush mountains loom over us. I roll down my window and feel the cool breeze wash over me, carrying with it the sweet scent of autumn.

My peace is disrupted by the obnoxious reggaeton music Maria has insisted we listen to. Despite the noise and peaceful drive, I can only think about the restaurant accidentally being set ablaze by someone. It's twelve o' clock now, which means they'll be in the middle of a lunch rush shortly.

"I should call. You know, check in," I conclude.

"Uh, no, you definitely should not." Maria looks over at me mid-sip.

"I'm calling."

"Isa, stop it, you psycho." Maria snatches my phone from

my hand. "I'll call them if it makes you feel better. Damn. Just keep driving."

The panic in my chest makes me want to sprint out of the car while it's still in motion and run back home. Instead, I wait patiently for Maria to speak.

"Hey, Faye, how's it going?"

I lower the music slightly.

"What? No way!" Maria exclaims.

"What?" I whisper yell at her, trying to keep my eyes on the road as I glance back and forth between her and the cars ahead.

"Oh *shiiit*, I can't even believe that."

"Maria, what?" I beg.

"That really happened? Shit. Okay. Yeah, I'll tell Isa. All right, bye!"

Maria hangs up and takes a sip of her stupid coffee.

"Hello? What happened? Should I turn around?"

"Oh, everything is fine. Faye said the morning went really well, and they were all ready for lunch. I got you, didn't I, pendeja? Relax! This is going to be such a fun week. We'll party, eat good food, drink, and hey, maybe even find you a hot date."

"First, you suck for that. Second, it's a wedding full of family. Who the hell am I going to date?"

"Oh, right. Well, there's always Valentina," she says, winking.

"Over my dead body," I mutter, though the words feel hollow.

"Why? Have you seen her recently? She's hot and successful! I think she's a chef or something."

Maria pulls out my phone and searches for her on social media.

"See?"

"I'm driving," I say, trying to glance at the phone. "She's all right, I guess." I try to sound indifferent, though the memory of her smile is more vivid than I want it to be. "But she's also a life ruiner, so there's that."

Maria snorts and continues to scroll through her phone. I keep my eyes fixed on the road, willing myself not to ask to look at the photo of Valentina again, even though curiosity gnaws at me.

Suddenly, we hear a sputter in the engine of my car. A noise I've become accustomed to. Maria? Not so much.

"I seriously hate your car," Maria whines.

"What? Why? What's wrong with Miss Piggy?"

"What *isn't* wrong with Miss Piggy?" She snorts.

Miss Piggy is the name I so endearingly have given to my old 2000 Volkswagen Beetle. It was a high school graduation gift from my father. He even took it to my cousin to paint it pink since that's my favorite color.

"This will take you to college and back for years and years, mija," he insisted, despite the car being over a decade old and already having over 170,000 miles on it at that time. That was six years ago. The poorly done paint job has been chipping off like my toenail polish—slowly and painfully.

"Don't dis the pig," I say. "She's doing great!"

I pat her on the dashboard a few times.

"You're joking, right? You had to jumpstart her before we even left the restaurant."

I swerve to the right lane, finally getting ready to merge off the highway.

"Don't you ever need a jumpstart in the morning after a deep sleep? She's a badass. Look how far she's gone with no issues."

The dashboard looks like a light show, with nearly every symbol turned on, alerting me that something is wrong. Most of them have been on for years. I survive off my measly restaurant salary. I can't afford to get her fixed, and I certainly can't afford another car. Plus, it's Miss Piggy. She's going to the grave with me.

"As long as we don't crash and die, I guess we'll be all right," Maria whimpers.

"We won't crash. Miss Piggy wouldn't allow it," I reply confidently.

Miss Piggy can't let us die. I literally cannot afford to die. Not only will we not make it to the wedding, but the restaurant will undoubtedly close. Oh, and we'd be dead. We drive past a green highway sign that reads, "Entering Lee." After another painstaking stretch of gravel, we finally make it to the exit and into town.

"We're *heeeere*," Maria says in a sing-songy voice. "Take it all in, Isa. It's super cute, isn't it?"

It really is cute. Driving into the Berkshires feels like you're stepping into a different world. One you'd only see on a show like *Gilmore Girls*, where everyone is super kind and they host random festivals in the town square. I suddenly start to feel the excitement I have been bottling in since yesterday, when Maria told me about the opportunity. I've been so worried about the restaurant and ensuring everything is perfect that I haven't even thought about how I'm finally fulfilling my childhood dream of going to summer camp, albeit as a twenty-five-year-old adult woman. Plus, I finally get to see my cousin again after ten years.

I lower the window and allow the cool breeze to touch my cheeks as we pass through a line of colonial houses. Finally, we turn the corner and reach the main street. I take in every single detail. There are lampposts every several feet marking the way down the road. I can already picture them covered with green garlands during the holiday season and feel the urge to book a return trip just to see the Christmas lights everywhere. To my right is a small park with a few gazebos to relax in.

Local shops are on each side of the road, nestled close together, leaving no room for error. People are walking on the sidewalks, shopping, eating, and enjoying the last few days of summer. We continue driving past.

"So," Maria says, breaking the silence. "Are you going to tell me what was in that letter you had yesterday?"

Miss Piggy sputters briefly, jerking us forward slightly, but chugs along.

"Come on, girl. We're so close," I tell my car. "It's a letter from my father," I finally say to Maria, trying not to let Miss Piggy's inevitable demise distract me. But, unfortunately, I recognize these signs all too well.

"Another puzzle? No fucking way. You have to show me!"

"Shit. Shit. Shit!" I shout as I bang on the steering wheel.

Miss Piggy begins to slow down just enough for me to get into the breakdown lane. We're not too far from the campsite; I can't believe she'd give up on me now.

"What's going on?" Maria asks.

"Miss Piggy," I say as I try the ignition with no success, "is fucking dying. Shit."

"Well, we saw this coming, didn't we?" Maria laughs. "Should we call Sofia?"

"Damn it!" I shout. "It's bad enough I'm showing up in this shitty fucking car, but it breaks down before I can even get to the wedding? Great first impression, Isabella. Thanks, Miss Piggy."

"Yeah, how were you going to justify this car anyway if you're 'so successful' with all your 'designer' shit?" Maria says.

"I was going to say my real car was in the shop, and this was a loaner from a coworker. Duh."

I grab my phone and hover my finger over Sofia's name. I haven't looked at this number in so long. In the past ten years, I've probably hovered over her name a total of five times. Curious if she'd reply—and wondering what I would even say. I hold my breath and send the text to Sofia.

After what feels like five minutes but is probably closer to one, she replies. "All right, she says someone is coming to get us," I say to Maria. "Back to the letter, I think I left it in my apartment; I couldn't find it in my bag this morning." My stomach twists as I say it, because I know I put it there. Did I leave it somewhere else?

"It was only a two-line letter, but it felt important—like a clue I was supposed to hold on to. It said that I will find the truth in his book and that I have the key."

"Oh shit. We'll have to figure this one out later. I fucking loved his puzzles."

My dad didn't just enjoy puzzles for fun. He had a knack for hiding things inside them—important things. When I was little, he used to make me solve a riddle or a puzzle before I got a gift or a special surprise, like it was some game between us. But as I got older, I realized it was more than that. He used puzzles to teach me how to think, to see beyond the surface. He used to say that in life, the answers weren't always obvious—you had to work for them, piece by piece.

And now, with his book and the clues he's left behind, I can't help but wonder if he's hidden something important again. Something I'll need to figure out to understand the bigger picture of what he's been trying to tell me.

After a few moments, our silence is broken by the sound of a car horn. I jump up and look through the rearview. I can't determine who it is, but it seems like a nice car. It must be Sofia.

Maria looks up from her phone. "This must be our knight in shining armor." She laughs.

"Stop," I groan. "It makes me feel like a poor peasant in distress being rescued by the rich princess who pities me and my stupid car."

"You're so dramatic." Maria chuckles, unbuckling her seatbelt and opening the car door. "We should go. Are you ready?"

I give Miss Piggy one more pat before exiting her. She'll be fine. She always is. Besides, I already called for a tow—they said they'll pick her up later today. Hopefully, she's back in action before all the wedding festivities start.

"I call shotgun," I whisper to Maria as we walk toward the gorgeous silver Volvo SUV staring back at us. The headlights are on, which must be some fancy automatic thing Miss Piggy would scoff at. I still can't see who it is.

My throat is dry, and my heart is pounding. I reach for the passenger-side door and pull the latch.

"Hi, thanks so much for picking us up. Miss Piggy—" I look up, my breath catching in my throat as my eyes meet the driver's. The air between us seems to thicken, and for a split second, I feel my pulse quicken, betraying the annoyance I try to hold on to. "No fucking way." Maria lets out a cackle.

"Long time no see," she says, her grin as sharp as ever, but it isn't just the smugness that catches me off guard. Something flickers beneath the surface—something I wish I could ignore as easily as the smirk.

Her car smells of vanilla. Her long dark brown hair drapes strategically down her chest in perfectly curled, thick tendrils. I would recognize that face anywhere, unfortunately.

"You've got to be fucking kidding me," I say.

"Of all the people who could pick us up." Maria laughs. "Who would have thought it would be—"

I exhale deeply, but it isn't just frustration that settles in my chest.

"Valentina Garcia," I say, my voice steadier than I feel, the name rolling off my tongue with far more weight than I intend.

Chapter Five

"So, this is exciting," Maria says, breaking the silence, but it doesn't stop the undercurrent of tension that buzzes between me and Valentina, unspoken but palpable.

I look straight ahead, determined to ignore the warmth that has spread through my chest, even though I can feel Valentina's gaze lingering longer than necessary. I turn around to glare at Maria, who only grins.

"It's definitely been a while, huh? Ten years, right, Isa?" Valentina says, her voice carrying that same easy confidence, but there is something softer in her eyes. I hate that I notice, and hate even more that it makes my heart skip a beat.

"Yes," I reply between clenched teeth, forcing myself not to look at her, even though I can feel her presence, unsettling and too close for comfort.

Driving toward the main gates of the camp feels incredibly surreal. The Berkshires are beautiful, and the towns here are so quaint and sweet. But this camp—it's something else, like an entirely different world. I didn't think feeling as excited, anxious, and utterly terrified as I feel right now was possible. I spent my entire life dreaming about spending my summer at this specific camp.

When I was incredibly young, every time Sofia would leave for her trip, I would throw what I would now describe as a simple temper tantrum, but my mother would so lovingly describe it as a possession. In hindsight, as an adult, I'm completely mortified. She thought I was just being dramatic, but it was heartbreaking for me. I didn't understand why I couldn't go with Sofia, and it was my mother's fault. As I grew up, when I was finally exposed to more American movies and stumbled upon *The Parent Trap*, my obsession with attending camp only grew. It wasn't until I was older that I realized it was because my family couldn't afford it, which made me angry, knowing I missed out on summer camp because of something out of my control. As I grew up, I started telling Sofia that I had plans for the summer so we wouldn't appear so poor anymore, and once she left, I'd lock myself in my room for a few days and cry. I didn't want my parents to feel guilty that they couldn't afford it, but I couldn't stop yearning for it. Now, here I am, slowly driving through the gates. With Valentina at the wheel, no less.

I first notice the obnoxiously showy decorations on either side. Large vases hold an assortment of tall white flowers and greenery. Garlands of ivy are wrapped around the top of the gates. On one side is a sign on top of a gold easel with a floral arrangement in whites, creams, and soft light greens cascading down. The word "WELCOME" is hand-painted in a bold, white cursive font, with the names "Sofia" and "Luciano" printed below it.

"This is so bougie." Maria chuckles, whipping out her phone to snap photos.

"Oh, it gets worse," Valentina groans. "I don't understand why she needs to have this extravagant performance of a wedding."

"What do you mean?" Maria asks.

"I just think it's too much. If it were me, it'd be different."

The gates open slowly, and it appears we've stepped inside a movie set. I can't help but gasp audibly.

Valentina laughs. "Yeah, I know."

I look up through the windshield to see a canopy of lights going down to the end of the driveway, creating a magical tunnel. White tulle draperies are strung across the trees, almost mimicking a fence. White rose petals cover the ground that tires have half trampled but still look beautiful.

"This is ridiculous," I finally say.

"Yeah, the circus only gets worse. This part ends at the check-in, thankfully. We'll be there in a few minutes. For now, enjoy the view, I guess."

"Can you believe it's been ten years?" Maria says. "It's so nice to catch up with friends and family again, right, Isa?"

"Well, you know we're not friends." Valentina chuckles. The sound is light, but there's something about it that makes me pause. Maybe she's nervous? Or just playing along? I can't tell if she's joking or if the laugh is covering something else.

"*Whaaat?* You and Isa? I can't even believe it," Maria says sarcastically.

"Maria, if you don't shut your face," I bark.

"Yeah, no. Isa hates me, actually," Valentina interrupts.

"Is that so?" Maria asks aloud, annoying me further.

"With good reason," I add, staring out the window, trying to get distracted by the dizzy tulle garland that sways up and down as we drive past it.

Valentina snorts. "Hardly."

I snap my head so quickly toward her I'm surprised it doesn't spin all the way around my head, *The Exorcist* style.

"You ruined my fucking dress, Valentina. And embarrassed me in front of the whole family at our quinceañera!" I finally shout.

"This is the best day of my life," Maria whispers.

"I *accidentally* tripped and fell. I didn't mean to grab your dress and rip it. It wasn't a big deal."

"First of all—" I shout again, my voice rising louder than

I intend. Valentina rolls her eyes, and for a second, I catch a flicker of something—frustration, maybe, or something deeper.

"Oh, boy—" Valentina groans, cutting me off before I can say anything else, as if we've done this a hundred times before.

"We were in the middle of our choreographed number," I say to Maria specifically, as if she wasn't there at the party and didn't witness the whole incident go down in person. "There was no reason for her to even be near me at that part of the dance."

"Okay." Valentina snorts, that halfhearted laugh she does when she doesn't want to admit she's wrong. Or maybe she's just tired of this argument, too.

"Second of all, there was nothing to trip on. She just randomly fell and ruined my fucking dress." My voice cracks, the memory still as sharp as it was that night. "The dress that cost my parents a lot of money."

I don't say the rest—that the dress was never really mine, not in the same way things were for Valentina and my cousin. They were the ones who were supposed to be celebrated that night, the ones who had everything. And me? I was just there, tacked on, like an afterthought. But that dress…it was the one thing that made me feel like I belonged. Until it was ruined.

"Couldn't have been that much," Valentina says, her voice casual, like it's no big deal, like she really means it.

"Screw you," I spit, my anger flaring at how easily she dismisses it.

"Okay, you love birds. Let's settle down!" Maria cuts in.

I turn up the music to drown my anger and crack the window open slightly. The sound of crickets is almost overwhelming. However, I have a feeling this will become a sound I will cherish for the rest of my life. I take it all in. All I have to do is check in, find my cabin, and hide away for a bit. Get myself situated. Figure out my game plan. I pull my bag closer to me, feeling the outline of my father's book on my lap. I grip it tighter.

After some uncomfortable silence, we finally reach the main

cabin. This must be where we are supposed to check in. We park in front of the cabin at one of the guest parking spots and sit in the car for a moment.

"We have arrived at your destination," Valentina says in a robotic GPS voice.

"Thank you so much for the ride. We really appreciate it. Right, Isa?" Maria glances over at me, raising her eyebrows to imply I should say something.

"Yeah, thanks," I mutter, stepping out of the car quickly, needing the distance from Valentina, even though the pull between us lingers.

Valentina just nods, her eyes lingering on me for a moment too long, and for a split second, I think I see that softness in her gaze again—something that makes my heart race.

I immediately step outside, eager to put space between us and shake off this foreign feeling. I don't even have a second to realize I'm actually here. At the wedding of my cousin I haven't seen in a decade. I grab Maria's hand and start walking toward the main office.

"Hey, she really is hot now," Maria says as she waves goodbye to Valentina.

"And still a life ruiner," I add, though I can't deny the pull of attraction simmering beneath my anger. I hate that Maria is right. Valentina has changed—grown into her confidence in a way that makes it hard to look away—but I can't forget what she's done. I won't let myself.

"Well, that seems dramatic. She ruined your dress, sure, but did that really ruin the party? I remember it being so much fun regardless."

"Of course you do." I sigh. "Technically, no. She just sucks for embarrassing me for life. Mariposa and Rosita ruined it."

"That's true. The elusive fight."

I stop and turn around to face Maria. She takes a step back, startled by my sudden movement. I look around the campsite to make sure no one is too close.

"That's another reason I have decided to come. No one has ever figured out what happened, and for once, I get to focus on something that isn't falling apart. This week, I'll uncover the truth—and maybe, just maybe, I can escape the restaurant's constant weight for a while."

"*Riiiight.* And how exactly do you plan on doing that?" she whispers as we walk up the porch steps to the front door of the main office.

"I haven't planned that far yet. One thing at a time."

"Welcome to Sofia and Luciano's wedding!" a deep voice echoes as the door to the cabin swings open.

I look up and squint my eyes past the sun's glare to see a young man, probably my age, staring at us and smiling. His wispy auburn hair falls perfectly on top of his forehead, complimented by his deep-brown eyes. His smile could blind the sun. For all intents and purposes, he's a dreamboat. McDreamy-Face, if you will.

"Come on in." He signals us to come inside.

The cabin looks exactly like the photos I looked at more times than I want to admit. It's woodsy, cozy, and warm. I mean, the walls are made of literal wood logs. It can't get any woodsier. The only difference is that Sofia has managed to turn it into the perfect welcome spot for any lavish wedding. As soon as I step inside, two men dressed in white suits holding trays of macarons greet me.

"Uh, hello," I say to one of the men and grab a pink macaron.

"Don't mind if I do." Maria cheerfully grabs three and immediately bites down on one of them. "I can already tell this is going to be the most epic wedding I've ever attended."

"Yeah, no kidding," I say.

We follow McDreamyFace to the counter.

"Help yourself to a strawberry or mango mimosa," he says,

pointing at the champagne flutes sitting on one side of the counter.

Maria grabs a mango one, so I grab the other flavor and take a sip. It's perfect, of course. It was probably made with fresh strawberries shipped all the way from France.

"It doesn't count as day drinking if it comes with orange juice, am I right?" He laughs. "I'm Daniel. I'll be your interim camp counselor and wedding guide for the rest of the week."

"What are those gift bags on the table in the corner?" Maria points.

There are at least fifteen white bags with white tissue paper sticking out slightly.

"Oh, those are the wedding favors for the day. Every day there are new favors, so don't forget to grab yours, or you'll miss out!"

"You're kidding, right?"

I watch as Maria runs over to the table and grabs two bags.

"Sweetie, I don't kid about free gifts. Names so I can check you in?"

"Maria Lobo and Isabella Valdes," she says.

He types methodically on the laptop he clearly brought from home, ignoring the office's actual computer.

"Are you, like, the staff here?" I ask.

"Oh, God, no. Could you imagine? Look at me. I'm wearing a Prada bow tie. I'm actually just a sort of close friend of Sofia who volunteered his services for exclusive access to her wedding. She only invited close family and select friends because she wanted to keep it intimate and special. I personally think she just wanted it to seem super exclusive and exciting, and I refused to be left out. Like, hello? Mimosas? Daily gifts? It's a literal dream."

As he searches the guest list, I peek inside the gift bag Faye handed me. There's a Chanel perfume box, a small skincare set from a French brand I wouldn't even be able to pronounce, a pack of more macarons, and a "hangover recovery kit" consisting of Advil, vitamin C, a granola bar, and a packet of electrolytes to add to water.

"This is amazing!" Maria shouts, opening the perfume box to give it a whiff. "We need more rich friends, Isa."

"Yeah, just wait. It only gets better. My laptop is a little slow right now, so let me just explain a bit about the itinerary for the week. Today is the first day, so it's just basically a check-in and a way to mingle with the guests and meet the family. There will be a special welcome dinner tonight cooked by our amazing caterer. Tomorrow is a bridal hike and brunch. We'll be climbing to the top of the mountain and having a lovely brunch at the top."

Maria and I just stare at him, completely speechless.

"It sounds primal, I know, but I promise it'll be so extravagant. Wednesday is Sofia's bridal shower, hosted by yours truly. Thursday is the bachelor and bachelorette day. The rest of the family will stay at the camp with on-site spa specialists, and the bridal party will be partying it up with some camp activities to mimic Sofia's childhood. There will be some paddle-boarding in the morning and river tubing afterward. We'll finish the night with some s'mores by the campfire. Friday is, of course, the wedding rehearsal, followed by the last big dinner before the grand finale, Saturday, which is the wedding. Duh. Any questions?"

"That...was a lot of information," Maria finally says.

"Oh, don't worry. Each cabin has a lovely printed itinerary, so you don't miss any event."

I immediately feel overwhelmed. That's a lot to do while also trying to impress Luciano with my father's secret recipes, find out the mystery behind my mother and aunt, and make everyone believe I definitely belong in this high-end world.

"Oh, looks like my laptop's running again. Maria, you'll be in cabin four, but I'm having a bit of trouble pulling up your cabin, Isa. I see you RSVP'd a few days ago, and we're kind of low on space for housing. Sorry about that."

"Wait, how? This campsite is huge. Is it because it's haunted?" Maria snorts.

"Uh, what?" I say, staring between Daniel and Maria. "Did someone die here?"

"Yeah, probably." Maria shrugs. "The killer is probably still here. Lurking. Waiting for you, Isa."

"Uh, no. I don't think so," Daniel says. "Well, Luc actually bought the camp as a wedding gift to Sofia a few months ago. He's started construction on a majority of the cabins, so they're closed off to the public. Sofia made him promise he wouldn't do any outside work until after their wedding so as not to ruin her aesthetic. Anyways, you'll have to speak to Sofia about this—it looks like she's the one who changed your RSVP status in the system and left a note to speak with her. She's somewhere around the site. Just look for the blushing bride."

"Seriously?" I groan. "I just wanted to go to my cabin and lay down. I'm so tired."

"I'm so sorry. I don't make the charts, girl; I simply relay the information. Here, have another mimosa on me!" He grabs a flute and hands it to me.

"I thought they were free?"

"Off you go!"

"Wait?" I pause. "How do we even get to the cabins or find Sofia?"

"You're in the woods now, sweetie. I also would love a personal driver, but you're going to have to walk. Don't forget to use the hashtag 'LoveAtFirstLuc' if you share the wedding on social media! Isn't that so clever? I thought of it." He grins and waves as we walk away.

"Well, that was interest—"

"Oh, I almost forgot," Daniel shouts as we open the office cabin doors. "Welcome to Camp Hollow Pines!"

Chapter Six

"You're in the woods now," I quietly mock as we make our way down the path toward the cabins. "I wouldn't even know how to get a personal driver. What's with this place?"

"I don't know, I thought he seemed nice," Maria replies half-heartedly as she looks back through the gift bag. "Plus, look at these amazing gifts. This place is awesome!"

"Well, you think everyone is nice," I mumble.

I can feel the sweet summer breeze race over my face. It's incredible how small the camp actually is. In my head, I pictured an extensive area with an enormous lake and maybe fifty cabins, one of them preferably having long-lost twin sisters in it. This place has around twenty cabins and resides on one of the smaller lakes in the county. As we walk through the area, I look at every single cabin. Some have their doors wide open to allow the breeze to flow inside. Some have a few people sitting on the steps, talking. A few guests wave at us, which feels friendly and welcoming. I wave back enthusiastically. I'm here to impress, right?

As we pass a few cabins, I see the main hall to my left, and on the right, several white folding chairs piled up near a cluster of maple trees. A couple of people, possibly vendors, are installing some string lights up in the trees. I see Sofia standing under them, pointing and directing them to the perfect spot to put each light. This must be where the ceremony is taking place. It's barely decorated, but it already looks magical. A pile of birchwood logs is at the end of the path near the lake. Those are probably for the arbor. It's going to be perfect, I already know it. Of course it is. Just as I am about to call out to Sofia to get her attention, I hear someone scream my name in a high-pitched shriek.

"Isabellita!"

An older woman with short, curly hair undoubtedly dyed a fake red heads in my direction. I can smell her overpowering perfume already. Her bold red lipstick and maroon maxi dress make me think she definitely has a favorite color.

"Who the hell is this?" I whisper to Maria, nudging her ribs.

"It's Tía Maritza," she says, laughing. "I know it's been a while and at least six different facial surgeries since you last saw her. With the new nose, facelift, and Botox, I'm not surprised you don't recog—Hola, Tía!"

Standing at nearly six feet tall, Maritza could have easily passed for a model. Her cheekbones are high, making her face look gaunt but in a high-fashion way. Despite the work, I can see her crow's feet peeking through and the dark circles hidden under fillers. I try not to be too surprised at how unrecognizable she is now.

"Tía Maritza! How are you?" I shriek back in the same fashion and lean in quickly for a hug. "You look amazing. What are your secrets?" I laugh with a fake smile. I would never, at any point in my life, be able to afford whatever her secrets are.

"Oh, please, Isa. As if you need any of my secrets. Look at you. You're gorgeous! I love that dress. Who's it from?"

This velvet midi-length dress with long sleeves and a scooped neckline comes from a very prestigious and fancy store called Target, actually. But I can't tell her that. Not when I've worked so hard to project the image of success. If they think I'm struggling, the investment will slip through my fingers. The panic rises in my chest, knowing I have mere seconds to answer before it looks too suspicious.

"It's Calvin Klein," Maria blurts out.

I shoot a thankful glance at her. I've got to keep up the act, no matter what.

"Oh, is it?" Maritza scans my body with her razor-sharp green eyes like a robot trying to discover a secret weapon somewhere on my body. I suddenly feel naked. "I've never seen it before. It must be new, then. I love it!"

"Yeah, it's part of his fall collection," Maria continues. "Where's Silvana?" she adds to change the subject.

"She's somewhere around here, probably tanning by the lake or drinking way too many free daiquiris. Oh my God, Isabellita. It has been so long. We didn't think you were coming. It really is a surprise to see you here. ¿Y tu mama como esta?"

"She's not coming," I say awkwardly. Is she playing dumb? She must know she's not invited.

"Oh, que pena. That's too bad. I haven't seen her in so long too. In fact, since your quinceañera. That was quite the night," Maritza laughs as she rummages into her purse until she finds her lipstick. It's Ruby Woo from MAC. I watch as she reapplies it to her full lips that were definitely once pencil thin.

"Actually, I wanted to ask you, and well, everyone, about that night—"

"Aren't you excited for Sofia? This wedding will be the event of the year, maybe even the decade. Rosita has been working overtime with her to make sure it looks perfect. But you know me. I'll always find the flaws," she says, winking. "Que pena that she doesn't have a father to walk her down the aisle."

"Yeah, that is a bummer. I know how that feels," I say softly. "Anyways, about that night, I was wondering if you had any information—"

"Well, chicas. I see an open bar there calling my name, so have fun settling in. See you at dinner, mis niñas."

We both watch as she saunters away toward one of the three full-service open bars.

"She did it," Maria whispers.

"Did what?" I look over at her, confused.

"She's the killer. In the parlor room, with a Ruby Woo lipstick canister."

"Don't be ridiculous," I laugh. "It would be in the powder room. She knows something, though."

"About the fight? You think so? Looks like we've got our first suspect, then."

I roll my eyes. "She's not a suspect, Mar. Just a person of interest."

"Oh, she's interesting all right."

We head toward Sofia, passing the bar tables with white cloth and tulle, most likely for happy-hour mingling. A few guests reside at one of the photo booths, which appears to be a rented old-school machine you sit inside to take photos. Next to it is another photo booth. This one is made of a boxwood hedge backdrop decorated with real roses and greenery throughout. In front of the backdrop is a red velvet couch, and there's a bright neon sign hanging above it that says, "The Smiths." That must be Luciano's last name, and now I can't stop picturing Sofia as Sofia Smith.

"Okay, we have to take photos there. It'll go with your 'I'm super lavish and successful' facade you're trying to put off," Maria says.

"Can you not mention that so loudly?" I cringe, looking around me. I notice Sofia making direct eye contact with me, and my throat suddenly dries up.

"Isa! Maria!" Sofia waves, her smile beaming from ear to ear. She jumps up and down and screams excitedly.

We walk over to her, considering the piles of string lights surrounding her.

"Sorry about the mess. These were supposed to be put up yesterday, but you know how it is," she groans. "I can't believe you're both here, especially you, Isa."

"Here I am," I say awkwardly. I haven't seen Sofia in ten years. I have no idea how even to act. Like myself? Myself as a fifteen-year-old girl?

Sofia rushes in for a hug. Her embrace is warm against my skin, in contrast to the substantial chill slowly approaching in the air.

"This is going to be an amazing week, I just know it. Maria told me about your business plan, and I'm so excited for you. Expanding the restaurant, huh? We had no idea you were so successful."

I look over at Maria, who just grins at me.

"Yeah, I was pretty surprised too." I glare at Maria. "Who knew we'd be expanding? We're just...doing so well. We thought it would be a great time to bring an investor in. You know, while we're at the top of our game."

I internally cringe. "Top of our game"? Seriously? But hey, they don't need to know how "well" we're actually doing. It's all about the illusion, right?

I glance at Maria again, who's still beaming like this was all part of some brilliant plan instead of a half-baked scheme we cooked up just yesterday. God bless her optimism. Sure, we're not there yet, but this isn't a total lie. It's a real plan. I'm not selling them where we are; I'm selling them where we'll be—once I figure out how to unlock those damn recipes and make everything work.

Kudos to me for keeping a straight face. Years of practice, I guess.

"Well, you're absolutely right." Sofia picks up a pile of the string lights by her feet and moves them aside, signaling to one of the employees to pick it up and start untangling it. "Luciano would be a great investor. He's amazing. Maria told me you'd need the kitchen to whip up a couple of samples for him to try, and that is totally fine. I already talked to my catering chef, and they're okay with sharing the space. Oh, speak of the devil—my *fiancé* is here."

"Hola, mi amor." Luciano picks up Sofia sweepingly and twirls her around. She giggles excitedly. They kiss passionately for what feels like an uncomfortable amount of time.

Maria and I look at each other, feeling like we're peeping at a private moment. Maria clears her throat loudly, alerting them.

"Sorry, ladies. I just can't help myself around her." Luciano smiles and pulls her closer. "I'm Luciano, but you can call me Luc."

"Amor, these are my cousins, Maria and Isabella. Isa is the one who has the restaurant I told you about."

"Ah, Isabella! So nice to meet you."

He shakes my hand, and it feels like he could easily break my knuckles with just an ounce more of pressure.

"Hello! It's so nice to meet you, too, finally. I've heard so much about you and your family," I fib. I really need to do my research. "I just want to thank you for the opportunity to tell you about our restaurant and plans."

"Absolutely. We'll set up a time to meet this week where you can show me your business plan, and I can sample a few dishes, but other than that, I'm excited just to learn more about you."

"Me?" I gulp.

"Yes, of course. I want to know who I may be working with. We'd be partners, after all. And also, family soon."

He reaches for a side hug and pulls Maria in on his other side.

My palms feel sweaty. Learning more about me? What if he learns too much?

"Sofia, could you come over here?" asks one of the employees, completely wrapped up in string lights.

"I'll be right there." Sofia sighs. "I can't catch a break. Anyways, Isa, again, I'm seriously so happy you came. I have so much to say. For now, though, you should definitely settle in. Your cabin is all ready to go. Also, please do not forget to say hi to Rosita and Abuelita before you go to your cabin, or I will not hear the end of it."

"You got it," I reach for the cabin keys from her as she scurries away to help untangle the helpless staff from the lights. Cabin 101.

Maria grabs the key to inspect it.

"Oh, damn. I recognize this cabin number! It's one of the renovated cabins—the nicer ones, single occupancy. What the hell? Clearly, she has a favorite cousin." Maria scoffs. "I'm taking back my birthday gift from last year that I forgot to actually give to her."

I squint at her, confused. "How do you even know that?"

"I used to stay here all the time when I was younger. My family came up to the camp a few times every summer. Guess that's what happens when you're family friends with the owners."

Her words hit me like a reminder of everything I'm not. This was my family too, but I never had a summer at the camp. While Maria and Valentina spent their summers in fancy cabins, I was back home helping my parents run the restaurant, making sure the bills were paid. The contrast between us feels sharper in moments like this.

"Why would she give me an entire cabin? Weird..."

We head toward the cabins, hoping to catch Rosita or my grandmother so we can end this introduction portion of the week early.

"Maybe it's an olive branch? She could be reaching out and trying to make amends." Maria shrugs.

"Maybe..."

We pass a couple more stand-alone open bars, and Maria grabs another mimosa for the road.

Maria stops at one of the cabins. "Oh, this is mine. I'll see you at dinner, Isa. I am so tired," she says, fake yawning.

"Excuse me? Why do I have to face family by myself?"

"Ugh, just…so tired." She scoots toward her cabin door. "Gotta go!" She rushes inside.

"You traitor! I hope your cabin is haunted! I hope the killer is in there!" I shout.

"Is that my little Isabellita I hear screaming?" a shaky voice squeaks from one of the Adirondack chairs in front of the next cabin.

I walk over to see my adorable grandmother enjoying the sun's rays while simultaneously protecting her skin under a light orange shawl. Her eyes are squinting, but they always look like that. Almost as if they're permanently closed. Her grey hair hangs down the sides of her face in waves.

"Abuelita!" I squeal and rush over to her.

I want to hug her tight, but I'm afraid she may break in half. I kiss her a few times on the forehead and sit beside her.

"Como estas, mijita?" she says slowly and softly.

A wave of guilt hits me, sharp and sudden. Abuelita was my father's mother. But after Rosita and Mariposa's falling out, she started to create some distance between us. When my father died, Rosita took her in like her own mother and took care of her. If you ask anyone in our family, she's everyone's Abuelita. I haven't seen her since my father's funeral—three years ago. Not because I didn't want to, but because Mami has made it clear she doesn't get along with this side of the family. Visits were few and far between, and then nonexistent after Papi died. But seeing Abuelita now, so much older in just a few years, so much frailer, it feels as if I've missed too much. She moves slowly, more methodically, as if she's taking her time as time slowly takes her. Tears well up in my eyes.

"I'm great, Abuelita. How are you? Eating well? Sleeping well? I missed you so much," I say, my voice cracking.

"Oh, mijita. Don't worry about me. I'm still kicking, verdad? I'm only eighty-four." She lifts her arms to show off her nonexistent biceps. "I even go to the gym."

"Oh, dang. I see." I pinch her biceps and nod approvingly, which clearly pleases her.

"I'm so happy you're here, mijita. We weren't sure if you were going to make it. Y Mariposa?"

I sit quietly for a moment, staring at the workers in the distance, finally setting up the curtain lights they untangled.

"She won't be coming, Abuelita. You know how it is."

"Si, mija." She pauses. "I know."

"I wish I knew what happened. You know, between Rosita and Mariposa that night."

I look over at my grandmother, her eyes wandering the sky, watching the chickadees fly by from tree to tree, singing her a sweet song as they pass by. A smile slowly creases her face.

"Are you bothering Abuelita?" A stern voice comes from my right, startling me.

I see Rosita standing with her hands on her full hips, grinning. Her thick straight black hair practically takes over her entire head, complementing her round face. I can see some greys shining through.

"Tía!" I rush over to her at full speed and reach my arms around her body, squeezing as hard as possible.

"Mijita, I missed you so much! I can't believe you're here. Look at you!"

She pulls me away to look me up and down. She grabs my hand and makes me twirl, which only makes me giggle. I feel like I'm fifteen again, at my quince, begging to dance with my favorite aunt.

Her warmth is like a balm I didn't realize I needed. I'd been dreading this trip, convinced I'd feel like an outsider, a fraud among family. But standing here with Rosita—feeling her genuine pride and joy—it's almost enough to chip away at the knot of anxiety that's been living in my chest. For a fleeting moment, I wonder if coming here might not be so bad after all.

"You look incredible, Isabella. I've heard so many amazing things about you. I heard the restaurant is doing well from Sofia, and you're looking to expand. Look at your gorgeous dress! I'm so proud of you, mija."

Her words burn a hole through my heart. My clearance-rack dress is really starting to feel like a pile of rags against my skin that everyone can tell is slowly unraveling at the hem.

"Yeah, I hope to impress Luciano enough this week to win an investment. I even brought Roberto's book," I say enthusiastically.

"El Libro Sagrado?" Rosita looks at me, shocked. "I thought it was locked. He always boasted about having his little secrets inside that no one could see. It would drive your mother mad. It made me laugh, but I was always curious."

"Well, I think I have the key. Somewhere," I say.

Currently, my only plan is to slice through the book cover to get to the pages. My father said I have the key, but I still don't know what that means.

"Your father was always full of secrets, wasn't he? Loved puzzles."

"Yeah, there are many things in my life that are a puzzle to me." I hesitate. "Like what happened at our quinceañera. Do you..."

"Ah, si. I remember."

My eyes widen. I can feel my heart start to pick up the pace.

"I remember you all looking so beautiful that night. You in your gorgeous royal-blue dress. My little Sofia in her one-of-a-kind designer dress. Oh, I'll never forget Miss Valentina."

"Oh, that's not what I meant, Tía—"

"Have you seen Valentina yet?" Rosita cuts in.

"What? Yes, I have. She picked me up when my—friend's car broke down."

"Oh, I see," Rosita says, grinning. "She's still as pretty as ever, huh?"

"Yeah, I guess?" I shrug, feeling a flicker of annoyance. I know where this is going.

"Maybe you two should finally stop bickering and..." Rosita raises her eyebrows suggestively. "You know, get together."

"Have you been speaking to Maria today?" I quip. It's as if they think just because we used to be close, there's some inevitable romantic ending waiting for us. But there's not. We're not like that.

Rosita shrugs. "I don't know. You two were so close growing up—a bond like that never disappears. Plus, you could use a little distraction from all that work, mija."

"Tía! No. Absolutely not. I have better things to do this weekend than spend time with her, especially after what she did."

"Ay, Isa. It was ten years ago. She's changed. You've changed. Give her a chance. Anyways, I have to go. Check out your cabin and get settled in before dinner."

Yet again, another family member walks away before I can finish saying what I need to say. Everyone must be busy and flustered about this big week ahead of us. I myself feel like I'm spiraling, and I just got here. I just need to get through this day. Then the next. And the next. I groan. Maybe a nap in my quiet cabin will be just the ticket.

My cabin is settled a bit off the main road, which is nice because it gives me a bit of privacy. My luggage sits outside, patiently waiting for my arrival. I fumble, trying to find the key in my pocket, before noticing that the door is already unlocked. I push the door open and step inside, and it's perfect. Does it probably look identical to every other cabin? Yes, absolutely. But it's mine. With string lights hanging across the ceiling, the bed sits in the center of the room in front of the door, with two old nightstands nestled tightly against the mattress. There's a huge trunk sitting proudly in front of the bed, probably full of extra blankets and pillows. Or a dead body. Even still, it's everything I would have wanted at summer camp, and it's all mine—my very own cabin. I do a little dance in place as young Isa finally cannot contain her excitement. I did it. I'm here.

As I step farther inside, I notice some things on one of the nightstands and a pair of shoes by the closet door. I suddenly feel hyperaware of my every movement. Is someone in my cabin? Oh my God, Maria is right. The place is haunted. Or worse. There really is a killer on the loose. What if they're in the trunk, waiting to pop out and slice my throat open? That would be my luck. No, maybe they're in the closet. Waiting for the perfect moment to jump out and slash my Achilles tendons, rendering me useless at running away. Then they'll drag my lifeless body under the bed, where I'll surely bleed out and die.

I sneak around the cabin slowly, making each step practically mute. I walk over to the nightstand and pick up one of the lamps. I blame Maria for this. I will return and haunt her for the rest of her life if I die. I walk toward the closet. My heart is beating so loudly that it's almost deafening.

"Come out now! No need to hide anymore. I know you're there. I have a weapon!" I shout into the air. My voice is shaky. I reach my hand out toward the knob—my pulse racing. Sweat piles up on my forehead. With all my force, I pull the door open and yell as loud as I can as I swing the lamp up, ready to hit my assailant.

No one is there. Duh. I must stop watching horror movies before bed and believing everything Maria says.

"What are you doing?"

I scream and turn around to see Valentina leaning against the doorway, sipping what looks like a can of kombucha.

"I'm just—taking precautions," I say, straightening myself out. “What are you doing here? Haven’t you bothered me enough for a day? Shouldn’t you go to your cabin and be your cool self over there?”

“Yeah, I am,” Valentina replies between sips.

“Okay, then go. I’m busy.”

I walk past her to grab my luggage and I get a whiff of her perfume. It’s a heavenly blend of amber and sandalwood with notes of vanilla. It’s almost intoxicating. I sniff outwardly as if it would help the scent shoot out of my nostrils and stop tempting me. On the other side of the bed, I notice a measly cot on the floor with a blanket folded neatly on one end. A pillow rests comfortably on top.

“What the hell is this for? Is something wrong with the bed?” I wonder out loud.

“That’s your bed,” Valentina declares coolly.

“Hah, good one, Val,” I say, clapping mockingly. “Is this about that one time I peed on the bed when we were kids? For the hundredth time, it wasn’t me, okay? But sure, keep making jokes. You’ve always been great at that.”

There was a time when jokes like this didn’t sting. When Valentina and I could tease each other and laugh it off like it was nothing. Sofia, Valentina, and I were inseparable once—always getting into trouble, sharing secrets, practically glued at the hips. And there was always something about Valentina… even when we were young. I’d never let myself think too much about it, but it was there, that magnetic pull. It’s still there, even though I wish it wasn’t.

But that was before. Before the quinceañera, before everything changed. Somewhere along the way, the teasing stopped feeling light, and every joke started to feel like a reminder of how far apart we’d drifted—and of things left unsaid.

I catch her eye for just a second too long, and my heart does that stupid flutter it’s been doing since we were kids. Annoyed, I break the gaze, glaring at her. “Can you please just go to your cabin now?" I say, my voice sharper than I intend. I need her to leave before I give too much away, before I remember what it felt like to be close to her in ways I still don't fully understand.

Valentina chuckles and walks toward the bed. In one fell swoop, she twists her body and lands on the bed. She kicks off her shoes and puts her feet up. I'm speechless.

Before I finally get to muster a word, she says, "This *is* my cabin."

Chapter Seven

"Good one again, Val. Have you considered stand-up comedy as a profession? You're on a roll today," I insist.

She looks up at me with a slanted smile and raises her eyebrows. With those two motions, I know immediately. I'm sharing my cabin with Valentina. Fuck. You have got to be kidding me. This is just my luck.

"I am not sharing a cabin with you, let alone a bed." I laugh, incredulous.

"Who said anything about sharing the bed?" Valentina points to the cot once more. "Like I said, that's where you'll be sleeping for the week."

"Ab-so-fucking-lutely not. This isn't a part of my plan." I rush to the door and scream out Sofia's name into the camp so loudly that I alert a few vendors to my direction.

"Someone get Sofia now!" I shriek.

Valentina winces. "Ugh, you're so loud."

I turn around to see Valentina put on her headphones and place a pillow over her head in the most obnoxiously dramatic fashion. I can't imagine sharing a space with this person for an entire week. I scan the room slowly, inspecting all of her things. The nightstand near her is covered in crumpled-up receipts, a wallet, and two empty mugs, undoubtedly dirty with coffee or, in her case, kombucha. I feel the urge to pick up the mugs and clean them, but I resist. There's a pile of clothes on the floor next to the nightstand, possibly whatever she wore the day before, which she stripped off before throwing her body onto the bed. I highly doubt she took a shower before doing that. The towel she used whenever she did decide to shower is lying on the floor. A sad, wet ball of 100 percent cotton. How could someone who has only been here a day longer than me have already made themselves at home so quickly? The bed looks as if she just rolled out of it in the morning and didn't bother to make it. I sigh hopelessly. There is just no way this is going to work out. We're absolutely different people. She's messy and unorganized. I'm…not that at all—the complete opposite.

"Hey, you two," Sofia pipes up as she enters the cabin. "I see you're getting acquainted."

Her smile drops quickly when she sees the look of utter dissatisfaction on my face.

"Okay, Isa, I know. I know. I'm so sorry, but this was super last minute for me, and all of the other cabins are taken," she whispers.

"So not only do I have to share a cabin, but it's with *her*, and there's only one bed? You're joking, right? Please tell me this is a prank you're playing on your prima because I haven't seen you in years."

"I wish it were." She smiles awkwardly. "At least you have your own little bed." She points at the cot. I look down at it—a mere few inches off the ground like an elevated dog bed. I'd probably end up spooning a few field mice from that height. I look back at her.

"I know, prima. But hey, it's just for a week. And you'll be spending most of your time doing wedding activities and talking to Luciano anyways, right? Or maybe you two can get… acquainted better." She winks.

"Sofia!" I whisper, turning around quickly to see if Valentina is listening, but she seems lost in whatever music is blaring loudly into her eardrums.

Sofia shrugs, her grin playful. "What? You two have always had—something, you know? You fight like you've known each other forever—and you have. We were inseparable. Maybe all this tension is because there's something more underneath."

I glare at her. "We fight because we can't stand each other."

"Sure, sure." Sofia waves her hand dismissively. "But sometimes the best relationships start with a little heat. Anyways, I have to go and get ready for dinner tonight. Bye!"

"Wait, I'm not do—"

But before I can finish the sentence, Sofia is already halfway to the other side of the camp. She couldn't have left any faster. I turn back toward the bed and see Valentina still lying there with the pillow over her head. I can hear the music softly escaping the earbuds. I yank one out of her ear.

"Are you seriously napping right now?"

Silence.

"Well, I really think I should get the bed, Val."

Silence.

I have half a thought to toss her off the bed and spread my limbs out toward each corner, taking over the entire mattress. Maybe I'll hide her blankets or steal them in the middle of the night and use them for myself. Perhaps I'll fill her pillow with wet leaves. I could just pee on the bed and assert my dominance. Thanks to Maria, my peeing on the bed wouldn't be out of the ordinary to Valentina. I walk over to my new bed for the week—the saddest little cot. I can already feel my back aching. Don't I have to deal with enough in my life? An overbearing mother, a failing restaurant, impossible puzzles from my dead father, and now a crappy bed? This just simply won't do. I march over to Valentina and poke her in the ribs.

"I deserve the bed."

She squeaks at the impact of my finger against her skin.

"Why the hell do you think that?" She lifts the pillow off her head slightly, revealing a singular eyeball staring back at me in utter surprise.

"Because."

The eyeball blinks.

"Because I do, okay?"

I know I sound absolutely ridiculous, but I don't want to tell this stranger that I'm just tired of getting the short end of the stick in my life. I grew up sleeping on an unbelievably uncomfortable twin mattress until I finally moved out of my parents' apartment. I just want to sleep in a nice bed all week. I don't think that's too much to ask.

"Why do *you* deserve it?" I squawk.

"Because," she says, smirking.

I blink.

"Because, I got here first. You were the last-minute addition. So why should I give it up for you?"

"Because I'm tired. I just drove three hours to get here. I don't want to sleep on a dog bed all week."

I can't help but feel silly as I argue my reasoning. I sound like a small child throwing a temper tantrum because I wasn't allowed to get the candy bar at the supermarket. I'm almost embarrassed by myself. Almost. Not enough to give in.

"Listen, Isa. It's Isa, right?" Valentina says with a tilt of her head, her tone just a little too casual, as if she's testing the waters.

"No, I changed my name as of five minutes ago," I shoot back, keeping my voice light but feeling the familiar heat rise. I know exactly what she's doing—subtle, almost playful, as if she's daring me to bite. And for a second, I almost do.

"If you can give me three valid reasons to give you the bed, it's all yours. But if your only reason is that you're a little tired, well"—Valentina points to the cot—"there's your bed."

I huff.

"I"—I pause, thinking of something clever to say—"broke my back."

"Well, you're going to have a hard time participating in the wedding activities, huh? Might as well just head back to New Jersey and leave me the bed."

Have I mentioned I hate this person?

"Well, fine! Whatever. Keep the bed, Val. I don't need it. I'll just sleep on the floor."

"Great," she says.

I stomp over to my luggage to begin unpacking my things. I look around the cabin and spot the dresser across the room next to the closet. Clutter has already taken up residence on top of the dresser, making me angrier. I scoot the candy wrapper, watch, and notepad to one side of the dresser.

"This is my side, okay?"

Silence.

"Ugh, whatever," I retort and open the top drawer. Thankfully, it's empty. I doubt she brought enough clothes to even need these.

"Why don't you just keep your stuff in your luggage?" I hear her mumble from the bed.

"Like some sort of wild animal?" I scoff. "I like to see my clothing, not rummage through my luggage like a city rat scouring the trash bins for food."

"Am I a sewer rat then?" This time, she sits up, looking half shocked and half amused.

"Well, if the shoe fits," I retort.

She smiles and lies back down, covering her face with the pillow again.

I grab the handful of dresses I stole from Maria's closet. If I am going to persuade the family to think I am successful and not panicking about overdue bills, I need to dress the part. Unfortunately, my closet is full of thrift shop pieces and definitely nothing designer.

I open the closet door and see a few dresses hung up—clearly expensive ones—a structured beige blazer, and brown corduroy trousers. So she *does* have style. I push her clothes to one side of the closet and hang my stack of clothing on the rod. I turn around to look at her, her head peeking slightly out of the pillow now, but her eyes are closed. She's probably spying on me when I'm not looking.

"My side," I state.

She gives me a cavalier thumbs-up.

I look up at the top shelf in the closet and notice a fleece blanket folded neatly in the corner. I pull it down and inspect it. It's soft—much softer than the crappy blanket on my cot now, but not as soft as the blanket on the bed already. I throw the blanket on Valentina's head.

"What the hell?" She finally emerges from under the pillow.

"Let's switch blankets."

She inspects the blanket I have thrown on her.

"I'm not sleeping in this burlap sack, but thanks for the offer."

"Oh, come on," I insist. "It's so soft."

I rub the blanket and nod approvingly.

"Nice try," she chuckles. "You can use it if you like it so much."

I tug on the blanket on the bed. She isn't even lying under it. So what's a simple switch?

"Listen, I think it's only fair that if you get to keep the bed, I at least get the nice blanket. Please?"

I tug even harder this time, determined to make this piece of fabric mine.

Valentina reaches down to grab the hem of the blanket, now hanging off the bed, startling me. I take a few steps back as I watch her quickly roll across the bed, bring the blanket with her, and turn herself into a human burrito.

"Are you fucking kidding me, Val?" I shout. "How old are you?"

"I'm twenty-five. How about you?" She mumbles underneath several layers of cotton.

"More like three." I scoff, kneeling on the bed to tug at the blanket some more. "You're being so immature!"

"Look who's talking," she yells back.

"I just thought it would be fair to give me the blanket since you get the bed. Is that so far-fetched?"

Silence.

"Ugh, whatever." I push Valentina, rolling her deeper into the covers. "Keep it, you child. See if I care."

I crawl off the bed and shake myself off. The fleece blanket isn't that bad anyways. It's certainly better than whatever sandpaper blanket Sofia placed on the cot, so I'll be fine. She can keep her stupid blanket. I walk back over to the dresser to keep unpacking and to distract myself from the brat I've been forced to room with for the week. She thinks she's so charming and funny. I scoff again, and I start to wonder if I will make it out of this alive. I guess it doesn't matter as long as I win the investment for La Mariposa.

"Are you folding your underwear?"

I snap my head around to see that she has unfurled herself from the burrito of immaturity and is now seated, leaning against the back wall for support and scrolling her phone.

"So what if I am?" I snap.

"It just seems a little…much. You're very tidy."

"Well, one of us has to be," I grumble.

She chuckles, gazing up from her phone and staring at me. I don't know why, but it makes my ears hot. That damn smile. I guess all those awkward teenage years in braces paid off.

"I bet you have a different designer underwear for each day of the week, too, huh?"

I look down at my lacy white underwear. Parts of the lace have come undone, leaving little gaps. These panties are so damn old, the tag has completely worn off.

"I do not. Mind your business, okay? We can't all be so… free-spirited like you," I say, rolling my eyes.

I can hear Valentina chuckle to herself as I turn around to

continue folding my underwear. Why do I feel so lightheaded? It's as if there's an emptiness in my stomach. Butterflies? Maybe the thought of Valentina as a burrito is making me hungry. Yeah, that might be the one. So what if I organize my underwear? It just means it's one less thing for me to think about throughout my day. I don't wake up in the morning trying to fish through the drawer and find the perfect pair to wear. And since no one sees them anyways, why does it matter what I do with them? She makes me so mad I could just—

"Neat book."

I turn around to see Valentina standing a mere few inches away from me. I didn't even hear her get up. I was too distracted with my thoughts about how much she sucks. I use my peripherals to glance behind me and spot El Libro Sagrado sitting on the dresser. I feel a sense of panic, but I can't move. I'm fixated on Valentina's eyes, staring back at me with curiosity and amusement. As if she's a tomb raider staring at an ancient artifact she's been looking for her entire career. I gulp, but my throat is dry. She pulls in closer, both of her hands on the dresser, trapping me in between. I smell her perfume again. The vanilla is practically hypnotic. I don't know what's happening right now, but I don't want it to end for some strange reason. I look back up at her. She's smiling slightly. Almost slyly. As if she knows exactly what she's doing. I hold my breath, glancing down at her lips. Her lips. *Fuck.* She pulls in even closer, reaching one hand behind me. Then she slowly pulls away from me, revealing a phone charger in her hand.

"Phone's going to die." She chuckles.

It feels like someone dumped freezing-cold water onto my body. The jolt is almost disorienting.

"Right. Your phone." I cough.

She lingers momentarily, licks her lips once, grins, and returns to the bed.

I'm frozen. I can't even move right now. I feel so ridiculous, but I can't have imagined that whole thing, right? Maybe I did.

"Don't forget, Friday comes after Thursday when you're organizing your thongs." She laughs.

"You're such a—"

"Hey, pendejas! Am I interrupting anything?"

I look toward the door to see Maria standing there. This is just what I need. A distraction from my already crumbling world and patience.

"No, not at all." I glare at Valentina, who only smiles back at me, seemingly amused.

"Mm-hmm," Maria says, unconvinced. Suddenly, her eyes widen. "Is that Roberto's book?" she yelps.

"Yes! Let's talk about it…outside," I suggest, trying to find any reason to get out of this stuffy cabin. I need some fresh air.

Finally, I'm able to peel myself from the spot, but I almost don't want to move. I want to linger in those weird feelings for a second longer. Figure out what the hell happened. Or maybe I'm just overthinking it like I do everything in my life. I grab the book and follow Maria outside.

We pass by a few guests, some of whom I don't recognize. One stares at me a bit too long, almost as if she's glaring at me.

Maria snorts. "Damn, Isa. You already made an enemy."

I scoff. "Shut up," I say. "She probably doesn't know who I am and was trying to figure it out."

Walking toward the dock, we're distracted by the staff running around preparing the area for dinner. There are even a few servers standing around holding trays of food.

"Oh shit. Hors d'oeuvres!" Maria shouts as she runs over to one of the servers.

"Maria! I'm sure it's for dinner, don't take any."

"Actually, we've been hired to have these trays available at any time of the day," the server says with a rehearsed smile.

"See?" Maria grins. "Damn, Sofia went all out."

I watch as Maria grabs nearly half the tray of smoked trout croquettes.

"Thanks! Keep 'em coming," Maria shouts to the waiter as we walk away.

I regret not bringing a jacket with me, as the temperatures have already dropped significantly. A shiver develops deep in my muscles. But despite it feeling so brisk, it feels…nice. Probably because I was getting so hot inside the cabin, but I need this—this wake-up call. I was so lost in that back-and-forth with Valentina that I had already forgotten my purpose for being here. I clutch my father's book tightly.

"So, are you two getting along?" Maria asks.

I shrug.

"That bad, huh?" She laughs.

"She's just so immature. Why can't I just stay with you? I'll bring my cot."

"Our cabin is full and I don't want to smell your feet all night."

"My feet do not smell," I protest.

"Besides, clearly Sofia put you with her there for a reason. Maybe she wants you to hash it out and be friends again? You've hated her since the dress incident, but before that we were all practically besties. Give her a chance, pendeja."

"She's messy, too," I say, ignoring her. "Did you see the cabin?"

"It didn't look messy to me." Maria chuckles, knowing we have different tidiness standards. "You're too picky, Isa."

"Well, it was to me. She refused to let me sleep on the bed instead, and when I finally caved and suggested she at least give me the blanket, she wrapped herself in it. Can you believe that?"

Maria laughs even harder.

"It's not funny! She's ridiculous. I just need to focus on why I'm here. To save the restaurant and prove everyone wrong."

"What are they wrong about?" Maria asks.

"About me. And my mother. Being poor, pathetic failures."

"I see. And what makes you think they think that?"

"Are you kidding?" I scoff. "Just look at the way they look at me. They scan my entire outfit as if they can detect I got it on sale at TJ Maxx because it had a rip. My mother has constantly told me what they've said about us. How we're not a real part of the rest of the family. How we 'don't fit in.' I've heard it all. And it's time that they eat their words."

"Ooh, feisty. I like it." Maria grins.

We arrive at the dock overlooking the lake. The sun is slowly setting, meaning it's almost time for the first dinner. Time flies when you're dealing with a child, I guess. We sit on the two black Adirondack chairs at the edge of the dock.

"Well, I still think you should give Valentina a chance. She's cute," Maria protests.

"Sure, if you're into that tall, effortlessly gorgeous bit," I grumble.

"Sounds like you're into her," she replies.

"Absolutely not. I can't—I need to focus on why I'm here. I can't have any distractions," I insist.

"Well, maybe you need the distraction."

I look over at her, curious.

"I'm just saying, Isa. When was the last time you let yourself have a little fun? What's some harmless flirtation going to do? You can still focus on impressing Luciano and tricking the entire family and allow yourself to enjoy this."

"Sh, sh. No more of that," I say, putting my finger near her mouth. "I will absolutely never flirt with Valentina. Anybody but her."

"Okay." Maria laughs. "Whatever you say, prima. So, it's time. Show me the book."

I hand her my father's book carefully as if, at any moment, the pages will just disintegrate into thin air, and I'll lose my only chance at finding out what is hidden in the leather binding of this journal.

"It's locked," she states.

"Yeah, I know. I thought I could rip it open or use a chef's knife from the kitchen to cut it. Is that bad?"

"You're asking me if it's bad to mutilate your late father's book just to see what's inside? The man who loved giving you puzzles to solve? No, it's totally fine. I'm sure he'd love how resourceful you are. I can hear him rolling in his grave now. *Isabella, you betrayed meeee.*"

"Okay, I get it." I roll my eyes and grab the book from her. I stare at the cover, looking at every crease in the leather made by wear and tear.

"What did the note you recently got from your dad say again?" Maria asks.

I reach into my pockets to try and find it again, to no avail. I definitely left it in the apartment back in Jersey.

"It said something like, 'You'll find the truth in my journal. You have the key.' I think. I don't remember exactly now. I don't even know what the key could be."

Maria laughs.

"What's so funny?" I look over at her, confused.

"You're the worst sleuth. After all these years growing up with your father, I can't believe you don't know the answer to this clue. You really are a pendeja."

"What do you mean!" I shout.

I search my thoughts quickly, trying to find the answer before she makes me feel stupid.

"Did you get it?" She chuckles as she watches me try to figure it out.

"No," I say, surrendering. "Tell me if you know."

"Stupid." She reaches for my neck and grabs my necklace.

I look down at the necklace, confused. It's the same necklace I've been wearing for months—the last thing my father left me. The pendant is small and simple, shaped like a delicate teardrop, with faint, intricate etchings along its surface. It always seemed decorative, but now Maria's expression tells me it's more than that.

"Wait, this is the key?" I ask, my pulse quickening. "How did you even know?"

Maria smirks. "Your dad told me once—well, sort of. Remember when we were kids, and he was always working on his little projects, hiding things around the house? I asked him why he never just used regular locks, and he laughed and said, 'Locks are too easy. Real secrets hide in plain sight.' He never directly said this was a key, but when I saw that necklace around your neck, something clicked. It looks like a pendant, but it has that hidden quality your dad was obsessed with. I had a feeling it was a key to something—I just didn't know what."

I frown. "But it doesn't even look like a key."

Maria holds the pendant up, turning it in the light.

"Exactly. Your dad loved puzzles, right? He probably made it look like something ordinary so no one would suspect. See these tiny ridges along the side?" She taps the pendant, revealing the delicate notches etched into its edge. "It's meant to fit into something more intricate—like the lock on that journal."

I stare at her, feeling like an idiot. "Oh my God," I groan. "I've been walking around with this key the whole time."

"Yeah, you have." Maria laughs. "Try it."

I unclip the necklace from my neck, my pulse quickening. The pendant feels heavier now, its significance suddenly clear. My hands tremble as I grab the journal, the lock small but intricate, just like Maria said. I line up the pendant's notches with the lock's grooves and hesitate. I turn to Maria, who's staring intently at the journal.

"Turn it, stupid," she shouts, growing impatient.

"All right, damn. I was trying to have a moment," I murmur.

I give it a gentle twist. There's a soft click, and the journal springs open.

Chapter Eight

As I finish getting dressed for the first dinner tonight, my heart is still racing. The journal. I finally opened it—after all this time. My father's secrets, his stories, everything I've been waiting for are right here, just beneath the cover. I stare at the open pages for a moment, feeling the weight of it all. This is it.

But before I can dive in, a vibration on my wrist snaps me out of the moment. It's an automatic email notification that La Mariposa's revenue report is ready to be viewed. *That's right. It's the beginning of the month. Oh, God. The report.* I quickly reach for my phone, which is lying peacefully on the dresser. I unlock the screen, and the report is there, waiting for me. Taunting me. I click it.

Fuck. It's worse than I thought. La Mariposa is officially… losing money. We were always close, but it was never this definitive. I feel a wave of panic swirl in my chest, picking up strength with every turn around my heart. If I don't secure this investment, it will all be over. My mother will be devastated. Everything she worked for—well, my father worked for—will be taken away. La Mariposa is the last thing we have left of him, and I don't want to be the reason we lose it. I can't be. She'd never forgive me. Any morsel of pride she has in me and herself would be gone forever. This investment needs to happen. I look through my contacts, and after making my selection, put my phone against my ear, listening to each trill, getting increasingly impatient with each one.

"Domino's."

I quickly glance at my phone screen to see the number I called.

"Faye, I swear to God," I snarl.

"Oh, hey! I had no idea it was you," Faye jokes. "What can I do for you?"

"Just checking in on the restaurant. How is everything?"

"Well, José quit, Carlos stole all of the inventory, and all the customers have decided to boycott the place. How are you?"

"Ha-ha, Faye. Can you please just tell me? Have you been getting my emails?"

"Isa, everything is still going fine. I helped José prep the food yesterday, so we're all set for tomorrow. I double-checked the inventory, and we're ready to close the shop in a couple of hours. I'm currently baking some empanadas and placing the flans in the display. Please trust me, okay? I wouldn't let you down."

"You're right," I say between gritted teeth. "I'm sorry."

"How's it going over there? Are you settled in?"

"Uh, yeah. Sort of." I glance over at the bed Valentina has taken possession of. "This is going to be an interesting week for sure. I'll try not to bother you too much. I do trust you, Faye. I'm just… I feel like I'm spiraling."

"Hey, just take a deep breath. You've got this. And I've got this. I promise. I'll talk to you later."

I put the phone down and take a deep breath. They're right. I got this.

I shiver in the crisp evening air as I approach the main hall in my slinky silver dress. How could it already be so chilly here? I pull my dark-grey shawl tighter around my shoulders.

As I walk closer to the building, I'm already picturing myself in my own corner of the kitchen, thanks to the chef and catering staff being so gracious to let me work there. In my own little world. No one to bother me. No one to distract me. I can focus on figuring out the secrets of my father's book and make some sample meals for Luciano to try. Maybe this week won't be so bad after all.

As I open the doors of the kitchen, my stomach sinks. There, in what is supposed to be my sacred haven, is Valentina. She's moving swiftly around the kitchen, reaching for a pan hanging from the ceiling, snatching a spoon to stir whatever concoction she has in a pot on the stove, and gliding over to her cutting board to chop some vegetables. Of course, she's the caterer. That would be my luck. I want to curse at the universe.

I walk silently toward the back counter to put my things down, trying to avoid the swift-moving staff. I'm almost dizzy watching them rush around to prepare everything for dinner. I grab an apron and start slowly tying it around my waist.

"I didn't know you were the chef," I say.

"Yep," Valentina replies quickly as she looks through some papers, probably making sure everything is going to plan for the dinner service, considering she also has to attend as a guest. "Is that all right with you?"

I stand there, slightly stunned, but I won't let her see that. A chef. It makes sense, though. I should have known. Back when we were teens, she'd always whip up those late-night snacks for me and Sofia—perfectly seasoned quesadillas, impromptu pasta dishes. Valentina always seemed so effortless in the kitchen, as if she belonged there. I used to think it was just another one of her talents, something I could roll my eyes at.

And now, seeing her like this—commanding a kitchen full of people, moving with purpose and grace—I have to admit, I'm a little impressed. But God, it's annoying.

"Yes. Of course. Well, I don't want to impose," I stumble. "I can go somewhere else."

"Where would you go? This is the only kitchen. And you need to make something for Luciano, right?" Valentina glances over at me, her tone casual but with just enough edge to make me feel flustered.

"Yeah, for the business plan," I reply, my face suddenly feeling hot.

"Well, as long as you don't get in the way, do whatever you need to do."

Valentina continues to move around the kitchen, this time reaching for a tray of duck from the steaming-hot oven.

I pull out my father's journal and place it on the counter. This is it. I can finally open his book and not get yelled at. Even now, I feel like I will get in trouble just for looking at it. I unclasp the necklace from my neck, feeling the familiar weight of the teardrop pendant in my hand. It's strange how something so ordinary hid the answer all this time. I insert the pendant into the intricate grooves of the lock, and again, it fits perfectly. With a soft click, the latch swings open, just as it did before. My heart races as I prepare to finally see what's inside.

I hesitate for a moment, with my thumb and finger on the corner of the leather-bound book, ready to turn to the first page. I feel as if I'm doing something wrong, something forbidden. I'm not, though. He wants me to open it. He wants to show me the truth. Whatever that could be. Still, after spending my entire childhood knowing this book was off-limits but never really knowing why, it's an eerie feeling that I could find out a lot of secrets just by opening it. I take a deep breath and hold it for a few seconds. Finally, I close my eyes and turn the book to the very first page. Knowing my father, he would want me to inspect each page of the journal, from beginning to the end. I can't miss any detail.

After what feels like a century, I finally open my eyes and

look down at the book. There, on the inside front cover, is a black-and-white photo of myself as a baby in a hospital crib with my father sitting by my side. The picture is ripped just by his right shoulder, but it's us—the two of us when I was born. I feel a pang in my chest—the one I get right before I start to ugly cry.

"Whoa, who is that baby?" Valentina says over my shoulder, and I jump.

"God! You scared me," I say, my hand over my heart. "It's my father and me."

"Well, weren't you a cute little one, huh?" Valentina winks.

"Duh, what else would you expect?" I roll my eyes.

"What happened?" she jokes.

"Excuse you. Have you *seen* me?" I spin around and use my arms to trace my curves.

Valentina walks closer to me, scanning my body from my toes, all the way to the top of my head. I swear I can feel her eyes on me.

She grins slyly. "Yes, I have definitely seen you."

"Well." I clear my throat. "Then you'd know. I'm still cute."

"I guess I can't deny that. You definitely had a glow-up. Remember the braces?"

I shrug. "I mean, you don't look too bad yourself."

My eyes shift back and forth from Valentina's honey eyes. I could melt in them. I instinctively glance down at her lips. A slight crease appears to form.

"Don't get any ideas, Valdes," she states as she starts plating some appetizers. One looks like crackers with mashed olives on top. I can almost taste the vinegar.

"What ideas?"

She stops, turns back toward me, walks a few steps in my direction, and smiles.

"Falling in love with me," she says matter-of-factly.

"Excuse me? Who the hell do you think you are? Please. You are not *all* that, Garcia."

She shoves a cracker with the olive mixture into my mouth, which had been open due to shock from her sheer audacity.

"I'm just warning you now. It's not a good idea."

I scoff. "You definitely did not need to warn me about that. I'm not interested."

Valentina gets distracted by a caterer dropping a sheet pan of zucchini. The pressure must be on since it's the first night of Sofia's extravagant wedding. I haven't seen Valentina in years, but even I can see how stressed she is. The last time I saw her, she was a teenager ruining one of the biggest nights of my life. Now, she's a chef leading a bunch of cooks to create a gorgeous event for Sofia. It's honestly kind of impressive. I turn to the next page in the book.

"Rice pudding?" I mutter to myself.

"What's that?" Valentina walks over after fixing another tray of zucchini to put in the oven, full speed ahead.

I turn my head over toward her, and she's, once again, standing undeniably close to me. I can feel the warmth of her body. Or maybe it's just the hot ovens in the kitchen. Whatever it is, I feel lightheaded. I look up quickly into her eyes and then shift my focus back to the book.

"Sorry, I was talking out loud to myself. This is my father's journal. It's supposed to be sprinkled with random things, but mostly recipes—ones I want to discover to impress Luciano and win the investment. But this one here…it's a recipe for arroz con leche," I say.

"And?"

"It's just weird." I pause, inspecting the little notes around the recipes.

One note in particular, written in small print, has caught my attention.

Valentina leans against the metal counter and crosses her arms, watching me, her eyes focused. I feel her presence next to me, and suddenly the air feels heavier. I try to ignore how close she is, but it's impossible. Her attention, so undivided and sharp, makes my throat dry.

This journal is deeply personal. It's my father's—his words, his memories. I've barely touched the pages myself, and now Valentina is standing here, watching me leaf through them as if she has any right to see inside. A mix of irritation and something else—something I can't quite place—flares up inside me.

She raises her eyebrows, silently encouraging me to continue. I shift uncomfortably but finally speak.

"Well, it's just—my mother hates rice pudding. Like, absolutely hates it. She never even lets me have any in the restaurant despite customers requesting it."

"So? Maybe he liked it, so he wrote a recipe for it. Or she used to like it." Valentina shrugs.

"No, it's not that. It's this." I point at the note my father left on the recipe.

"'Her favorite,'" Valentina recites. "Now that's interesting."

She turns around and scooches closer to me, inspecting the recipe closer—the smell of her is, again, slightly intoxicating. Maybe there's no "slightly" about it. I shake my head.

"Who could this be for then?" Valentina asks, but to no one in particular. Like a detective would, hoping the answer would appear out of thin air.

"I'm not sure," I say, shrugging. "It has to be someone we know, right? Maybe even a guest here at the wedding?"

"It's possible. He could have had a totally secret life, too, though."

"Shut up," I groan, almost insulted by the mention that my father would be a two-timing player with a double life.

"I'm just saying." Valentina lifts her hands in surrender. "I'm sure it's someone here, honestly. All of the family that is here was at our quinceañera. Even if it isn't someone here, there is bound to be a cousin, uncle, or aunt that has the information we need. So what do you plan to do now? Ask every guest who likes rice pudding?"

I look down at the recipe. I considered doing that. Just interrogating every single person. But that wouldn't get me much closer to an answer—lots of people like rice pudding. But maybe, just maybe, someone really loves *my father's* rice pudding. I need everyone to try my father's recipe and gauge their reactions. Then, maybe I'll know who he's talking about and be one step closer to figuring out…whatever he's trying to tell me. It's a bit of a stretch, but I have to start somewhere. This is the first major clue and seems easy enough to get this investigation started.

Plus, as a bonus, Luciano can sample it too, bringing me one step closer to securing his investment.

"I have an idea," I finally say as Valentina takes a sip of some leftover cafecito one of her staff made earlier.

They've all started tidying up the kitchen and getting trays of hors d'oeuvres ready to be brought out as the guests wait. God forbid they should have to sit around and wait for food. If I had asked my mother for a snack while she was preparing dinner, I don't think I'd be alive right now.

Valentina just continues sipping her espresso, knowing I'll elaborate eventually, which irritates me.

"Don't you want to know?" I bark.

"Aren't you going to tell me anyways? Who cares if I want to know or not," she says with a sly smile.

My face feels flushed.

"Okay, anyways"—I huff—"I was wondering if we could make my father's rice pudding recipe for dessert tonight. I think it would really impress Luciano."

Valentina laughs into her coffee, causing herself to choke a bit.

"I'm serious."

"You want to step into *my* kitchen? During the service? And make an entirely new dessert for your little mystery puzzle? I said you could use the kitchen for your little business plan, but changing the menu for tonight?"

"Well, I—"

She raises an eyebrow, clearly amused but skeptical. "You know my team is already prepping everything, right? This isn't some random home kitchen. It's a finely tuned machine."

"I get that, but this is important. It's my dad's recipe. It could help me make a connection with Luciano." I pause, trying to gauge her reaction. "Please, Val. Just this once?"

"Hey, you two. Getting along?"

Sofia saunters in, wearing a gorgeous white tulle dress with mesh details on the bodice. It has a short train that gracefully follows her every step. Her hair is curled to perfection and cascading down her shoulders and back. She's wearing a tiny but exquisite tiara, because of course she is.

"Oh—hey." Valentina clears her throat. "You look great."

"You think so?" Sofia giggles and twirls.

Valentina smiles and nods.

"Obviously. Always the cutest in the room."

I look between both of them. Why is Valentina suddenly acting so different? I want to roll my eyes, but I can't look away, even for a second.

"So I see dinner is just about done. So excited! And you're making the—"

"The duck confit, just like you requested," Valentina replies.

"Ah, perfect! You're amazing," Sofia squeals, putting her hands on top of Valentina's.

Valentina looks down at their hands touching, as if she's caught in a daydream. I watch her softly caress Sofia's fingers before Sofia pulls away quickly.

"And is everything okay for you, prima? Are you excited about the hike and brunch tomorrow? I know how much you've always wanted to attend this camp."

I almost forgot I was in the room as I watched their exchange. I come back to reality for a second to respond.

"Yep! Everything is great. I'm honestly so excited to be here. Everyone is so nice, and it's nice to catch up and let everyone know how I'm doing. Actually, Valentina just agreed to help me make Roberto's famous rice pudding recipe for dessert tonight." I smile innocently at Valentina and then look back at Sofia.

"No. Fucking. Way." Sofia gasps. "Are you serious? I haven't had that for at least ten years now! Are you really going to make it, Valy?"

Valentina glances at me so fiercely, I'm pretty sure I can see daggers shoot out of her eyes and into my soul. I can't help but smile, though.

"That wasn't really a part of the plan, Sof," Valentina grumbles.

"Oh, *pleeeease*," Sofia begs with her hands clasped together.

She makes a whimpering sound like a helpless puppy.

"You can't always get away with this behavior, ya know," Valentina complains. "You're getting married soon."

"Oh, please, Val. Do it for me," Sofia pleads.

Valentina laughs softly and nods her head.

"Thank you, babe! You're the best." Sofia jumps up and hugs Valentina, throwing her arms around her neck. Her dress lifts slightly off the floor. "I must mingle with the guests, but I'll see you soon, right? Bye!"

We watch as she prances away, as a moment of silence grows between us. All you can hear is the clinking of dishes behind us and the murmuring of voices as the kitchen staff finishes the final touches. I watch as Valentina stares at the recipe, slowly biting her lower lip.

"So," I say.

"What?" Valentina replies, almost surprised I'm still standing here, clearly lost in her little world.

"You're in love with Sofia," I state.

Valentina snaps her head so quickly in my direction I'm surprised it didn't break right off.

"Excuse me?" She scoffs. "What the hell are you talking about?"

"Oh, please. The tension was palpable. You can see it all over your puppy-dog face. How long has it been? Does she know?"

"There's nothing to know," Valentina says between clenched teeth.

Clearly, this is a touchy subject for her, but I'm unbelievably amused.

"Did you ever plan on telling her?"

"Don't you have some mystery to solve? That you've now involved me in it," Valentina retorts.

"Oh, my God. You weren't going to tell her. You're just going to let her get married and never confess? Are you also going to appear at her doorstep during Christmas with big white cardboard signs expressing your love, à la *Love Actually*?"

Valentina sighs deeply.

"So I'm right," I say.

"Whatever," Valentina replies. "It's not a big deal anymore. She's getting married, and I'm catering her wedding. Not to mention I'm her maid of honor."

"Why are you even working at your best friend's wedding?"

"Because she asked me if I could. Her caterer dropped out at the last minute, and she begged me one night, crying on my couch. How could I let her down, you know? I wanted to show her that I was there for her till the very end."

I sit on the metal counter, facing the staff, and watch them move swiftly around the kitchen.

I snort. "That's rough. I wouldn't be able to do it. Watch the love of my life be with someone else. I'd go crazy. Probably ruin the wedding or something."

"Well, actually"—Valentina looks around us to ensure no one is nearby—"I do plan on ruining the wedding."

Suddenly, my stomach flips. I have to grab the edge of the counter to keep myself from spinning into a panic.

"Uh, come again?"

Valentina's eyes narrow, but there's something behind her expression—a quiet desperation. "Luciano is not good for her. She deserves to be with someone who has known her her whole life. And would do anything for her. And well, that person should have been me. So I'm going to stop this wedding."

The calm with which she says this is mindboggling, but I can see it now—the love that blinds her. The way she talks about Sofia isn't just about protecting her. Valentina really believes she's the only one who should be with her. I leap off the table, snatching the book from her hands to force her to look at me.

"Are you fucking insane? I was *joking*. You can't destroy the wedding. Sofia is your best friend; why would you want to ruin something she's spent so much time planning?"

"Because," Valentina murmurs.

"Because what?" I reply impatiently.

"It's my last shot, Valdes. I should have tried to do more when they started dating but I didn't think it was serious. Then they got engaged, but I didn't think it would last. Now they're about to actually get married. I just—I can't let that happen. She deserves to be with someone who appreciates her the way I do. So I need to end it now before it's too late."

"How do you even plan on doing that?"

"Well, I have a few tricks up my sleeve. But I need some help. An ally, if you will." She grins mischievously at me.

I know that look way too well.

"Absolutely not."

"Oh, come on. We'd make a great team! Listen, I'll make you a deal. You help me end this wedding, and I'll help you solve whatever silly mystery is in your father's book, starting with the rice pudding recipe."

"I can't!" I exclaim. "I'm supposed to win an investment with Luciano, remember?"

"Don't worry. I'll make sure no one knows you were an accomplice. You'll be my silent partner. Listen, it will happen regardless, so you either help me and I help you, or you figure your stuff out yourself and I still go on with my plan. So what do you say?"

I can't lose this investment. If I do, the chances of me losing everything increase exponentially. I won't be able to pay Gabriel the back rent and get us caught up. If I'm exposed, I'll lose the chance to show everyone I fit in with them. That I'm not just the poor pitiful niece or cousin they probably mock as they eat caviar and drink expensive wine I can't pronounce. I'm somebody. I have a restaurant, and to their knowledge, I want to open another.

I know they don't say it to my face, but it's there, under the surface. My mother used to say that's why we never quite fit in with them—why there's always been that invisible gap. It's as if no matter how hard I work, how much I try, I'll never quite catch up to their world of wealth and success. Maybe they don't even notice, but I do. I feel it every time they talk about designers out of my price bracket, or when they would buy me extravagant gifts when I was younger and forget to take off the price tag, and I had to remind myself not to look at the cost.

But having Valentina help me with this book will make it so much easier to go through with my plan. She's been with the family longer than I have, thanks to my mother. Valentina may have information I don't have. I can't lose that chance, either. So, maybe I'll lie. Keep your friends close and enemies closer, right? The closer I am to her, the better I can be at foiling her plans without her knowing.

"All right," I finally decide. "Maybe I can help a bit."

Valentina turns to me and smiles.

"I knew you'd do it—so, deal?"

She extends her hand out, waiting for mine. I take a deep breath and shake her hand.

"You've got a deal."

She tosses me an apron, and I catch it, fumbling slightly. "All right, let's see if you actually know what you're doing," she teases, her tone light but challenging. "I'm not doing all the work, though. This is a team effort."

"Deal."

As I tie the apron, the strings get tangled in a knot, and I mutter a curse under my breath.

"You're a mess," Valentina teases, stepping behind me. "Here, let me."

Her fingers brush lightly against my back as she untangles the strings and ties them in a perfect bow. I try not to shiver at the contact. "Thanks," I mumble, avoiding her gaze.

"Don't mention it. Can't have you tripping over yourself while we cook."

"Ha-ha," I deadpan, rolling my sleeves up.

We start working in sync, with Valentina expertly crushing a cinnamon stick while I zest an orange and lemon. The air fills with a mix of warm spices and bright citrus, and I can't help but feel a sense of ease, even in her presence.

"Smell that?" she asks, holding the crushed cinnamon under my nose.

I lean in, inhaling deeply. "It smells incredible."

Valentina smiles, her voice soft. "Kind of like home, doesn't it?"

Something about her tone makes my chest tighten, and I nod, suddenly lost in the memory of my dad's kitchen. "Yeah. Exactly like home."

We rinse the rice together, Valentina nudging me with her elbow as I swirl it under the water. "You sure you know what you're doing? Don't want to mess up this sacred recipe."

I smirk at her. "I'm a professional, remember? I run an actual restaurant, Garcia. I think I can handle a pot of rice."

As the rice cooks, we take turns stirring it to make sure it doesn't scorch. Valentina leans over me, her shoulder brushing mine. "The trick is to stir just enough, but not too much," she murmurs.

Her proximity makes my pulse quicken, and I glance at her. "You don't think I know that?" I ask, keeping my tone light.

She grins, her eyes glinting with amusement. "Just checking. Don't want to lose the big investment."

"Please," I retort, rolling my eyes but smiling. "I've been making arroz con leche since before I could reach the stove."

"Guess I'll let you take the lead then," she replies, stepping back with a playful shrug.

We add the three milks one at a time, stirring constantly until the mixture thickens. Valentina hands me a spoon to taste it. "Well?" she asks, watching me closely.

I take a bite, letting the creamy, cinnamon-infused flavors melt on my tongue. "It's perfect."

Her lips curl into a small smile. "Told you we'd make a good team."

I roll my eyes but feel a warmth spreading through me that has nothing to do with the stove. "Yeah, yeah. Don't let it go to your head."

As we spoon the pudding into ramekins and top each with a sprinkle of cinnamon and orange zest, Valentina glances at me. "You know, I think your dad would be proud."

I look at her, struck by the sincerity in her voice. "Thanks, Val. That means a lot."

She shrugs, but her gaze lingers. "Don't mention it. You can head out to mingle with everyone. I just need to clean up a few things here."

I turn around to see that the staff has already left. I didn't even hear them. We must have been so caught up in our own work that they sneaked right by.

I rush to remove my apron and grab my things. I take a look at my dress in the reflection of the cooler. Could anyone tell that it's cheap? I wish I knew more about fabric. Maria said it was fine, but who knows with her. This is the first night, and I should have dressed to impress with one of the dresses I borrowed from her.

As I'm about to leave, I pause for a moment. *Don't do it, Isa.* Leaving Valentina to clean up our mess at the last minute would mean she'd be late for dinner, and I need her there to help me sleuth. I groan loudly and head back into the kitchen, throwing my stuff onto the counter. I remove my shawl, collect all the dishes, and put them near the sink, where she's already begun to wash them.

"What are you doing?" She looks at me, bemused.

"I'm helping you clean your dishes," I reply. "I'm surprised your staff didn't wash them. They did all the rest of them."

"I always tell them to leave mine. I never want them to feel like I'm taking advantage of them. You don't have to help me, Isa."

"Yeah, I know. But then you'll be late, and I need you."

"You need me, huh?" Valentina jokes. "I like being late. That means I'll miss most of the event and can just go back to the cabin and sleep while I dread tomorrow's stupid hike I couldn't get out of."

"Well, I need you to help me figure out who the rice pudding is for. And, more importantly, I need to refresh my memory on family members so I can keep tabs on everyone. I have to solve this mystery," I say, my voice more serious now. "This journal—it's not just recipes. There's something buried in here that could change everything. I need to figure it out."

I pause, glancing at Valentina. "And of course, I also need to secure that investment. That's the only way I can save… I mean grow the restaurant. So yeah, I'm juggling both," I add with a hint of sarcasm. "Plus, you could, I don't know, figure out new ways to ruin their wedding. And I'm actually happy to go on the hike tomorrow."

Valentina stays quiet for a moment, pondering my words. "Why are you helping me right now?"

Honestly, I'm not entirely sure why I am. It's not as if I did this to her. She's the one who has poor time management. Plus, she's practically forcing me to help her destroy my cousin's wedding. And after her rude comment about not falling in love with her, I should want to see her suffer. But for some reason, I just want to be here. Maybe it's our history. Perhaps it's the smell of vanilla in her hair.

"You helped me with the rice pudding. Just say thanks."

"Oh. Right. Thank you. Seriously. This is nice of you. Even after I ruined your dress when we were younger. I'm seriously sorry about that. I promise I didn't mean to."

I freeze for a moment, caught off guard by the sudden apology. This is something I've been holding on to for so long, and now that she's finally bringing it up, it feels too quick, too easy. I let the words hang in the air for a second longer than I should. "I know," I say slowly, feeling my words come out a little too stiff. "I forgive you…for that."

I take a small step back, fiddling with my shawl as I look away, making sure not to get too comfortable with this moment. "But don't think this is some big thing between us," I add with a shrug, my voice light but guarded. "We'll call it a truce. For now."

Valentina's eyes flicker with something I can't quite place, but she just nods. "A truce it is," she says, a faint smile tugging at her lips. I force a small smile back and turn toward the dishes, the moment passing, though the weight of it still hangs in the air.

While Valentina washes the dishes, I quickly dry them and put them away. It's incredible how quickly one can move when they have someone helping. I wonder if my time prepping in the morning at La Mariposa would be cut in half if I just scheduled Faye to help me.

"So, why are you so excited about this hike?" Valentina asks, breaking the long silence as we meditatively clean the kitchen.

"I've always loved the idea of camp. Hiking, getting outside, doing something completely different—it's kind of like my childhood dream coming true. I know Sofia used to come here a lot, and I always wanted to join her, but I never got the chance."

I glance out the window at the foliage blooming in the mountains, a smile tugging at my lips. "There's something about being out here, you know? It feels like an adventure. I think it all started with watching *The Parent Trap* when I was younger. I became obsessed with all the fun activities—like fencing, the campfires, the freedom. I guess this hike is my way of finally living a piece of that."

Valentina chuckles softly. "Well, I don't think there's fencing, but you'll definitely get some adventure. Maybe even a little *Parent Trap* magic."

I snort. "Yeah, I just need to find some Oreos and peanut butter to bring it all together."

"Is that from the movie?" Valentina asks.

"Of course it is. Don't you remember watching it?"

She shakes her head.

"We watched it when we were kids. I remember it vividly. You and Sofia were on the bed, and Maria and I were lying on the floor on a bunch of blankets and pillows. Tía Rosita ordered pizza, and we ate it straight from the box."

Valentina tilts her head, thinking. "You know, that does sound kind of familiar."

"It was one of those nights, you know? When we all hung out together, no drama. Just us, the movie, and way too much pizza." I smile, thinking about how easy everything felt back then. "You used to always make fun of the way they ate Oreos with peanut butter in the movie. You said it was disgusting."

Valentina puts a hand to her chin, her eyes softening as if the memory is slowly coming back. "I guess I did say that, didn't I?"

"Yeah, you did. But you still tried it. You always did stuff like that—mock it, but then dive in anyway. That's what made it fun."

"Well, it must not have been that great if I can't even remember it," she says, though her tone lacks its usual edge.

I chuckle. "You were too busy trying to be cool to care about a camp movie."

She smiles at that, and for a moment, I see a flicker of the girl she used to be. The one I used to laugh with, back when things were simple.

"It's a great film about long-lost sisters and family and falling in love. What do you know about romance anyways?" I take a handful of bubbles created by the dish soap and blow it in her face. Valentina laughs as she wipes it away, her eyes beaming.

"Whatever you say, Isa," she says, rolling her eyes.

"You know, I don't need to help you." I throw the towel down abruptly. "I can leave you to your mess."

"No, don't leave!" Valentina says in between giggles.

"Give me one good reason I shouldn't," I tease, feeling a strange sense of warmth creeping up my neck.

She wipes some sweat off her forehead with her shirt, and the movement sends a jolt through me. Maybe it's the way her muscles flex, or the small veins on her forearm exposed by her rolled-up sleeve. My eyes linger longer than I'd like to admit.

"Well"—she grins, her voice softer this time—"I like your company."

Her words hang in the air, and suddenly the room feels smaller. I try to laugh it off, but something about the way she says it—so sincere, almost intimate—makes my heart skip. I look away quickly, hoping she doesn't notice the heat rising in my cheeks.

Chapter Nine

I didn't mean to walk into the dinner with Valentina, and it feels like everyone's eyes are on us. I clear my throat lightly to try and swallow the lump developing. I almost regret staying behind to help her clean. I would have had more time to mingle and find my seat. Now it looks like I'm making some grand entrance with Valentina. As if we're some power couple. Oh God.

"You've got this," Valentina whispers. "Just pretend you're a detective on a secret mission to uncover the truth. Like a regular Nancy Drew."

"You can't think of any other detective? How about an actual adult? Like Carmen Sandiego," I argue.

She smiles. "All right, all right. Carmen, it is."

We walk toward the long wood table set up under a canopy of string lights. I must look like an absolute pauper next to Valentina. Her crimson satin dress hugs her every curve as if it was specifically designed for her body. Then again, I wouldn't be surprised if it actually was. I remember Sofia gloating that her quinceañera dress was created especially for her by some French designer I had never heard of. Valentina probably got the same treatment since they were "besties." My parents bought my dress from the discount section of a gaudy dress shop. Even though my mother tried to alter it, she's no seamstress. I spent the rest of the night lifting the bust while it continuously slid down with every movement.

I feel like I'm fifteen again.

"You clean up nicely," I whisper. "You know, from the chef's costume."

Valentina laughs and puts her hand on my back, pushing me slightly forward to walk around the table. A chill shoots up my spine. I hope she can't feel my goosebumps. She continues to lead me past the servers until we're standing in front of two chairs next to each other.

"Hey, cuz!" Maria pulls my arm and drags me down to the seat beside her. I nearly trip on my heels in the process.

"Rip my arm off, why don't you?" I groan.

"What a coincidence you and Valentina are sitting beside each other, huh?" she whispers in my ear.

"Yeah, it is," I say.

She moves closer to my ear.

"It's not a coincidence," she whispers again.

"Yeah, I know," I retort.

"I did this," she whispers even closer to my ear.

"Yeah, I get it, pendeja. Get your breath off me," I say, pushing her with my shoulder.

Maria giggles as she settles back in her seat.

Voices overlap as I scan the table. This is my first time seeing everyone attending Sofia's exclusive wedding. The top-tier people in her life, I assume. The people who weren't invited probably have a severe case of FOMO. Something about knowing that friends of Sofia didn't make the cut makes me feel incredibly smug. I haven't seen her in ten years. Sure, I'm family, but it's been a decade. Surely, she could have invited anyone else.

"So, how about we break down everyone that's here?" Valentina says to me while the appetizers arrive.

"Okay, that's a great idea." I take a bite of the soft bread a waiter brought in a basket with garlic butter.

"All right, so we have the obvious, of course. Your aunt and Sofia's mom, Rosita. She was siblings with Mariposa and friends with Roberto. Could be a suspect."

I shrug. "Possibly, but doubtful. She hated drama, from what I remember."

"Next to her, we have Abuelita. An innocent old lady or a conniving menace to society? Also Roberto's mother."

"Excuse me," I yelp. "Abuelita is an angel."

"You're right." Valentina chuckles.

"Okay, next to her, we have my Tía Maritza and her daughter, Silvana," I add.

"Also my ex," Valentina mumbles quietly.

"Wait, what?" I glance over at Silvana, who just happens to be looking directly at me, almost as if she could hear our entire conversation clear as day. There's no way—there are too many people talking at once. It sounds like a high school cafeteria out here.

"Yeah, let's not get into that one." She sips her wine. "Next to her, we've got your cousins and Sofia's bridesmaids, Yolanda and Araceli. Doubtful they're suspects, but we can't rule anyone out."

"Fair," I play along. "You can never be too sure."

We lean over subtly to check out the other side of the table.

"Okay, I'm sure you met Daniel, Sofia's man bestie and guide for the whole event."

"Yes, definitely," I say, nodding. "Who is that guy next to him?"

"That would be Luis. He's Luciano's best friend and the best man for the wedding. Next to him are the two twins, Ramon and Rafael. They're also groomsmen."

"Okay, they'll probably be pretty useless to me," I say, laughing.

Valentina grins. "Undoubtedly so."

I point my chin in the direction of the far end of the table. "That's my cousin Alessandro—I could never forget that face. He was practically designed to be a handsome movie star."

"If you say so. Then lastly, we have Luciano's parents, John and Sarah, and of course, the bride and groom."

"Right. What about the other guests? I don't recognize any of them."

"They're probably a mixture of Luciano and Sofia's college friends and some coworkers. No one important. We need to focus on the family more than anything. That's where we will find our answers."

I nod, a determination settling in my chest. "This is about figuring out who my father's special recipe was for. If it wasn't for my mother, then there's something—someone—he wanted to remember. Tonight, we'll gather as much intel as we can."

Fireflies begin to wander near the table, which only makes the area look that much more magical. I watch their lights flicker on and off as they move through the bushes. I don't think I've ever seen a firefly in person before. Yet, I want to catch one and put it in a jar as my night-light.

"I can't believe there aren't any mosquitos or flies out here. How does that happen?" Maritza says.

"That's because I had my dear fiancé treat the entire place so they wouldn't attack us all week." Sofia looks at Luciano lovingly.

"She's a murderer," Maria whispers and laughs at her own stupid joke.

"That must have cost a fortune," Maritza replies, almost as if she's calculating how much it would actually cost. So nosy.

Luciano laughs. "Anything for my Sofie."

I can hear Valentina groaning under her breath.

"That's a lot of chemicals," she finally says. "Isn't that harmful to the environment, Luc?"

Everyone looks over at Valentina, then back at Luciano and Sofia.

"Oh, Val, don't be such a tree hugger." Sofia snorts. "It's only for this week. They'll be back in no time, I promise."

"I just don't know if I could do that." Valentina shrugs. "But that's just me," she says as she sips her wine.

Sofia laughs awkwardly.

We all sit in silence for a moment. All you can hear is the clanking of spoons against the bowls as we eat our first course: spiced pumpkin bisque. A nod to the upcoming season, I'm sure. I take my first slurp, and I'm immediately transported to a pumpkin patch. It's cozy, warm, and perfectly spiced. The nutmeg dances lightly around the heavy cinnamon. A dash of cloves adds some much-needed depth. It's perfectly balanced. I could sit here in silence forever, just slurping up my soup.

"Cute dress," Silvana states blandly.

I'm too distracted by my bowl of heaven to realize she's even talking to me. Maria nudges me lightly in the ribs with her elbow. I look up to see Silvana staring directly at me. It takes me a second to remember what she said.

I look down at my dress and back up at her. A slanted smile creeps onto her face.

"Thanks," I reply.

"Where's it from? Forever 21?" Silvana laughs.

A rush of heat swells in my cheeks.

"It's Calvin Klein," I say quietly.

Silvana leans closer across the table, squinting her eyes as if it would make her vision clearer. It feels like she can see right through my dress and find that it's just tattered rags sewn together by my mice friends.

"Doesn't look like anything I've seen from him. Must be old," she finally says.

"You mean like the Prada dress you're wearing from four seasons ago?" Valentina chimes in.

She doesn't look up from the wine she's been swishing in a circle. Her long, slender fingers envelop the glass, keeping it comfortably secure in her grasp.

Silvana huffs in her seat and returns to stabbing pieces of lettuce from her side salad to shove into her mouth.

"Thanks," I murmur loud enough for Valentina to hear.

"Anytime," she says, pressing her leg against mine lightly.

I can't help but wonder if Valentina was trying to defend me or just wanted to shut her ex up for once. Either way, I feel grateful. I was sure I was just about to get exposed as the liar I am, especially considering the dress I'm wearing is a random one I found at TJ Maxx a year ago and hung up in my closet, never to be worn.

How does Valentina even know Silvana's dress is four seasons old? I didn't even know there were seasons for clothing. It's easier to fake it with accessories; a designer bag, even if it's not real, does most of the talking for you with all those obvious emblems. But clothes? They're more subtle. No logo to flash, no easy shortcut to convince people you belong. I usually don't have to think about it—I spend my days in my usual work clothes. Dior and I aren't exactly on a first-name basis.

I glance down at my dress, one I brought from home instead of from Maria's closet. I had tried on a few of her pieces, but none of them felt like me. They were stunning, sure—sleek cuts, luxurious fabrics, and designer labels—but I felt like I was walking around in someone else's life, wearing their choices, not mine.

This dress, at least, is mine. It might not have cost more than my monthly rent, but I know every thread and seam. I know how it moves when I walk, how it feels against my skin. It feels safe, even if it doesn't scream "luxury." Still, I can't help but wonder if my family's trained eyes can tell the difference. The thought makes my throat tighten. I don't know if I can keep pulling this off.

I grab some water to keep my throat from closing up. Immediately, a waiter appears and refills it.

"Oh, thanks," I mumble, startled by his attentiveness.

I guess I shouldn't expect anything less from an event organized by Sofia.

The main course starts to come out of the main hall, where several servers walk down in unison, holding plates. One of the servers places a dish in front of me. It's the duck confit, and it looks divine. In fact, it looks like something I probably couldn't afford to eat otherwise. Maybe because it's duck, and I wouldn't even know where to get a duck. Your local pond? It could be because Valentina does an excellent job at plating dishes to make them look like literal works of art. It's nothing compared to the Cuban sandwiches I serve at La Mariposa. Even our fanciest flan doesn't compete. I might as well be serving slop in comparison.

"So, mija. How's business?" Rosita asks in between bites of the duck. The pieces are so soft they practically melt in your mouth.

I try to swallow a bite before speaking. This is my time to shine. Or lie. Mostly lie. Oh God.

"It's going well."

I hear Maria snort silently next to me, but I ignore her.

"We're looking to expand to help grow our customer base and footprint in our small New Jersey area. In fact, I was hoping to talk to Luciano a bit about it."

"I'm looking forward to hearing your big plans for the new space," Luciano adds.

I muster a small smile, trying to project confidence. "Actually, you'll get a little preview tonight. It's something special, and I think it'll give you a taste of what La Mariposa is all about."

Luciano raises his brows, intrigued. "Now I'm even more curious about your restaurant."

"It's so great to see you and Mari are finally doing well for yourselves," Maritza says.

Her words are nice, but the tone has an edge to it. Almost as if she's trying to remind me how poor we once were. Well, still are.

"Yeah, it's interesting. La Mariposa, you said it's called?" Silvana says as she scrolls through her phone.

"That's correct."

"Weird, your social media channels are pretty bland. Not a lot of followers."

"So?" Maria pipes in, offended since she's the one who manages most of it.

"I'm just surprised that someone about to expand their business has such a small footprint on the internet. Where does your marketing come from?"

"Since when are you a marketing expert?" Valentina barks back, startling Silvana.

"It's mostly through flyers, ads in the local paper, and word of mouth," I reply.

"I just find that a bit surprising. You can't possibly get enough business just from word of mouth."

I stare at my half-eaten duck, trying to think of what I could say to stop this line of questioning.

"What do you plan to do about—"

"Oh my God, will you shut up?" Maria shouts. "You're so fucking nosy. It's none of your business, Silvie. Just eat your fucking duck. Damn."

For a moment, everyone is quiet. Their eyes shifting back and forth between each other. Then, almost as if it was rehearsed earlier, they all begin laughing. Luciano nearly spits out his wine. Abuelita is giggling so hard, her eyes are completely closed from the grin on her face. Rosita has tears falling down her face.

Maritza and Silvana, on the other hand, are unamused. Silvana's cheeks are flushed, probably from embarrassment. I can't say I'm unhappy about this.

"Maria, you nailed it right on the head," Rosita says, laughing even louder. "These two are the nosiest putas in this place."

Everyone laughs so much harder. Even I can't help but join in.

I look over at Silvana, who is just glaring at me. Something tells me I just became her new target for the week.

I was never close to Silvana or Maritza, who, like Rosita, is my mother's sister. She and my mother were so different that they never got along. I barely saw my aunt and cousin, but when I did, I remember thinking what an absolute snob Silvie was. It looks like she still is one, if not worse now.

The first dessert course arrives, and it's the original one they planned before I came and added another one. It's a merlot-poached pear. I don't even know how to eat it. Do I pick it up and take a bite? It's all soggy. There's no way. I see everyone using a fork and a knife to slice into the pear. I'm suddenly incredibly excited about the rice pudding afterward.

"Interesting dessert choice," I whisper to Valentina.

"Only the best for your highness," she mutters.

"Do you normally make desserts like this at your gigs?"

Valentina nods. "This is the norm for me. I get a lot of... bougie clients, for lack of a better word. They like to eat fancy dishes to make themselves seem important. To them, a simple plate with a random pear is decadent. A symbol of class."

"And for you?" I say, glancing up at her eyes. The string lights above us make them sparkle.

She smirks. "I hate pears."

I can't help but smile back. The way her eyes crease every time she grins makes me want to melt. Maybe it's just the merlot in the pear getting to me or the second glass of chardonnay I had earlier. I feel a buzzing in my head, hyperaware of her presence next to me. The way her thigh presses up against mine, even though there's definitely room. The sweet scent that wafts in the air whenever she flips her hair back to reveal her long neck.

"What the fuck is this?" Maria whispers, breaking my trance.

"What do you mean? It's obviously a fancy dessert for fancy people like us," I joke.

"We need some flan or tres leches up in here. Who do I speak to about this?" Maria laughs as she pokes the pear with her knife.

"Just eat it, you child," I demand. "We need to play the part."

If it weren't for Silvana, I would be in a perfect position to continue talking to Luciano. Now is the time, before the real dessert—Roberto's arroz con leche—that I should gather some more information about him. I need to know everything I can to impress him with my business plan.

"So, how did you two meet?" I ask, pointing back and forth between Luciano and Sofia.

They look into each other's eyes in perfect unison and smile like a couple of almost newlyweds, blindly in love.

"Oh, brother," Valentina mumbles.

"Should I say or do you want to, mi amor?" Luciano coos.

"You can say it. Or I can say it." Sofia giggles.

"I think you should."

"No, no, you should!"

"I'll say it then," Maria squawks. "It all started in the men's bathroom at Olive Gard—"

"That's okay," Sofia chimes in. "Luciano will start."

"We met at a holiday party my parents threw in NYC. They invited all their friends and colleagues, including your aunt Rosita. She does all our accounting."

"And he ignored me the entire night." Sofia snorts. "I kept trying to get his attention, and he kept looking the other way. Acted like a total prick."

"How chivalrous," Valentina murmurs with a faint smile,

keeping her tone light. "You spent the rest of the night complaining to me about it, desperate to go home. Remember? I recall you feeling really rejected."

"Yeah, but right before we left, he finally approached me." Sofia's eyes light up as she feeds Luciano a slice of her poached pear.

Luciano smiles, putting an arm around her. "I was just so nervous to talk to such a beautiful woman."

Valentina's lips curl into a small smile.

"Well," Sofia says softly, "it all worked out in the end."

"I still think my version was better," Maria mutters, causing a few guests nearby to snicker.

"And your parents, sorry I haven't been able to meet them yet. Hi! I'm Isabella." I lean over to see them past a few of the other guests. They lean in and wave back.

"Hi, I'm John, and this is my wife, Sarah," Luciano's father replies in a surprisingly deep voice. "Actually, I wanted to thank you all for inviting us to the wedding. We know it was pretty exclusive. We weren't sure we would make it on the list."

"Dad..." Luciano rolls his eyes.

A sense of longing circulates in my gut. I miss my dad's dumb jokes.

"We really are so grateful," his mother says. Her voice is smooth, like honey. "It's so nice to meet people from a different culture. We tried our best with Lucie here, but we can only do so much."

Luciano holds her hand and squeezes it. She smiles back at him.

"He's adopted," Maria whispers in my ear.

"No shit, pendeja," I whisper back.

"I think that's why he's most excited about you, Isa," Sarah says.

"Me?"

I watch the servers come by to take our empty dessert plates away. That means the rice pudding is coming up.

"Yes, absolutely. We invest in many restaurants, but you'll be his first one, and he's so excited it's a Cuban restaurant. It's like a way to be in a different part of the world he's been missing."

"Wow, I'm honored. Thank you."

Honored, and now there's a giant indestructible boulder on my shoulders. He's going to be exceptionally disappointed if he finds out the truth. I should just come clean now. Let everyone know I'm a fraud.

As I consider it, I see the servers come back, now holding trays with small ramekins on top. I can smell the cinnamon as they approach us and start putting one down in front each of us.

There it is. My father's arroz con leche. It's almost as if he made it himself in the kitchen. I have to actively stop myself from running back into the main hall to see if he's in there, whipping up more pudding for us to enjoy. The top layer is dusted with cinnamon. There's a lone cinnamon stick leaning against the ramekin, as if it's relaxing in a warm, gooey hot tub. I take the smallest spoon and scoop some of the rice, my excitement growing. Slowly, I bite, allowing the flavors to coexist in my mouth simultaneously, feeling the rice's softness and the pudding's creaminess. It's perfect.

"What is this amazing concoction?" John says in utter awe as he takes another bite.

"It's delicious," Luciano chimes in.

"Arroz con leche," I say proudly.

"Valentina, did you make this?" Rosita replies, her eyes wide.

"Isa and I did, but it's not my recipe."

"It tastes like Roberto's, doesn't it, Rosita?" Maritza squeals.

"It really does," she agrees. "Abuelita, did you try it? Here, take a bite."

Rosita cautiously feeds Abuelita a little spoonful of the pudding.

"Ah, si. My Roberto made this. I remember this," she says gleefully, opening her mouth for another bite.

"It's his recipe," I finally admit.

They all stop and look at me like a deer caught in headlights.

"No mientes!" Rosita says.

"I'm not lying! It's really his recipe. Valentina and I made it together tonight to surprise you all. It's my way of saying thank you for having me here."

Rosita starts clapping with excitement.

"Wow, you nailed it, Isabellita. This is my favorite dessert!"

Valentina and I both look at each other quickly as if we had the exact same thought.

"Oh, shut it, Rosita. This was my favorite first," Maritza replies. "You discovered it after me."

We look at each other again. If only eyes could speak, they'd say, "what the fuck is going on right now?"

"No, it's my favorite." Sofia laughs. "He made it for me all the time when I would visit."

I can't believe this is happening right now. I also don't know why I'm surprised. Why wouldn't this recipe be everyone's favorite? I remember how much everyone loved it. Except for my mother, I guess.

"No, es mía," says small, shaky voice in the background.

We all turn to look at Abuelita, giggling to herself, holding the empty ramekin. We all laugh in unison.

"I guess it's Abuelita's favorite," Rosita says.

"It's my favorite now too!" Luciano states. "If this is how the food is at La Mariposa, I'm already impressed, Isa. I can't wait for more."

I can't help but smile. I've already impressed Luciano.

I turn to Valentina. "I don't know why you hate him," I whisper to her. "He seems great."

"It's not about him," she mumbles, but I ignore her, still riding the high of the possibility of saving La Mariposa.

That was easy enough. I can't say I'm surprised—my father's food is the best. But there's something else lingering for me now. We have four potential suspects: Rosita, Maritza, Abuelita, and Sofia, who all said the dessert was their favorite. It could be any of them.

I glance at the list of names, the possibilities swirling in my mind. I'm not even sure where this path is taking me, but I need to figure out who it was meant for and why my father thought this recipe mattered enough to hide it. Maybe this will lead me to something bigger—something that could finally help me make sense of all the pieces he left behind. Or what happened the night of the quinceañera that forced me away from my extended family. Maybe even something that could help me save the restaurant.

Chapter Ten

"Is that what you're wearing?"

I look down at my outfit. My brown corduroy trousers pair beautifully with my grey top and flannel. I even managed to wear hike-appropriate boots under my rolled-up pants. I tied my thick curly hair back in a high ponytail. I can't find anything wrong with my look.

"Yeah, is that a problem?"

"No, I'm just…surprised, is all."

I look over at Valentina's outfit. She's wearing black leggings, probably from Lululemon, and an oversized Gucci hoodie.

"You're wearing a Gucci hoodie on a hike?" I gasp. "That's risky."

"What else would I wear? It's all I brought, and I don't even want to go to this stupid bridal brunch. Besides, we're changing at the top. Luciano was supposed to set up several small changing tents and portable showers for the guests."

"Are you serious? That seems excessive," I say.

"That's Sofia for you. Never misses an opportunity to dress her best, even after a hike," she laughs.

I open my closet and pick out a lavender slip dress and a pair of strappy flats to put into a bag.

Valentina's Chelsea boots will not be a good choice for the terrain, but what do I know about hiking? Nothing other than that possibility of seeing Sasquatch at any given moment. At least, that's what I was always told growing up by pop culture and the internet before it was monitored better. The amount of cryptid urban legends I read about as a child has probably directly contributed to my anxiety in some way. Anyways, the point is, how could she possibly have an opinion on my outfit when that's what she's wearing? And I hate that I feel silly now wearing my corduroy pants. Sure, they weren't pricey, but at least I look like I might be going for a hike. They're brown! Brown is the color of dirt—and cuddly bears.

"Should I change?" I finally say after inspecting myself in the mirror of our cabin, twirling back and forth, trying to see if there's a patch or brand on my clothing that says "POOR" on it.

She smirks. "No, I like it. You look cute."

"Oh."

I don't know what to say. A warm feeling bubbles up inside my gut. Valentina must sense my awkwardness, because I hear her chuckling softly. I watch as she grabs her brown cross-body bag and slings it over her shoulders and across her chest.

"Have you ever been hiking before?" I ask.

"Not even in my imagination," she groans. "I'm not excited about this. I'm just not much of a 'let's go camping in the middle of the woods with no electricity and surrounded by bugs' kind of girl. Neither is Sofia. Anymore, at least. She just wants everyone to relive her childhood with her."

"Well, I personally don't mind," I say, grinning. "I want to live these dreams for the first time."

"Fair enough." Valentina smiles.

I pull my father's journal from my bag and set it on the dresser. We need to find another clue. I open the book to the rice pudding recipe and turn the pages until something stands out. There could be clues anywhere, but I need something obvious. As I flip through the pages of recipes, journal entries, and random photos glued inside, I stop at one specific page. There's a yellow note taped on it with a lipstick stain, as if someone kissed the paper.

"Whoa, look at this."

Valentina walks over and inspects the note.

"Do you think it was from your mom?"

"I'm not sure," I say, shrugging. "I don't remember her wearing makeup, let alone red lipstick like this. I think...it's from someone else."

"Well, fuck."

"Yeah. Who do you think it could be? Maybe someone here?" I look up at Valentina, suddenly realizing how much taller she is than me. Maybe it's just her boots. I feel dizzy.

"Could be Maritza. She wears lipstick all the time. We'll have to bring this with us and see if she's wearing lipstick when we get to the brunch. Then we can compare."

"Oh, God. What if my dad had an affair with Maritza," I groan.

"Maybe it was more than an affair. Maybe...it was love."

"Stop. Please. I'm begging you."

Valentina laughs, and I can't help but roll my eyes. But the way she's teasing me—there's something almost playful about it, as if she's enjoying the mystery as much as I am.

We have our next clue, and it's not something I would have wanted to find. I'm not sure exactly what my father is trying to show me, but I really hope it's not some "one that got away" type of love with my aunt Maritza. I slowly rip out the note, trying not to damage the page.

I glance over at Valentina, still smiling, and there's a spark in her eyes I haven't seen before. It's making me curious, maybe even a little bold. She seems different, more open, as if she's holding back less. I wonder if there's more to her than I thought.

"So," I say as I put the note in my pocket. "If you're not a hiking girl, what kind of girl are you?"

"Wouldn't you like to know," Valentina teases, a mischievous grin on her face.

"Yeah, actually, I would."

I step closer to her, trying to act like I'm confident when I can actually feel my knees trying not to buckle from the weight of my nervousness. I can almost see her eyes light up. I swear she's looking at me in a way she's never looked at me before. It's hard to pinpoint what it is. Amusement? Disdain?

"Oh, well, I don't think you're ready for that," Valentina coos.

"Try me," I say, way too confidently. I immediately regret it.

Valentina starts walking toward me, and I take a few steps back, which completely ruins how cool I just looked. She laughs softly, and I know full well she just called my bluff. What the fuck am I doing? This is Valentina Garcia. I hated her for so long. Now I'm…flirting with her?

"I'm just the kind of girl who prefers to go shopping, eat at nice restaurants with electricity and an amazing chef, and spend time at home in my condo with a view of Manhattan in the distance. Camping is…blech. I'm only here for Sofia and, well, to ruin her entire wedding."

I nod slowly, listening to every word. Or trying to, anyway. I'm still replaying her walking toward me just now.

"Well, it's unfortunate." I shrug.

"What is?"

"That you're such a Grinch about camping. We have all these outdoor activities planned while we're here. On top of us having to share a cabin. And a kitchen. This will be a hellish week for you, isn't it?"

"You know it. So let's hurry up and get it started, so it can be over faster."

She signals me out the door, and we head to the far end of the camp, where the rest of the guests await instruction.

"Good morning, wedding guests! I hope everyone slept amazingly and got their beauty rest," Daniel begins. "I will be guiding the hike this morning. We have about two miles to the top."

A few guests groan. Some are still yawning as if they just woke up. Or perhaps they never went to bed.

"I know, I know. But I promise the view and the brunch will be worth it. And we have changing stations and portable showers ready, so we can all look our absolute best for the bridal brunch. You may notice a few people missing, like Abuelita. Obviously, we won't be forcing our sweet grandma up the hike, but don't worry. Sofia has assured everyone that if they don't want to partake in the hike, they can stay behind and enjoy any services she's hired for the week. There's a massage therapist on site, two estheticians, a manicurist, and waiters bringing bottomless drinks to guests by the lake."

I almost regret not just staying behind and enjoying those amenities, but I have a mission—today, we need to figure out if the lipstick print on the note matches Maritza's.

"So let's start hiking and get to the top. Everyone ready?"

A few guests cheer. Luciano and Sofia are at the front of the group, with Maritza and Silvana near the middle. I can't get a good look at Maritza's lips, which is the strangest thought I've had about my aunt. Valentina, Maria, and I are hanging back, the last of the group. Everyone else could be models for a specialty outdoor store where a simple rain jacket costs $600. I look down at my corduroy pants and sigh. I should have changed.

Our hike begins at the trailhead closest to the lake. The sign at the front of the path says the route is four miles long, out and back. I'm not exactly sure how long that is, but it sounds like it will take forever. I groan at the thought. Despite how badly I want to be here, I'm not exactly what someone would describe as "outdoorsy." It's comical I even decided to go on this hike, but that doesn't mean I'm not unbelievably excited. I wish I could just run to the top of the mountain and cheer at the peak.

I also wish I could have trained for this to look less like someone who has never stepped foot on a mountain before in her boring life.

"I can't believe I agreed to go to this," Valentina grumbles.

As we begin our trek, my footsteps crunch on the carpet of fallen leaves and twigs. The dappled sunlight filters through the trees overhead, casting a warm glow on the forest floor. I inhale the fresh, earthy scent of the forest, noticing the smell of damp soil and pine. I hear the rustling of leaves in the gentle breeze, the occasional bird chirping, and the soft gurgling of a nearby stream.

As we continue through the trail, I'm thankful I wore my waterproof boots. Some areas are incredibly muddy, and the last thing I want is to get my shoe stuck in it. Valentina, on the other hand, is, unsurprisingly, a bit unlucky. She walks awkwardly around, looking for the driest spots, hoping the mud won't touch her ankles. Her logic is that the more awkwardly she walks, the less weight will be pressed into the dirt. Is it sound logic? No. Is it hilarious and slightly satisfying to watch her move like a marionette? Yes, absolutely.

"You're doing great, sweetie," I shout behind me as Valentina slows down during a particularly muddy section.

"Can you waddle any faster?" Maria complains. "We're losing the group!"

"Listen. I'm going as fast as I can. You two go on ahead. Leave me to my demise. I can only hope my death by mud drowning will be quick and painless."

I wave to Maria to go ahead and catch up with the group while I wait for Valentina.

She steps one foot forward, and I hear it plop into the mud

and sink slightly. Valentina waves her arms around in a circle to regain her balance.

"This is pathetic, Val." I snort. "Get your hiking legs! Put your back into it!"

"What do you think I'm doing, Valdes? Having a little puppet show in the mud for you?"

I'm trying incredibly hard not to laugh.

"Come on, pick up the next foot. You got this!"

"Isabella—" She grabs her thigh with both hands and swings her leg ahead of the other foot. "You just wait until I get over there."

"Will it be today? Because we've got things to do, you know. Brunch will be over by the time you're done making mud pies." I mockingly look down at my watch. "We all got through this part just fine. So why did you choose the muddiest part to walk through? Did you think you were Indiana Jones?"

"Why don't you come over here and help me?" she shouts and reaches her hand out toward me.

There is something so pleasing about the confident, charming Valentina looking like a newborn giraffe walking through the mud.

"Absolutely not. You're going to just pull me in with you. I know that trick."

"I won't. Get me out of this quicksand!"

"You're so dramatic." I sigh and reach my hand out toward her. "If you pull me in, I'm not speaking to you for the rest of the week."

"Oh, please, as if you wanted to speak to me anyways."

"Okay, fair."

I grab her hand and begin pulling her toward me. She lifts her back foot and lands on a dry part of the trail, but the other foot is still in the mud. She loses her balance and begins to lean backward. I grab her hand with both my arms now to prevent the fall.

"Isabella!" Valentina screams as we both fall into the mud.

I land right on top of her, but my boots, knees, and hands are covered in mud. I can't complain, considering Valentina's entire body saved me from the messy fall.

I look down at her face and realize we are perfectly at eye level, our noses practically touching. Considering how much taller she is than me, it is odd to see her so closely. Her eyes dart back and forth between my own. For a moment, it feels like we're the only two in the woods. No trail to hike. No family to impress. No investment to win. Just…us.

Sinking in the mud.

I smirk. "Thanks for breaking my fall, Val."

"You were supposed to save me, not throw me in the mud, Isa!"

"I thought you needed a mud bath. Your skin is going to be so soft after this."

"Maybe you need one, too, then."

"Oh, no, Val. I'm okay. Thanks, anyways."

I try to get up, but she wraps her legs around my waist and locks me in. I'm completely stunned, but I don't pull away. She jerks me toward her, pushing my face even closer to hers. I feel a jolt run through my body. With one fell swoop, she swings her body on top of mine, landing my back into the mud. This time, she is looking down at me.

"Who's dirty now, Isa?" Valentina laughs.

We stare each other down for what feels like an eternity and then suddenly break into laughter.

"Valentina! I'm supposed to be impressing Luciano. Now, look at me."

"Hey, at least we're both in the same mess," she says, grinning.

I can almost melt into the mud at the sight of her from this angle. The way the sun casts a halo around her hair. The little pieces of mud drying on her cheek and forehead. I could stare at her forever.

For a moment, we are silent, our eyes lingering. I watch as her eyes dart back and forth between mine again, but I can only imagine her thoughts. Butterflies quickly form in my stomach. My lips feel dry but achy, as if they need something. Something Valentina could provide. My heart is beating loudly in my chest. I'm almost certain she can hear it unless she miraculously has mud stuck inside her ears.

"Hey! Are you two all right?"

I lift my head to see Maria looking over at us.

"Yeah, we just fell in the mud," Valentina says, then turns around and gazes at me for a moment longer. Her eyes shift toward my lips and then back to my eyes. I freeze. She chuckles, climbs off of me, and stands up. I quickly become aware of the fact that I was lying in a disgusting pile of mud. It's the cold, icky dose of reality I need. What the hell am I doing? I need to get a grip.

"You go ahead. We'll catch up!" Valentina shouts.

"Good, because I don't want a part of any muddy mess," Maria cackles.

We stand up, and I look down at my clothes. Then, I look over at Valentina, who is completely covered.

"Your hoodie! I told you not to wear it."

I can only imagine how much it cost.

"Eh, it's fine. I'll get it dry-cleaned when we get back. Or buy a new one."

Right. I forgot. She's one of them. I'm the odd one out here.

We start to hike over to catch up with the group.

"At least we have the showers and a change of clothes, right?" I recall.

"Oh. Right. About that." Valentina chuckles.

"What did you do?" I groan.

"It's all part of my plan."

"Val…"

"Okay, so I may have moved the changing stations and portable showers yesterday. Hid them somewhere in the back of the woods at the top."

I stop and stare at her, feeling both annoyed and impressed. The sun casts a glow on her cheek.

"Are you fucking serious? Why did you do that?" I shout.

"Sh. Luciano was in charge of the tents and showers. So, I figured if I hid them, Sofia would get pissed that he ruined the brunch, and everyone had to eat in gross, sweaty clothes. It's genius, actually."

She isn't wrong. It does seem like a solid plan for her. It just sucks for everyone else, including me. The girl covered from head to toe in mud. What a great way to impress the rest of the family. At least they'll all also be sweaty and gross, right?

"You seriously suck. Why do you need to do this, anyways? Do you still love her?" I finally ask, unable to keep the annoyance out of my voice.

Valentina's gaze shifts, softening just a little. "It's not just about how I feel about her. I just think she deserves better. Luciano isn't right for her, and maybe she just needs a reminder of what that looks like."

I feel a pang of something—jealousy, maybe?—and quickly shake it off. "Whatever, dude. I just wish I didn't have to suffer through brunch because of it," I mutter, frustrated.

Valentina looks away, a hint of wistfulness in her eyes, but the determination remains. She's convinced that if Sofia just sees things clearly, she'll make the right choice—her. And now, I'm caught in the middle of her plan.

As we continue walking the path, slowly catching up with the group, we spot flashes of vibrant green ferns and brightly colored wildflowers. The woods are alive with the sounds of wildlife, and I can hear the distant calls of squirrels and the shuffling of chipmunks through the fallen leaves. We even pause for a moment to examine a spider's web, glistening with dew, and admire the intricate design of its delicate silk threads. If we weren't muddy, wet, and miserable, this would be such a gorgeous hike.

"Damn, what the hell happened to you?" Sofia asks as we quickly approach the rest of the guests.

Valentina is occupied with Silvana, who comes to her "rescue." I can't help but roll my eyes.

"What? Oh, right. Nothing. I was just saving Valentina from the mud she fell in." I shrug.

"Looks like you fell in yourself. A little mud wrestling, perhaps?" Sofia snickers.

"Shut up—it was not like that. Wait, where's Luciano?"

"Oh, he's somewhere at the front with Daniel. Probably chatting away about boring stuff, like mushrooms or football. I just got tired of trying to catch up to their steps." Sofia drops her gaze to my legs. "Cute pants! Where are those from?"

"Oh, they're from—"

"Dude, what the hell! You smell." Maria pokes me.

"Shut up. I do not. Do I?" I grab my shirt and take a whiff, but I smell nothing but dirt.

"Yeah, you smell like mud and caca."

"Maybe it's your upper lip," I retort. Very mature of me.

As we approach the mountain's peak, my excitement and anticipation build within me. The trail has become steeper and more challenging, but the breathtaking views along the way have made the effort worth it. The air is thin, and each step requires a little extra effort, but I'm determined to reach the summit and see the brunch setup. I can see the site up ahead between the trees—the linens flowing in the wind. Finally, we reach the top.

I pause to catch my breath and take in the stunning panoramic views of the mountains and valley below. The sky is a brilliant shade of blue, and wispy clouds cast soft shadows on the distant trees.

I look at the brunch setup, and I'm already in awe. A large, elegantly arranged table is decorated with fresh flowers and accented with crisp white linen and gleaming silverware. In the center of the table are various gourmet breakfast and lunch items, such as poached eggs with hollandaise sauce, artisanal cheeses, juicy grilled vegetables, and baked goods, such as croissants and pastries.

A light breeze rustles through the trees as a harpist plays lightly near some trees. Near the musician is a bar area for guests to enjoy cocktails, including refreshing mimosas made with freshly squeezed orange juice or some sparkling rosé with a fresh strawberry inside each glass.

"Holy crap. This is incredible," I whisper to Maria.

"It's like a set from a movie. You better believe I'm stuffing some of those chocolate croissants in my bag for later, so come to my cabin if you want one." She rushes to the bar to grab a rosé.

"Goddamn it."

I turn around to see Valentina staring behind me. I turn around and see a line of tents set up and people walking into them to change and shower.

"I thought you got rid of those," I whisper to her.

"I did."

"Oh my gosh, you guys will not believe this," Daniel says. "I came up here early this morning to make sure everything was all set for the brunch, and all of the tents and showers were gone."

Valentina and I exchange a quick look.

"Well, I happened to find them over there in the woods and put them all back. Must have been a gust of wind or something that blew them away. Could you imagine if they weren't here? It would have completely ruined Sofia's vision for the brunch!" He smirks and flips his imaginary hair. "I literally just saved the day. Hopefully, the bridal shower tomorrow runs more smoothly."

"Yeah, that would have been terrible," Valentina says between clenched teeth. "We should get changed, Isa. So glad you were here to save the wedding, Daniel." She grabs my hand and pulls me toward the tents, where I wait for the next available shower.

When it's finally my turn to step into the shower to get this mud off, the warm water envelops me, easing the tension from my muscles after that hike. I can already tell I'm going to be sore tomorrow. The steam rises, surrounding me in a cocoon of warmth and relaxation. I close my eyes, allowing the water to beat down on my skin, washing away the mud and sweat of the hike.

After drying off and changing into my slip dress and flats, I head over to Valentina, who has already taken up residence on one of the seats. I notice Silvana waving at Valentina to sit next to her and see Valentina shake her head. I sit down next to her and can almost feel Silvana burning my skin with her glare.

"Your ex doesn't like me very much," I say.

"You mean your cousin?" She smirks. "Yeah, she's intense. We dated for a summer. It was just a fling. This was also, like, five years ago."

"What happened?"

"She just became too much. We weren't on the same page. Always texting me. Getting mad if I spent too much time with Sofia. Complaining I didn't give her enough attention."

"So, like a normal girlfriend?" I laugh. "It sounds like you were just maybe caught up on someone else. As we both know."

Valentina pauses, a flicker of something crossing her face before she shrugs. "Maybe," she says, her tone softer. For a moment, she almost seems lost in thought, as if there's more she could say but won't.

Maria sits down to my right, which relieves me from the daggers Silvana is sharpening to throw in my direction soon. Rosita sits in front of me, next to Maritza and Sofia. Luciano sits on the other side with Daniel, the groomsmen, and Alessandro. I'll have to find a way to get to him this week, but I can't stop thinking about the lipstick stain.

Maritza is wearing a bold red lip, just like Valentina said she often does. An empty feeling resurfaces in my gut. The air feels especially thin as I try to take a deep breath.

As everyone begins to dive into the array of foods on the table, I think of ways to bring up my father in conversation without appearing like a mood killer. No one wants to hear the dead-dad trope while enjoying a fresh mimosa.

"So Tía," I say to Maritza. "How was it growing up with my mom?"

"Que cosa? What do you mean? She was a pain in my culo. Always wanted what I had."

Rosita laughs. "Now you've got her started."

"It's true, and you know it too, Rosita. Every time we had something new and shiny, Mariposa wanted it too. Or she wanted a better version of it. It was so annoying! Maybe it's because she was the baby. Maybe it's because I'm only her half sister, so I spent most of my time with my father. Whatever it was, I was over it. Nothing was ever good enough for her."

Damn, I clearly struck a nerve.

"That sounds a lot like her." I laugh awkwardly.

"Maritza," Rosita shouts. "Be nice. That's your niece."

Maritza looks over at me almost apologetically.

"I'm sorry, Isa. I know she's your mom." She turns to Rosita. "But she's my sister, and I've known her longer. A pain in my damn culo."

We all laugh.

"So you must have been happy when she met my father, right? Keep her busy?" I pry.

"That shotgun wedding? I *wish* that were the case. Her getting together with your father was the worst thing that could have happened to this family. It brought nothing but drama. She was just greedy. Mari wanted everything. She even—"

"Maritza!" Rosita shouts more sternly.

Maritza looks over at her and then back at me again.

"I mean, not the worst thing to happen to the family, mija. You're here now." She grins, but it feels forced.

Silvana holds back a snicker, but I can hear it escape slightly, almost as if she did it on purpose. My ears feel hot. Did Maritza say shotgun wedding? I was right.

"She just…caused a lot of drama. That's all I'm saying." Maritza sips her mimosa and looks away.

"Mija, don't listen to your Tía. You know how she is. Your mother and father were great together. No one had a problem with it. We loved Roberto."

Maritza scoffs.

Her lipstick leaves a stain on her glass. It looks nearly identical to the stain I have on the note, but not an exact match. Still, I can't eliminate her as a suspect.

"Oh God," I whisper to Valentina.

"That was a train wreck, wasn't it? What's up?"

"I think my father had a love affair with my aunt."

Chapter Eleven

The next day, my mind is still reeling from the possibility that my father had an affair with Maritza. It's unsettling, and I can't seem to shake the thought. But with the bridal shower later, I push it to the back of my mind. There's too much at stake today.

What does a bridal shower even consist of? I've heard of baby showers, and those are usually where you ogle at the new mother's pregnant belly, eat tiny sandwiches, and buy baby gifts. I can only assume a bridal shower is the same, sans belly ogling and baby items. I feel like I should know this kind of stuff, especially if I'm trying to show everyone that I belong.

"Two iced coffees with oat milk and vanilla, please," I say to the on-site barista.

In the early mornings, the open bars have mimosas, coffee, and tea available to drink, and so far, it's been my favorite part of the wedding. The sun is just rising, casting soft golden light over the campground. It's one of those moments when I remember this isn't just a wedding venue. The air is cool and fresh, filled with the sounds of chickadees and the rustling of leaves in the gentle breeze.

Guests start to stir, stretching and yawning as they emerge from their cabins. Some head to the dining hall for breakfast, complaining of their stomachs rumbling with hunger. Others gather in groups, chatting and laughing as they plan for the exciting bridal shower party later this afternoon. The smell of sizzling bacon and brewing coffee drifts from the kitchen, drawing guests toward the dining hall. I follow suit.

Inside is a spread of hot breakfast foods, from eggs and toast to pancakes and bacon. Guests begin to fill their plates, chatting and laughing as they head back outside to sit at long picnic tables covered with silky white linen and surrounded by the sounds and sights of nature. I head straight into the kitchen. Where the magic happens.

"Morning!" I yell to grab Valentina's attention.

Her head whips up, and a grin immediately grows on her face. For a second, I almost forget why we're here, caught in her smile. But I shake it off. This isn't a peace offering—it's a temporary truce, nothing more.

"For you." I hand her the second iced coffee.

"You got me a drink?" she says, smiling.

"Don't get used to it—it's a thank-you for all your help so far." My voice is light, but I make sure she knows this isn't me letting down my guard.

"Got it," she replies, nodding, as if she understands the unspoken terms.

In the kitchen, the catering staff moves with purpose, each person focused on their task. The air is filled with the sounds of sizzling pans, clanging pots, and the occasional shout of a cook calling out an order. The servers, dressed in crisp white uniforms, bustle in and out of the kitchen, picking up food trays and heading out to the dining area.

My eyes drift toward the kitchen activity, my thoughts lingering on the rice pudding Valentina and I made. Was it good enough? Did it stand out among all this polished perfection? The idea of Luciano tasting something my father created feels monumental, like I'm bringing a piece of him to this table of luxury and expectation. I need it to succeed—not just for the journal, but for the restaurant. If Luciano sees the potential in my father's recipes, maybe he'll believe in me, too.

And what next? I can't stop at just one dish. My mind races as I mentally comb through the recipes in my father's journal, thinking about which dish could be the next to wow Luciano. Maybe the ropa vieja? It's simple but bold, the kind of meal that embodies comfort and tradition while still packing a punch. Or the lechón asado, marinated for hours with garlic and citrus. It's a showstopper when done right, the type of dish that could make someone feel like they've been invited into our family kitchen.

But would that be enough? What if he's looking for something modern, a twist on tradition? I could take my father's recipes and elevate them somehow, blending his authenticity with something unexpected. My stomach tightens as the ideas swirl. Every decision feels like a gamble—like every plate I present could tip the scale between securing this investment or losing everything.

"All right, I'm pretty much done here." Valentina wipes her hands with a rag. "Are you ready to find our next clue?"

I nod, excitement bubbling under the surface, though my mind is still half in the kitchen. As I pull out my father's journal, I glance back at the bustling staff. Solving the puzzle in this book feels inseparable from saving the restaurant now. Each recipe is more than a dish—it's a piece of the story I need Luciano to see. If I'm going to make him believe in me, I need the next dish to be perfect.

"So far, we know that he definitely either had an affair or was in love with someone that wasn't your mom. Why it matters? That's what we need to find out."

I turn the pages slowly, and we inspect each one. She stands so close to me. She places her arms around my body, gripping the counter and leaning closer to see the journal. I'm trying to focus on the pages, but it's all becoming a blur. I'm so aware of how close she is to me right now. Her breath rhythmically caresses my shoulder as she peeks over it. I want to turn around and see what happens if I look into her eyes, but I don't.

"Wait, go back," she shouts.

I turn the page to a recipe titled "Flan de Perdón."

"Flan of forgiveness? That's a weird name, isn't it?" I ask.

"That's not the only weird thing about it. Look at the recipe closely."

I start to look at all the words. The ingredients. The directions. The notes. There are random letters capitalized throughout.

Valentina laughs. "Roberto was quite the puzzler, huh?"

"He really was. When I was twelve, I found a note inside my lampshade with random numbers on it. At the bottom was a tuft of hair. I realized it was fur from our little poodle, so I hurried to my closet and found a polaroid hanging from his collar there. I rushed over and started rummaging until I found a small box. It had a brand-new phone inside. The numbers were the passcode to unlock it. My birthdate. He could have just gifted me the phone for my birthday like a normal person, but he knew how much fun the little puzzles were."

"It seemed like you had a nice relationship with him," Valentina says. "I can see why you like doing these puzzles. Well, I think I figured this one out. We need to circle all these capitalized letters and see what it spells out."

I watch as she meticulously scans the recipe, looking for each letter that seems out of place. Finally, she finds all of them. Eight letters. BLTIAEUA.

She chuckles. "I feel like I'm back in school again, trying to unscramble words during English class."

"It's Abuelita," I say.

"How did you get it so quickly?" she replies, shocked.

"Oh, please, Garcia. This isn't my first rodeo."

"She says at her second rodeo."

"Excuse you. I happen to be an expert sleuth at this point."

"Oh, my apologies." Valentina chuckles. "I would say intermediate at most, though."

I lightly punch her in the arm, and she flinches away before laughing.

"So what now? Do we kidnap Granny? Throw her in the back of the car, drive to an unknown location, and ask her the tough questions? 'Where were you August 26, 1998?'"

"Maybe we can just casually bring it up in conversation?" I suggest.

"That's way less fun, but fine. We can do it at the bridal shower. Did you bring your gift for Sof?"

Fuck. Gift. Of course. It's like a baby shower but for a bride.

"Do you think she'd notice if I gave her today's wedding favor as a gift? Who doesn't want a nice Tiffany bracelet and MAC lipstick with candied almonds?"

"How about we go into town and pick something up? There's an outlet mall nearby," she says, laughing.

"Wait, like, leave?"

Valentina takes off her white chef's coat—her costume—and grabs her bag.

I watch as she shrugs off the coat like it's nothing, transforming from chef to casual chic in seconds. It's so easy for her, shedding layers and revealing a different side. I get it, though. We both wear costumes. Mine's the life I pretend to lead around my family—the successful restaurant owner, the one who's got it all together. Her chef's coat? Just another role she plays. It's only when she takes it off that I feel like I'm seeing the Valentina I have known my entire life.

"Yeah, we're not prisoners here, Valdes. We're free to leave." She winks.

"What about sabotaging the wedding? Shouldn't you be planning your next attack?"

"For you? That can wait." She smiles. "Shall we pick up Abuelita and bring her along? She might be more open to questioning if she's away from family, especially Maritza. Major gossiper."

"Yes, definitely."

"It's a date, then. I mean—that's not what I meant," Valentina stumbles, her usual composure slipping as she fumbles over her words. I catch a faint blush on her cheeks, which, surprisingly, is kind of endearing.

I raise an eyebrow, leaning in just a little. "A date with Granny, huh? Not exactly how I pictured our first date, but I guess it's memorable."

She laughs, trying to brush it off, but I can see the fluster lingering in her expression. "Oh, please. Like you'd ever take me on a real date."

"You'd be surprised," I counter, letting a grin tug at my lips. "I've been told I'm an excellent date."

Valentina rolls her eyes, but the smile she tries to hide betrays her amusement. For a brief moment, there's an ease between us, something almost comfortable.

"Come on," she says, shaking her head as she leads the way to the car. "We've got a granny to pick up."

As Valentina navigates through the narrow roads of Lee, I can't help but be captivated by the quaint charm surrounding me. I spot a few historic buildings, each with its own unique character and story to tell.

"Que lindo," Abuelita says, pointing out the quaint boutiques and cafés we pass by.

"I still think we should have taken Miss Piggy," I joke.

"She's dead."

"She's just sleeping at the mechanic's!" I yell back. "Like a coma for cars. She'll be up in no time. She has to be, anyways, so I can leave this place on Sunday."

As we approach the outskirts of the town, I can see the large outlet mall in the distance, a beacon of consumerism in contrast to the charming small town.

The car turns in to the parking lot, and Valentina pulls into a spot. We step out, excited to leave the campground and experience some retail therapy. I wrap my arm around my grandmother's, and Valentina follows suit on her other side.

"This is so nice," Abuelita coos.

We make our way through the mall, passing several stores featuring everything from clothing and accessories to home goods and electronics. I take in the sights and sounds of the mall, enjoying the thrill of the hunt for bargains—or designer stuff, I guess. I'm not used to this. Usually, I'm shopping for counterfeit accessories. I don't think I've ever stepped inside an actual designer store.

Finally, we come upon the Coach outlet. It's housed in a large, inviting space, with its logo prominently displayed above the entrance. The elegantly appointed interior has warm lighting and sleek fixtures showcasing the luxurious leather goods and accessories. Basically, anything that I can't and will not ever be able to afford. When we step inside, my eyes light up at the sight of the beautiful handbags and wallets on display. Abuelita also seems impressed, admiring the quality of the leather and the attention to detail in each piece. I pick up a pair of black loafers—$120. The discounted price. I nearly faint at the thought of paying so much for a pair of shoes.

"These shoes are $120," I say to Valentina, trying to hide my surprise.

"Yeah, it's crazy, isn't it?"

"That's one way to put it." I laugh.

"It's the outlet store, so everything is so cheap."

Suddenly, I realize we have different opinions on what constitutes a good deal. These are cheap to her—a bargain if you will. For the first time this week, I realize just how different our worlds are. Maybe too different. How would I fit in?

"So, you know Sofia well. What do you think I should get her?"

Valentina browses around, picking up wallets and bags that make my wallet sweat.

"It's tough. Sofia can buy herself anything. I always have a hard time coming up with a good gift to get her. You could get her this bag."

She shows me a chalk-colored satchel with gold accents and the signature logo on the front. It's chic, classic, and perfect for her.

"She could bring it on her honeymoon. What do you think, Abuelita?"

Valentina shows her the bag. Abuelita manages to find a bench to sit on and watch us shop. She nods happily.

"Muy lindo, mija," she says.

Can she even see from that far? She'd probably say that about any item here. I think she's just happy to be included. I grab the bag from Valentina and inspect it closer. It's cute. It's stylish. It's…$150. I can't tell her that I can't afford it. It'll give me away.

"Okay, I'll get this one," I say, praying my credit card has enough of a limit available for it to go through.

"You go ahead to the register. I'll catch up," Valentina says as she continues to browse through the wallets.

I take my walk of shame to the register, just waiting for those big, bold red words to appear on the screen: DECLINED. It's a word I am all too familiar with regarding my credit cards. I'm so used to it at this point that I don't even feel embarrassed. I just move on. But this. This is just not the time for it to happen.

"I'm going to sit outside," Abuelita announces to us both.

She points to the bench just outside the door. It's a beautiful day not to enjoy the breeze and sun.

I step up to the cash register with the Coach bag in hand, determined to buy it as a gift for Sofia's bridal shower. I hand over my credit card, trying to hide my nervousness as the cashier swipes it. A moment passes—then another moment.

"Sorry, sometimes the computer is a little slow." The cashier giggles.

"Yeah," I say, laughing nervously.

As I wait to see the dreaded words, my phone buzzes. I pull

it out of my pocket to see my mother's name show up on the caller ID. Fuck.

"I'm sorry, ma'am, but your card has been declined," the cashier replies in a lower voice.

"What?" I put my phone away. "That can't be right," I lie. "Let me try another one."

I pull out my second card I deemed "In Case Of Emergency" and hand it to the cashier, trying to act as if it's not a big deal. A moment passes. Another moment. Then there is that big, mean word again: DECLINED.

The cashier looks at me, clearly with a sense of pity.

"I'm sorry, ma'am, but we'll need another form of payment."

I can feel everyone staring at me. My pulse is racing. My palms are so sweaty I can barely put my cards back in my bag.

"I—I don't have any cash on me. I thought I had enough in the account."

I start to fumble through my wallet, trying to come up with a solution before Valentina comes over and finds out the truth. I feel the cashier getting impatient as a small line of customers begins to form behind me.

"I'm sorry, but I'll need to see another form of payment, or I'll have to put the item back," she says.

"I—I understand. Let me just run to the ATM real quick."

I quickly gather my things from the counter and rush out of the store, hoping to escape the prying eyes of the other shoppers. A wave of embarrassment and disappointment washes over me. I haven't felt this in a long time. I have been trying so hard to act like I am doing well financially, but now my lack of funds has been exposed for all to see.

"All done, mija?" Abuelita coos, patting the bench to get me to sit beside her.

I sit down since I feel like I may faint if I stay up any longer. I try slowing my breath. My hands won't stop shaking. What the fuck am I going to do? I can't even buy Sofia a gift. They'll all know the truth, that the business isn't successful and neither am I. My phone buzzes again. I pull it out, bracing myself. This time, it's a text from my mother.

Mija, call me when you get this message.

"Hey! Everything okay? I saw a line start to form when you were checking out while I was browsing, and then you sprinting out of the store."

Valentina walks toward us with a shopping bag in one of her hands.

"Yeah, I'm fine," I say, putting my phone away once again. "I forgot I maxed out my credit card on some Prada shoes last week. Whoops."

"Oh yeah, that's a bummer. Well, hey, here." She hands me the shopping bag and sits on the bench next to Abuelita and me.

I open it and see the white Coach bag inside.

"Did you buy this for me?"

She smiles. "Well, to give to Sofia, yeah."

"What? No, I can't let you do that. I already feel embarrassed enough as it is."

"It's not a big deal, Valdes. It happens to all of us. There was a time when Sofia and Rosita couldn't even afford Coach. I want you to give her a nice gift. You haven't seen her in a decade. It'll make a good impression. Don't worry about it."

I stare at the bag, tears forming in my eyes.

"I'll pay you back," I finally say, my voice quivering.

"Eh, don't worry about it. Think of it as a thank-you for keeping me entertained during this torturous week. I don't know if I'd still be standing by now if it wasn't for you and your mystery."

"I don't know what to say..."

"Just say you'll let me treat you to lunch. Well, Abuelita too, of course." She smiles.

"I'd like that."

"Great. I just need to go back in quickly and get something I was eyeing earlier. Be right back!"

I watch as she rushes back into the store. The butterflies in my stomach make their presence known.

"You like her," Abuelita whispers.

"What?" I look over at her, but she keeps looking straight ahead, her eyes appearing closed.

"I may be old, mija, but I'm not blind." She smiles. "You like each other."

"No." I scoff. "She does not *like* me."

"Ah, I see. So you must be blind then."

"Abuelita! She really doesn't. She's in love with someone else," I say, shrugging.

She stays quiet momentarily, making me wonder what she could be thinking.

"Bueno, this has happened before, and it didn't stop your mother from making a move," she finally says.

"What? Abuelita, are you talking about Papi? Did he love someone else?"

Abuelita coos as she looks up at the birds that fly by.

"Abuelita, what is 'el flan de perdón'?"

She finally looks over at me as if I have said the magic words that'll open Pandora's box.

She sighs. "Oh mija, I haven't had that since that night your father came home drunk, crying."

"What was he crying about?"

"Mariposa told him the news about her being pregnant."

"Oh. Interesting. Tears of joy?" I hope.

"Ah, mija. No, he was blabbering like a baby. I was shocked when I found out."

"Why is that?"

She doesn't respond.

"Abuelita?"

Nothing.

"Abuelita." I shake her softly, causing her to jump.

"Oh perdón, mija. I fell asleep."

"Abuelita! Why were you shocked when you found out my mother was pregnant?"

"Ah, si. Because I swore your father was dating someone else."

I feel as if I'm floating through Sofia's bridal shower, my thoughts tangled in the past instead of the lush greenery and floral arrangements that adorn the white tent. It's beautiful, but all I can think about is Abuelita's words. My father…with someone else?

How Sofia managed to turn a basic campground into an outdoor venue suited for a bridal shower to defeat all bridal showers is impressive, to say the least. The white tent, taking over the spot where the first dinner took place, is accented with an elegant chandelier, which sparkles and casts a warm glow over the shower. Lush greenery and blooming flowers are hanging off each support pole and across the top, creating a frame of foliage. There's a white photo booth in the corner to take some photos as souvenirs.

We are welcomed with glasses of pink champagne as soon as we walk inside the tent. I sip and admire the details throughout.

As we make our way to our seats, a beautifully decorated table with white linen and delicate flower arrangement greets us. The centerpieces on each table are tall and grand, featuring a variety of blooms in shades of pink and cream, with candlelight adding a warm and inviting touch.

"Candles? It's literally two in the afternoon," Valentina says with an eye roll.

She's probably used to these kinds of events, but to me, it feels as if I'm in a fairy tale. This is something straight out of my childhood imagination when I'd play with my dolls, picturing them having an extravagant tea party.

Sofia is a vision in a stunning cream-colored gown, her hair styled in loose waves and adorned with a delicate flower crown. I notice Valentina stare at her for a while before getting distracted by Silvana approaching her. Even Silvie looks gorgeous, wearing a stunning pink tulle dress.

"Cute dress, Silvie," I say.

It doesn't hurt to try and be friendly to her.

"Nothing you could afford," she says with a scoff.

Okay, I guess it does hurt.

"Oh, please, Silvie. Everyone knows that's a last season Tom Ford," Maria pipes in.

"Yeah," I echo. "It's from his—"

Maria stands behind Silvie, mouthing a word to me.

"—spring collection. Not my cup of tea, but it works on you, I guess."

Silvana strolls toward me until she's a mere few inches away from my face.

"Good guess, but you're not fooling me, Isa."

She walks away to stand next to her mother, probably to insert herself in needless gossip. Or talk shit about me—or both.

Valentina's staff prepared a gourmet feast. A long table features smoked salmon and caviar, artisanal cheeses, freshly baked croissants, and a variety of fresh fruit and juices to choose from. We each grab a small plate and add a few pieces before sitting down and waiting for the bride-to-be to open her gifts—the moment I've been dreading all day.

One by one, Sofia opens the gifts. Guests ooh and ahh as she reveals the items inside. Lingerie from La Perla risqué enough to make even Maria blush. White Louboutin heels to wear to dinner on their European honeymoon. Rosita even gifted her an additional week in France. I'm fucking doomed.

"Ooh, I wonder who this one is from."

Sofia picks up the white shopping bag with the word COACH on the front. My face starts to feel hot. She ruffles through the tissue paper and pulls out the white bag.

"Oh my gosh, this is so adorable! I haven't owned anything from Coach in so long. So nostalgic! Who is this from?"

"It's from me," I say, raising my hand meekly.

Silvie snorts. "Figures."

"Thank you so much, Isa! It's beautiful and such a throwback. I feel like a teenager again shopping for my first designer bag."

"A teenager buying a $150 bag?" I whisper to Maria. "Oh, my God. I'm screwed. What did you get her?"

"A Tiffany necklace."

"Cool. I'll just die over here in my shame."

Sofia opens a smaller white shopping bag, unwrapping one of the tissue papers.

"Oh my God, Val! Did you get me a Coach wallet? I am having some major flashbacks right now—you guys are amazing. Thank you for this!"

Silvana rolls her eyes, but everyone else seems unbothered. I can't tell if they're judging me internally or if they really don't care.

"Why did you get her something from Coach?"

"They have cute stuff," Valentina says.

"Did you buy that while we were there today with Abuelita?"

"Maybe."

I look over at her, but she looks straight ahead. I can see a smile creasing her lips.

"Did you do that for me?" I ask.

"Maybe."

I can't help but feel a flutter in my chest, something that feels both exciting and terrifying. It's a small gesture, but it's enough to make me wonder if there's more to her than I've let myself believe.

The air between us feels charged, and for a moment, I can almost forget about everything else—about the lies, the secrets, the tension. Right now, it's just me, Valentina, and a stolen smile that makes me want more of this side of her.

Chapter Twelve

I'm not the type of person who is woken up very easily during the night. I usually sleep through most of it unless there's a literal tornado tearing through my bedroom. This is why it's a complete shock to me when I look at my phone and see that it's 4:30 a.m. I'm not sure exactly what woke me up, but I can only hope it wasn't something with sharp teeth or a knife. I stare at the ceiling, trying to listen for any odd sounds. Perhaps a bat is flying around the room and slapped me in the face with its wings. Maybe a deer has barged into the cabin and trampled my body, and the adrenaline has kept me from realizing my entire skeletal system has collapsed. Perhaps it's that killer Maria mentioned on the first day finally returning for his revenge. Maybe it was Valentina?

I try to peek at the bed, but the cot is too close to the ground. I push myself up to a seat with my hand. She's not here. I scan the room, checking to see if she's in the bathroom or perhaps standing in the corner with no head, waiting to take me as her final victim. Nothing. I'm almost too scared to look around now. I need to stop buying into Maria's stories, but this place does give me the creeps at night.

It's clear that Valentina is not here, so where the hell did she go? Maybe she left to get snacks in the main hall. That must mean she'll be coming back any minute. Should I pretend to be asleep? Or maybe I should hide and pop out when she least expects it. Give her a little scare for practically forcing me to be an accomplice in destroying the wedding. Actually, I have a better idea. Probably the best idea I've had in a long time. I'm going to steal the bed from her.

The millisecond the thought enters my head, I jolt off the cot onto Valentina's bed, giggling and rolling around like a small child finally getting what they wanted. I stretch out my limbs in each direction, as if trying to reach every corner of the bed. I crawl to the top of the bed and rest my head on her pillow. It's so much softer than mine. I could sleep here all day. I tuck myself inside the covers. How can they feel so cool yet so warm at the same time? It's as if this bed is enchanted. That, or maybe I've been sleeping on a dinky cot for too long.

I can smell her on the pillowcase—a mixture of her perfume and shampoo. Maybe even a little bit of the vanilla-and-amber lotion she puts on every night. If I could bottle up this combination of scents and sell it as a pillow mist, I could probably close down La Mariposa and live a wealthy life after selling out on my new product. I take a deep breath as I try to soak in the remaining scent of her on the bed.

I startle myself awake. I must have dozed off slightly. Just enough to have that weird dream where it feels like you're falling. I look at my watch—3:50 a.m., and she's not back yet. I start to think the worst. What if she got attacked by a bear and she is currently dragging the top half of her body back to the cabin to seek help? What if she was kidnapped and is now living in someone's shed? Oh God, I'm gonna be sick.

I throw the blankets off my body and rush to the closet to grab my boots and jacket. I could have switched to leggings, but something about walking around in chunky boots and a white-and-red-striped pajama short set makes the situation feel less scary to me. If anyone sees me, I can try to convince them I'm a chronic sleepwalker. I swing the cabin door open almost too loudly. I look around to see if anyone else is awake or if a lifeless Valentina is lying on the dirt. Nothing. I breathe a sigh of relief.

I shuffle quickly through the campsite, practically giving myself whiplash with how quickly I turn my neck. She has to be here somewhere. She wouldn't have just left. I approach the main hall, pull the doorknob, and step inside. It's completely dark—there's no way she's in here. I look over at the double doors leading to the kitchen. If the light were on, I'd definitely see it through the crack between the doors. It's off. No one is here.

Against my horror movie—watching instincts, I keep looking and step back outside and look toward the direction of the lake. I can't really tell, but it looks as if there may be some sort of figure over there. My heart begins to pace faster as I walk toward it. It could be Valentina, but it could also be a bear. Or the kidnapper. The closer I get, the surer I am that it's a human. I can see the shape of their head. The way their neck curves into their shoulders. It's Valentina on the dock. Thank fucking God.

"Are you trying to give me a heart attack?" I ask, startling Valentina.

"Ay, you scared me. What the hell are you talking about?" she replies, clearly annoyed.

"I woke up, and you were gone. I thought something had happened to you. I was freaking out. I waited for a bit, and you never came back, so I decided to come out looking for you to make sure you were alive or not stuck inside someone's basement."

"Aw, you missed me?" Valentina coos.

"No! I mean, I just thought you were dead or something."

"That's cute."

"What are you doing out here in the middle of the night?" I ask.

"I mean, technically, it's early morning," she says, grinning. "I'm just enjoying the silence and looking at the lake. Thinking. Join me."

She pats the empty spot next to her, her feet dangling off the side of the dock facing the water. Without thinking, I sit down next to Valentina.

The lake is calm and still, with only the occasional ripple to disturb its surface. The moon casts a soft silver light across the water, illuminating the shadows and creating a tranquil atmosphere. In the distance, the silhouette of trees and hills stands out against the night sky. The stars twinkle overhead, and I can hear Valentina's quiet and rhythmic breathing, breaking the silence of the early morning. I think I found my new favorite time of day.

Now that I know she's alive, I can finally look at Valentina. She is stunning, even under the moonlight. She is wearing grey sweatpants and a matching button-down top. It looks soft. *She* looks soft.

"So, are you excited about paddleboarding? It's the first event of Sofia's ridiculous bach party today," Valentina says.

"You already know I am. I can't wait!"

"Have you ever actually done it before?" she asks teasingly.

"Well, no, but I'm a fast learner, and I never make mistakes."

Valentina laughs. "I can't wait to see you fall face-first into the water."

"I will not. You will. When I push you in." I laugh at the thought.

"Oh, is that so?"

"Yeah, it is. You better watch yourself, Garcia. I'm coming for you."

"One can only hope," she says, winking.

I ignore her innuendo because I refuse to give her the pleasure of knowing that it made me blush. Valentina is not into me. She's in love with Sofia. I just need to keep that mantra in my head whenever she's giving me even a morsel of extra attention.

"You really like it here, don't you?"

I nod.

"Have you been living your *Parent Trap* dreams to your full satisfaction?"

"Not yet. Our days have been filled with so many wedding activities it hasn't even felt like a camp. That's why I'm so excited about the bach—all the activities! It's what I've dreamed about. Also, I still need to get some Oreos to recreate the scene with the peanut butter. It's a mind-blowing combination, and I'm determined to have it again before I leave."

She laughs. "That sounds....disgusting."

"You are such a grouch, you know that?"

"I am aware," she replies, amused.

I take a breath, remembering my conversation with Abuelita. I still can't believe it, that she actually thought my dad was with someone else before my mom. I glance at Valentina, wondering if it's worth bringing up. But something about this quiet, surreal moment at the lake makes me want to spill a bit more. Maybe she'd understand. "You know, Abuelita told me yesterday that she thought my dad had someone else in his life before he started dating my mother. Someone he was serious about."

Valentina raises an eyebrow, turning to face me fully. "Wow. That's...unexpected. Do you think it has anything to do with what you've been finding in his journal?"

I shrug, hugging my knees to my chest. "I don't know, but I can't stop thinking about it. It's like every time I uncover something, I find out I knew even less about him than I thought. It's scary. And it makes me wonder if I'll ever really get the full picture. But I feel like I have to try."

Valentina nods, her expression softening.

"It must be hard, not knowing. But it sounds like you're starting to piece things together, right? Maybe this whole thing, as weird as it is, will help you finally understand who he was."

"Maybe," I say, smiling faintly. "It's just…there's so much I didn't know about him. And now I have to figure it all out while I'm here, pretending I've got everything together."

"You're not pretending with me," Valentina says quietly, almost to herself. For a second, I feel exposed but also comforted.

I nod, grateful for the moment but also ready to move on, the weight of the conversation still lingering. "Enough about me," I say, forcing a small grin. "So, what's your next step?"

"What do you mean?"

"To sabotage Sofia's wedding. So far, your plan has failed hilariously. I mean, insulting him at the first dinner didn't work. No one knew you had even stolen the tents at brunch. I'm curious about what else you have up your sleeve."

She laughs at that last part. Then, she stays quiet for a moment. As if she's thinking of what to say. Or if she's considering telling me something secretive. I hold my breath.

"All right, there is something."

"Okay, tell me," I say, trying not to appear too eager.

"How about I show you?"

Valentina reaches into her pocket and pulls out two gold rings.

"My precious," she says in a hiss.

"Uh, are those what I think they are?" I look at her, eyes wide.

"Maybe." She grins. "The ultimate sabotage. Luciano is in charge of the rings. Sofia's going to be really upset when she realizes he lost them."

"But…you stole them. He didn't lose them."

"Well, he shouldn't have made them so easy to take," she retorts.

I stand up, slightly slipping on the old moss collected on the dock.

"Val, you have to put those back," I demand.

"What? No. Listen, Valdes. I'm just doing what needs to be done."

"Give me the rings, Val," I yell.

"No!"

She stands up and dangles the rings in front of me.

I reach for them, but she locks them into her fist. As we struggle for the rings, our grunts and gasps fill the still morning air. I'm strong, but Valentina is more agile and manages to wriggle out of my grasp.

"Why can't you give up this stupid plan?" I grunt.

Valentina freezes, her grip on the rings tightening. "Because it's all I fucking have!" she shouts, her voice cracking slightly. She looks away, but I can see the pain in her expression.

"What do you mean?" I ask, my own anger softening as I realize there's more to this than I thought.

She takes a shaky breath, her gaze fixed on the rings interlaced between our hands. "It's like…everything's slipping away. Once she's married, that's it. It's over. She gets her happily ever after, and I'm just left behind. I know it's selfish, but I can't just let her go without a fight. I've invested so much of myself into her. Into our friendship. My feelings. And now, this is all I have left to hold on to."

Just as Valentina seems to be getting the upper hand, the rings slip from our fingers, bounce off the dock, and fall into the lake with a splash. We both freeze, our eyes fixed on where the rings have fallen.

For a moment, no one speaks. The only sounds are the gentle lapping of the water against the dock and the birds singing in the distance. Then, without a word, Valentina dives into the lake, disappearing beneath the surface. I watch in horror, my heart pounding in my chest. What if Val can't find the rings? What if she's hurt or stuck between two rocks and slowly drowning?

Just as I was starting to panic, Valentina's head pops back up above the water. She has a grin on her face, and her fist is held above her head in triumph.

"Got 'em!" she yells, splashing back to the dock.

I breathe a sigh of relief, but I'm also pissed.

"Why did you do that? You could have been hurt."

She climbs back onto the dock, looking down at the rings in her hand. "Well, I had to save them, didn't I? If anyone finds out they're missing, I want it to be on my terms." She pats the pocket where she stashes them, and for a moment, I see something like doubt flicker in her eyes.

"There. Safe and sound," she mutters, almost to herself.

"It's not all you have, Val," I finally say.

"It feels like it is."

"Is there really no one else you can see yourself with?" I ask, my voice louder than I intend. Her eyes widen slightly at my tone, and I feel an unexpected flutter in my chest. I shake it off, focusing on the urgency of the moment. "Maybe you should just let her go and move on. Stop this wedding sabotage. Enjoy the week. Help me solve the big mystery in my father's journal. Just…stop."

She tilts her head, studying me, a playful smirk tugging at her lips. "Oh, so now you care what I do with my time?"

"Well, it's not like I want to be dragged into your mess," I retort, though the words feel hollow. There's something else keeping me here, an almost magnetic pull that I'm not ready to name. "Besides, it might be nice to not have to look over my shoulder every time you're scheming."

Valentina grins, clearly amused. "You're right," she says, but I can tell she's not ready to let me off the hook just yet. "Maybe I'll take a break from all this plotting. But only because you asked so nicely."

She steps closer, her gaze meeting mine. For a heartbeat, the air between us thickens, and I wonder if she can sense the quickened pace of my breathing. I want to say something—anything—to break the tension, but I can't find the words.

"All right, all right. I'll stop," she finally says, breaking the spell with a laugh. I release a breath I didn't realize I was holding, a mix of relief and something else I can't quite place.

"Good," I reply, trying to sound nonchalant. "Now, let's get back to the cabin. The sun's going to rise soon, and we have paddleboarding to conquer."

I look up to confirm my suspicions. The sky is painted with a warm palette of pinks, oranges, and purples. The sun's rays slowly inch their way over the horizon, casting a warm golden light over the lake and the trees that surround it.

"All right, fine," she finally agrees.

As I turn to head down the dock, I feel her hand wrap around mine, pulling me back. I spin around, our eyes meeting. There's something in her gaze—an intensity that I'm not prepared for.

She hesitates, just for a second, before a faint smile curves her lips. "And maybe I do see myself with someone else."

The words hang in the air, and I feel my heart skip, then start hammering in my chest. I'm not sure if I heard her right, and I don't trust my voice to respond. For a moment, everything else fades, and it's just us, standing together as the sun rises. The implications of her statement settle over me, shifting something between us. I don't know what to say, so I just nod, barely managing to hold her gaze.

Finally, I turn away, hoping the blush creeping up my cheeks isn't as obvious as it feels. My mind races as I try to process what just happened as we walk back, her words echoing in my thoughts like a melody I can't quite shake.

Chapter Thirteen

The morning sun streams through the window, and I groggily sit up, rubbing my eyes. Today is the day we're supposed to go paddleboarding, but my mind is elsewhere. Luciano casually mentioned after the bridal shower that he'd love to try a few more dishes from La Mariposa.

"Maybe something savory this time," he had suggested with a smile. "It'll give me a better sense of what your restaurant could bring to the table."

It's barely seven in the morning. The idea of making something spectacular feels daunting, especially since I know I'll need help. And that means waking up Valentina.

I push myself up on the cot, the springs creaking beneath me, and look over at Valentina. Her hair is an untamed mess, splayed across her pillow as she lies sprawled out like she hasn't a care in the world.

"Val," I whisper.

Nothing.

"Valentina," I try again, louder this time.

She groans and pulls the blanket over her head. "If this isn't an emergency, I'm going to end you."

"It is an emergency," I reply, standing and tugging on a

sweater. "Luciano wants to try another dish today. We need to cook something savory. I need your help."

"Seriously?" she mutters from beneath the blanket. "It's barely sunrise, Isa, and we have to pick up Miss Piggy before paddleboarding. Can't this wait?"

"We have time to do both," I insist, pacing the small space. "Please, Val. We made a deal."

She lets out a dramatic sigh and sits up, her hair sticking out in every direction. "Fine. But you owe me—big time."

"I'll make it worth your while," I promise. "I'll… I don't know…carry your paddleboard later?"

She does not seem impressed.

The kitchen feels almost eerie in its stillness. The catering staff isn't here yet, and the space seems too big, too empty, but also charged with potential. I glance at Valentina, who's leaning against the counter, cradling her a fresh coffee like it's the only thing keeping her upright. Her hair is still a wild, tangled mess.

"Okay," she sighs, setting her mug down with a dramatic thud. "What's the game plan, Chef?"

"We're making ropa vieja," I say, pulling out the flank steak and vegetables from the fridge. "It's a classic Cuban dish, slow-cooked shredded beef in a tomato-based sauce with peppers and onions. It's hearty, flavorful, and exactly the kind of dish Luciano will appreciate."

Valentina tilts her head, studying me. "You've clearly thought this through."

"I have. This dish means a lot to me. It's one of the first recipes my dad taught me how to make. It's simple but soulful."

She smiles faintly at that, and I feel a flicker of warmth in my chest before I shake it off.

"Okay, what do we do first, boss?" she asks, rolling up her sleeves, clearly letting me take charge this time.

"First, we need to sear the meat," I say, reaching for a cast iron pan and placing it on the stove. "Grab the olive oil."

Valentina rummages through the pantry, pulling out the oil with a flourish. "Your wish is my command."

"Try not to spill it everywhere," I mutter, pouring a thin layer into the pan.

She smirks. "You're so uptight. Relax."

The steak sizzles as I lay it in the pan, and the aroma fills the air almost immediately. Valentina stands beside me, leaning a little too close as she watches the meat brown.

"You're crowding me," I say, nudging her with my elbow.

"Am I?" she teases, not moving an inch. "I'm just trying to learn from the expert."

"You run a kitchen too, Val. Don't act like you've never browned a steak before."

"True," she admits, grinning. "But it's more fun when you do it."

I roll my eyes, but I can't help the small smile tugging at my lips.

As the steak sears, we chop the vegetables together. Valentina slices an onion with quick, confident movements, while I tackle the bell peppers.

"Your knife skills are impressive," she says, glancing at my precise cuts.

"Thanks," I reply, focusing on the rhythm of the chopping. "It's called practice."

"Or obsessive perfectionism," she quips, and I glare at her.

"Do you always have to get under my skin?" I ask.

"Only because you make it so easy," she replies, her grin widening.

I shake my head, unable to suppress a laugh. "You're impossible."

Once the vegetables are prepped, we remove the steak from the pan and set it aside. I toss the onions and peppers into the same pan, stirring them as they soften and release their aroma. We add garlic, tomatoes, and spices to the pan, the rich aroma building layer by layer. The chaos of cooking grows around us—used utensils, spilled spices, and vegetable scraps scattered across the counters. I feel the familiar urge to stop and clean, but Valentina's voice interrupts my thoughts.

"Leave it," she says softly, noticing my hesitation.

"But it's a mess—"

"Let it be," she insists. "Sit down for a minute."

Reluctantly, I sit on the counter beside her, the clutter surrounding us. I glance at the chaos, my chest tightening, but when I look at Valentina, her calm presence steadies me.

"It's just a mess, Isa," she says gently. "Not the end of the world."

I take a deep breath and lean back, letting myself be still for a moment. The kitchen feels alive, the chaos humming around us, and for the first time, it doesn't feel overwhelming. It feels...peaceful.

When the dish is finally done, we plate it carefully. The shredded beef is tender and coated in the flavorful sauce, the vibrant colors of the peppers and tomatoes making it look as good as it smells.

As we step back to admire our work, Luciano enters the kitchen. His presence immediately fills the space, his confident stride a stark contrast to the messy kitchen and our slightly disheveled appearances.

"What's this?" he asks, his eyes lighting up as he sees the dish.

"Ropa vieja," I say, handing him a fork. "We thought you might like to try something new."

He takes a bite, his expression shifting to one of pure delight. "This is incredible," he says, savoring the flavors. "The depth of the seasoning, the tenderness of the beef—it's exactly what I look for in a dish. The two of you make quite the team."

I glance at Valentina, who gives me a small, knowing smile.

My heart flutters, but I quickly look away, trying to focus on Luciano's reaction.

"This," he continues, gesturing at the plate with his fork, "is the kind of food that tells a story. It's rooted in culture, in family. That's what I love to see in a restaurant. It's what makes it stand out."

His words land heavily, and I feel a wave of conflicting emotions—pride, relief, and a gnawing sense of imposter syndrome. My palms feel clammy as I force a smile.

"I'm glad you like it," I say, my voice steady despite the storm inside me.

"I more than like it," he replies, his tone serious now. "This is the kind of dish that makes people come back for more. If this is the level of care and quality you bring to your food, I can see a lot of potential for La Mariposa."

Potential. The word hangs in the air like a challenge, and I feel the weight of it settle on my shoulders. I glance at Valentina again, and for once, she doesn't say anything, letting me process the moment.

Luciano's expression shifts slightly, his brow furrowing. "But I need to see more than just good food, Isa. Running a restaurant is about vision, about being able to plan for the future. I need to see your business plan—how you intend to expand, what your numbers look like, and how you'll make this sustainable."

I nod, swallowing hard. "Of course. I'll have it ready soon."

Luciano holds my gaze for a moment, his intensity unwavering. "This is about showing me that you're ready to take this to the next level. Don't just impress me with your cooking—impress me with your strategy."

The gravity of his words hits me like a punch to the gut. This isn't just about one dish or even one meal. This is about proving that I belong here—that La Mariposa belongs here.

"Understood," I manage to say, my voice barely above a whisper.

As Luciano leaves, I feel a knot tighten in my stomach. The stakes have never felt higher.

Valentina steps closer, her teasing grin returning. "Well, that sounded serious."

"You think?" I snap, my nerves getting the better of me.

"Hey," she says gently, placing a hand on my arm. "Relax. You've got this."

"I don't know how to write a business plan," I admit, my voice trembling. "I've been winging it this whole time, Val. What if I can't do it? What if he sees right through me?"

"You're not winging it," she says firmly. "You know this business better than anyone. I'll help you figure it out."

I'm not so convinced. She bumps me on the shoulder. "Come on, let's go pick up that piece of junk you call a car."

Her playful tone breaks through my tension, and I can't help but laugh despite myself. "I'm telling her you said that," I say, shaking my head.

It wasn't until I arrived here at the camp that I realized what paddleboarding is. I mean, I've seen the photos of fit people on social media living their best life, making it look super easy. They just stand on these flat boards on the water. Some would say it's like lazy surfing. That someone would be me.

Now, with Miss Piggy safely back at camp, I take in the paddleboards lined up along the shore. It feels different standing in front of one in real life, but I'm excited to try it out. It can't possibly be that difficult, right? It's not like I have to worry about sharks or large waves pummeling me into the water. My biggest concern is figuring out how to get back on the board if I fall off. How does one climb up on a floating surface without the ground to boost themselves up? Maybe I finally understand why Jack couldn't get on the door with Rose after the *Titanic* sank.

"So, are you ready?"

Valentina looks me up and down, framing my body with her hands, pretending that she's taking a photo. I decided to wear a bright yellow Chanel bikini top with high-waisted bottoms I borrowed from Maria, worn under my hiking shorts.

"No. I have no idea what the hell I'm doing. I am fully in freak-out mode right now."

"You've got this, Valdes. It's just like standing on a board. Except you're on top of the water. And said water is probably freezing like it was earlier this morning."

"Great," I take a deep breath. "Okay. I can do this. This is fine. Right? I've got this." I pause, then add, "But if I fall in, I'm dragging you with me."

Valentina gives me two enthusiastic thumbs up, and I can't help but smile, though I avoid meeting her eyes. Ever since she said those words—"maybe I do see myself with someone else"—I've been thrown completely off balance. I keep replaying it in my head, wondering if I misheard her, but the way she looked at me makes me think otherwise.

My nerves feel as if they're buzzing just under my skin. It's not just the paddleboarding I'm nervous about—it's her. Every time she's close, my heart races and my palms sweat. I'm sure she can sense it, but part of me hopes she can't. I've been avoiding her gaze, worried that she might see through me, that she'll catch on to how much her words have unraveled me.

"Hey, everyone," Sofia begins. "Welcome to our Jack & Jill Bachelorette Party Shindig Extravaganza—okay, I don't have a cute name for it."

A few guests laugh, mostly her bridesmaids.

"First of all, I want to thank you all so much for joining me. I know it's going to be a tiring but also a super fun day. Okay, Daniel—it's all you."

"Thanks, babe! Morning, friends! So, the first activity on today's schedule is paddleboarding. We'll be grabbing our boards and paddles and launching from the beachy part of the lake where the Adirondack chairs are."

He points across the camp, making me wonder why they'd set up the boards over here if we would have to carry them so far.

"After a few hours of paddleboarding and relaxing on the lake, I'll rally everyone up, and we'll move on to river tubing. I'll give more instructions when we reach that point, so don't fret. After that, we'll finish the night with a campfire and s'mores! Sound good?"

Everyone cheers.

"Sorry, I can't hear you. This is Sofia and Luciano's wedding. We just got cashmere scarves in our wedding-favor bags this morning. Can I get a little bit more energy?"

The men start whooping loudly, pumping their fists in the air like a pack of wild wolves. The girls scream at the top of their lungs with *woos* and *ahhs.*

"That's more like it! Follow me!"

As we are about to head out with the group, Valentina nudges me in the ribs.

"What?"

"Did you forget already? We need to find the next clue."

"Oh! You're right. I can't believe I forgot. I guess I'm just so excited about today. The real camping experience I've been looking forward to all week. All right, let's look for the next clue."

I rush over to my bag and pull out the journal, placing it on one of the picnic tables.

Silvana sneers. "Are you two coming?"

"Yeah, Silv. A little later. Just go on ahead," Valentina replies blandly.

Silvana scoffs and keeps walking. I can't help but feel smug.

I flip through the pages slowly until I feel something strange on my finger. I immediately pull my hand out and step away from the book.

"What happened?"

"There's something in there," I whisper in horror. "It touched me. It was hairy."

"What?" Valentina chuckles.

"Check for me, please?" I beg, feeling completely freaked out.

"Seriously?" She laughs. "All right, fine."

She reaches through the pages until she finds the page with the furry creature inside. She turns to the page. There's a lock of hair taped to one of the pages.

She smirks. "I found the monster."

"Shut up," I whine. "It felt weird."

I step closer to inspect it further. There's writing above it in Spanish.

"First haircut, 2001," I read.

"Is this your hair?"

I look closer at the hair. It's pin-straight and brown.

"Have you seen my hair?"

I hold up a few strands, showcasing the tight tendrils from my thick head of hair.

"What about your mom?"

"She also has curly hair, and wouldn't it be weird if he kept a lock of her hair?"

"Maybe." Valentina pauses. "Unless it was her first haircut since moving to the country. That would be a cute memento."

"You're probably right, but it's not her hair either. But it could be either a child's or a woman's hair from when they came to the country."

"So if it's a woman's hair, a lover, if you will—"

"I will not," I insist.

"—then it could be either Mariposa, Maritza, or Rosita. We've already ruled out your mom. So Rosita or Maritza."

"Or someone we don't even know," I note.

"Correct, but unlikely. We're Latino. We know everyone in the New Jersey area. I doubt he was having an affair with some random person and kept a lock of their hair in his journal for years."

"Okay, fair," I say. "If it's a child's hair, it's either from me, Silvana, or Sofia."

"What about Maria, Yolanda, and Araceli?"

I shake my head. "They were already older by then. Like, practically teenagers. The note about it being the first haircut? That's obviously the kind of thing you say about a toddler or a little kid. And the hair is so fine—like baby hair. Plus Silvana and Sofia are both the closest to my age. It wouldn't make sense for it to belong to an older cousin."

"That makes sense," Valentina says.

"And we know it's not me," I add. "I have baby pictures of me with hair so curly I looked like a little grandma with a perm. So it's Silvana or Sofia. But why?"

"That's the second thing we'd need to find out. For now, let's try and find out who it belongs to and get this dreadful activity-filled day over with."

I stuff the lock of hair into my bra, making Valentina chuckle. We grab our boards and join the group.

"How cold do you think that water is?" I ask, remembering the scene from *Titanic*.

"Probably the same as a few hours ago," Valentina says.

"Morning, prima," Sofia says. She and Luciano wave as we approach them.

She looks so effortlessly bridal in her white one-piece and matching cover-up. Luciano looks like a Greek statue come to life. If you looked up the definition of a power couple, I'm almost entirely sure it would just be a photo of Sofia and Luciano wearing these outfits.

"Hey! Paddleboarding, huh?"

"Yeah! This will be fun," Sofia says, beaming.

"Have you ever done it?" I asked.

"Would you be shocked if I said no? I was too scared to do it with the other campers when I was younger, so I'd sit it out. I always wanted to, though. Have you?"

"I've done it once or twice, actually," I lie.

The second the words come out of my mouth, I instantly regret it. I can't stop it—like word vomit.

Now I have to show off any skill I learned from the videos I watched the day before and this morning, prepping for this specific excursion. Luciano can't see me as a liar. I mean, any more than I already have been to everyone here. Valentina looks over at me and raises an eyebrow. *Crap.* She definitely knows I can't paddleboard.

"I'm not very good, though," I blurt, trying to save myself.

Sofia grins. "I'm sure you're great."

"Yeah, Isa. I bet you're practically an expert," Valentina adds, grinning mischievously at me.

She is thoroughly enjoying this train wreck.

"Well, maybe you can teach Luciano and me a few things?" Sofia insists.

"She already promised to teach me," Valentina chimes in and winks at Sofia.

"Oh. I see! Well, I'd still like to join. It's been a while since I've had some cousin time with Isa."

She was right. It has been years. The last time I was in the same place as these two was at our quinceañera, and, well, we all know what happened. Ever since our moms had that falling-out, we've kept our distance, whether we wanted to or not. Being back here now, with both of them, feels like stepping into a past I thought was long gone.

Since I arrived at camp, I felt as if I was invited out of pity, thanks to Maria. It didn't even occur to me that Sofia might actually want to spend some time with me. I feel the pressure to impress her, but there's also this nagging desire to just have fun, like we did when we were kids—staying up all night, watching movies, and eating way too much pizza.

After Daniel gives us thorough instructions, we rush toward the lake with our boards, our toes digging into the sand the camp placed at the edge of the shoreline to mimic a beach. The water is freezing. The sensation shoots through my spine like a jolt of electricity, and my stomach immediately sucks in. I try not to show it. We place our boards on the top of the water and climb on. Daniel instructed us that we could stay on our knees or stand up and use the boards traditionally, but I start on my knees since I am still unbelievably terrified. I hope I am doing a good job of hiding that fact.

Valentina gets on her board almost effortlessly, stands up, and begins paddling around. I roll my eyes. Of course, she can paddleboard. Valentina can do anything.

"Are you ready?" Sofia asks excitedly.

"Let's do it, prima!" I cheer like a war cry, waving my paddle in the air.

Paddleboarding is relatively easy while on your knees. You have a lot more stability. It almost feels too easy. For the next hour, I build the courage to stand up on the board like Valentina. Now is my time to shine. I hold my breath and put one foot on the board. I use it to push my body upward and immediately feel unstable. I pause for a moment, catching my balance. Finally, I get both of my feet on the board, and I'm standing upright. I can't fucking believe it.

"Whoa, impressive." Sofia claps. "Should I do it too?"

"Definitely. The view is way cooler up here. Do you need help?"

I hope to the heavens themselves she does not ask me for help. I wouldn't even know the first thing on helping someone stand up on their unstable board while mine is bopping around like one of those rusty metal horse rides in the front of supermarkets.

Luciano paddles to her side and helps her up, and I couldn't be any more grateful. Valentina snickers as she floats by me.

"You're so funny, Isa," she whispers. "Don't forget the hair."

"Shut up. And I won't," I whisper back.

Valentina, Sofia, and I start to paddle around the shoreline. Most guests have paddled on ahead or skipped out from the activity entirely. Probably because who the hell wants to swim in a New England lake in September? I can still see a few of them sitting on the Adirondack chairs by the sand. I wave humorously at them and get a few thumbs-ups.

The lake stretches out in all directions, a vast and shimmering expanse of dark blue. The sun is high in the sky, casting a warm golden light over the calm waters. The air is fresh and clean, carrying the scent of pine on a gentle breeze.

"So, when did you learn how to paddleboard? I thought you never left the restaurant! Well, that's the chisme from Maria," Sofia says.

Shit. I didn't even consider that she might want to know where in the world I may have learned how to do something in a body of water, since it's not as if I was paddleboarding in the Hudson River. The thought alone makes me shudder.

"Oh, I went on a little beach trip with… Faye. My assistant. It was like a work thing," I fib.

Valentina and Sofia look at each other for a moment before breaking out into roaring laughter.

"What's so funny?" I yell.

"Isa, I know you don't know how to paddleboard. You practically live inside La Mariposa. There's no way you found time to do anything but work," Sofia says gently.

"Hey, I resent that. I could have gone in college or something," I grumble.

"You're right, but based on how you got up on the board, I think it's safe to say you're a newbie. You don't have to impress me, prima. We're not kids anymore."

For the first time, I feel a sense of relief. She's right. Why the hell do I need to impress her? She's my cousin. Sure, I've been putting on this whole show of success for her, making it seem as if I've got everything figured out with my business, but it's not just for her. It's for Luciano, too. He's the one who can secure my future. But maybe impressing them both doesn't have to mean putting on a front all the time. Maybe I can just...have fun. What a thought.

I notice Valentina drift a little bit away from us. Almost as if she was trying to give us some privacy. I see her point to her boob, which confuses me at first, but then I realize she's reminding me about the lock of hair in my bikini top. I shoo her away.

Sofia sighs. "Isa, I just want to say something."

"What's that?"

"I missed you so much. It was different when we were younger. We have led different lives. Our mothers have this unspoken feud. No matter how hard my mother tried, she couldn't get into Mari's good graces."

"Yeah, I know," I say.

The sound of the paddles hitting the water breaks the sudden silence between us.

"In hindsight, though, if I had known I wouldn't see you again for so many years, I think things would have been different. I wouldn't have let them govern our relationship too. It would have been different."

"You really think so?"

Sofia nods.

"As I got older, I noticed myself wanting to know more about you and how you were doing. Like, did you end up going to college? Did you have a dream career? I can't believe I wasn't around when you had to come out to the family. That must have been so difficult to deal with on your own. It's not like you had siblings to support you through it. I was supposed to be there, and I wasn't. I mean, I just didn't know."

"Sofia, it's fine. I grew up just fine, can't you see?" I point to myself and grin. "Besides, I never actually came out to anyone. They just started to notice I was 'different' and never brought it up. It's a touchy subject for my mother. She just kind of ignores it. It goes against her idea of perfectionism and success. She mentions wanting to see me with someone, which I guess I can appreciate, but she never specifies the gender. I just wish she'd say 'with a woman.' Sometimes I feel like she's just hoping one day I'll bring a man home and be able to continue our family line for my father's memory."

"Damn, Isa. That's really serious stuff." Sofia exhales. "I wish our mothers weren't so petty and could resolve whatever stupid issue they have going on that's caused all this separation. I'm so tired of acting like it's some big family secret we're not allowed to know about."

"I know. I always try to pry with my mother, but she's not budging."

Dare I tell her about the journal? The lock of hair in my bikini top?

"Oh God, prima. I've been trying for years. My mother refuses to say anything too. All I know is that she's hurt by something. I just have no idea what. Maybe it was something Tía Maritza did, but maybe it was something Mami did herself. Who fucking knows?"

"Well." I pause.

"What? Do you know something else?" Sofia urges.

"No, no. Not yet. But that was kind of a goal of mine while I was here. To find out the truth. Get some closure. I don't have the best relationship with my mother, so asking her has been completely impossible. But, I figured, maybe, just maybe, I could figure it out while I was here."

Sofia stays quiet for a moment, thinking.

"I hope you do, prima. I miss you." She smiles softly.

"I miss you too."

"Can I be honest about something?" Sofia asks.

"Of course." Even though it's something I've been terrible at all week.

"I don't have the best relationship with my mother either. Granted, it's not at all like what you have to deal with, but she can be overbearing. I don't know what happened between her and Mari, but it's like a switch flipped in her head during our quince. She always wants to have nice things. Put on a certain facade to complete strangers. Make sure I have the most extravagant wedding. That we have the most expensive rings. The most expensive dress we could afford. It's too much. Luciano and I—we're not really like that."

I nod slowly, taking it all in. I hear laughter in the distance, the sound of splashing water, and someone falling into the lake. I think about the wedding rings, and I'm so grateful Val found them again. Though I don't recall getting a good look at them when she plucked them back out of the water.

"I remember her once saying, 'I have to win, Sofia. I just have to,' and I'm like, win what? Who are you competing against? So I grew up with the same mindset for a long time. Always needing the best things. The nicest designer stuff. When you bought me that Coach bag, I felt like me again. It was the first bag I ever got myself. Cheap by her standards, but it was so special. Your bag brought back a lot of memories for me."

"I'm glad to hear it, Sof. I hoped it would be a good gift."

I remember Valentina buying me the gift I couldn't afford for my cousin and handing me the shopping bag. I'll be eternally grateful. Something that probably cost nothing to Valentina meant the world to me and apparently, Sofia too. For a grump, she definitely has a soft side. I smile softly.

"I have another confession while we're at it." Sofia laughs.

I laugh back. "Lay it on me, prima. I'm ready."

"I was jealous of you. Growing up."

"What? You were jealous of me?" I cackle, unable to even comprehend the thought.

"Yeah, I was. Roberto was always a great uncle to me, but it would have been nice to grow up with a father—a real one. I remember being so envious of you and him when you did your father-daughter dance at our quinceañera. I wished I had someone I could have danced with."

"Oh, Sof. I don't know what to say. I'm so sorry."

"No need to apologize. Like I said, he was a great uncle to me. He was there for me a lot. Cheered me on at events. Went to my school plays. I only wish—"

"What?"

"I wish I could have been there. For the funeral. I'm sorry, Isa. I really wanted to. I sent a letter to your mom, and we sent flowers, but it's all we could do. She refused."

"You sent flowers? I didn't even know. She didn't tell me," I say softly, feeling hurt.

"Moms, am I right?" She chuckles softly, but there's sadness in her voice. "I only hope we can continue moving forward together, despite their issues. What do you think?"

I smile. "I would love that."

"Mi amor," Luciano shouts and waves Sofia over to him.

"I'm going to go annoy my future husband for a bit. Can you believe the wedding is in two days?"

I watch her go, and suddenly remember I forgot to check her hair to see if it matches the lock I have stashed in my bikini top. *Shit.* It's not like I can just ask her, though. I need to see if it has that same reddish-brown tint in the sunlight or if it shimmers with those subtle golden streaks, just like the one I found. I glance down to make sure it's still tucked safely inside my top, nice and dry.

"Do your breast screenings somewhere else, prima," Silvana remarks.

I look over to see her paddling by me. She's on her knees, making me think she's never done this before. I figured she would keep paddling by, but to my surprise, she stays beside me. She doesn't say anything for a solid minute. I sit awkwardly, waiting, watching the tiny fish swim under the board.

"What are you doing with Valentina?" she finally asks. "You're spending a lot of time with her here."

"She's helping me with something," I reply, trying not to sound defensive.

"Do you like her?"

"Why do you care?" I retort.

"Because she's mine."

"Okay, Silvie." I snort. "It sure seems that way. She's *veeery* affectionate towards you."

"Oh, fuck off. She just doesn't want everyone to know. So you need to back off, or you'll regret it."

"Is this high school? Grow up, Silvie."

She sneers and adds, "I guess losing your father made you extra defensive, huh? I suppose it's not like you'd understand loyalty."

Her jab hits harder than I'd like, and I feel the sting.

"Where's your dad, anyway?" I quickly snap back.

"Excuse me?" She turns and glares at me.

"I said, where is your dad? I'm just saying, family loyalty goes both ways, doesn't it? You'd think he'd be around if it mattered so much to you."

"What the fuck do you know about my family? Mind your own business."

I'm surprised that I'm actually shocked by her attitude. I have no idea where this is coming from. Granted, she's always been a bit of a jerk to me, but this is a whole different level of Silvana I'm not ready to put up with.

"Why do you always have to be such a bitch? Honestly. We could have been closer. You know I didn't grow up with two sisters like my mother did. I was by myself often, and it would have been nice to have cousins around."

"Two sisters? What the fuck are you talking about?"

"Mari, Maritza, and Rosita? Who else?"

I look at her as if she has five heads. I can't tell if I've really thrown her off or she's just trying to mess with me.

"Rosita isn't related to my mom and your mom. How do you not know this?" She scoffs. "I guess it's clear you're not that important in the family if everyone is keeping secrets from you, huh? I don't even know why you're here, but I can assure you, it won't end well for you. So back off and stop asking questions."

"Wait, what?"

But Silvie turns her paddleboard away, her back toward me. I quickly remember the lock of hair and pull it out of my top. She begins to paddle out, and I reach my arm out as far as I can to compare it to her hair. I keep reaching until I slip off my board and fall into the water. I panic as I swim to the surface quickly.

"Hey! Are you okay? I saw you fall in."

Valentina paddles quickly toward me.

I hold on to my board and clear the water from my face and lashes. I look around at the lake, then below me, into the darkness.

"Fuck. I lost the hair."

"Oh damn, really?"

Valentina looks around the water, but it's long gone.

"Well, that blows," I groan.

Valentina shrugs. "Well, I guess it wouldn't have been super helpful if Sofia dyed her hair or something, right? All is not lost."

"I guess you're right," I sigh. "I fucking hate paddleboarding. I'm ready to go river tubing now," I say in utter defeat.

Between Sofia's heartfelt words, Silvana's threatening message, and the possibility that Rosita isn't even my real aunt, I think I've learned enough to earn myself a moment on dry land before our next activity. The thought still plagues me, though. If Rosita isn't my real aunt and not my mother's sister, then who is she? Who is Sofia?

As soon as we're back on shore, I pull Maria and Valentina aside. I can't hold this in any longer.

"There's something I need to tell you both."

They both look at me, concern etched on their faces.

"I just found out that Rosita might not actually be my real aunt."

Maria's mouth falls open, and Valentina stares at me in disbelief. "Wait, what do you mean?" Maria asks, clutching my arm.

"Apparently, she isn't my mom's sister. I don't have all the details, but it's starting to feel like everything I thought I knew about my family might be a lie. If Rosita isn't my aunt…then who is she? And what does that mean for Sofia?"

The weight of it hangs between us. Valentina places a hand on my shoulder. "We'll figure this out together."

"Yeah," Maria adds, nodding firmly. "But first, let's get through this day. We'll sort through all of it later."

I take a deep breath and nod, trying to focus on what's ahead. I need to keep it together.

Chapter Fourteen

"Yeah, I'm not wearing this."

I look over at Maria holding up a T-shirt that says, "I got washed away at Sofia & Luciano's Bach," printed with some cheesy cartoon photos of them.

"This can't possibly be Sofia's handiwork," I say, throwing the shirt on the bed in protest. "The entire wedding has been so bougie and extravagant. These shirts…the penis hats…the penis glasses. What is going on?"

"I am not wearing a dick on my head. It's bad enough I have to put them in my—"

"I'm gonna stop you right there," I groan.

Valentina comes out of the bathroom wearing the shirt with an exaggerated grin plastered across her face. This is the happiest I've seen her this entire week.

"Uh, you seem pretty pleased with the uniform for the bachelorette."

"It's pretty fantastic, isn't it?"

Maria and I look at each other as if Valentina had been replaced with some random stranger.

"'Fantastic' is not the word I'd use," Maria says.

"'Heinous' would be mine," I chime in.

"'Atrocious' is mine," Maria adds.

"Perfect." Valentina smiles.

"For someone who has been so miserable, why is this penis adornment the thing that has shifted your mood?" I ask.

"Because, you guys, I'm the maid of honor."

"Okay?" we both say in unison.

"I was in charge of the bach party." She grins, showing off her entire look. The baseball cap has a small penis superglued to the lip, standing straight up. The shirt is oversized, not designer, and has the ugliest illustration of the couple I have ever seen.

"Valentina, was this part of your...plan?" I ask, side-eyeing her.

"No! Okay yes, it was. But I had decided on this long before I agreed not to do it anymore, so I need to follow through. Besides, I hadn't planned anything else, and it's too late to change it. It's going to be great."

"'Great' is also not the word I'd use," Maria says. "But I can't wait to see the look on Sofia's face when everyone's wearing these shirts and hats."

"Oh, that's not all," Valentina laughs.

She pulls out a box from the closet and pours out a bunch of random stuff. There are bags of straws where the end you drink out of is a literal penis, and they're all in different funky colors. There are glow-stick necklaces and face paint. There's a "pin the penis on the man" board.

I gasp. "What the fuck?"

"I have never seen so much dick in one place in my entire life," Maria laughs. "Well, there was that one time in Cabo—"

"Maria!" I shout.

"So what did you do? Look up the world's cheesiest bachelorette decorations and buy everything listed?" Maria asks as she grabs the glow sticks and begins cracking a few to make herself a necklace.

"Actually, yes, I did. I was stressed about how to host and

decorate the perfect bachelorette. I spent months trying to figure it out. She always does everything over the top, with the utmost elegance one could muster. So how could I possibly compete? Well, I finally decided the best way to ruin—I mean, enhance—the week was to do the complete opposite of what she'd expect. I was nice enough to wait until the river-tubing activity to bring it all out."

Maria laughs. "Well, this is going to be interesting."

River tubing is more my speed. There used to be this old water park where I lived called Splash City. I didn't get to go often when I was younger because my parents couldn't afford it, but one year, I was finally able to go, and I fell in love. I was too scared to go on any of the more dangerous water slides, and my mother would absolutely forbid it. However, the one ride I would go on over and over again was called the Lazy River. It lasted about twenty minutes, but I'd go on it for hours. I would bring a drink and put it in the cup holder. I sneaked in a packet of Goldfish once, but I accidentally dropped it in the water. The workers were furious, but all the guests laughed as they watched the crackers swim in the river like fish. I imagine this will be a lot like that, with just a little bit of turbulence in some parts, I'm sure. Easy.

But standing next to the river now feels intimidating. The river itself is wide and flowing steadily, with gentle ripples on its surface reflecting the sunlight that filters through the trees that line its banks. The trees are tall and lush, their branches providing shade to the river below and creating a natural canopy over the water. Slightly different shades of green, orange, and red are represented on the leaves as the season changes.

The sound of the river is constant and soothing, with the water flowing over the rocks and boulders providing a peaceful background melody to the chatter surrounding the hyped-up crowd.

"Most of the river is pretty timid," Daniel begins. "But this one section gets a little crazy, so be careful going down there. Make sure you unhook from your party, or you'll all go down together. Now just have fun, and we'll have a little campfire at the end. I already left the van on the other side so we can easily return. Sound good?"

The group collectively cheers.

"What the hell is this, Sof?" Silvana moans as she looks down at the oversized shirt covering her expensive bathing suit underneath.

"What's the problem?" Valentina asks.

Silvana's face flushes.

"Nothing. I just think it's…different than what I expected."

"It's just Valentina messing with me," Sofia laughs. "It's funny!"

Sofia puts on the penis hat and drinks her spiked tea through one of the straws. Valentina snaps a selfie with her. I feel a pang of envy inside my gut. Based on her grimace, I'm sure Silvana feels the same way right now.

Silvana grabs her tube and walks over to the other bridesmaids.

"We should hook together. The three of us," Sofia exclaims excitedly.

"That's a great idea! The Three Amigos!" I add.

I grab one of the already-inflated tubes and hand it over to Valentina. Sofia grabs herself one and hands me another. We dock our floats near the shoreline and walk back near the group. Everyone is either applying sunscreen, taking selfies, grabbing some last-minute drinks, or waiting for more instructions. Valentina leaves for the snack station to grab two more iced teas. I walk over to my bag and pull out Roberto's journal while Sofia's distracted by her bridal party. It's weird seeing her in a normal, albeit ridiculous, shirt. She almost looks like an average person who doesn't have a ton of money. It's kind of nice. Like we could actually be related or something.

I flip through the pages, passing all the delicious recipes, random journal entries about his day, photos of me as a kid, and one picture of my mother holding me. Nothing is sticking out to me. I turn the page once more and find a phone number written in the book. It's his handwriting, for sure, so it's not someone else who wrote it. There's a star scribbled on each side of the number.

"I got our drinks."

"Sh," I say, pulling Valentina down to the picnic table with me. "Look."

"A phone number. How intriguing! Should we call it?"

"There's no way it's still in service," I conclude.

"Isa, hasn't our family had the same numbers for decades? I mean, isn't your mother's phone number the same as it has been since you were a baby?"

"Okay, yes," I admit. "You call, though. I can't. I'm scared."

"All right." She chuckles and pulls out her phone.

I hold my breath, and she presses the numbers and puts her phone against her ear.

"Valentina? Why are you calling me?"

I hear the muffled words spoken, and panic rises in my throat. Valentina knows the person. Maybe she's been hiding something from me this entire time. Have I been trusting the wrong person with this information? Has she been leading me astray this whole time?

Valentina, confused, looks down at her phone, and her eyes widen.

"Oh, hi, Maritza! It was an accident, sorry."

She quickly hangs up and stares at her phone.

"I didn't even notice that the number was already saved on my phone when I dialed it. It's your aunt Maritza's number."

I stare at her phone, trying to process this information. Why is her number in my father's journal? Why is it labeled as "important?" What am I missing here?

"Do you think—"

"That my father was in love with Maritza? Maybe they had a secret love affair? God, I fucking hope not. I'm going to investigate a little bit."

I consider asking Valentina what she knows about Silvie, but I don't want to even hear her talk about her ex. I need to ask Sofia.

It is scorching today, even though the water will probably still be too cold for comfort. I can already feel the beads of sweat developing on my forehead. I grab the iced tea Valentina brought us, twist the top open, and take three long gulps. The ice-cold black tea coats my throat with sugar and lemon. I have to physically stop myself from chugging the whole bottle and subsequently giving myself a cramp.

We crowd the beach just off the riverbed, with our floats in tow. We are instructed to just walk into the water, and when the river reaches our knees, and there are no longer any obstacles, we can hop on our tubes and float down. First go the men. They lift the tubes above their heads one by one and race into the water, lifting their knees toward their chests as if they are about to jump across the river. Once they get about a third of the way in, they slam the floats on top of the water and, in the same motion, jump right on top. We watch as each one waves and begins to float away.

"Wait for us!" Araceli shouts as she clumsily climbs into her tube.

She has her arms in the water to paddle herself faster toward the men.

"You can do it!" Alessandro shouts from a distance, paddling against the water to slow himself down. Finally, Araceli latches in and they keep floating away.

A few more people go before us, but it is finally our turn.

"Rock, paper, scissors?" I suggest.

Valentina scoffs. "Isa, what are we? Five?"

"Uh, yeah," I assure her.

"You're on, then."

Valentina makes a ball with her right fist and places it on her left palm. I follow suit. We both look at Sofia.

"Fine." She sighs and puts her hands in.

"Rock, paper, scissors, shoot!" I shout.

I hold out my hand flat, like paper. Valentina has a paper as well. Sofia holds her hand out with two fingers in a shape of a V, meaning scissors. She cut our hands with her scissors.

"Looks like it's down to you two," she says, amused.

"Loser goes first," Valentina states.

"Rock, paper, scissors, shoot."

I hold my hand in a fist to signify rock. Valentina has her hand out flat. Paper. Paper beats rock. *Damn.*

"Looks like it's you first, Isa," Valentina says, giving me a thumbs-up.

I grab my tube and walk into the water. This is definitely not like the lazy river in Splash City. Splash City had Goldfish crackers floating in it. There are real fish in this one. Maybe even…piranhas. No, that would be ridiculous. Right? They wouldn't put us in a river full of man-eating piranhas. I think. I hope.

"Are you going to go?"

"Shut it, Sof. I'm concentrating."

"You should just brace yourself and make the jump," Valentina says.

Her words of encouragement are surprisingly effective. With this newfound burst of energy, I hold my breath, sprint into the water, and jump on my float. I look around and watch as the scenery starts to move around me. I did it.

"Let's go, ladies!"

As if I had shot a gun for a horse race, they look at each other and race into the water after me. Sofia slips, and Valentina pulls ahead. Valentina has trouble getting onto her tube, allowing

Sofia to catch up. The two are neck and neck for the final round of the race. They climb onto their floats and paddle toward me as fast as possible. It is a tough race, and it is anyone's game. Valentina is clearly stronger. Those biceps could lift me in an instant. The thought tempts me. I'm not sure what Sofia does for exercise, but she looks like she'd beat me in any race with those quads. Who is it going to be? I watch the water splash around as they slap the river with the sheer force of two determined women. With just a few seconds left on the imaginary clock, two hands slap my tube. But whose are they? Is it the bicep queen, Valentina, or the possible deadlift fanatic, Sofia? The verdict is in. The winner is…both of them! It is a tie!

We hook our floats to each other and settle into our tubes. It is finally time to sit back, relax, and enjoy the scenery. Unlike that famous Jersey water park, there are beautiful views here. At Splash City, you'd see drunk grown men being loud and obnoxious. You'd see bandages floating around the kiddie pools. You'd see teenagers screaming at the top of their lungs as they shot down the waterslides. You'd see overpriced hot dogs and warm Pepsi. Here? Instead of crying children floating past you, there are sounds of crickets and birds singing their favorite tunes. I lean my head back against the inflated pillow attached to the tube and stare at the blue sky above me. I watch as the clouds drift by, making out their different shapes each time. One looks like a teddy bear. Another one looks like a boat.

These past several days at camp have been a stressful and strange blur. Sofia's wedding is happening so quickly that it's hard to keep up. I still haven't secured the investment with Luciano. I need to work on the business plan tonight. I haven't figured out my father's big secret yet. Meanwhile, tomorrow is the rehearsal dinner. I'll be leaving in a couple of days. I'm not ready to go just yet. I feel like I haven't made sufficient memories with Sofia now that we've reconnected. My to-do list looms over me, like a dark cloud, in contrast to the fluffy white ones passing me by.

"Whatcha thinking about?" Sofia's voice startles me as my eyelids already begin to feel heavy with each blink.

"Me?"

"No, Valentina." She giggles.

I look over at Val, who has already been taken over by the soothing rocking of the river and lulled into a deep nap.

"Oh. Nothing really. Just…stuff I need to do."

"Like what?"

I hesitate for a moment. Do I tell her everything that's plaguing me? Do I pretend everything is fine and silently suffer?

"What do you know about Silvie and Maritza?" I say, slightly changing the subject.

"What do you mean? I know they're my cousin and aunt?" She laughs softly, staring up at the sky.

But they're not. It seems Sofia is unaware of the news Silvana just told me.

"What about Silvie's dad? Where's he?"

"I think she divorced him about six years ago? Ronaldo, right? Yeah, she took more than half his money. That's basically how she and Silvie have lived so comfortably without working. That's probably why they're so snotty too."

I snort.

"Do you know why they divorced?" I ask.

"Prima, I didn't peg you for such a gossiper," she says, laughing. "Maria must be rubbing off on you."

"She's like a parasite, really," I joke.

"Well, it is kind of scandalous."

I lean in. We both look over at Valentina, who is still fast asleep. Or wins Best Actress for her role in pretending to be.

"He found some letters between her and her lover. Allegedly, it had been going on for years. We're talking, like, decades at this point. She finally admitted that she was in love with someone else for their entire relationship. It was a whole thing. They dislike talking about it because it makes them look bad."

My stomach churns.

"And you said this was six years ago?"

She nods. So it was three years before my father passed. She must have felt like she needed to be true to herself and him before he got too sick.

"And is she still with him?"

"I have no idea—we never found out who it was. That was kind of the last thing we heard about her alleged lover. The whole story could be fake, for all we know. You know how they are. Always making shit up to be the center of attention."

"Well, I don't, really. I haven't been around much to know." I laugh softly, but even I can hear the pain in my voice.

"Shit. Sorry, Isa. You know what I meant. I promise you haven't missed much. You're lucky not to have been around for all that drama. It's all she'd talk about for a year. Then suddenly, she stopped mentioning anything about it and her lover. It's a blessing in disguise you missed it, honestly."

I chuckle weakly. "I guess so."

I turn around to see if Valentina has woken yet. Nothing.

"So—" I say.

Sofia begins reapplying suntan lotion to her shoulders, knowing I'll continue talking regardless of what she replies.

"Silvie and Val," I continue.

Sofia looks up at me, raising her eyebrows as if the conversation got disproportionately more interesting.

"Yeah?" she says, amused.

"How long ago did that happen?"

She smiles at my words, knowing exactly why I'm asking.

"It's been years too. Silvie is still caught up on her, but Valentina never liked her. I think she was trying to fill a void."

I wonder if Sofia knows what the void was.

She looks over at Valentina and pokes her leg with her toes. Her body moves, but she's still asleep.

"She had feelings for me," she finally says, softly.

The fact that Sofia knows shocks me right to my core. I guess I can't be too surprised. I knew immediately after seeing the way Val looked at her for just a mere moment.

"It was sometimes awkward. I felt bad often. Sometimes I wished I was queer just so I could date her." She chuckles softly. "But I'm not. And she's truly my best friend. I hated seeing her suffer. Nothing I did would change it. I was hoping my wedding would help her move on. Maybe even seeing Silvie would help jolt her from her trance of being in love with me."

"I see."

"And here you are," she says, grinning.

"What? What do you mean?"

"Oh, please, prima. She clearly likes you. You've been hanging out all week, and I haven't seen her this happy in years."

I laugh. "No, there's no way."

"Uh, why would you think that?" Sofia asks.

"Because—" I hesitate again. "She told me not to fall in love with her when we first met. So why would she say she likes me? Plus, she's in love with you still. Or maybe she even still likes Silvana. Who knows. She's kind of a flirt, I feel like."

"She really said that?" she whispers back, playing along.

"Not to fall in love with her? Yeah, it's exactly the type of thing a player would say, anyways. So."

"And did you?"

"Did I what?"

"You know." Sofia laughs and splashes me with river water.

"No, I did not. I am just curious. About things. And her relationship with Silvie. That's all. And again, she's in love with you. Even if I was remotely interested, I don't have a chance. She's stuck. She'll probably end up back with Silvana anyways."

I try to keep my voice steady, but the words sound hollow

even to me. The thought of Valentina choosing Silvana doesn't feel right—it doesn't even make sense. But still, I let the lie settle, using it as a shield against the truth I'm too scared to admit.

"I can't risk getting hurt," I finally say, more quietly this time, my voice tinged with vulnerability.

Not to mention, I'm keeping secrets from everyone in the family, including her. She's been nothing but helpful to me, and I've just been a fraud, making her think I'm a moderately wealthy and successful restauranteur.

A flock of geese flies ahead in the distance in an iconic V shape. I wonder where they're going. I doubt they have to deal with love problems like this. Maybe if I believe hard enough, I can grow wings and fly away from all my responsibilities. I tilt my head back and watch them slowly fly away. I swish my hands in the water, leaning back on my tube to feel the cold river against my fingertips. Maybe I'll turn into a fish instead.

"Oh, my sweet, sweet cousin," Sofia says, patting my head. "You don't know Valentina at all. She's not some sort of player. Sure, she puts on a facade, but she's the most hopeless romantic person I know. She's also my best friend, and I can tell when she likes someone. And you, prima, she likes."

I double-check Valentina's tube to make sure she hasn't been awake this entire time, listening to our conversation.

"So what should I do?"

Sofia laughs. "Are you serious, Isa?"

"No, no. I'm not." I shrug, making Sofia laugh harder.

"Oh my God, you two are perfect for each other," she says, rolling her eyes.

Sofia lays her head back against the inflated pillow on the tube. I can't help but laugh at the penis standing up on the top of her head. I lie back on my pillow as well.

My eyelids start to feel heavy. Each time I blink, it feels like I'm adding half a pound to each one. The soothing sounds of the river flowing and the birds chirping, combined with the knowledge that I'm safe with Valentina and Sofia, is the perfect recipe for a quick nap. And so I do.

"Isabella! Wake up!" Valentina shouts as she shakes me awake, startling me.

"What the hell, Val? I was having the best nap."

"We're approaching the rapids!"

I immediately perk up. Suddenly, the river doesn't feel as safe as it once did. We all look ahead like meerkats, trying to see when to brace ourselves. I can see the part where the water begins to get rocky, and it is quickly approaching. If I were by myself, I would be terrified. But since I'm with Val and Sof, I somehow feel better. As if we are on this adventure together, and we're going to go out together. Everyone else has gone through just fine, so why won't we?

Just as quickly as it approaches, we start getting rocked by the choppy waves, shaking us up in every direction. We hold on to the handles on the edges of our tubes and keep our legs inside for extra stability. The river is creating a ripple effect between us. When Sofia gets pulled away, Val and I follow suit. When Valentina gets jerked to the left, Sof and I follow suit.

"Ow!" Valentina yelps.

"What happened?" I shout.

"I think this area is a bit shallow. Watch out for rocks!"

I look down into the water and notice the taller rocks passing by. It is only a matter of time before we all get bruised butts from hitting so many of them. But, for the most part, we are able to navigate through the rapids. We start to settle down, feeling more confident in our abilities. Valentina laughs, enjoying the ride now that it isn't as scary. Her amusement makes me laugh too. Then Sofia joins in. It isn't so bad and certainly isn't like Splash City.

"Iceberg, straight ahead!" Valentina shouts.

A large boulder begins to make an appearance, and it is heading right toward us. If we don't move out of the way, we'll slam right into it and get stuck between the rushing water and the rock.

"We need to move!"

In unison, we all start to paddle away from each other, but we can't seem to move. The boulder continues to be in our path. Now I am beginning to panic.

"Why can't we move?" I shriek.

"We're still hooked!" Sofia screams.

We forgot Daniel's instruction to unhook ourselves before entering the rapids—the most important rule. Sofia quickly unsnaps herself from Valentina and starts working on unsnapping from my tube.

"It's not unlocking!"

"Let me try mine," Valentina cries out.

I watch as they both desperately try to unhook from my tube. The boulder is too close at this point. It is time to brace for impact. Within a second, my tube smashes into the boulder. The sheer force breaks the hooks and sends Sofia and Valentina flying down the river. I try to push off, but the river pins me into the rock. This must be how the *Titanic* felt. I try again to pull away, this time managing to slide around it slowly. When I reach the edge, the water pressure shoots me out and causes me to flip over, off the tube and straight into the water.

"Isa!" they both yell.

I alternate between having my head above the water and being fully submerged. The river is deep enough at this point that I am not too worried about slamming into another rock, but my legs keep bumping into smaller ones, giving me nicks and scrapes. I need to get a grip on something. I don't even know where my tube is anymore. The river looks completely different from this angle. The water begins to slow down, which helps me calm down, knowing the rapids are nearly over. However, I still can't seem to keep my head above water and continue bopping up and down like a hopeless buoy.

"Isabella!" Valentina shouts, her voice sounding close by.

"Val!" I try to shout but choke on the river water and dip back into the water.

As I float underwater, for a moment, everything is still. I feel peaceful. As if I have nothing to worry about anymore. Something in the universe is telling me that everything will be okay. Or it's my brain preparing for my untimely death.

Just as I have those thoughts, I feel an arm slide around my waist and another grab my arm and pull me out of the water. When my head reaches the surface, I take a deep breath and cough up river water. I rub my eyes and frantically look around. Valentina saved me. She is hanging off the outside of her tube, using it to keep herself afloat so she can easily rescue me. Sofia is not too far ahead, paddling against the current to stay close. For the first time in my life, I am the damsel in distress. And I have a knight in shining armor.

"Isa, are you okay? You scared me half to death." Valentina wipes my hair out of my face and grabs my chin to make me look at her. "You can go on, Sofia—she's fine!"

"I'm fine, I'm fine," I say in between coughs.

Valentina starts to inspect all of my limbs and then gasps.

"What?"

"Isa...you're bleeding!"

I look down at my forearm to see a long scratch going down toward my elbow. It isn't deep at all—just a surface wound.

"Val, I'm fine." I chuckle. "I promise."

Valentina paddles closer to the river's edge, where the water is still and shallow, so we can catch our bearings.

"Thank you for saving me. I don't know what would have happened if you weren't here to rescue me. I don't know if I would have come out of that water. It just...kept holding me down. I was getting so tired. It was terrifying. But you were there for me. You managed to swim against the river just to save me. I'll never forget that."

"I'm just glad you're okay. Let's get you patched up. I have a first aid kit in the cabin."

As we step clumsily out of the water, we finally make it onto the riverbank. Up ahead, I can see a dirt path. I pick up my foot to get past a section cluttered with branches and debris from the river but lose my footing and begin to fall. Then, like a supernatural instinct, Valentina swings around and catches me, resting my back against her forearm. I look up at her, completely shocked.

"Be careful, Isa," she whispers as she pulls me back up to stand. "What am I going to do with you?"

The question intrigues me.

Since we didn't make it to the end of the route where the van is, we begin our trek back to the cabin, and it seems to take forever. We're barefoot, wearing these silly T-shirts Valentina made, and somehow the fucking penis hat survived the crash and stayed securely on my head. Valentina has several glow stick necklaces around her neck and the same hat on her head. We look ridiculous.

The dirt path is surrounded by the lush, green vegetation winding alongside the river. The trail is narrow and well-trodden, with soft, brown earth packed tightly underfoot. The dirt is rich and fragrant, scented with the smell of the surrounding forest, and damp from the nearby river, making it soft against my toes.

The path is engulfed by tall trees that reach toward the sky, their branches providing dappled shade to the path below. Sunlight filters through the leaves, casting its warm, golden light on the path.

"That was fun," Valentina says. "Besides the whole you almost dying part."

"Yeah, sans drowning, it was awesome. It would have been

nice to get to the end with the rest of the party. I heard there was going to be sparklers and goody bags."

"I like this better, though." Valentina smiles.

"It's nice," I agree. "Nice and quiet. I wish I lived somewhere where there were trails I could hike through like this. Makes me appreciate nature a bit more."

As we continue to walk, our conversation trails off, and the only sounds are the crunch of the dirt under our feet and the gurgling of the river. I am lost in thought, thinking about how much I enjoy just being near Valentina, even in silence.

"So," Valentina says, breaking the silence.

"So," I repeat.

"You like me, huh?"

I turn my head so quickly I nearly give myself whiplash.

"What?" I cough, choking on my saliva.

Valentina chuckles. "I asked if you like me."

"Were you awake the entire time?" I groan.

"No, I woke up right around the point where I heard you and Sofia talking about me loving her and you liking me."

"Oh my God, Val. I'm so sorry. I—"

"You don't need to apologize. Weirdly, I feel relieved. Relieved that she knows—or has known—and like I can finally relax knowing I don't have to figure out how to tell her anymore. It can just be this unspoken truth between us we never mention."

"Still," I say. "That must have been hard to hear. I'm sorry."

She smiles. "Thanks."

A critter runs through the woods, breaking tiny twigs and rustling dry leaves along its path. I can't see it, but even the sound is cute.

"So, you never answered my question."

I shrug halfheartedly, which only makes her laugh.

"You told me not to fall for you," I say.

"But did you?"

"Maybe I did." I shrug again.

She shakes her head, amused. "Even though I specifically said not to."

"Yeah, well. You don't control me. I have free will, you know," I retort.

Valentina stops. Our gazes lock as we stand on the dirt path.

"I'm happy you're here, Isa. This week, I've had more fun than I thought I would. I know I've been pessimistic about this entire thing. I just wanted it all to be over…tired of feeling this unrequited love. Forced to be near Silvana again. Pretending like everything is okay. Then you came along. This bright light in my gloomy life. I'm glad you didn't listen to me, because I can't handle another unrequited love again."

She moves toward me slowly, and I find myself holding my breath. Valentina takes my hand in hers, and I look up at her. Her eyes shine with emotion.

Slowly, she leans in and presses her lips to mine, our kiss soft and tender at first. Her lips warm against mine. She wraps her arms around my waist, pulling me in close.

The world around me fades away, and all that remains is the two of us, lost in a moment of pure, unbridled bliss. My kiss is filled with all the emotions I've been holding back, and I pour all of myself into it.

As she finally pulls away, I feel breathless, my face flushed with the moment's intensity. She pulls me into her embrace, and I can hear her heart beating fast. I don't want this moment to end. Forget the wedding. Forget the puzzle. Forget the investment. She lifts my chin and smiles.

"Do you want to make some s'mores with me?"

Chapter Fifteen

The smell of the woodsmoke and the sounds of the fire crackling fill the air. The entire bridal party sits on various large wood logs and camping chairs, chatting and laughing, their voices echoing through the quiet forest. Despite the chill in the air, the fire keeps us warm. That, and the fact that Valentina's thigh and shoulder are pressed tight against me. I can't help but steal glances at her. She looks beautiful in the firelight, her hair shining like gold and her eyes sparkling with happiness. I wonder if she's replaying the kiss in her head a thousand times a second or if it's just me.

Next to me are Luciano and Sofia. They lean close to each other as if they're telling secrets no one else can know. I hear her giggle softly.

"I really did decide to stop my big plan, by the way," Valentina whispers low enough for just me to hear.

"Oh you did, huh? Why's that?"

"Well, I realize I was doing it for the wrong reasons. Holding on to something that was never really mine." She looks over at Sofia and Luciano for a moment. "Luc is obviously perfect for her. He's a nice guy and I had to actively try to make him a bad person for it to work. It was just doomed from the beginning. Plus—"

"Yeah?"

I look up at her, her eyes shimmering in the fire.

"I learned that there is someone else that could see the love I could give." She grins.

I smile. "Well, I'm glad."

I hold a long, thin branch in my hand. On the end is a jumbo marshmallow, waiting to be roasted into oblivion. I submerge it in the fire until it completely lights up in flames. I watch it for a moment, allowing the outer layer of the marshmallow to char. Finally, with one big breath, I blow it out.

Valentina laughs. "That's burnt."

"It's how I like it! Watch."

With my fingers, I pull the charred marshmallow layer off, exposing a gooey center. I put the whole shell into my mouth.

"That cannot be good for you," she says, watching in awe and slight concern.

"I mean, probably not. But it's delicious. I usually do it a couple more times before I eat the rest. You should try it." I smile, grabbing a marshmallow and handing it to her.

"You're supposed to roast it lightly and melt the inside so you can make s'mores, Valdes." She rolls her eyes.

She grabs another marshmallow and puts it on the end of my stick, then directs it toward the flames. Placing her hand on mine, she twists it slowly, making sure not to light it on fire as I did.

"This is taking forever," I groan.

She chuckles. "Patience, babe."

Excitement bubbles in my stomach at the sound of the word "babe" coming out of Valentina's mouth and being directed at me. I try to play it cool, but I can't stop smiling like an idiot. I look across from me for a mere moment, and the feeling immediately washes away.

Silvana looks across the campfire with a deadpan stare at both of us. The flames dances around her, making it look like she's on fire. Or some sort of fire demon who has come to punish us for flirting around her.

"Your girlfriend is getting jealous," I whisper.

"Huh?" Valentina looks at me, confused.

I purse my lips and use them to point in Silvana's direction. Valentina looks over at her and shakes her head.

"She's ridiculous," Valentina mutters. "I wish she'd take the hint and move on."

"Hmm, I wonder if Sofia has ever thought the same thing about you," I tease.

"Fair point. I'm going to use the restroom—don't burn the camp down while I'm gone."

Moments after Valentina walks away, Silvana stands up and heads in her direction. I try not to be bothered by it. Valentina has made it pretty clear she's not interested in her. Right? Unless she is just a flirt and is willing to mess around with Silvana for the sake of the thrill. My palms feel sweaty.

"Did you have fun today?"

I turn to my left to see Luciano staring at me, waiting for a reply.

"Yes. Sorry, I was lost in thought for a second there." I laugh. "It's been amazing. Thank you so much for having me. It's been an honor."

"We wouldn't have it any other way. You're family, Isa. Sofia was really excited to have you come. I wondered why. I was curious what about you could be so special. Then she told me about your restaurant, and I became even more intrigued."

"Wow, that means a lot, Luc," I say.

"So tell me. What makes you and your restaurant special?"

I clear my throat and sit up straight. Now is finally my time to shine. I've been silently rehearsing to myself how I would win him over. Do I just cry and beg for the money? Do I tell him how much debt I'm in or wait until he agrees to work with me? Do I pretend everything is great? I've been torn all week about it, but this is it. I have to decide. I take a deep breath.

"Well, it was originally my father's restaurant. He's had it since I can remember. I distinctly remember running around the store as a toddler, giggling as he chased me because I stole a croquette. It was his croquettes, actually, that first made me realize how special La Mariposa could be. They weren't just snacks—they were magic. Customers would come in just for those. Some still do."

The warm fire casts a glow on Luciano's face as he listens to my story.

"As I got older, I started being way more useful," I say, laughing. "I could take customers' orders, help him bake pastries, and make all kinds of sandwiches. But it was the recipes that really fascinated me. My dad always said they were the heart of La Mariposa. The croquettes, the ropa vieja, the flan—everything was made with so much care. He'd stay up late tweaking the spices for the arroz con pollo, insisting it had to be just right because it was my abuelita's recipe. It became my haven. We were a team. I even remember sponge-painting the wall with him despite my best efforts to convince him it was ugly. Of course, my mother hates it, but now it makes me smile."

"I bet it's a fond memory you have with him every time you look at it," he says.

"It is," I say as I stick another marshmallow at the end of my branch. "Then he got sick, and I had to take on even more responsibilities. It became super stressful for me when I left for college. I didn't want to leave him behind. He urged me to get an education and then come back. He promised me he'd be here when I did. Then I got the call while I was in my dorm."

I can feel the tears filling my eyes.

"I'm so sorry, Isa," Luciano says softly.

"It was really tough. I had to drop out of college and continue running the restaurant. I refused to let it fall. It would be like I let him fall too."

"And your mother? Did she help out a lot too?"

I snort. "No. She hated being in there. She spent most of her time shopping or having lunch with her friends. But, of course, she'd always boast about the restaurant and what an achievement it was for her that she *owned* one."

"It seems like the restaurant means a lot to you."

I blow out the marshmallow I, once again, have lit on fire. "It's everything to me. I wake up thinking about it and go to sleep thinking about it. I don't do anything else but work, really. I think about my father's recipes—how I can modernize them without losing their soul. I think about new recipes to add, new ways to market the business, and new decorations to add. La Mariposa is the last thing I have of my father. If I lose it, I don't know what I'd do. I'd be lost—a part of me would be lost. Gone. The only part that keeps me going these days."

"Well, it's a good thing you're doing so well then, right?"

"Right." I laugh nervously. "Of course. That's why we're expanding. To bring more people to La Mariposa so they can enjoy my father's delicious foods. His recipes are what makes it special, and I want to share that with the world."

The moment the words come out of my mouth, I regret them. I should have come forward with the truth. Now he'll never invest. It already feels like a lost cause. What do I expect him to do when he finds out we actually can't afford to expand?

"If I'm being honest, we struggled a lot," I say, lowering my voice to an almost whisper. "My family didn't grow up as Sofia did. We were really poor. I was lucky if we had something to eat other than rice and beans for dinner every night. We never went out to eat. I never got new clothes—only thrifted and on clearance. I don't...fit in here. And I can tell. I'm sure everyone else can tell too."

Luciano stays quiet for a moment, biting into the s'more

he smushed together with a piping-hot marshmallow. I watch as he chews, enjoying the combination of flavors that make s'mores so great.

"Can I be honest with you too?" he finally asks.

I nod.

"You know I'm adopted—I'm sure everyone here knows. It's pretty obvious. My parents are white. I'm a really, really tan Hispanic man." He laughs, then reaches for another marshmallow.

"Well, my parents didn't adopt me until I was about sixteen years old. So before that, I was in and out of the foster system since I was a toddler. The older I got, the harder it seemed to get adopted. I know what it's like to grow up with nothing—not even having a bed to call your own. Sharing a home with ten other kids you don't know, all going through something serious and personal. I owned the same pair of pants until they turned into capris. As I got older, I became more and more bitter. Then, I started going down a bad route."

He pauses momentarily, almost as if the memory itself is too hard to remember.

"I started stealing money from other kids, my foster mom, and stuff from stores. I just wanted to have something that was mine for once. It felt great. Like I finally owned something. I bought my first pair of shoes with money I stole. It wasn't until my foster mom found out that she sat down with me and explained that I was lying to myself. I didn't own those shoes. I stole someone else's hard-earned money to buy them. From that moment on, I stopped stealing. I didn't want to own things that weren't mine. I wanted to earn them. Then I met my parents."

"Luc, I had no idea. That sounds rough. It's amazing you persevered."

"I did." He nods. "Thanks to my parents. I was lucky to find parents who wanted me and were also so successful. They did grow up with money. They lived in a gorgeous house with six bedrooms. I finally had my own bedroom and bed. My parents would buy me whatever I wanted and needed."

"Wow, that sounds amazing."

"You'd think, but it made me super uncomfortable. I felt like I didn't earn any of it. It was all luck. I was just in the right place at the right time when they came looking for a kid to adopt. Now I have this nice house, I go to a private school with a fancy uniform, and I know my college tuition is set. I went from not knowing when my next meal would be to being able to ask for whatever food I wanted and practically have it appear in front of me in mere seconds. Once I got into my parent's investment business, I started to feel the nepotism."

I watch a few people get up and dance to the soft sounds of Alessandro playing the guitar across the campfire.

"So, what did you do to combat those feelings?" I ask.

"Well, I decided I wanted to branch out on my own and start my own investing. Granted, I still needed a start-up fund from them, but this is my only opportunity to feel like I have a choice in investing in something I believe in and grow my own business. Would I be self-made? No. Am I ashamed I'm not self-made? Sometimes. But my parents worked incredibly hard for me to have the things I do, so I try to remember that I'm just honoring their hard work by expanding on it."

"That makes sense." I nod slowly, taking it all in.

"That's why I'm so excited about your restaurant, Isa. They expect me to find something that'll be a surefire success. Something that doesn't require a ton of work on my end. But I want to find something that I truly believe in. And your story, I believe in that. I believe in your food. I believe in your relationship with your father before and after he passed away. I believe in your ideas to expand the restaurant and make it even more successful. But most importantly, I believe you. You are special, Isa. Your story. Your life. I just feel like I can relate to it so much."

"Wow, Luc. That means a lot to me that you believe so much in the business." I'm touched, but the guilt twists in my stomach like a knot. Part of me wants to confess everything right now, to tell him that the restaurant isn't the thriving empire I've painted it to be. But I can't bring myself to do it. Even though he says he believes in the story, what if that belief crumbles once he finds out I've been lying? I've gone this far—backing out now might just ruin everything.

"So, when you finish the business plan, send it my way."

"Right. I'm almost done. I'll have it ready for you tomorrow." I force a smile, but I'm already dreading how long I'll have to keep up the facade.

"Hey, there's no rush. You can wait until Sofia and I get back from our honeymoon. We'll be back in New Jersey in about three weeks. I know it's a long trip, but since I'll be busy with my new investment, I wanted to make sure we had a nice break before the craziness begins."

Three weeks. I can't wait three weeks. I'll receive an eviction notice before they even get back from Greece or Italy or wherever the hell they decided to vacation to.

"I'll have it for you tomorrow. I'd like a definitive answer about the investment before you leave, if that's all right."

I immediately feel guilty. Who am I to tell him what to do at his own wedding? He should be focusing on being in love, not work. But if I don't find out soon, I won't know what to tell Gabriel.

"That's fine with me. Just send it whenever it's ready, and I'll take a look."

"Thanks, Luc. Seriously. For taking a chance on someone like me. I'm sure you could invest in literally anyone."

"Probably." He laughs. "But I wouldn't want to. This just feels right."

I should be feeling ecstatic right now. I practically have the investment locked in. But it's based on a lie. Does that mean the investment isn't mine? Did I actually earn it? Would he still invest if he knew the restaurant was currently months behind on rent and slowly failing, and in no position to expand?

"I'm back!" Valentina announces. "Did you burn any more marshmallows?"

"Yes, at least three," I say with a laugh.

Valentina sits back down next to me. Shortly after, Silvana joins in and sits down across from me. She has a discernable smile on her face. It's slightly unsettling. Chills creep down my spine, and my throat feels dry. Did she follow Valentina into our cabin? Did they—no. She wouldn't.

"How was your trip? You were gone for a while, it seemed," I say.

"Was I? It didn't feel that way. It was fine. I just used the restroom and double-checked tomorrow's rehearsal dinner menu with my staff. It's the second-to-last big day for us, so I want to make sure everything goes right."

"That makes sense," I say blandly.

"Is everything okay?"

I want so badly to ask her if she was with Silvana. Did she kiss her? Are they back together? But I can't. It's what Silvana wants. She wants me to doubt Val. And I refuse.

"Everything is great." I sigh happily.

"Well, good," Valentina says, smiling.

She cups my jaw with her soft, slender fingers and slowly brings my face to hers. Our lips meet for a tender kiss. One that I know will get Silvana riled up and other people talking. I'm surprised she did something so public, but it must be a good sign.

When she pulls away from me, I see her slightly bite her bottom lip before smiling. I turn away, suddenly feeling shy. I look up and see Maria staring at her with wide eyes. I shoo her away, hoping she'd just mind her own business, but she comes right over and sits between us.

"Oh, Jesus, Mar," I groan.

"Hey, you two." She looks at each of us and smiles. "How's it going?"

Valentina grins. "It's going great."

"It was until you came along, pendeja."

"Listen, I didn't want to be the one to bring it up, but I'm sure you two will forget. But remember that I was the matchmaker here between you two. If it wasn't for me, this wouldn't have even happened. So I'll take my thanks at your wedding as a heartfelt speech."

She's not technically wrong. If she hadn't convinced me to come here to the wedding, I probably wouldn't have ever seen Valentina again in my life. Or if I had, it would have been too late. So, I really do have to thank her for it. I just refuse to give her the satisfaction.

"You're giving yourself way too much credit. It's not like you put us in the same cabin or forced us to spend every day together. I could have ignored her and kept my grudge about my dress from our quince."

"One day, you'll admit it. And I'll be here. Waiting to say, 'I told you so.'" She laughs, reaching over my shoulder to hug me.

"All right, all right. We'll see. I'm going to go get more marshmallows."

"Did you eat them all while I was gone, Valdes?" Val asks in mock horror.

I stand up, stretching my lower back by twisting my body from side to side. Sitting on a log is not as comfortable as they make it seem in the movies.

"Maybe I did." I laugh and head towards the snack station near the main hall.

I step away from the campfire and into the darkness of the campsite. The fire was the only light source, casting flickering shadows across the trees and bushes surrounding them. The rest of the grounds are shrouded in darkness, the only sounds being the soft rustling of leaves and the distant croaking of frogs.

I make my way toward the station where Sofia has stored the extra marshmallows, my hand outstretched in front of me as I feel for any obstacles in my path. The darkness is absolute, and I can barely make out the shapes of the trees and bushes surrounding me. A small light outside the main hall creates a beacon of safety. I walk toward it, feeling more at ease. I'm not sure how Valentina walked through here without feeling creeped out. Then again, she probably wasn't convinced by Maria that there is some killer on the loose in the campground.

As I walk, I feel a shiver run down my spine. The darkness is palpable, and I can't help but feel a sense of unease. As if someone is watching me. I quicken my pace, eager to reach the safety of the snack station. Finally, I reach the cart and open the cabinet door on the side, feeling around for the bag of marshmallows. I grab a handful, close the cooler, and turn back toward the campfire.

When I turn around, I see a shadowy figure lurking in the corner. I gasp and let out a half scream, clutching my chest. The figure steps forward into the light.

"Jeez, relax," Silvana says, rolling her eyes and taking a long drag from her cigarette. "I'm not going to murder you. I was just sneaking a smoke."

"Oh. Right."

I breathe a sigh of relief, trying to act casual even though my heart is racing.

Silvana flicks some ash off her cigarette and gives me a look that could cut glass. "But I do know things, Isa. Things you probably wouldn't want getting out. Like the truth about your so-called booming restaurant. You think you can just stroll in here and play pretend?"

"What are you talking about?" I cross my arms, trying to look unfazed, but Silvana just smirks.

"I told you to leave Val alone. I told you to stop asking questions. I know you're dirt poor. I know you owe Gabriel three months of back rent. I know you can't afford to pay him without Luciano's help. I know everything."

"How do you—"

"What's that? You're wondering how I know?" Silvana flicks her cigarette into a nearby planter. "My mother has been dating Gabriel for years. She left my real father for him. I just happened to see some paperwork on our table from La Mariposa. Oof. It is not looking good for your father's restaurant, is it?"

I freeze, my mind racing. That must have been the man Sofia was talking about. Maritza's lover was not my father but his best friend, Gabriel. That must be why he has her number in his journal, to help the both of them stay in contact while she sneaked around. If Maritza wasn't the one my father was in love with, then who was it?

Silvana raises an eyebrow. "Oh, and don't worry—I also overheard your little lakeside chat with Valentina. Gotta say, I'm shocked you'd go along with her little sabotage plan, considering how much you have to lose. You must really like her, huh?" She gives me a smug grin, obviously loving every second of this.

The shadows on her face caused by the dim lighting make her look distorted.

I roll my eyes and take a step back. "What do you want, Silvana?"

"Oh, Isa, relax," she says, leaning casually against the wall. "I'm not planning to throw Valentina under the bus. But you?" She narrows her eyes. "Well, I really couldn't care less. If you keep playing around here, I might just have to mention your little deception to Sofia and Luciano. How do you think they'll feel when they find out the truth about your restaurant? About the investment you so desperately need?"

I sigh and cross my arms, forcing myself to sound braver than I feel. "Just spit it out, Silvana. What's your endgame here?"

She gives a fake gasp, as if she's shocked I haven't figured it out yet. "Oh, come on. It's simple. Stay away from Valentina. You can't just waltz in here, swoop in on my girl, and act like you're suddenly one of us," Silvana hisses, a hint of desperation undercutting her usual bravado.

"This family—it's mine. I've been here through everything, and you? You disappear, then show up and suddenly everyone's fawning over you like you're the next best thing? So, do as I say, and I won't blow your little cover." She steps back with a smug smile, clearly satisfied with herself.

"You can't boss me around, Silv." I scoff. "You're deluded."

"Oh, come on, Isa. Be smart about this." Silvana sneers, stepping in close and giving a smug smile. "You really want to risk it all? I mean, once everyone finds out about the real Valdes family—the fake designer bag, the restaurant on its last legs, the father who's not here anymore—well, it's not exactly the picture you've been trying to paint, is it?"

"Go to hell," I retort, pushing her away and turning to walk back. I'm done with her games.

But before I can take more than a step, she grabs my wrist and holds it, her nails digging in. "Are you seriously going to let some silly crush ruin everything you've built? Risk being exposed as a fraud?" she hisses. "Do you really think Valentina would still want you if she knew the truth? That you're barely holding it together?"

I yank my arm free, but her words sting. I've come too far to let this all crumble now. My mother's pride, the family's approval, this second chance at success—it's all on the line. And she knows it.

She steps closer. "Break it off with her, Isa," she says in a mock whisper. "Spare yourself the humiliation. You really want to lose everything just to chase after a girl?"

I look at her, taking in the twisted glee in her eyes. She knows exactly where to hit, and she's right. If I don't end this, she could destroy everything I've worked for. I close my eyes for a second and take a deep breath, knowing there's only one choice left to make. "Fine. If that's what it takes, I'll end it."

"Good," she says, letting go of my wrist with a little shove. "Remember, Isa, I'm always watching." She turns and struts away, leaving me alone under the moonlight, feeling the weight of what I've just agreed to.

Chapter Sixteen

"Hey! I thought you got lost."

Valentina stands up from the log and walks toward me. She puts her arms around me in a warm embrace. It feels so good to be held by her, but I know it's a fleeting feeling. I want to hold on for a moment longer, but I pull away awkwardly.

"Yeah, I found them—it was pretty dark, so I had a tough time."

"Well, I'm glad you made your way back," she says, smiling warmly at me.

Every word she says digs and twists into my heart like a sharp knife. I thought I had found my way back, but here I am, getting ready to push it all away. I feel trapped. I know what I want, but they are two different things. I want to be with Valentina, but I can't lose the restaurant. It would be like losing my father all over again.

"Yeah, well, we should get back to the group," I reply coldly.

I walk toward the campfire, but Valentina grabs my hand and stops me. I notice Silvana watching as she roasts another marshmallow. I bet she wishes she had supersonic hearing to get the pleasure of listening to me break this off with Valentina. I turn around to face Valentina. Her brows are furrowed. She looks confused.

"Is everything okay?" she asks.

"I just think we need to take some time apart."

"Wait, what?" She laughs nervously. "I don't understand. We *just* started this. Tonight. Why do we need time?"

I don't even know how to respond, and I can't get myself to even look into her eyes, worried I'll burst into tears and look even more pathetic than I do now following Silvana's orders.

"That's the thing. I don't think we should start anything, Val," I say in an exhale. "We're different people. Living different lives."

"Why are you doing this? I thought things were going great," she says, her voice rising as her panic grows.

"I won't need your help with the investigation anymore, either. So you won't have to worry about seeing me for the rest of the week."

"Isa, what the fuck? I don't understand what happened between you leaving to get marshmallows and now, but are you under some sort of spell? This doesn't make sense, and frankly, I'm hurt."

I know she won't stop until she has real answers, but I can't give them to her without exposing myself as a liar. What's worse? Breaking up with her because Silvana has blackmailed me, or her breaking up with me because I've been lying this entire time about who I am. We're from different worlds, and she could be with literally anyone else. Someone who is more on her level. Someone who doesn't carry the baggage of a failing business and an empty bank account.

Valentina has the world at her feet—opportunities, success, the kind of freedom I can barely imagine. I can't afford to offer her the experiences she deserves, the travel, the adventures, and the luxuries that she could easily find with someone else. I barely scrape by as it is, and I know what it's like to be with someone who can't keep up. The long hours, the stress of constantly trying to stay afloat—it's broken down every relationship I've ever been in.

I can already feel the strain it would put on us. She'd end up resenting me, or worse, I'd start resenting myself for not being able to give her what she deserves. By walking away now, I'm giving her the chance to live her life without that weight, free to find someone who can give her the world without compromise. She deserves a love that isn't burdened by overworked nights and canceled plans. Maybe by letting her go, I can do something right for her.

"Val, I just don't want to be with you, okay? Just drop it. Go live your best life with a rich girlfriend who can give you whatever you want. Sleep in your luxury condo and have amazing dinners with world-renowned chefs. I can't do this anymore."

I notice through my peripheral that the campsite has gone silent. Everyone is looking in our direction. I turn my head and see Silvana grinning. I wish I could slap that smile right off her face. I just need to remind myself of the big picture. Why I really came here.

"I gotta go," I say, tears filling up around my waterline.

"Isa, please don't go like this. Can we talk?"

This could be it. The moment I tell her the truth. I want to. I do.

"No. There's nothing to talk about. Just move on."

I walk around her and head down toward the lake, past the campfire.

"Isabella!" Maria shouts from her seat.

I start running until I make it to the dock, slowly losing the light from the campfire. I stand on the pier's edge and gaze at the still and silent lake. It is a chilly late summer night, and the water is probably freezing. I take a deep breath and step off the dock, plunging into the darkness below. A sense of weightlessness washes over me as I sink deeper into the water. The icy water envelops my body, and I feel a sense of freedom and release that I didn't realize I have been longing for. Trying to keep up this facade to every guest. Securing the investment. Trying to solve my father's puzzles. Trying not to fall in love with Valentina. The silence of the water is a welcome change from the constant noise of my thoughts and emotions.

As I swim deeper, my eyes adjust to the darkness, and I see the shimmering outlines of fish and plants beneath the water's surface. The moonlight dances on the ripples above, casting a soft, ethereal glow across the lake. Despite the beauty of my surroundings, my heart is heavy. I broke up with Valentina, and we have only seen each other for a day. We just kissed for the first time a few hours ago. I sink deeper into the water, letting it bring me down.

Suddenly I feel something grab my shoulder. I scream, losing all my air. I kick my legs until I reach the surface. As I emerge from the water, gasping for breath, I see Maria leaning on the dock, reaching into the water to save me.

"What the hell are you doing, pendeja? Don't you think this is a bit dramatic?"

I grab onto the dock and pull myself up.

"No, I'm pretty sure it's the appropriate amount of dramatic," I say, squeezing my hair to release the lake water it's absorbed.

"Dude, what happened? We all went from laughing and having a good time to watching you two yell in the darkness. Everything okay?"

"No, everything is not okay," I say, and begin to cry.

"Damn, you're crying now too? I did not sign up for this," she groans, scooching closer and putting her arm around my shoulder. "Tell me everything."

"We kissed."

"Yeah, we all saw," she quips.

I nod slowly.

"And that's bad?"

"No, it was great. I thought we were going to, I don't know, start dating or something. But I just broke it off."

"Uh, why? Don't tell me it's because of your stupid quinceañera dress, or I will throw you back into the lake."

I sway my feet around in the lake water. They're almost numb from the icy temperature, but it feels nice.

"Silvana knows."

"About you two?"

"Yes, but also about me. The restaurant. My mother. She knows everything. She knows I don't know shit about this fancy stuff. She knows we're still poor and struggling. And worst of all, she knows the restaurant is behind on the rent."

"Holy fuck, how did she find out?"

I groan and lay back on the dock, staring at the clear sky. The stars shine like diamonds against the inky blackness of the sky, twinkling and sparkling as if they are alive. The longer I stare, the more stars I see until it seems the entire sky is alight with their brilliance. They make my problems seem so small and insignificant.

"Hello? Are you going to tell me, stupid?"

"Maritza is dating Gabriel. The landlord," I whine.

"No fucking way. This is some telenovela shit right here. I wish I had a camera so someone could record my dramatic reaction to the news."

I look up to see her posing with different shocked faces.

"Can you take my life seriously for once?" I shout. "I'm spiraling."

"All right, all right. You really want to know what I think?"

"Yes, of course."

"You need to get your ass up and apologize to Valentina."

"What? Why?" I yell back, sitting up on the dock.

"Because she's a good person, Isa. You acted like a total dick, and she doesn't understand why. You must apologize and explain everything—or at least some of it. You don't have to go into the details, but she deserves to know what happened. Wouldn't you want to know?"

I stay quiet for a moment, scraping a piece of wood from the dock with my fingernail, ultimately chipping the fresh manicure I got from the on-site manicurist.

"All right, fine," I finally agree.

"Good. Now get up and go. I think I saw her go back to your cabin."

"Okay, I'm going. Damn."

I step off the dock and take a deep breath, feeling a sense of nervousness wash over me. An uneasiness looms over me as I trek back to the cabin. Everyone has dispersed from the campfire, and all that remains are soft embers glowing in the wood. Walking along the dirt path, I feel the cool night air brush against my skin. The full moon casts a delicate and ethereal glow across the campsite. The scents of pine and wood smoke fill the air.

I try to shake off the nervousness, but it lingers. The last time I walked alone in the dark in this direction, I was practically attacked. I want to sprint to the cabin at full speed just to feel safe, but I'm not entirely ready to see Valentina's face. She must hate me already. As I make my way back to our cabin, I hear the distant hooting of an owl. A few fireflies make their presence known by some bushes. Finally, the cabin draws near. I pause for a moment to take in the view. The cabin is cozy and inviting, a warm glow emanating from its windows. A soft lantern lights the porch, and I can picture Valentina inside, relaxing while reading a book. If tonight hadn't happened, I would smile and crawl into her space, resting my head on her shoulder and pretending to read. I'd slowly fall into a deep sleep, and she'd keep me safe and warm in her arms until the early morning. This thought alone excites me into hastily walking up the steps and opening the door.

"Isa!" Valentina shouts, her eyes wide.

"Oh my God." I can't believe what I'm seeing.

Chapter Seventeen

I close my eyes for a moment, hoping that I'm dreaming. Maybe I'll wake up, and this won't be happening. But when I open them again, my fear is confirmed.

Silvana is cupping Valentina's face, their lips clearly still tingling from the kiss I just interrupted. Now, Valentina looks at me in complete shock, and Silvana just smirks.

"What the hell is going on here?" I ask, my voice trembling, a raw mix of hurt and confusion leaking through. Valentina quickly pushes Silvana away.

"Isa, please, let me explain," Valentina stammers. "I promise it's not what it looks like."

I shake my head, trying to hold back tears. "Save it. Really."

I grab my bag and run out of the cabin, tears streaming down my face. I don't know where I'm running to, but I need to get the hell out of here. I rush toward the dock, but it seems too easy. She'll know I'm there, and I'll have nowhere to hide. I turn around and head for the kitchen but stop promptly. I'd be trapped in there, too, if she found me, forced to listen to her words. I wish I could run into my father's arms. He'd lift me and take me away with him to wherever his soul lives now. We could spend all of our time together. He'd save me from ever feeling hurt again. I'd never have to let someone get this close, only to feel like this.

While my mind races at thoughts of being rescued by my father, I find myself subconsciously standing right in front of my rusty old car, Miss Piggy. Of course. He gave me this car. It's a part of him too. Maybe he led me here. I look up at the night sky. Tears continue streaming down my face. I don't know what I'm hoping to find when I look up. A giant cloud of my father forming to convince me to be the king of Pride Rock? A few stars twinkle extra brightly, which I take as a sign that he's watching me. Helping me.

I fumble with the keys, my hands shaking with anger and frustration. I have to shimmy the keys rapidly just to unlock the car. At some point, I'll have to Thelma and Louise it with this car and just get rid of it—sans me in it, of course. Finally, I get the door open. The creaking of the hinges echoes loudly in the darkness of the campsite. Miss Piggy is old, and it's almost always a challenge to start her up. I insert the key into the ignition and turn it, but the engine only sputters a few times before giving up. I take a deep breath and try again, this time pumping the gas pedal, but it only makes the car backfire loudly. I wince at the sound, knowing that it could alert other guests at the camp, or worse. It could alert Valentina where I am.

My heart sinks as I try again and again, each time met with the same disappointing result. I slam my hands on the steering wheel in frustration and scream, tears streaming down my face. I can't believe what I have just witnessed, and now my car is failing me too. I lay my head on the steering wheel, letting my tears fall onto my thighs. Maybe I can hide inside the car and she won't find me. I could hide in the trunk. I did that once when Maria and I were trying to sneak into a drive-in theater without paying for an extra ticket or snacks. I know exactly how to get out if I need to. I can even pop the brake light out slightly for some oxygen without drawing any attention to my car. I could hide in here for the next couple of days, skip the wedding, show up at the last minute to secure the investment, and then leave. I won't ever have to see any of them again.

I won't have to feel this terrible again. I'm tired of pretending, of lying about my life and my business. I'm exhausted from trying to keep everything from falling apart, only to end up here, heartbroken and alone. The thought of just disappearing, even for a little while, feels like the escape I need. Maybe I'll finally be free from the stress of saving a failing restaurant, from the lies, from all of it.

But I can't. I need to get the fuck out of here. I sit up and wipe the tears from my eyes.

"Come on, Piggy. You can do it. I know you can!" I yell at my car as I put the key back in the ignition.

Come on, Dad. Help me out here.

I press down on the gas and turn the key. It sputters, and sputters, and sputters, but I persist. Finally, after what seems like an eternity, the engine coughs to life. My relief is palpable, and I quickly put the car into gear and slowly maneuver my way out of the crowded parking lot, trying not to bump into any of the expensive Lexus or Mercedes cars around me. Seeing my rusty old tank next to these pristine vehicles is almost comical. How could anyone believe I'm not just some poor Jersey girl trying to keep her dad's restaurant afloat and failing miserably? Maybe they all know and have been taking pity on me. Treating me like Cinderella. Giving me a week of feeling as if I belong before I go back to turning into a pumpkin. I drive out of the campsite parking lot. Miss Piggy sputters and kicks forward, making my heart race with every jolt.

"Isa!" I hear a faint shout.

I look through my rearview and see Valentina standing outside near the parking lot as I drive away. The tears begin to collect again, but I shake them off. I step on the gas slightly, trying to accelerate Miss Piggy, but I'm only met with some extra sputters and kicks. Maybe I expect too much from her. She's an old gal, after all. Probably not the ideal getaway car after a breakup.

Through the rearview, I see Valentina's silhouette in the distance, just standing still, watching me leave. It somehow makes my heart break even more. As I approach the gate, it begins to open automatically. I'm so close to returning to my regular life in which I don't fall in love, don't get hurt, and just keep trying to save a sinking ship. Miss Piggy sputters again and then suddenly shuts down. My heart drops as I realize I'm stuck. I try to start the car again, but she refuses to turn over.

I hear Valentina calling my name. I glance at the rearview mirror and see her running toward me. I can't see her right now. I need to get out of here. I try Miss Piggy again, tears blurring my vision.

"Isa, wait. Please!"

I jump at the sound of Valentina trying to open the passenger side door.

"Jesus, Val!"

"I'm sorry; I didn't mean to scare you. I panicked. Please, just talk to me."

"I have nothing to say to you," I say, trying the ignition again but being met with pathetic sputters.

"You're going to kill Miss Piggy if you keep trying. Just let me in so we can talk."

I sit in silence, staring at the steering wheel. I blink to clear my eyes from the tears lingering on my lashes.

"I can't," I whisper.

With one quick motion, Valentina grabs the roof of the car and slides feet first through the window of Miss Piggy.

"Val!"

"Just hear me out, and then I'll leave your life forever. Please."

I take a deep breath and exhale. The silence in the forest is almost deafening now that Miss Piggy has completely shut down. Despite how badly I wanted to run away, I deserve some answers. She should explain herself to me. I deserve that.

"Fine. Go," I finally say.

"Thank you."

I can hear a sigh of relief in between her words.

"If you had just waited ten extra seconds, you would have seen me push Silvana off me with full force and scream at her for assaulting me. She was unbelievably wasted. I returned to the cabin after our fight to have time for myself. I didn't go in there with her, Isa. I need you to know that. She came in to talk and then kept trying to kiss me."

I freeze, Valentina's words sinking in. "Assaulting you?" I echo, a mix of anger and shock tightening my chest. I want to reach out, to comfort her, but I'm too tangled in my own hurt. I can barely look at her, knowing what I thought I saw. "I—I'm sorry. I didn't realize."

"I don't want to be with Silvie," Valentina adds.

I can't help the morsel of relief I feel creeping in at the thought.

"Well, you can't be with Sofia either, so I guess you're shit out of luck." I sniff, the sadness leaking through despite my efforts to hold it back.

I pick at the peeling leather of the steering wheel, focusing on each little piece and letting it drop to the floor. I've been anxiously peeling this wheel for so long that I'm surprised it hasn't completely disintegrated.

"I want to be with you, Isabella. Not Silvie. Not Sofia. You. I know that now. But honestly, I think I've known it for a long time. Maybe even since we were kids. It's always been you."

"You don't even know the real me. Everything—" I pause.

"I already know."

I look over at Valentina. Her eyes glisten in the moonlight.

"Know what?" I hold my breath. What could Silvana have said to her?

"Everything. Silvie mentioned it earlier, after she saw me heading to the bathroom, and she went on about it when she came to the cabin later. About your restaurant struggles. How you're not super successful. How you don't have any money—you or your mother. She was trying to get me to stop wanting you. Trying to show me how different you and I are. But I don't care. And I already suspected you were different when you pulled up to a $500,000 wedding in Miss Piggy."

I want to argue and defend Miss Piggy. Tell her she's more than worthy of attending this fancy wedding.

"She's right. We are different, Val. I don't have a fancy condo with a view of New York City. I don't go to nice restaurants where I know the chefs by their first names. I don't own real designer things. My mother has no idea we're about to lose the restaurant. You? You're a successful chef. You deserve to be with someone who's in your league."

I take a breath. "Besides, we don't just live different lives—we are different. I'm always obsessing over every detail, trying to control things. I freak out over the smallest mess. You're free-spirited, you let things happen naturally, and you don't get hung up on stuff like I do. I don't know if someone like you should be with someone like me."

"You're in my league," she says, grabbing my hand. I don't pull away. "Be with me, Isa."

I let myself sit in the moment, enjoying the warmth of her hand against mine. Her long, soft fingers caressing mine. She traces the lines on my palm lightly. I try not to look at her, worried I'll cave.

"Val, I can't."

"Yes, you can," she argues.

"No, I really can't." I pull my hand away. "I can't risk losing this investment and everyone knowing the truth if Silvana sees us together and decides to spill the truth."

"Are you serious?"

I finally look into her eyes, almost in awe.

"Yeah, Val. I'm serious. I don't live your life. You don't get it. You don't understand what it's like to struggle. To be months behind on rent. To be two unfortunate events away from being homeless with your cat. To want so badly to keep your last memories of someone who meant so much to you."

Valentina scoffs.

"What?" I snap.

"You'd rather have people believe a lie about you than be with someone who cares about you for who you are and not for what you have? It's just a restaurant, Isa."

"It's all I have left of my father, Val!" I shout, alerting a young couple walking on the sidewalk a few feet before the front gate.

"It's just a stupid building that sells food. It's not your father. He doesn't live in the walls, Isa. Your father is in your heart, but you're too damn scared to let go to see that. The people who care about you the most are in your heart."

I lay back on the headrest, staring up through the moonroof. The tall trees huddle over the sky, creating a dark canopy. The moon shines between the branches, sending streaks of light into the car.

"So you're really going to turn your back on something real here for a restaurant that's already breaking you?" She pauses, searching my face. "I know it's not easy. But can't you see what we could have? Don't you want something that's just for you?"

"Val, please," I whisper. "You just don't get it."

"Oh no, I get it. You're little miss perfect in your mother's eyes. She thinks everything is going swimmingly because of you. You can't risk that. What will you have if you don't have the restaurant, right? Because there's nothing else you could see yourself having or doing." She shakes her head, now avoiding my eyes. "You can take the cabin until we leave. I'll sleep somewhere else."

"Where are you going to go?" I ask.

"Don't worry about me. Since it seems like there's only one thing you care about."

Valentina pulls the handle and opens the door, whose rusty hinges break the silence in the forest, causing a few birds to fly away in fear. She slams it shut and leaves. I watch her slowly disappear through the rearview mirror. I take a deep breath and try to calm myself down.

As the tears begin to well up in my eyes, my breath hitches in my throat. My chest tightens, and a lump forms in my throat, making it hard to speak or swallow. I try to fight the tears, but they spill down my cheeks like a broken pipe. Sobs shake my entire body, causing me to tremble and shake.

The tears keep coming in waves, and I can't control them. My face is red and puffy, and my eyes are swollen, making it difficult to see. I gasp for air, trying to catch my breath between sobs, but my crying only worsens. My emotions are consuming me, and my thoughts are racing a mile a minute. No matter how hard I try, I can't stop the flood of tears. Each sob is a painful reminder of what I lost. What I let go of.

The sound of my crying is loud and guttural, like that of a wounded animal. My heart aches, and the tears won't stop flowing. I haven't felt like this since the day I heard the news about my father. I cry for what feels like an eternity, until finally, my sobs slowly begin to subside. My breath is still ragged, and my face is still wet, but the tears have stopped. I wipe my face with my sleeve, trying to clear away the evidence of my outburst. But the pain in my heart remains. I know that I will cry again, that this won't be the last time. But for now, I just sit here, feeling raw and exposed, trying to catch my breath and calm down. I reach into my bag and grab my father's journal for some comfort and distraction.

I slowly skim the pages. A photo of him standing in front of the restaurant appears. A handwritten caption below says, "My dream came true." This is why I need to win this investment.

This simple sentence solidifies it for me. I can't lose my father's dream. Valentina would never understand. I continue flipping through the book and reach a page that causes me to stop instantly. It's an envelope taped to the paper. It has my name and dorm address from college on it. I slowly rip it off the paper, trying not to damage the journal. I tear the envelope open and pull out a letter written by my father. This must have been a letter he was going to send me right before he passed away. I rub my eyes as they continue to blur from my tears.

My dearest Isabella,
I wanted to tell you how much you mean to me. You are the light of my life, and I am so proud of the strong, kind, and beautiful woman you have become. I hope college is going well, my brave little girl.

I know that I haven't been feeling well lately, and it's difficult to talk about, but I wanted to let you know that even though I may not always be here with you, I will always be in your heart. You have brought so much joy and love into my life, and I am grateful for every moment we have shared.

I want you to know that I believe in you and know that you have the strength and resilience to overcome any challenges life throws your way. You have proven time and time again that you are capable of achieving great things, and I have no doubt that you will continue to do so.

As you go through life, my dear, I hope you find a love as strong as I once had. A love that will support you through thick and thin, a love that will make you laugh and cry, and a love that will stand the test of time. You deserve nothing but the best; I know you will find it.

I may not always be by your side, but I will always be with you in spirit. I know I couldn't be the most successful man for you and your mother, but please know I tried.

I only wanted the best for you. You deserve it, my Isabellita. I love you more than words could ever express, and I will always be proud to call you my daughter. I hope you'll always be proud of your father, despite all his faults. Your strength will get you through everything, but your love will help you soar.
Forever and always,
Dad

I flip the page and find a small poem written on the back.

As I grow old and tired, my dear,
Please know that I am always near,
Even when I am gone,
My love for you will carry on.

I hope you find a love as strong,
As the one that's carried me along,
A love that's true and pure and rare,
That will always be there to care.

My Isabella, my precious gem,
Your heart and soul are bright and brimmed,
With love and kindness, grace and light,
May you continue to shine so bright.

I close the letter and slowly put it back in the envelope. I hold it tightly against my chest as I break down once more, my heart breaking all over again.

"What if I'm not strong enough, Dad?" I say, clutching the letter to my heart as if it will bring me closer to him.

Chapter Eighteen

I lay on the bed of our cabin, staring up at the ceiling. The wooden planks above me are stained with watermarks from past leaks hastily missed during the renovation, and the occasional spider crawls lazily across the rough surface. The early morning sunlight shines through the window, casting a glow on the walls. The room is quiet except for the sound of my breaths, which come out in short, shallow puffs. I can feel the weight of the last night on me, each hour adding a little more until I feel as though I'm sinking into the mattress. My thoughts swirl in my head, a jumbled mess of worries and regrets. I know I should get up and do anything to distract myself, but the effort seems too great. So, I lie here, still and silent, and let the thoughts run their course.

As I stare up at the ceiling, patterns emerge in the wood's knots. I trace their lines with my eyes, following them until they blur and I'm lost in thought once more. My breathing begins to slow, my muscles relaxing as I surrender to the room's quiet. The worries and regrets fade away for a moment, and I'm left with a sense of peace. I think of my father's words and feels his love wrap around me like a warm blanket. I imagine his smiling face and the sound of his laughter, and for a moment, I feel as if he is here with me, watching over me.

Eventually, I force myself out of bed. The empty cot across from me is a stark reminder of how things have unraveled. I reach for my laptop on the dresser, crawl back in bed, and open a blank document labeled *Business Plan—La Mariposa Expansion.*

The cursor blinks, taunting me.

I type a few words: *Mission Statement.* Then I delete them. I try again: *Goals.* Another delete. I lean back in the creaky chair, letting out a frustrated sigh. Why is this so hard? I've been running La Mariposa for years. I know the business like the back of my hand. But every time I try to write something, my mind veers to last night—to the way Valentina's lips touched Silvana's, to the look of shock and regret on Valentina's face when she saw me standing there.

I shake my head and force my fingers back to the keyboard.

La Mariposa is more than just a restaurant—it's a place where culture meets comfort, where the rich history of Cuban cuisine is celebrated in every bite. I stop typing and read it back. It sounds sterile, like something ripped from a corporate brochure. It doesn't capture the heart of what my father built.

I close my eyes, trying to summon his words, his passion. He'd always said the food was just as much about the people as the ingredients. "Every dish tells a story," he'd say. "Every customer leaves with a memory."

I try again.

Our goal is to preserve the legacy of La Mariposa, a family-owned Cuban restaurant that has served our community for over two decades. Through authentic recipes passed down through generations, we strive to create a welcoming space where people can gather, share stories, and savor the flavors of home.

It's better, but it still feels incomplete.

I scroll to the section labeled *Financial Projections.* My stomach churns as I consider whether to include the full extent of the restaurant's debt. My finger hovers over the keyboard. Would Luciano still be interested if he knew the truth?

The thought paralyzes me. I can't lose this opportunity. I can't let my father's legacy crumble because I was too honest for my own good.

Instead, I focus on crafting optimistic projections based on potential revenue from an expanded customer base, improved marketing strategies, and the introduction of catering services. I pull numbers from the best months we've had and project growth trends as if those months were the norm. It's not technically a lie—those numbers exist—but I know it's not the whole truth either.

Projected Growth, I type. *With the expansion, La Mariposa is expected to increase its customer base by 40%, generating an estimated 25% profit margin within the first year.*

I pause, staring at the sentence. It's bold but plausible—at least on paper.

I finish the plan an hour later, my fingers trembling as I hover over the Send button on the email to Luciano. My heart pounds as I click it, watching the email disappear into cyberspace. It's done. Now all I can do is wait. The knock at the door jolts me, breaking my moment of reflection. "Isa, are you awake?"

I slither out of bed and saunter toward the door as if any energy I had was already depleted for the day.

Standing at the doorway is Sofia, with mascara streaks down her face. Her appearance almost startles me, but I try not to make it obvious. She immediately runs into my arms and begins to sob uncontrollably. Does she know about my fight with Valentina? Is it that big of a deal?

"Hey. Is everything okay?" I hold her tightly, not realizing how badly I need this hug.

"It's all a mess," she mumbles into my shoulder. "This is all a mess, Isa. I don't know what to do."

I shush her softly as I rub her back slowly.

"Okay, back up. Sit down, and let's talk."

Sofia runs inside and throws herself on the bed exactly like a princess in a cartoon would have done it.

"Sof, it's only nine a.m. How did you manage to have a crisis already before I got an iced coffee?"

I sit down at the edge of the bed and wait for her to finish sobbing into my pillow.

"It's Luciano," she says into the pillow.

"What about him? Did he break up with you? Is he gay? Did he run away with Daniel?"

"No!"

"Okay, okay. So what happened, then?"

She sits up abruptly, her makeup even more smeared than before.

"Jesus, Sof," I say as I try to fix her smudged lipstick.

"He lost the wedding rings," she cries as she throws herself back onto the pillow.

The wedding rings? The ones that Valentina stole? Did she not give them back?

"Like your wedding bands?"

"Yes, Isa. What else? The rings we're supposed to wear, signifying we're married! The rings we got at Tiffany together. The rings we engraved our names into. We're getting married tomorrow!"

"Okay, sorry! Are you sure? Did he say he lost them?"

"Yes! I went to look at them in the ring box, and they were gone. So I asked him about them and he's playing dumb. Like he has no idea where they could even be. We got into a huge fight about it."

She sits up, wiping her face from falling tears, making her makeup look even worse.

"A fight? Why? It's not like he lost them on purpose, right?"

I'm starting to believe Valentina did lose the rings in the lake. How stupid was I to believe she found them? It was a fucking lake in the middle of the night. Unless she has some secret superpower where she can see underwater in the dark, there's no way she could have found those rings. I don't doubt that Sofia and Luciano's $30,000 wedding bands are at the bottom of the lake at Camp Hollow Pines.

"We fought because I told him that it was obvious he didn't think they were important if he could lose them so easily. They're expensive rings, Isa. You know how Tiffany rings are."

"Right, right," I mumble.

"If he can't take care of this one task, how can I expect him to take care of other things in the future? This was his one responsibility. I've done everything!"

"I thought you had a wedding planner and assistant?"

"Okay, they did everything, but I've been making all the decisions! I just feel like he doesn't care. What are we going to do now? We can't get married without wedding rings! And I won't pick up random rings from some random jeweler in town. Could you imagine?"

"Sof." I sigh. "I think you're putting too much importance on the rings and their value."

I stand up and start pacing the room, thinking of the right words to say to the cousin I have just reconnected with after ten years without offending her.

"It doesn't matter if the rings are from Tiffany's or if you made them yourself during metal shop class in middle school. They won't define your marriage. They won't make or break your relationship. They're just stupid rings."

She stares down at the comforter, taking in my words.

"So what if he lost them? Maybe that was a sign that you cared too much about status, anyways. Remember young Sofia? The one who shopped at Limited Too with Valentina and me? The one who got her ears pierced at Claire's? The one who thought Juicy Couture was the equivalent of Fendi?"

"Oh God"—she laughs so hard she snorts—"don't remind me."

"What happened to that girl? The one who didn't care what

people thought about her? The one who would roll her eyes if someone was crying about a bunch of lost rings?"

"I don't know." She shrugs, tracing circles on the blanket with her finger. "I guess it's easy to get caught up in the lifestyle. I feel like I lost myself."

I lean against the bedpost and cross my arms.

"You're still there, Sof. You know how I know?"

She sniffles. "How?"

"Because you could have had your wedding anywhere. Literally anywhere in the entire world. You could have had an amazing wedding in Manhattan that would have ended up in the *New York Times* for some reason. Or a destination wedding in Italy. Instead, you chose to have it at your dinky summer camp."

She laughs, and it feels like a small victory. I feel a little lighter.

"Even with all the money you have, you still wanted to have your wedding somewhere that has meant something to you for your entire life. Is it a little over the top? Yes, definitely. But it's still camp. Your childhood memories are here, and you wanted to share that with everyone. That's how I know you're still you."

"You're right, Isa," she says softly.

"So you need to clean your face, because you look ridiculous right now, and go patch things up with Luc. He loves you, Sof. I can see it. The rings? They don't matter. Your relationship does."

Sofia sits quietly on the bed, smiling softly at my words. There's a moment of silence between us.

"I always wanted you to come here with me, ya know? I begged my mom every year. Valentina refused to come."

"Really? I always wanted to come. I would cry to my parents every year to let me come." I sigh, sitting beside her on the bed.

"I think I wanted you here because I knew how much it meant to you," she says, a hint of nostalgia in her voice. "I just wanted us to have that experience together, like we dreamed about when we'd watch *The Parent Trap.*"

"You remember?" I laugh. "It's practically all I've been thinking about since I arrived. I can't believe I'm finally reliving my childhood dreams of being here and pretending I'm in that movie. I mean, sans the on-site manicurists and massage therapists, I'm sure."

"Yeah, I know I went a little crazy with the wedding." She laughs. "But it's supposed to be my only one. So I wanted it to be memorable, with everyone I cared about here with me."

Sofia lies on the bed, her head propped against her hand as she looks at me.

"So," she says, stroking the bed softly. "Have you and Valentina done the nasty here yet?"

"Sofia!" I shout, my face flushed with embarrassment.

"Oh, come on. Don't be such a prude."

"No, we have not done 'the nasty' there," I groan.

"What? Why not?"

"Because we're at a wedding full of family, for one. And two..." I hesitate. "We broke up, or whatever it would be called when you just start seeing someone after a day."

Sofia sits up quickly and gasps. "Why? You just started dating, right? I saw you two getting all cozy at the campfire."

"Yeah, well. It's just not going to work out. We're too different."

"How so?"

I can't reveal the reason we ended it without revealing the secrets I've been hiding from everyone for years. I can't.

"It's just personal. Let's talk about something else."

Sofia hesitates but quickly shrugs. "Okay, how about this? I have an idea. It just occurred to me."

"Oh yeah? What's that?" I say halfheartedly, still thinking about Valentina.

Should I have even said anything? It's not as if we were dating or anyone knew it was something official. I shouldn't have even said we broke up. I get an uneasy feeling in my stomach.

The one I usually get when I regret saying something and so badly wish I would have said something else, but it's too late. Maybe I just don't want to think of it as a breakup.

"We should recreate the most iconic scene in our favorite movie."

"Do you mean the—"

"You know I do!" She screams and laughs, standing up on the bed and jumping up and down.

I stand up and join her, and suddenly we're twelve again, having a sleepover and eating junk food without a care in the world. No responsibilities. No restaurant to save. No rings to cry about. Just two kids.

"Okay, you wait here. I'm going to go get them." Sofia runs off the bed, slips slightly when she lands and rushes out the door.

I plop down on the bed, the springs bouncing back with me. I can hear small birds chirping outside, embracing the new morning. I slide off the bed and walk around, looking to see if Valentina left any sign of her behind—even just a crumpled-up receipt. I walk toward her nightstand and open the drawers. Empty. I stroll towards the closet, but only my clothes are left, looking lonely. My eyes were so swollen last night to not have noticed that she had taken everything with her. I remember just crawling into bed and crying myself to sleep.

I walk over to the dresser. I don't think she ever emptied her luggage to even fill these with anything. I open each one, only to find my own clothes inside. Sitting on top of the dresser is my father's journal. I reach for the journal, feeling a fresh wave of sadness wash over me. The letter he wrote for me still echoes in my head. I close my eyes and whisper again, barely audible, "What if I'm not strong enough?"

I grab the journal and sit back down on the bed. With or without Valentina, I still need to figure out what my father is trying to tell me. I need to find another clue. Something to distract me from the pain I feel inside. I begin flipping the pages slowly, passing ones with clues I've already discovered with Val. I reach a page I haven't seen yet with a photograph from the quinceañera. Sofia is dancing with Rosita, I'm dancing with my father, and Valentina is dancing with hers as well. There's a handwritten note taped to the page in my father's handwriting.

"Para mi florecita, I'm sorry I couldn't do it, but please know I wanted to."

His little flower? Who could that be? He's never called me that, so it can't be me. It's definitely not Valentina. So it has to be either Rosita or Sofia. Since he wasn't secretly in love with Maritza, that I know of at this point, it's got to be Rosita. Was Rosita his secret lover?

"I'm back! I had to run to the snack closet to grab the essentials."

Sofia runs inside, kicks off her slippers, and jumps on the bed. I quickly slam the book closed and stuff it into my bag. My thoughts swirl with questions, but I hold back from asking Sofia about what Silvana said earlier—that Rosita isn't really our aunt. I'm not ready for that conversation, especially not here. There's too much I still don't understand, and I need to piece things together first.

"What did you get?" I jump on the bed next to her.

"Only the best snack in existence, duh."

Laid out in front of us are several packets of creamy peanut butter and a few packages of Oreos.

"Oh my God, we're really doing this?" I shout gleefully, unable to contain my excitement.

"We can't have a summer camp experience without it. I never actually got to do it with anyone else when I would come to camp, but now we get to do it together."

I've always loved the classic chocolate cookie with its creamy white filling, but tonight I'm feeling a bit adventurous—and nostalgic. I rip open one of the peanut butter packets and take a deep breath, the aroma of the rich, nutty, and creamy spread filling my nose. Gently pulling an Oreo out of the package, I squeeze the packet of peanut butter and carefully spread it on top of the cookie.

I take a bite, then another, each one more delicious than the last. The creamy peanut butter adds a layer of richness and depth to the classic Oreo cookie. It's a flavor combination that is both indulgent and satisfying.

Sofia sighs. "It's truly the perfect combination of flavors, right?"

I nod slowly, close my eyes, and savor every last bite, feeling utterly content and happy. Even though I know it's only temporary.

"I can't believe we're doing this. Together. You and I. Can you believe it?" I exclaim.

Sofia giggles. "I really can't, but I'm so happy."

"All that's missing is for us to get our ears pierced. Should we go find a Claire's?" I wink.

"Very funny. Never doing that again," she says, laughing. "But I'm always up for an adventure with you."

I can't help but smile. It feels as if nothing has changed. As if there hasn't been ten years of silence between us. I want to know everything about her. How her life went after we stopped seeing each other. Her love life. Friends. College. Everything. I feel like I missed out on so much, and I don't want to waste another second not knowing everything about my cousin.

Suddenly, the mattress vibrates. I look around and spot Sofia's phone lighting up. I grab it and see a text from her mother.

Mi Florecita! Where are you? We need to do a final dress try-on for the seamstress.

My heart beats so loudly I can barely hear Sofia speak. That name. *Florecita.* The one from my father's journal.

"Who was it?" she asks nonchalantly.

"Your mother." I clear my throat. "Dress fitting."

"Oh crap. Right. I must get that done, but this was so much fun. Thanks for doing this with me, Isa."

She pulls me in tightly for a warm embrace. At first, I resist, but then I melt into her arms.

"I love you, prima," Sofia whispers.

"I love you too. See you at the rehearsal dinner."

As she walks out of the cabin, I can't help but wonder if Sofia is "the little flower" my father was talking about, or if the nickname was passed down to her from Rosita. Regardless of who it was, I need to find out what it was that he couldn't do and why he couldn't do it.

Chapter Nineteen

As the sun sets behind the trees, Sofia and Luciano's rehearsal dinner is officially coming to life at the campsite. The main seating area is decorated with elegant white tablecloths, high-backed white chairs, and thick, plush cushions. String lights are strung up on poles and hanging across the trees, creating a canopy and giving off a warm, golden glow that illuminates the entire area. Luscious bouquets of white roses, periwinkles, hyacinths, and dahlias adorn the tables, with large and incredibly tall centerpieces cascading over the vessels' sides. Flickering candles placed between the flowers add an extra layer of coziness. At each place setting, delicately folded white napkins and silverware glisten in the light. A small vase with a single white flower is placed on each plate. A garland of greenery and white flowers, delicately interwoven with a sparkling string of fairy lights, runs down the center of the serving table.

Maria snorts as we stare at the immaculate setup. "That's a lot of white for a place full of dirt."

We spent the last couple of hours getting ready while the bridal party rehearsed their entrances for the ceremony. Maria is wearing an emerald-green pleated Badgley Mischka gown. The sleeves are long, reaching down to her wrists, but mesh, so she can probably still feel the slight chill in the air. The frock's plunging V-shape neckline is perfect for displaying her diamond necklace.

As for me? My burgundy off-the-shoulder dress clings to my every curve. The cap sleeves lie just below the top of my shoulders, perfectly displaying my collarbones and the tiny key necklace my father gave me. It's not designer, but it's so stunning I may just be able to get away with it tonight. I catch myself thinking I could say it's Vera Wang, and part of me is ready to. The truth, though, is so close to the surface now that I wonder if there's even a point.

But then, the fear creeps back in. I've protected myself from Silvana's threats, but what if someone still finds out? If the wrong person catches wind of my truth, I could lose everything—the investment, the restaurant, and my last chance to save my family's legacy. So maybe, just for tonight, I'll keep pretending. Because as much as I want to be real, I can't afford for anyone to know the truth—not yet.

"I wish you would have told me you would wear a burgundy dress. We look like fucking Christmas over here."

We walk in unison toward the dinner. Unsurprisingly, Sofia has set up a cocktail hour beforehand. Several bar tables covered in white linen have been placed around the center of the path, keeping the guests away from the seating area until all the food is ready. Maria reaches for two glasses of pink champagne a waiter is carrying on a tray and hands me one. We stand around one of the tables and begin surveying the situation. I can't help but look for Valentina.

Maria smirks. "She's probably in the kitchen finishing up."

"Who?"

"Oh, please, Isa. The woman you're so desperately searching for right now. Valentina's not here. Plus, she was probably at rehearsal, so she had to return to the kitchen and ensure the staff was okay."

I scoff. "I'm not looking for her."

I was, but I wouldn't admit that. The trees surrounding the dinner tables are wrapped in twinkling lights and draped with more garlands of greenery and flowers. White paper lanterns are strung from tree to tree, creating a canopy of soft golden light that bathes the entire area in a romantic glow.

As guests slowly arrive, they are greeted by the servers, who are dressed in crisp white shirts and black pants. The servers, equipped with trays of hors d'oeuvres and drinks, quickly circulate among the guests, offering them delicious treats and refreshing cocktails.

"There's Satan," Maria mumbles and points with her eyes.

I look over to see Silvana in a bold red satin dress that drapes gracefully down to her silver strappy heels. She spots us and begins walking over as if she is gliding on air.

"Look at you two," she says, smiling. "You look great. Is this another Forever 21 dress, Isa?"

"Silvie, you look like my period blood," Maria retorts.

Silvana's eyes widen, and I can see her face flush. How incredibly satisfying.

"Isa is wearing a red dress too," she whines.

"No, it's burgundy, and it's classic. You look like a firetruck. Or Clifford."

"Fuck off, Mar," Silvana huffs and leaves to go stand with her mother, no doubt to throw shade at everyone.

"Have I ever told you that I love you?" I laugh. "Thank you."

"Oh, please. Anytime. She's such a twat."

A band begins to play soft jazz music, adding an extra layer of ambiance to the night. Almost as if it was rehearsed, Sofia and Luciano appear just around the corner and glide onto the dance floor. All the guests begin to clap, and some of the groomsmen let out a few whoops. Luciano lifts his arm to allow some space for Sofia to twirl.

Maria laughs. "Leave it to Sofia to have multiple wedding

dresses to change into for the next two days," she says, but there's a tinge of judgment in her voice.

Sofia is a vision in white, her dress crafted from a soft and flowing fabric that swirls beautifully with every movement. It is practically designed to catch the light, and the shimmery fabric glints in the setting sun as if sprinkled with fairy dust. The top of the dress is simple and elegant, with a fitted bodice that hugs the curves of her torso. The fabric flows down in layers, gathering at the waist before cascading to the floor in a frothy cloud of white. The skirt has just the right volume to create an enchanting twirl that seems to transport her to another world. Delicate details add to the dress's ethereal quality. A scattering of tiny white pearls graces the bodice, while lace details trace the neckline and hem. The back of the dress is particularly stunning, with a delicate row of buttons running down the length of Sofia's spine.

"Jesus, I wonder what her wedding dress will look like," I say in awe. "I don't think anything can top this."

Maria chuckles. "Her wedding dress will probably have a twenty-five-foot train and require a crane to lift her to the altar."

"Thank you so much for coming to our rehearsal dinner," Luciano announces. "I hope you enjoy the wonderful five-course meal Valentina and her staff has prepared for us. Please find your seats when you're ready, and we can begin eating the delicious food."

I look around frantically, again trying to spot Valentina. Finally, I see her in the back, walking toward Silvana. My heart drops into my stomach like a heavy boulder falling off a cliff. Silvana laughs at something Val says, but they're too far away for me to hear them. I can't tell if Valentina is playing along or if she's simply putting on a facade. Part of me wants to believe she has her reasons for talking to my nemesis, but it's hard not to feel betrayed.

Just as I am about to turn around, Valentina's eyes meet mine. She smiles slightly, her expression hard to read, and begins to walk toward me slowly. The uncertainty twists in my gut—why is she engaging with Silvana like this after everything? I need answers, but as she gets closer, I wonder if I even want to hear them.

I try to distract myself with my champagne, taking too many sips. Her dark-grey gown drapes down to the floor, dragging on the dirt path, but she doesn't seem to mind. The cowl neck on the satin neckline creates a subtle sweetheart line I can't stop staring at. As she moves toward me, I notice a high slit on her dress that gracefully exposes one of her thighs every time she takes a step. Underneath, she wears silver strappy heels tied up just below her knees.

Valentina smiles. "Isa, you're a knockout."

"Thanks. So are you," I say shyly. "Listen, Val. I just want to say—"

"You don't have to say anything, Isa. I get it. I'm sorry I reacted the way I did in the car. I was upset."

"The car?" Maria whispers to herself, raising her eyebrows.

"I know—I'm sorry. Please know that this isn't what I want to do. It's what I have to do," I say.

"What could she have to do?" Maria whispers to herself while taking a sip of her champagne and flagging down a server to get a few more for the table.

I look at Valentina, hesitating before finally asking, "Val, can I ask why you're even talking to Silvana after what happened?"

She sighs, casting a quick glance in Silvana's direction before looking back at me. "She did apologize to me about it when she sobered up. I guess I'm just trying to keep the peace. She's not someone who lets go easily, and the last thing I want is for things to escalate even further. I didn't want you to worry."

"I guess," I murmur, unconvinced but trying to understand.

Valentina's eyes soften. "I'm sorry if it seemed like more. I promise, it's not." She reaches out and squeezes my hand.

Maria, watching intently, continues her whispered commentary. "Oh, so now they're holding hands. This is better than the movies."

"I'm sorry. For the things I said. About your father. I know he means a lot to you."

"Oh shit, she talked about her father," Maria says, whispering again.

"Maria!" I shout.

"Sorry, shutting up." She mimes a zipper being closed on her lips.

"I know, Val. It's okay. I really do forgive you. And I hope you forgive me. I—don't want to end things like this."

"Or at all," Maria whispers, even softer this time.

"I don't either. But I respect your decision and will be here if you need me. Like the investigation or any troubles you have. I'm always here for you, Isa."

I smile softly. "I know."

Valentina looks me in my eyes, her gaze unwavering. Her mouth opens slightly, as if she's about to say something. My breath catches in my throat as I anticipate her next words.

"Val! Let's go find our seats."

I look over to see Silvana waving Valentina over to their table. My stomach twists, and a poisonous rage is starting to ruminate inside me. Of course, they're still seated together—it's part of the original seating plan. I can't believe I let this person—this monster—take the one thing that has made me happy in such a long time. I want to run over there and snatch Valentina away. Maybe even expose Silvana and Maritza's story before she can expose mine. But I can't. Not only will I be known as the poor lying cousin, but I'd be the backstabbing one too. The one who would willingly bring down someone else for their gain. And that's not me. Oh, but I wish it were.

"Let's go find out seats, prima," Maria urges as she pulls my elbow to get me away from the situation.

The guests begin to find their name cards and sit comfortably in elegant chairs arranged around the tables in a symmetrical pattern, with soft music playing in the background. The servers move gracefully around the tables, offering glasses of sparkling pink champagne and presenting carefully curated dishes. The plates are like pieces of art, each dish crafted with exquisite attention to detail.

The first course is a beautiful salad with fresh greens, grilled peaches, and crumbled goat cheese, all dressed with a tangy vinaigrette. The peaches' sweetness contrasts with the goat cheese's saltiness and perfectly blends with the sourness of the vinaigrette. I'm not the kind of person that enjoys or even thinks about salads, but I could eat this every day and live a very happy life.

"How does she manage to make salads fancy?" Maria snorts, shoving a huge mouthful of greens into her mouth.

"That's all Val." I smile, shifting my eyes toward Valentina, who must have heard me because she is looking right at me. Those little butterflies I know so well begin to flutter inside my stomach. That, or I'm seriously allergic to goat cheese, and this is the first sign.

"Valentina, you never cease to amaze me," Maritza says as she savors each bite of the perfectly grilled peach. "You'll have to make this for Silvana and me when we return home."

"The only thing Valentina is going to make when you get home is pancakes the morning after your stay at her place," Maria whispers.

"Maria!" I nudge her with my elbow and look around to ensure no one else heard.

Every so often, I find myself glancing over at Valentina, and almost without fail, she manages to look at the same time.

The main course begins to arrive. It's a choice between two

options: pan-seared salmon with a citrus glaze, served with roasted asparagus and creamy mashed potatoes, or grilled filet mignon with a red-wine reduction, served with garlic mashed potatoes and sautéed green beans.

Everything looks delicious, but something feels off. "Why aren't there any Latin food options to choose from?" I finally ask. Everyone looks up at me, almost shocked I would even ask such a question.

"Well." Maritza laughs. "I may not have planned this wedding, but I think I can speak for everyone when I say that most Latin foods just aren't…up to our standards for this event."

"What's that supposed to mean?" I retort, my words sharper than I intend.

Maria hits her foot against mine, trying to keep me from making a scene, but I can't help myself.

"Oh, right. You're saying the Cuban food we grew up on isn't fancy enough. Got it."

As I slice into my steak, a surge of pride bubbles up, mingling with the resentment I feel. I know the food we serve at La Mariposa is special. It's rooted in our history and culture, and it has a soul that this polished steak could never hope to touch. Yet here I am, trying to fit in, feeling like a fraud with each bite. My thoughts drift to the ropa vieja and croquettes we make—the dishes that may not cost much, but they mean everything to me. Their dismissiveness just reinforces the chasm between us, one that feels deeper with each passing moment.

"Get ahold of yourself, pendeja. I don't want to get kicked out before I can pick up the last wedding favor," Maria mumbles.

"Sorry," I say dryly.

"Isa is right," Sofia finally says. "I wanted to create a menu that would feel extravagant to match my wedding, but I'm kind of craving a Cubano, aren't you?"

Everyone laughs in agreement.

"Thanks to my almost-husband's investment, I promise my

next party will be delicious Cuban food from the best Cuban restaurant in New Jersey: La Mariposa!"

The whole table begins clapping and cheering. My face is flushed with embarrassment. I look over at Silvana, who is staring daggers at me. A crease forms at the corners of her mouth, creating an unsettling smile. I turn back to my steak, focusing on cutting it and enjoying every bite I can. Who knows when I'll eat another steak that costs more than my rent?

I take a small cut of the filet mignon and bring it to my lips. The tender, juicy meat melts in my mouth, bursting with rich flavors. The perfectly cooked steak has a charred exterior that gives way to a pink center. I close my eyes and savor the flavors. The accompanying roasted vegetables are equally delicious, adding a hint of sweetness to the savory flavors of the steak. I take another bite, enjoying the mashed potatoes' smooth buttery texture. Every element of the dish is cooked to perfection, and it's clear that Valentina has put a lot of care into every aspect of the meal. It might not have the Cuban flavors I crave, but she is a gifted chef. I can't help but smile, remembering all the moments I shared with Valentina over the week. A warmth spreads through my belly as I think of telling her about the new clue I found, or even just admitting how much I miss her already.

But then, I stop myself. Valentina left the door open, yet I'm the one who locked it shut. If I reach out to her now, it'll be like stepping back into something that might hurt us both all over again. So, instead, I keep silent, unsure if I'm protecting her or just myself.

"Valentina, you outdid yourself," Rosita says as she wipes her mouth with her napkin.

Valentina gives a modest shrug. "Thank you, but I wasn't the one who originally planned to be here. The team has been incredible, picking up all the details on such short notice."

"Still. It came from your brain, verdad? That's what makes it so special. It's what makes *you* so special."

Rosita stands up, holding her wine glass.

"I want to give a toast. The wedding is tomorrow, which means you all have spent several days with us. Ready to leave yet?"

A few chuckles break out in the crowd.

"I just want to thank you all for taking time off to watch my amazing, gorgeous, talented, and incredible daughter get married. Some of you I have known my entire life. Some of you I just met this week," she says, nodding at Luciano's parents. "Regardless, you are all so special to me. Each of you has been placed in my life for a reason. Whether it was to heal from the past or see how bright my future could be. Some of you have been with me through the hardest moments of my life, and now you're here, supporting and celebrating with me in the best one so far—"

As Rosita continues her speech, I notice a white glow from a distance. It's moving up and down in a rhythmic bopping motion. It's getting brighter and brighter. Soon, other people start to notice it as well.

"—Love is so easy to find but so difficult to keep, and I'm just so happy my daughter, Sofia, has found it—"

A yellow taxi cab pulls into the campsite in front of the front desk. At this point, we've all completely stopped listening to Rosita's speech.

"Who is that?" Silvana asks.

Rosita stops and turns to look.

"Is there someone on the guest list that didn't show up, Sofia?" Rosita asks.

Sofia shakes her head as she leans forward, trying to catch a glimpse of who it could be.

We all stare in silence, watching a shadowy figure inside the car shuffling around. Then, finally, the door opens. Two feet step outside. Then the rest of the body. They close the door and begin heading toward us, but we still can't tell who it is.

Daniel gasps. "Oh my God, is this a wedding crasher? How dare they?"

The closer they get to the dinner, the more nervous I get. Until…

"Holy shit," I whisper.

"No fucking way," Maria whispers back.

"Is that—"

"Mami!" I exclaim as I stand up abruptly.

Murmurs are heard across the table. Silvana's snickers can be heard a mile away. Rosita looks as if she's looking directly at a ghost. Maritza won't even look up from her wine glass. Sofia opens her mouth in complete shock.

"Thanks for the invite, putas," my mother seethes.

She's wearing a long black gown with black heels. On her arm is the Prada bag I bought her. Her hair is done professionally, I have no doubt. There's no way she could have gotten those curls on her own. Even her makeup looks like a celebrity artist did it. My mother would do anything to impress, especially this crowd.

"Well, if it isn't the infamous Mariposa," Rosita finally says, shaking out of shock. "So glad you're here. Someone get her a chair."

"Oh, I won't be staying," she replies coldly. "I'm here for my daughter."

"Me?"

"Si. Tu. Would you like to explain to me why you've been ignoring my calls and texts and tell me where your father's journal is?"

A burning sensation overwhelms the skin on my face and ears. I probably look as red as a beet right now.

"Uh, well—"

"Don't bother. I already know you stole it. You had no right,

Isa. That journal was the last piece of him I had, and you just took it."

I glance at Valentina, who is looking directly at me. I almost want to cry just at the sight of her. She's the only one who knows the contents of my father's journal and the secret we were trying to uncover.

"Would you like to explain what the hell this is?"

She holds up a sheet of paper. I squint to try and make out the words. It's my father's note about his journal and finding the truth. I must have left it in her bedroom when I left in a rush. *Fuck*.

"It's a letter," I say softly.

"I can see that, Isabella. Where did you get it?"

"From Gabriel."

Silvana and Maritza both look up at the same time, eyes wide.

"He handed it to me when he came to collect the rent. It's a letter from Dad. For me."

"What the hell was Gabriel doing with that letter? What's the truth then, mija? What's the secret truth he had to keep from his wife and only tell you about?"

"The truth?" I cough, looking over at Valentina again, knowing we haven't actually figured out the truth. "It's—"

"I can tell you!" Silvana shouts in a sing-songy voice.

Everyone's eyes whip over to her as she slowly stands up, loving the attention. She's going to tell them everything. *Fuck. Shit.* What do I do? I'm frozen in shock.

"I already know the truth, and I think it's time everyone else did too. The real truth about the Valdes family."

Mariposa crosses her arms, waiting to hear more. Rosita shuffles on her feet nervously. I feel like throwing up. Maybe I can cause a distraction if I projectile vomit all over Silvana. Valentina tries pulling Silvana back down, but she snatches her arm away and walks around the table.

"You see, Isa here has been lying about something huge. To

all of us. But especially to Rosita and Sofia." She stops before me and smiles.

"Silvie, please," I beg in a whisper so only she can hear.

Silvana's smile gets even larger.

"I mean, Luciano hasn't found the rings yet, right? I wonder why."

"What?" I say, looking over at Sofia and Luciano.

They both look confused but as if they understand what Silvana is implying. That I stole the rings. I'm the thief.

I glance over at Valentina, hoping she'll speak up, but she's staring at the floor, fidgeting with the corner of the tablecloth. She opens her mouth as if to say something, but Silvana steps forward, cutting her off.

"Isa and Mari are liars. They're deceitful. Always have been. And Luciano, if I were you, I wouldn't invest in someone who would be so fake, like Isabellita is. The fact that she's been here this entire week, lying to everyone and acting like it was okay… I don't know, it seems kind of sketchy to me. Would you trust them with your life? Money? Rings? I know I wouldn't."

"Silvana, shut up, that's not—" Valentina shouts.

"No, esta bien," my mother cuts in. "This is why I stayed away from you people. Isa, this is why I told you not to trust them. They're all liars and cheaters. They only know how to take, take, take. They act all nice until they stab you in the back. Vámonos."

"But—"

"Now, Isabella. It's over. We're not welcome here. We're leaving."

She grabs my arm and pulls me away from the table. I turn around as we walk away, looking at Sofia, Rosita, Luciano, and Valentina—everyone I let down.

Chapter Twenty

"Pack your things, Isabella. We're leaving tonight."

"But the wedding is tomorrow," I mumble.

"Y que? I don't care, and you shouldn't, either. These people are poison. I told you from the start, didn't I? I have always told you."

I don't answer her. I slowly start grabbing my luggage from the closet and placing it on the bed. I finally feel grateful that I'm the kind of traveler who completely unpacked all her things. The more time I can waste figuring out my next step, the better chance I have of convincing her to stay. I can't leave yet. Not until I solve the secret. I'm so close.

"And look at you," she continues. "Dressing like you're some high-class Latina, finally. I've been trying for years to get you to look presentable, and you wait until you're with the 'other' family to do so? Who are you trying to impress? Because it better not be them."

I continue ignoring her and walk into the bathroom. The space is compact yet efficient, with everything I need in arm's reach. The walls are painted a pale shade of green, which Valentina so endearingly described as the color of puke after a dog overeats grass. I personally like it. I start grabbing my toiletries, one by one, and placing them neatly into my bag.

"What are all these gift bags doing here? They're full of expensive things, mija. Where did you get these? Did you buy these as gifts for them? I can't believe you would do that when your poor mother is at home, lonely and sad. I like gifts too, mija."

"They're wedding favors, Mami!" I shout.

I grab my toothbrush off the holder on the sink. My eyes drift to the little empty space next to it where Valentina had hers. I sigh deeply.

Above the sink is a large, frameless mirror that stretches from one side of the wall to the other, reflecting every detail of my face. I look at my reflection. My dress. My elaborate updo the on-site hairstylist did. My makeup. It's all so much. Even the necklace I'm wearing is from one of the wedding favors and cost at least $500. I look like I belong, but I feel like such a fraud.

The shower, tucked in the opposite corner of the room, is enclosed with a clear glass door. A small shelf is built into the wall, holding soap, shampoo, and conditioner bars. I grab them all and shove them in my bag, starting to care less about the mess the soap will make against the rest of my products.

I step outside to see my mother sitting on the bed, looking through all of the wedding favors, probably finding things she wants to keep for herself. At this point, I wish she'd take them all and leave. I slowly approach the dresser to start filling my luggage up.

She scoffs, struggling to put on one of the tennis bracelets. "I just can't even understand why you wanted to come here in the first place."

Should I just tell her the truth, finally? That we're dirt poor, and the restaurant will undoubtedly close now? That I came here in hopes of saving the restaurant and being the hero? That now everything is ruined because of her?

"I—"

But I hesitate. I already failed at impressing everyone here as

I planned. I failed to show them how successful I was and how great we were doing. The last thing I need is for my mother to think I genuinely am the failure she's been worried I am. I refuse to give her the pleasure of being right.

"—I knew there'd be free gifts. I wanted to grab some for you," I finally say.

"Hmm. Well, that's the one thing you've done right in a long time, Isa." She laughs. "Maybe next, you can change the horrid paint job in La Mariposa and make me proud. Or finally, get a new car, so we don't have to go home in that basura your father gave you. I can't even believe you showed up in that. I'm so embarrassed they saw it."

"Miss Piggy," I murmur low enough that she doesn't hear me.

"What was that?"

"I said, how is the restaurant? Everything running smoothly?"

"Oh, I didn't check on that, mija," she says while lying on the bed, looking at how the bracelet glimmers in the light.

"You haven't even gone in to see the restaurant? What if they didn't open? Or there was a robbery? Or the employees all quit and left the place?"

"Eh," she says, shrugging. "I'm sure it's fine."

"You don't care, do you?" I turn around to look at my mother, my blood boiling.

Just as I was about to say something I would undoubtedly regret, I hear a banging on the door, jolting me back to reality.

"Isa. Open up."

I rush to the door to find Sofia standing there, her makeup ruined again.

"Sofia."

"You ruined everything!"

She barges inside and starts pacing around as if she's looking for something but is not sure what it is.

Mari perks up and watches as if she just started her favorite telenovela.

"Sof, please. I didn't—"

"Save it. I don't want to hear it. I just want to know one thing."

She grabs a note from her pocket, unfolds it, and holds it to my face. I take a few steps back to read it and bump into the bedpost.

Isabella will have the answer. You just need to trust her.

"So what is it then, Isa?"

I grab the note from her, inspecting it closer. It's my father's handwriting.

"Where did you get this?"

"Doesn't matter. Tell me the answer."

"Sofia, please. Where did you get this?"

"Gabriel gave it to me. He said it was a letter from Roberto to me. I didn't believe him initially, but I have felt a lingering emptiness since our quince. Since that fight. So I thought maybe he was talking about what happened that night and why we stopped talking. So I invited you to the wedding, hoping to connect and finally get some answers."

"So you only invited me to find out the truth?"

"At first, yes. I just needed to know. But then I realized how much I missed you and wanted you in my life. You seemed so happy and excited to be back with the family. Now I realize it was all a lie."

"It wasn't a lie, Sof," I cry.

I step toward her, but she moves backward, closer to the door.

"You single-handedly managed to ruin my wedding, Isa. And you embarrassed me. Don't even worry about giving me the rings back that you stole. You can keep them. Use them for the inv—"

"Sofia," I chime in quickly. "I didn't take the rings."

"Isa, stop lying to me. And to yourself. Aren't you tired of it at this point? Just be real for once. All I wanted was closure, but I guess I'll never get it. Neither of us will since it seems you don't have the answer like he said you would."

"I'm so sorry for everything. I didn't mean to hurt you, Rosita, or anyone."

"Well, you did," Sofia cries.

"I know. I fucked everything up. I'm so sorry."

Sofia's face crumples, and for a moment, I think she's going to say something else, but instead, she spins on her heel, her dress swishing around her ankles. She storms out of the room, leaving a trail of silence in her wake. The door slams behind her, echoing loudly in the empty space. I stand frozen, staring at the spot where she was just moments ago.

The weight of everything presses down on me—the lies, the secrets, the guilt. I've destroyed her trust, shattered the fragile bond we had. My stomach churns as I replay her words in my head. She wanted closure, answers, and all I gave her was more pain.

I stand there, frozen, my breath catching in my throat. The tension in the room hasn't lifted. It's heavier now, because even though Sofia's gone, my mother is still here—watching everything. She's been standing in the corner this entire time, silent, her arms crossed over her chest, her eyes piercing into me, just waiting to remind me why I should listen to her.

I don't dare look at her, but I can feel the weight of her judgment bearing down on me. The knot in my stomach tightens, twisting into something unbearable. I want to leave. I want to run out of this room, out of this mess I've created, and never look back.

I sink slowly onto the edge of the bed, burying my face in my hands. The urge to flee is overwhelming, but my legs feel like lead. What would be the point? Wherever I go, she'll still be there. She always is. Her silence is louder than any words she could say. I can almost hear the thoughts running through her mind—*You're a disappointment. You've ruined everything.*

I steal a glance at her, and she's just standing there, unmoving. Watching me unravel. I half expect her to say something—to yell at me, to scold me—but she says nothing. And somehow, that's worse. The shame crawls under my skin, itching, burning, making me want to disappear.

I close my eyes, willing myself to breathe, to think, to do something. Anything but stand here and crumble under her gaze. But nothing comes. Just the crushing weight of failure and the unbearable presence of my mother's silent disapproval. There is nothing left to do but pack.

Chapter Twenty-One

Trying to fold my clothing into my luggage through blurry eyes is proving to be quite tricky. Since Sofia left, my mother and I have been sitting in silence. She's been browsing her phone and taking photos of the wedding favors. Probably showing them to her friends as things she bought herself. I want to rip up all of the gift bags. Smash all of the Chanel and Dior perfumes. Cut up all the gift cards and just run away.

"Hello?" Mari shouts.

"Huh?" I look up, and she's staring right at me.

I hadn't even realized she had said anything to me. I was so lost in my own thoughts and misery.

She frowns. "I said you must give me his journal back."

"What? Why?" I ask defensively.

Panic begins to bubble in my chest at the thought of giving the journal to my mother. I know I'll never see it again after that. She'll find someplace to hide it away. I won't ever get to see his words. The photos. The recipes. It'll be as if I lost him all over again. This whole week I have felt closer to him than I ever have. I'm not ready to let that go.

"Mija, you need to give it back," she says, sitting up as she packs all the gifts into one of the gift bags.

"Why?" I ask again, this time with more defiance in my voice.

She must have heard it because she looks up at me in shock.

"Because it needs to be preserved. There's no reason for you to have it. You'll ruin it by opening it and closing it all the time. So just give me the book, Isabella."

"I won't, though! I'll keep it protected. It's not going to get ruined," I state.

"Mija, I'm not debating this."

Her voice gets sterner.

"Papi would have wanted me to have it. You know he would have. Please, Mami. Just let me keep it."

"Isabella, this isn't a negotiation. You don't need the journal. There is no 'truth' to find out. There never was."

"What about what happened between you and Tía Rosita?" I shout, tears starting to form in my eyes.

"What about it? You won't find that in ese maldito libro, Isabella. There is no big secret you need to discover. Your father would create puzzles to keep you entertained and distracted while he battled his sickness. There is no big secret you need to solve. He was so sick by the time he finished his journal. Nothing in there makes sense."

"That's not true!" I scream.

"Isabella! Do not raise your voice at me! I'm telling you the truth. There is no great answer to his puzzle. I promise. Please, mija. Don't make this harder than it is. Just give me the journal, finish packing, and we'll return home. We can pretend none of this ever happened."

"It's not true," I whisper, feeling defeated.

Mariposa stands up and walks over to where I am standing.

"Oh, mijita," she sighs, pulling me into her arms.

I can't help but sob into her shoulder as she slowly caresses the back of my head.

"I know how hard his death was for you. You two were so

close. Closer than you and I could ever be. I know that. I resented that for a long time. You've been swept up in his journal, being led into a cat-and-mouse chase with these random clues he's put throughout it."

She pulls me away to wipe my eyes.

"But I know the truth, mija. I know how hard it's been for you to let him go and move on. That's why you won't paint the restaurant for me. That's why you don't want to let go of this journal. But you need to let him go—my Isabellita. I know you can do it. He would want you to move on and live your life managing the restaurant and caring for me. He wouldn't want you to be chasing words in a book."

She pulls me in again, squeezing as hard as she can.

I pull away and stare at her, my chest tightening. Managing the restaurant and caring for her? Is that what she thinks my life is supposed to be? My entire existence, reduced to running the restaurant and making sure she's okay? That's not living. It's surviving. It's waking up every day trapped in the same routine, in the same walls my father built, with no room to breathe, to dream, to do anything more than keep things from falling apart.

I swallow hard, trying to keep my voice steady. "That's not what he would've wanted. Not for me."

She tilts her head, her eyes softening as if she's trying to comfort me. But all I feel is suffocated. "He loved the restaurant, Isa. And he loved you. He would've wanted you to carry on his legacy. I think it's time you give me the journal, mija, and move on from this little hunt. The restaurant is what keeps him alive."

Without saying another word, I slowly walk past my mother, toward the dresser. Have I been using his journal as another way to keep his memory alive for a little longer? Has it all been fake? Was there ever a big secret to discover? I start to feel silly, as if I made everything up. As mad as it makes me, my mother isn't wrong. I haven't been able to move on from my father. I never coped with his sickness, and I felt so much guilt when he suddenly passed away. I wasn't there for him. I was away at college, trying to get a degree in business so I could help him run the restaurant, and then he was gone. This journal has brought so much of him back for me. I've learned things about him that I haven't ever known. Even if the puzzle is fake, his words are still real to me—all of them.

I slowly pull the journal out of my bag. I give it a good look. The leather-bound cover is wearing down around the edges. A few pages inside have unattached from the spine and stick out slightly. It may be in somewhat rough shape, but it shows how many adventures it's been on. How many of his memories live inside. I open the cover and see the photo of him sitting beside me as a baby. I look over my shoulder slightly and see if my mother is staring. She's back to taking pictures of the stupid new tennis bracelet she took. I turn back around and slowly peel the photo out of the journal, trying my best not to tear the page. Finally, I pull the photograph out, sighing in relief that she didn't notice. I hide it in my bag for a moment.

"Here," I say. I toss the journal to her on the bed and return to the dresser.

I pull the photo slowly out of my bag to look at it closer. To see my father's large grin under his thick, black mustache. I feel warm. He seems so excited to be next to me. I rub my hand slowly on the perforated edge of the ripped side. I wonder who else was in this photo. Maybe it was my mother, and he didn't want her in the shot? If he had a secret lover, as I may have found out with his clues, it's possible he resented her as well. The way he's sitting in the photo, though. It's strange. The picture is cut right by his right arm, as if he was holding something else in his hand. Or someone else. It could have been my mother, but why would she sit on his other side and not next to me? I can't seem to shake these thoughts. I wish I could have the journal for a moment longer to figure this out.

What is my father trying to tell me? Some of the pages felt like memories he wanted to preserve—simple snapshots of our lives, like the ones from my quinceañera. But others…they feel like more than that. Almost as if he wanted me to find something. As if he left a trail on purpose. It's hard to tell where the memories end and the clues begin. Maybe that was his intention all along—to show me a mixture of both.

Without thinking, I turn the photo around to see if anything is on the back. To my surprise, I see my father's handwriting, but half of it is cut off by the rip. I look closer to see what it says.

os hijitas

Os? I'm not sure what that is. But hijitas. That's the plural of daughter. Could it be dos hijitas? Two daughters? Do I… have a sister?

My heart pounds in my ears as I reread his words in my head. It's not Silvana. It's not Valentina. There's only one person I'm sure it can be: Sofia. I feel sick. I hold on to the dresser, trying to contain my anger as I process this realization. That's why Sofia has a letter from my father too. He was in love with Rosita. They dated. Sofia was born. I have so many questions, and only one person in this room can answer them.

"I know the truth," I say.

"Que dices?" My mother looks up at me, confused.

"The big secret Papi was trying to reveal to me. I finally figured it out. You took the journal to prevent me from figuring it out, but you were too late."

The expression on Mariposa's face begins to shift from confusion to realization.

"Isabella, there is no big secret. I told you."

"Stop fucking lying to me!" I shout, startling her.

"Isabella!"

"No. I'm done with your manipulations and lies. Your fakeness. Your obsession with pretending to be perfect. Your constant disapproval of me. And now you're gaslighting me into thinking that everything my father wrote in his journal doesn't mean anything when I know it does. I have been reading it all week. I've discovered things already. You're too fucking late. I know the truth, Mari."

That is the first time I have ever called my mother by her first name to her face, but it just felt right.

She stands up and crosses her arms, a slight smirk growing on her face as if she's caught my bluff.

"Okay then, Isabellita. What's the big secret?"

"Why don't you tell me?" I retort.

"But you said you already know, verdad? So just tell me."

I shake my head and laugh. "You really think I don't know?"

"Isa, I think you're just too caught up in trying to make something up to make yourself feel better."

"Is that so?" I chuckle. "Then explain this."

I dangle the photo in front of my mother's face.

Mariposa inspects it and smiles.

"It looks like an adorable photo of you and your father. So what's the big reveal?"

"I can't believe you're going to continue playing dumb. I know you know exactly why this photo is ripped."

I see the smile slowly start to fade from her face. She reaches for the photo, but I snatch it away.

"You can't take this one away from me, Mari. Now, look at the back."

I turn it around and watch as the color flushes from Mariposa's face. It is, by far, the most satisfying moment of my life.

"Sofia is my half sister, isn't she? Rosita was my father's true love, wasn't she? I know everything. You can't keep these lies from me anymore. I figured out all the clues. From her favorite arroz con leche recipe to the lock of hair from Sofia's first haircut."

I never did figure that out, but based on my mother's facial expression of shock and terror, she hasn't called my bluff for that, which means I'm right.

"Isabella, I did what I needed to do to protect you from these people. They're liars. They only care about money, class, status, and all the nice things they buy. It's not a real family."

"Oh, and we are? Pot? Meet kettle. Look at you. You're covered in all the wedding favor gifts that aren't yours. You showed up here in your nicest gown and even got your hair and makeup professionally done. You're going to sit here and say things about this family as if you're not exactly the same."

"It's not the same, Isabella. You don't understand the pressure I'm under."

"Pressure from who?" I shout. "No one gives a fuck what kind of designer bags you own. Only you do. You just have to prove yourself to Rosita and Maritza because they have more money. But news flash, they don't fucking care. No one cares."

"I care. I just wanted to live the life they did! I wanted to have nice things too, Isabella. I wanted to make good money and live a life where I could buy Chanel perfumes just because. I just wanted to fit in!"

"You don't have to be rich to fit in with them! If you took the time to be yourself and get to know them, you'd realize their opinions don't matter. And even if they care about your status, who cares? I know I don't anymore. I spent this entire week trying to impress them, making everyone think that I—that we—were super successful when really, no one seemed to bat an eye that I showed up in a shitty car or that I stumbled when asked about expensive things. I even got Sofia a gift from the Coach outlet, and they all loved it. You have a warped view of how you should be to fit in, and you're wrong."

Mariposa starts pacing around the cabin, her breath growing heavier. Her mood is getting angrier.

"Isabella, you just don't understand. You didn't grow up with them. Maritza was the spoiled one. She got everything she wanted from her father. My father was broke and couldn't care for my mother and me. Rosita was my best friend and made a name for herself without a man."

"You mean the man you stole from her?" I snap.

She looks up at me, her eyes wide but her eyebrows furrowed.

"Yeah!" she screams. "That's right. I stole Roberto! And it was the biggest mistake of my life. I wanted to take something from her for once, and he was the only thing I could take. So what!"

"So what? You ruined their relationship. You're a home-wrecker. Rosita was pregnant already, but you must have already known that, didn't you?"

"So what if I did? She was only a few weeks along, so I knew I still had a chance. I didn't want her to have everything while I lay in the dust. That's how it always was with us. And Roberto had all these dreams of being a successful and rich business owner. I knew if I could just get him alone one night, I would be able to convince him to be with me."

"You're unbelievable," I bite out, my disbelief swelling into anger. "You really think you could just convince him to leave her?" I pause, the pieces clicking together. "What—did you get him drunk, Mari? Try to trap him into being with you? That's—" My voice falters, disgust creeping in. "That's messed up."

I look away from her and back to the dresser, at my own reflection. Am I just the result of a bad memory? Did my father ever resent me?

"Is that what you think? That he was drunk when we had sex? Isabella, he was not drunk. He knew what he was doing. He's not the angel you think he is. He loved both of us."

"But he loved Rosita first. You led him on. You didn't have to do what you did but you still did it. You took him away from who he really loved."

"It's not that simple. He always had a thing for me. But getting pregnant with his child—that was the biggest mistake of my life. Not because I didn't care for him, but because it tied me to this small life. I thought we'd have more. More success, more money. I wanted to be like the rest of the family—wealthy, powerful. Instead, I got stuck in a modest restaurant, stuck with responsibilities I never wanted. And now look at me—I'll never catch up to them."

"You ran to his mother to tell her before Rosita could, and that's when you got married. You thought you'd won, right?"

"I did! I beat her to the punch!"

"Do you hear yourself? Your pregnancy was a mistake? My father was a mistake? Wow, we really did ruin your amazing, perfect, potentially prosperous life, didn't we?" I scoff.

"Maybe you did! What's so wrong with me admitting that for once in my life? This isn't the life I wanted. I didn't want to struggle with one little restaurant. I'm grateful it's doing well enough, but this isn't enough."

Suddenly, I'm fuming. I snap around and walk toward her until I'm inches away.

"The restaurant isn't doing well. We're three months past due on rent. The restaurant is fucking failing. It's been slowly failing for years. Not that you fucking cared even to check."

"What? What do you mean?" Mariposa says, panicked.

"You heard me. The one thing you thought you had that proved your success? It's not real. Just like the rest of you. I came here hoping to get an investment with Luciano to save the restaurant and buy it from you so it could be under my name instead."

"Why would you do that? And why would you lie to me about the restaurant?"

"So I can get the fuck away from you. What don't you get? You were never there for me growing up. Roberto was. You just showed up when you wanted to show off something new you bought yourself. Then I grew up and became responsible for making sure you looked successful, buying you nice things, and lying to you about the restaurant so you could gloat to your friends. And here I was, spending this entire week trying to convince the whole family we were doing great so that you could feel proud of me that I managed to do that. But even that wouldn't have been enough for you. So now you know the truth."

"You think you're better than me, Isa? No. You're exactly like me. You buy yourself designer things all the time just to put up a facade around people. Look at you now! Wearing this fancy dress and trying to play a part." She laughs. "You're just like your mother."

"You're right. I was. Not anymore. And all these designer things I bought myself? Fake. Every single one of them. So yeah, am I a fraud? The biggest one. I lied to you, to the whole family, and myself. I lied to you about the restaurant and our success. I lied to the family about how well we were doing. And most importantly, I lied to myself that I needed to be this type of person to be accepted. Someone important to me has taught me that I would rather be with someone who loves me for who I am and not what I have. Something you never understood about Roberto—but I do. So you need to leave because I'm not going anywhere."

"Excuse me?"

"You heard me," I seethe.

"You can't talk to your mother that way, Isabella."

I start to steer her toward the door, but she resists.

"You're right. That's not the way to talk to your mother. But you were never a real mother to me, so I guess we're even."

"Stop pushing me! I can leave on my own." She shakes me off her and turns around to face me.

"Leave," I say between clenched teeth.

"You're making a huge mistake, Isabella. These people are

not going to accept you. They never accepted me. What makes you think you're so special?"

"Because, unlike you, I will come forward with the truth and be myself for once. The real Isabella. Not the one who buys fake designer wallets while being months behind on rent because she's too busy trying to keep her mother happy with material objects."

"I should have let Roberto dance with Sofia at the quinceañera and left him there with you. I should have just run away and never come back."

"That's what the big fight was about? You didn't want him to dance with Sofia for the father-daughter dance?"

"Of course not, Isabella. What would people have thought? There would have been so many questions and judgment."

I can't help but laugh.

"Are you fucking kidding me? Even now, you're still worried about what people may have thought if they saw that happen. You're vapid, and I hope one day you grow up out of this. You may be my mother, but that doesn't mean I don't get to tell you the truth about how crappy of a mother you were. I'm done. I'm done with the guilt, the shame, and the pressure that it is to be your daughter. The restaurant will close, and that's my last memory of my father. You'll have to figure out what you'll do next because I have my own problems once that's all done. Now, please leave. I have a lot to do."

As my mother opens the cabin door, I walk outside with her and stand on the porch.

"Oh, by the way," I start.

She turns around, and I snatch my father's journal directly out of her arms.

"This is my fucking journal now. It always was, and you hated that. You knew I'd figure out the truth, and you'd lose your control over me."

"Isabella, I didn't want it to come to this."

"I know you didn't. You wanted to continue living your lavish lifestyle and keeping me under your thumb. Well, it's over. It's finally over. I'm done being a fraud. You, on the other hand, can do whatever you want."

"I'm not a fraud, Isa. Everything I have is real. Everything I have done is real," she insists as she walks away.

"Oh, Mom?" I call out.

She turns around again, seemingly annoyed, which only makes me smile. I look down at the black Prada bag I bought her.

"That Prada bag I bought you? The one you show off to everyone you know as the highlight of your daughter's life for you?"

Mari looks down at the bag and then back at me.

"It's a fucking fake."

Chapter Twenty-Two

My head is still buzzing from the fight with my mother. I sit down on the wooden porch of the small cabin, my father's journal resting on my lap. The cool night air sends shivers down my spine as I look into the darkness. I can see Mari's silhouette by the main office, waiting for a cab. I watch as she waits, not once turning to look in my direction. I have never spoken back to my mother before. She probably would have hit me with a sandal or wooden spoon if I had done that when I was younger. My mother is not the type of woman you prove wrong or rebel against. At least, I always felt that way. A part of me is proud of myself for finally standing up to her. But the other part of me—the guilt—is eating my insides. I just want to run over to her and apologize for everything. Try to act like it never happened and have things go back to how they were. But I can't. Not anymore.

My father was a soft-spoken man. He kept to himself, had minimal hobbies, and spent most of his time raising me. Whenever my mother had a problem, he'd just nod and listen to her rants. He had so much patience. At least, I always thought he did. But now, I wonder if it was more than patience—if his silence was really his heart aching. How much did he really love my mother? Did he at all? Was his staying with her a choice or a sacrifice? Did he stay because of me? I have so many questions now that will always remain unanswered. If he had left, what would have been left for me?

The campsite at night is eerily quiet, with only the occasional hoot of an owl breaking the silence. The darkness shrouds everything in a cloak of mystery, making it difficult to discern the shapes and objects around. The only light sources are the dim bulbs attached to the poles that line the walkways and the glowing lanterns hung from the eaves of the cabins. The trees cast long shadows that dance and sway in the gentle breeze, and the rustling of leaves is the only sound in the air. They create almost a claustrophobic feeling. I take shallow breaths. Despite the chilly air, the night is still and calm. Soon, tomorrow, this place will be filled with loud music, guests celebrating, and me trying to redeem myself after this horrible night.

As I sit on the porch of my cabin, the lantern illuminates my lap, reflecting a comforting glow on my father's journal. A sense of relief pours over me, knowing I finally have it in my possession for good. The journal's pages rustle as I turn the cover, and the sound echoes across the quiet campsite. I don't care what my mother says. I know my father finished this puzzle for me. And I do want to let him go and move on. But there's a reason he did this and a reason he did it behind her back. She would have never told me the truth about my possible half-sister. He was probably too scared to do it himself. This is the only way he truly knew how to communicate. She doesn't understand it, but I do. It's all here.

I turn each page slowly, inspecting all of its contents, ensuring I don't miss any clues. I pass the arroz con leche recipe. The one that started it all. "Her favorite," it says. It must be Rosita's favorite, but it's possible it was just about Abuelita or Maritza, as Valentina and I discovered. I pass the page with the lipstick stain on the note. We still never figured out whose lips that could be. I keep turning the pages, passing the photograph of my father standing in front of the restaurant. His dream came true. The guilt envelopes me, but I try to shake it off. I keep skimming through the book, but we may have found all the clues. Just before I reach the last page, I notice a photo we must have missed. Was it here before? I swore I checked for additional images, but maybe I didn't get this far into the journal.

In the photo, Mari, Roberto, and Rosita are sitting on a bench. They're laughing. Roberto's arm is around Mariposa's shoulders. It's clear they were dating at this point. Except… I look even closer at the image, squinting while using the dim cabin lighting to try to make out what I see. It's subtle, but you can't miss it. Roberto is holding Rosita's hand between their laps, slightly hidden from the camera's view. I can see it as clear as day. My father was in a love triangle, but there's no mistaking who his real love was. Roberto was absolutely in love with Rosita.

I used to think my mother got him drunk on purpose, tricking him into getting pregnant with me, but now… I'm not so sure. Maybe it wasn't that simple. Maybe I've been putting my father on a pedestal. Maybe he made mistakes too, just like everyone else. Maybe he loved both of them in different ways. But there's one thing I know for sure now—Sofia isn't just my cousin. She's my half sister. That's why our birthdays are so close. That's why we shared a quinceañera.

My heart pounds deeply as I stare at the photograph, confirming the journal's ultimate secret: Sofia is born from the same father as me, and she never even knew. Shock and disbelief course through my veins, but as the truth sinks in, there's an overwhelming sense of sadness and betrayal in my heart. This lie has gone on for too long. I need to tell Sofia.

After watching *The Parent Trap* for so many years, I have always longed for a sibling to share memories with and who would always be there for me. Someone to share Oreos and peanut butter with as I did with Sofia the other night. Now, I have finally found one, but the circumstances of our relationship are not what I expected. I can't help but feel angry at my parents for not being honest with me. Yet, despite this lingering feeling, I'm also…relieved. The puzzle pieces have finally come together, and the questions that have plagued me for so long have finally been answered. This discovery is going to change everything. Can Sofia and I bridge the gap that's been formed between us, or will our shared connection only remind us of the hurt and betrayal we both experienced because of our parents?

As I sit here, my thoughts and emotions swirling inside me, I know that one thing is sure: my life will never be the same again. I can't help but wonder what the future holds for my newfound sister and me and, if we can ever truly be family, and most importantly, how I will tell her. How will she even react? Can I even face her to tell her what I finally figured out? The truth she's also been searching for. I have to. She deserves to know, just like I did. I turn to the last page of the journal to find another letter from my father. My breath catches in my throat—the final note. I look up momentarily to see if my mother is still standing there. The silhouette of her figure still waits. I turn back to the letter.

My dearest Isabella,

I always knew you wouldn't turn to the last page until you discovered the big secret. That's my girl, always curious and determined. You never give up until you get what you want, and that's what I love about you. You have always been the most authentic version of yourself. I truly am so proud of you, mija.

I know that you have discovered something life-changing. It's hard for me to express how difficult it was to keep this from you. I have always wished to tell you everything, but circumstances never allowed me to do so.

I wished I had fought for the one I truly loved, but I let fear and uncertainty get in the way. If you ever feel the same way I did about someone, you fight for them with all your heart. Never let anyone or anything stand in the way of true love.

I know it was hard for you to find out, but I want you to be brave and confident. You are so strong, and you have the power to change your life and the lives of those around you. I made a huge mistake when I was young and dumb, my little Isa. But I don't regret what happened because it made you, my Isabella. I loved you so much, and I always will. You are the greatest gift I could have ever received. I only wish Sofia could have had the same experience you did. That's something I will always regret.

Remember to stay true to yourself, mija. You are enough just as you are. Please know I am always with you, even if I'm not physically here. Keep my love in your heart, and know that I am proud of the person you have become.

Be strong, my little girl, and don't let anyone tell you you can't do something. You can achieve anything you set your mind to, and I know you will make me proud.

I love you more than words could ever express.

With all my love,

Dad

As I think back on my father, I realize something I hadn't fully understood until now. Maybe he stayed because of me. My mother was difficult—manipulative, even—but he didn't leave. He stayed and raised me, gave me the best parts of him, and maybe that was his way of making sure I had the love I needed, even if his heart had always been somewhere else. Maybe, in a twisted way, he felt like he was doing right by both families.

I look up from the journal, tears streaming down my face. A

yellow cab has finally arrived, the headlights beaming into the void of the campsite. My mother walks toward the back seat of the car. She pauses for a moment. Then, with a motion so subtle it could have been missed by anyone who wasn't paying close enough attention, she looks slightly over her shoulder in my direction. She quickly opens the door and slides inside the car.

That one motion, despite feeling so minimal, means so much. She's angry. She's hurt. And she probably won't ever forgive me. I'm part of the enemy line now, according to her. How I wish she'd see things differently. I don't know what will happen to our relationship, but I can't think of that now. I need to be brave, as my father says. I need to tell Sofia the truth.

Chapter Twenty-Three

I feel my heart pounding as I take off running through the campsite, my feet slapping against the dirt path. The only sounds I can hear are my own ragged breaths and the crickets chirping in the distance. I keep my head down and my eyes trained on the path before me, not wanting to trip on any rocks or roots. Maria's words, warning me about a possible killer lurking in the darkness, echo in my mind. I curse her for saying that stupid joke. I haven't been able to shake off the thought. The memory of Silvana sneaking up on me makes me shudder, but I don't stop. I can't stop. I have to find Sofia.

As I run, I feel the cool night air brushing against my skin and causing my hair to whip around me. I can hear the rustling of leaves as the wind picks up, and I feel a chill run down my spine. I feel exposed and vulnerable, like a small animal scurrying through the woods. Or when, as a kid, I would run up the stairs, convinced a monster was chasing me. The memory makes my heart race.

But despite my fear, I keep running. I can't let anything stand in the way of finding Sofia and telling her the truth, and she won't have time to see me or hear me out tomorrow. Plus, I don't want to wait that long. She needs to know now. As I approach her cabin, I can see the glow of a lamp shining through the window, and I know that Sofia is inside, still awake.

Her cabin has been transformed into a wonderland of delicate decorations that flutter in the soft breeze. The porch is draped with fairy lights that twinkle like stars, casting a warm glow on the wooden planks below. The door is adorned with a garland of lush greenery, woven with delicate white flowers that seemed to burst with life against the dark wood. I can't help but marvel at the intricate details. The windows are framed with gauzy white curtains that billow in the wind, and the porch is dotted with whimsical lanterns that sway with each gust of air. It is as if the cabin has been transformed into a magical realm of wonder and enchantment.

I slow down as I approach the door, trying to catch my breath and gather my thoughts. I take a deep breath and raise my hand to knock, but I hesitate. What if Sofia doesn't want to see me? I wouldn't blame her. What if she doesn't believe me? I try to shake the doubts from my mind and knock on the door. There is a moment of silence before I hear Sofia's voice from the other side.

"Who is it?" Sofia says, mid-laugh, as if she is in the middle of watching a funny video on her phone.

"It's me, Sof."

There's another moment of silence. I swallow, feeling how dry my throat has become from the chilly air.

"I'm not going to open the door," Sofia says, her voice muffled through the wood. "Just leave, Isa."

I feel a wave of disappointment wash over me. Sofia doesn't even want to talk to me. But I know that I can't give up now. So I take another deep breath and try to sound as confident as possible.

"Sofia, please," I say, my voice trembling slightly. "There's something important I need to tell you."

There is a long pause, and I hold my breath, waiting for a response. Then, finally, I jump as I hear the lock on the door click, and the door slowly opens. Sofia stands in the doorway, her arms crossed over her chest and a look of suspicion on her face, her eyes dark and guarded.

"What do you want?" she asks, her tone cold.

"Sofia, please. I'm so sorry about everything. I didn't mean to cause you or Rosita or... Valentina, any harm. That wasn't my intention for coming here. I came to find out the truth. I didn't have the answer when you asked me earlier, but I finally do. I know what it is."

"It's too late for that, Isa. I don't care anymore. You've done enough. Please, just leave," she says.

I feel a lump in my throat, and tears prick my eyes. I can't leave, not without telling Sofia the truth.

"Listen, I know I fucked up. There are lots of things about this week that I regret. But I have waited ten years to see you again, and if this is the last time I see you, I need to say what I came here to say. You can ignore it, pretend I don't exist, and move on with your life if you want. But let me say what I need to say. We both need this."

"Isa, you were always one of my favorite cousins, but it's all too much. I thought you were someone who cared about me and my wedding, not someone who was spending the entire week trying to sabotage it."

"That's just it, Sofia. I'm not your cousin."

"Oh, so what? You're disowning me already?" Sofia scoffs.

"No, Sofia. I'm not your cousin because I'm actually your sister. We have the same father."

Sofia's eyes widen in shock, and I can see the emotions flicker across her face: disbelief, confusion, and finally, anger.

"What are you talking about?" Sofia demands, her voice rising in pitch.

I take a step back, feeling the weight of Sofia's anger. I knew this would be hard, but I have to keep going. I have to make Sofia understand.

"Roberto, he was in love with Rosita," I say, my voice trembling. "He had you and your mother. Then he slept with my mother and they got pregnant. She beat Rosita to the punch at telling Abuelita, knowing she would insist they'd get married. She wanted to steal Roberto away from Rosita. That's why we were born at the same time."

Sofia's face contorts in anger and hurt. "How could she do that?" she spits. "How could he have another family and just leave us like that?"

"I don't think it's as simple as that," I say, my voice still shaky. "He might have felt trapped. Maybe he didn't know how to choose between them, or maybe he was scared to stand up for what he really wanted. I know it's easy to be mad at him—believe me, I've been mad at him too—but I don't think it was all manipulation. I think he made choices, Sofia. Bad ones, maybe. But they were his."

I pull out his journal.

"He gave me this journal, and so many letters and notes lead to the truth of how much he loved your mother, Sof. How much regret he had for not fighting for the one he truly loved."

"Why would your mother do this?" she says with tears falling down her cheeks.

"I don't really know. I think she just wanted to take something from Rosita because she always felt like she got the short end of the stick in her life. It was selfish, greedy, and not at all the type of person I am. I just want you to know that."

Sofia stares at the wood floor, lost in thought.

"Why couldn't he tell us himself?"

"I don't know," I say softly. "Fear, mostly. My mother was a good manipulator; you know how obsessed she is with her image. I also doubt Rosita would have said anything to prevent unnecessary public drama that could affect her work. But there is one thing I absolutely do know. He loved both of us. He loved all of us. And he would want us to be sisters, to be there for each other."

Sofia doesn't say anything for a long moment, and I fear that I have made things worse. But then, to my surprise, Sofia opens the door a little wider and invites me inside.

The inside of the cabin is even more breathtaking. The walls are draped with sheer curtains, the delicate fabric catching the breeze through the open window and billowing like waves. I see touches of Sofia's vibrant personality everywhere, from the bright flowers that adorn the tables to the playful fairy lights that dangle from the ceiling.

My eyes are drawn to the magnificent display of flowers adorning the room. It is as if a magical garden has sprouted up inside the cabin, with blooms of every shape and shade of white bursting forth in a riot of beauty. I can smell the sweet scent of roses and lilies mingling with the heady aroma of fresh pine, which reminds me of the forest around the campsite.

Every detail has been carefully planned and executed, down to the smallest detail. As I look around, I'm in complete awe. I can't help but feel a twinge of envy at the thought of Sofia's wedding tomorrow and the magical celebration that awaits her.

Sofia sits on the bed, looking shocked and confused, as if she's still digesting the news. I sit down next to her.

"Where's Luciano?"

"He's out by the lake having drinks with the groomsmen. The last night, ya know."

"I see," I say, looking around the room.

Sofia sighs.

"So what now?"

"Do you want me to show you the puzzle pieces in his journal? It might help," I suggest.

She doesn't say anything but nods her head slowly. I pull out the journal and put it in between our laps.

"The first clue Valentina and I found was this recipe. It's for rice pudding, and he noted it was 'her favorite.' We weren't sure who he was talking about, because my mother hates rice pudding."

"Is that why you and Valentina made rice pudding the first night?"

"Exactly," I smile. "But Maritza, Rosita, Abuelita, and you all said it was your favorite. Now we had suspects."

I go through each clue with Sofia, explaining the details Valentina and I discovered and the ones I found on my own—and, finally, the last one.

"I can't believe you both did this all week. Now I know why I could never find you two." She laughs.

"There is one more clue. The one that helped solidify all my doubts. The one that answers the big question."

I reach into my pocket and pull out the ripped photograph of Roberto and me.

"You see the back? It says 'two daughters,' but part of it is ripped off. I'm unsure what happened to the other side, but I think you were in it."

Sofia gasps. "Oh my God."

I watch as she gets up and walks over to her dresser. She pulls out a blue velvet storage box and slowly opens it.

"Look at this." She walks back over and sits down, holding a ripped photograph.

It's of her as a baby. There's an arm on the left side and Rosita is on the right. I hold up my photograph and place it against hers—a perfect match.

"Holy crap," I say.

"We're sisters, Isa!"

"I can't believe we figured out the big secret."

"Wait." Sofia pauses. "What about the night of the quinceañera? What was the big fight about? Did you figure it out?"

"I did. My mother blurted it out during our last fight before she left the camp. She said Roberto wanted to dance with you for the father-daughter dance, but she refused to let him because people would ask questions."

"So I would've been able to dance with my father, huh?" Sofia sighs.

I put my hand on her knee.

"I'm so sorry you missed out on having a father figure like him in your life. But I know Rosita did her best to be the greatest parent she could be for you."

"She was amazing," Sofia says, smiling softly. "I'm glad you were able to have him in your life. I feel like he made up for your lack of a good mother, and my mother made up for the lack of a father. We both missed out on things and also had amazing memories. I'm really happy about that."

"You're right. And Sofia, I really am sorry about everything that happened tonight. But I promise it wasn't my intention to ruin your wedding. Well, originally..."

"What do you mean?" Sofia looks up at me, confused.

"Well, I should probably tell you that when I first got here, Valentina convinced me to help her sabotage the wedding in exchange for helping me solve the puzzle in the journal. Of course, I wasn't actually going to help her, but I think I inadvertently was involved. But I promise I did not steal your wedding rings."

"She tried to sabotage my wedding? Why am I not surprised?" Sofia laughs lightly but quickly narrows her eyes. "So what happened to the rings? Does she have them?"

"Well..."

"Oh God, what?"

"She accidentally dropped them in the lake. She acted like she found them, but I think she lost them in the water when we were having an argument. I was trying to grab them from her and convince her to return them. She was trying to make you think Luciano lost them so you'd call off the wedding."

Sofia lets out a loud cackle, though there's a bit of tension in her voice. "Oh my God, I knew she could be dramatic, but... the rings? Valentina really has no chill. Do you know how much those things cost?" She sighs, pinching the bridge of her nose. "I loved those rings. I'm not gonna lie, I'm pissed about that."

"I'm so sorry, Sofia. I really tried to stop her."

Sofia waves a hand dismissively but doesn't hide the frustration in her voice. "Valentina actually tried to talk to me about something the other day. She was acting weird—like, really nervous. But I got caught up in all the wedding chaos and told her we'd talk later. I thought it was just her usual dramatics, so I brushed it off. Guess I shouldn't have done that."

I bite my lip, the guilt bubbling up again. "I think she might have been trying to confess about the rings."

"I'm glad you told me. At least now I know what happened. It's just…damn. They were custom-made. But, I guess…what's done is done. We'll get new ones. Luciano will probably freak out more than I did when he finds out." She pauses, shaking her head. "Look, I've always known Val had a thing for me, and yeah, it stings that she'd go this far, but honestly, her feelings have never really affected me. I didn't see her that way, and she knew it. It's just… I don't know, sad that she's still trying. But I never saw her as a threat. Luciano and I are solid, and this isn't going to shake us. Still, the rings…that really sucks."

She glances back at me with a small, tight smile. "But, you know, I think you're helping her move on. She might have lost the rings, but she's slowly letting go of me. Maybe you're what she needs to finally move forward."

"I don't know, Sof. We got into a huge fight, and I saw her kiss Silvana."

"Oh, please. You and I both know Silvana is a dirty snake and drunk-kissed her."

"You know about that?"

"Of course I do. Valentina is my best friend. She tells me everything."

"Everything?" I groan.

"Yes, everything." Sofia giggles. "I'm not just saying this because I'm your sister, and she's my best friend, but you two are perfect for each other. I can just tell. Can't you?"

"I don't know. I think so. She's the only one here who knows the real me and doesn't care. I've never experienced that before. I've always put on a facade. With family, strangers, and people I've dated. She's the only person I've been able to finally be myself with, and my biggest fear of rejection didn't happen. And then I messed it all up."

"You didn't mess it all up," Sofia reassures me. "Valentina's already forgiven you, hasn't she? There's still a chance. You just need to show her that you're willing to fight for this. A grand gesture or something. She's still hung up on you, Isa. I can tell."

"I don't know if I can fill your shoes in her eyes. I don't want to spend the rest of my life being compared to you because she was in love with you for so long."

"She won't. I've seen the way she looks at you. She's never looked at me like that, trust me. She can be a total grump and honestly would have spent the entire week miserable, but she didn't. She had fun. You brought the light out in her. You're like her sunshine. You need to tell her how you feel. Don't let this one go, Isa. I don't know much about your past relationships, but I do know Valentina. And I know this—she's great, and what you two have is special."

I look up at Sofia, and we both smile at each other. I can hear the chatter of men approaching the cabin from a distance.

"It sounds like the men are officially done, so I'll leave," I say, standing up. "Tomorrow is the big day!"

"I know, I'm so nervous. But I know I'll be okay because my sister will be there with me. Right? I'll see you at the wedding?"

I stay quiet momentarily, pretending I'm thinking really hard about the decision.

"Isa!"

"Okay, I'll go. But only if you help me do one thing…"

Chapter Twenty-Four

I exhale. "This is it."

Standing in front of the cabin door leading out to the campground, I can feel the butterflies fluttering. I smooth out my dark orange dress, fluffing the flowy pleated skirt and exposing my right leg through the slit. I look down at my dark grey heels before looking back up at the door. I can do this. I hold my breath and open the door.

I walk along the path. My heels dig slightly into the ground as I approach the wedding area. I can't help but feel a sense of anticipation building inside of me with every step I take. Then, as I turn the corner, the sight before me takes my breath away.

The ceremony is situated in a small clearing surrounded by towering trees. The sun is beginning to set, casting a warm glow over the entire area. The chairs are arranged in neat rows, each one adorned with a simple white lace ribbon. The aisle is lined with delicate white flowers, their petals soft against the green foliage. In front of the chairs, a wooden archway is decked with flowers, vines, and delicate fairy lights.

As I approach, I can see the intricate details of the decorations, the soft pastels of the flowers and the twinkle of the lights.

Above the seats, string lights hang across the trees, creating a warm canopy—Sofia's signature look.

The ceremony is bathed in a warm and welcoming atmosphere, with a subtle fragrance of sweet flowers filling the air. The setting is intimate yet grand, with every tiny detail taken care of to make the day perfect. Walking closer to the archway, I can see the stunning view beyond it. The afternoon sun casts a golden light over the distant hills and the sparkling lake resting through the valley. The birds chirp in the trees as if adding their own music to the ambiance.

It takes me a moment to realize that dozens of staff members are running around, getting into their places. The bartenders are cleaning their counters, preparing for the rush of guests who will flood the area after the ceremony, during cocktail hour. As the guests arrive, they go to the white chairs facing the altar in neat lines. I watch as family and friends of Sofia and Luciano take their seats, each person dressed in their finest attire. Some are wearing flowing dresses, others sharp suits, but all with smiles of excitement and joy. I know she won't be in the crowd, but I can't help but scan the area to find Valentina. I wish I could see her for a second before the ceremony starts. The imaginary pill in my throat is impossible to swallow.

I finally follow suit and sit among the other guests, feeling a wave of emotions wash over me. The hired harpist begins to play, filling the space with soft music. I tightly grip the notecards in my hands, worried that with a strong enough breeze, they'd all float away, along with me. The sound of people murmuring keeps me distracted from my nerves. I can only imagine how Sofia is feeling right now. Should I have stopped by to see her before the big moment? No, that's not what we planned. *It's okay, Isa. You can do this.*

"It's finally here," Maria says, sauntering in, and then sits down next to me. "Damn, pendeja, you couldn't get a seat in the front?"

"What? This is fine."

"We're in the next to last row. Let's go closer to the front."

"Maria, no—"

But it's too late. She is already grabbing my hand and pulling me up the aisle to the third row. It's a much better seat, but I can't help but feel incredibly vulnerable being so close.

The harpist begins to play a slightly different tune, her fingers plucking at the strings of her instrument, filling the air with soft, melodic music. The guests fall silent, and I can feel the anticipation building in the air. I watch as the first bridesmaids appear, one by one, walking down the aisle in their burgundy satin dresses, each one more stunning than the last. The fabric flows gracefully, creating an elegant and timeless look. The neckline is a gentle scoop, the bodice fits each of them perfectly, and the skirt flows out in layers of tulle and silk. Their hair is styled in loose waves and pinned back with simple white flowers, which adds to the natural beauty of the ceremony decorations. Each bridesmaid carries a small bouquet of white flowers, which complements the bold burgundy of their dresses. Silvana glares at me as she walks by. I just roll my eyes while Maria gives her the finger. Valentina is the last to appear, and I must keep myself from staring at her too long. But I can't help it. She looks gorgeous. For a quick moment, our eyes meet, but I quickly look away.

The groomsmen stand at the altar with Luciano, waiting for the bride to make her grand entrance. They look sharp in their grey suits, each detail perfectly tailored to their forms. Their ties are a matching shade of burgundy, which ties the whole color scheme together beautifully. Luciano shifts back and forth on his feet, clearly anxious about seeing his glowing bride. We all are.

The harpist changes the sweet and tender melody once more, signifying that it's time for the bride to join the rest of us. We're all transfixed, watching in awe as Sofia slowly appears at the end of the aisle. You can hear a few gasps in the crowd.

"Damn, Sofia ate," Maria whispers, ruining the mood.

Sofia's wedding gown is a stunning work of art. The mermaid-style dress hugs her curves as if it were painted onto her body, before flaring out in a dramatic train. The bodice is adorned with delicate lace appliqués, which create a beautiful and intricate pattern. The lace trails down the skirt and train, adding to the dress's overall beauty and detail. The tulle layers of the dress add a soft and ethereal quality, while the detailed beading gives a touch of sparkle and glamour.

Her veil was equally beautiful. It is long and flowing, made of the same delicate tulle as the dress's skirt. A small and subtle blue comb secures the veil to her hair. Her hair is styled in a loose, romantic updo, with rogue strands framing her face softly and naturally. Her makeup is soft and feminine, with a focus on her eyes. Her makeup artist created a subtle smoky eye with shades of brown and rose gold, bringing out her eyes' natural beauty. Her cheeks are kissed by a soft blush, which adds a gentle flush of color to her complexion. Her lips are a muted shade of mauve, which complements the overall look perfectly.

"Her wedding gown is a masterpiece," I hear a guest murmur behind me.

Maritza scoffs lightly. "It's not as pretty as her rehearsal dinner dress."

She's wrong. Sofia's dress is elegant, timeless, and gorgeous. My heart swells with pride and joy as Sofia makes her way down the aisle. She looks absolutely radiant in her white gown, which flows gracefully behind her as she walks. Her veil trails behind her, softening the edges of her dress. We watch as she slowly approaches Luciano, taking his hand as he helps her up onto the stand. Suddenly, I feel sick to my stomach. I know what's coming up.

I watch Sofia whisper something to Luciano and the justice

of the peace. Oh, God. Is it too late to run away? Sofia grabs the microphone and faces us.

"Thank you all so much for attending our wedding and participating in such a special day. It means so much to me to have so much family willing to share this moment with me. Speaking of family, my sister wants to share a few words before we get started."

Fuck. Fuck. Fuck.

"Sister?" Maria looks around at the guests, who are doing the same thing.

I take a deep breath and stand up.

A mixture of gasps, whispers, and murmurs is heard throughout the crowd. I try to ignore them, attempting to keep my feet from buckling under the weight of my body.

"No fucking way," Maria gasps. "Bitch, you should have told me!"

I scoot by Maria and head over to Sofia, my eyes transfixed on her. I'm afraid if I look anywhere else, I'll pass out. I don't even consider tempting fate by looking at Valentina.

"Hey, you got this, okay?" Sofia whispers as she hands me the microphone. "Tell your truth and get your girl back."

I nod, unable to speak, and turn to face the guests. I look down at Rosita, whose face has completely changed colors. She looks like she's, quite literally, seen the ghost of Roberto appear in front of her. I reach for my notecards and realize I have left them on my chair. *Fuck.* I can't go back, that'll look weird, and everyone's staring. I'll just have to wing it.

"Hi, everyone." I clear my throat. "You're probably wondering why I'm standing up here, crashing Sofia's ceremony."

A few soft laughs can be heard from the crowd. I look at Maria, who just gives me a double thumbs-up.

"I'm standing here to tell you I'm a fraud. I was convinced to go to this wedding by my cousin Maria. I was told it would be a great way to secure an investment for my family's restaurant. The reason I so desperately need this investment is that La Mariposa is failing. It's not successful like I said it was. We're not expanding to create a franchise. We're three months behind on rent."

I turn around to face Luciano.

"Luc, I'm so sorry for lying to you. When you told me your story, I felt even more guilty, but I also felt like you'd understand, as someone who knows what it's like to struggle."

I turn back to the crowd.

"I have spent this entire week pretending to be someone I'm not. You all think of me as this successful, rich woman with a booming restaurant, but that's not me. So let me reintroduce myself. My name is Isabella Valdes, and I'm poor."

The murmurs in the crowd continue. I can hear Silvana snicker behind me.

"I can't afford to buy the things you do. This entire wedding cost more than I will ever make in my entire life. Not only that, but I've lied about what I've been wearing. I've spent this entire week desperately trying to be accepted by all of you, but I'm done trying. This is me. This dress is from a second-hand bridal shop, and I got it in the clearance section for $30. Yes, that means someone else wore it before me."

I turn to Sofia, who nods in approval for the next thing I'm about to say. I look forward and down at Rosita.

"I also just learned that my mother is the biggest liar of them all. She's been keeping a secret from me my entire life, and that secret is that Sofia is my half sister. Roberto, my father, was madly in love with Rosita. Now you can gossip about us all you want. I don't care. Because being with family and being true to myself is more important than what any one of you thinks of me. I'm tired of living a lie and hiding my true self."

Finally, I turn to Valentina. Her eyes are glossy as she holds back tears, presumably to keep her makeup intact.

"Val, I am so sorry for what I did to you. Silvana blackmailed me, threatening that she would tell everyone the truth about me if I didn't leave you. Well, Silvie, it looks like I win. There's nothing left for you to say, or is there?"

Silvana rolls her eyes and looks away.

"That's what I thought."

I look back at Valentina, my legs shaking.

"I never wanted to break things off with you. You were the only person here who saw the real me almost instantly. And you didn't pull away. You didn't look down on me. You saw me, Val—just me. And I don't want to lose that. It's all I've ever wanted."

I turn back to the crowd.

"That's me. You can accept me for who I am or not at all. It doesn't matter to me. Because the people who truly matter in my life love me."

I hand the microphone back to Sofia. I half expect a roaring applause to end my big speech, but everyone looks confused and uncomfortable. Maria cheers and claps, which prompts a few people to join in on halfhearted claps. I can't tell if they're unimpressed or appalled by my existence. I walk back down the aisle to my seat when I hear the microphone screech slightly.

"Wait!" Valentina says over the speakers.

I turn around.

"I have something to confess too. I tried to sabotage Sofia and Luciano's wedding because I was in love with her while we were growing up. When Sofia told me she was engaged, I was in shock. It's been hard for me to move on, but after meeting Isa, I feel like I finally can."

She turns to face the couple.

"Luciano, I'm sorry for getting you in trouble. I stole the rings, not Isa."

The crowd collectively gasps.

"Isa tried to convince me to give them back to you and even

fought me for them until we accidentally dropped them at the bottom of the lake and I lied to Isa about finding them."

Valentina pulls two rings from her pocket and hands them to Luciano.

"I got these at a gift shop nearby for $20. I know it's not your designer rings you spent a fortune on, but I hope you'll find the memory of these to be more valuable than the money spent?"

Luciano pulls her in for a hug, laughing softly. "Well, Val, I guess we'll just have to see which ones hold up better over time."

Sofia joins in with a smirk. "Yeah, I suppose we'll be telling this story at every anniversary, so thanks for giving us something priceless. The actual rings…well, that's another conversation," she adds with a playful wink.

Luciano chuckles. "Either way, thank you, Val. This week wouldn't have been the same without you."

"Take care of my best friend, okay?"

"I will. I promise."

Valentina turns back to me.

"Isa, I never loved Silvana."

Maria lets out a cackle, making Silvana's face change to a dark shade of red.

"I don't want to be with her. I never did. The time I have spent with you this week has been the happiest of my life, after spending so many years of loving someone who didn't love me the same. I did see you. The real you. And I hope everyone can see it, because the real Isa is amazing. She's friendly, compassionate, and driven, and she will do anything for her family, even if it means lying about her entire life so they'd have her around. Everyone here has secrets they're not sharing out of fear of rejection. We're all the same. You're just the one who was brave enough to admit it. So I have to ask you. Can we please un—break up now?"

I laugh as I rush down the aisle to her, leaping into her

arms. Much to my surprise, all of the guests begin to clap. The groomsmen let out a few whoops, and I can hear Maria screaming at the top of her lungs above the rest. I pull back and place my lips against Valentina's, sharing a kiss with her in the middle of my sister's wedding.

Sofia rushes over and hugs both of us.

"I love you guys. But it's time for me to get married." She laughs and shoos us away from the altar.

After the justice of the peace goes through the first part of the ceremony, the moment finally arrives for the couple to exchange their vows. The atmosphere is electric with anticipation as the guests look on, eager to witness the exchange of heartfelt promises.

The harpist plays a soft and romantic melody, slowly building it into a crescendo as the couple faces each other, their eyes locked in an intimate gaze.

Sofia and Luciano hold hands, their fingers interlaced in a gesture of love and commitment. Sofia's eyes sparkle with emotion as she begins to speak her vows, her voice soft and sincere.

"I promise to love, cherish, and support you through life's ups and downs. I promise to be your partner, confidante, and best friend. I promise to always strive to make you happy and be there for you in good times and bad. I also promise never to let material things come between our love for each other ever again. I would rather get married to you with $20 rings than not at all. You're my everything, Luc. I love you."

Luciano's eyes fill with tears as he listens to Sofia speak. Then, he takes a deep breath and begins to say his own vows, his voice shaking, filled with love and determination.

"I promise to love you with all my heart, to stand by your side through thick and thin, and to cherish you for the rest of my days. I promise to be your rock, support, and comfort in life's challenges. I always vow to be faithful, loving, and true. I vow to ground you when you get upset over silly rings getting lost and remind you how much stronger our love is than any amount of money in the world. I love you, Sofia."

As they exchange rings, their hands trembling with emotion, we all watch in awe, moved by the moment's beauty. Finally, the harpist plays a triumphant melody, signaling the end of the ceremony, and the newlyweds share their first kiss as husband and wife, sealing their love for the rest of their lives. We all stand up, cheering, shouting, clapping, and throwing flower petals in the air as they walk down the aisle. The bridal party soon follows, but as Valentina approaches my row, she reaches for me to walk down the aisle with her.

"Walk with me?" she asks, smiling.

"I'd love to," I say, feeling a sense of peace I never thought was possible.

Chapter Twenty-Five

Walking through cocktail hour on Valentina's arm feels like I have won the grand prize at a high-end casino. The event is set up next to the reception area, and there are multiple bars decorated with flowers, vines, and white linen. Bartenders in crisp white shirts and black vests stand behind the bar, ready to whip up any drink we desire. A string quartet plays soft classical music in the background.

We head toward one of the bars to pick up some already prepared his-and-hers drinks. Valentina picks up the spiced pear gin and tonic, and I choose the apple cider Moscow mule. The drink is served in a beautiful crystal glass, garnished with an apple slice and a cinnamon stick.

"That was a pretty incredible thing you did at the ceremony," Val says between sips.

"Well, let's just say I learned I can be strong. And brave."

I think of my father's letter about fighting for the ones you love.

"Well, color me impressed. It's so nice to see the real Isa. And for everyone else to see her too." Valentina smiles.

"Hear I am!" I do a spin, my dress flowing half a second behind me.

"I can't believe you put together the big secret in your father's journal. You and Sofia are half sisters! This is insane."

"I know; I couldn't believe it until I saw the other half of the photograph."

I reach into my clutch and pull out the photograph Sofia and I taped together and show Valentina.

"Oh my God, this is incredible. I'm so happy for you, Isa. Look at you two little babies!" she coos.

I can't help but look up at Valentina's eyes. The way they glisten under the starry lights. I reach up toward her, pull her closer, my hand behind her neck, and place my lips against hers.

"Ew, get a room!" Maria shouts as she walks over to us. "What a crazy week, huh? Sisters. Who would have thought? Aren't you glad I forced you to come? This all happened because of me, you know. You're welcome."

"Yes," I say, laughing. "I know you're just being a pendeja right now, but none of this would have happened if you didn't get me out of my fake little world. I can't thank you enough."

"Oh, stop it," Maria says, grinning. "I'm just happy to see my prima finally happy with someone. Treat her well, Val. Or I'll find you. I know where you live."

"I promise I will," Valentina says with a chuckle.

As they hug each other, someone taps my shoulder. I turn around to see Maritza standing there with her arms crossed.

"Hola, Tía," I say cautiously.

"I just wanted to say that I thought your speech was nice." She looks away, trying to appear uninterested.

"Thanks, Tía."

I wait for her to leave, but she lingers.

"Is there anything else?" I wonder out loud.

"I also wanted to say that...you're not the only one with secrets."

At this point, Valentina turns around and stands next to me, wrapping her arm around my waist and pulling me closer.

"This might seem hard to believe, but I haven't been with my husband for many years. I've been...dating someone...else."

Valentina and I both look at each other, trying not to laugh.

"Oh yeah? Who is it?" I ask, knowing full well who it is.

Maritza looks around to see if anyone is close by.

"It's Gabriel. Roberto's best friend," she says, wincing.

"Wow, really? That's surprising. I had no idea," I stifle a giggle.

"I know it seems far-fetched. Why would someone amazing like me be with someone like Gabriel, a measly landlord? But he makes me laugh. And I...love him."

"That's great, Tía! Don't be ashamed of it. Gabriel is a great guy, and I don't think anyone cares. Even if they did, whatever. Love him with all your heart, okay?"

Maritza tries to maintain her pose as she stiffly leans in for a hug. It feels like I'm hugging a tree, but I try my best to embrace her. Her sharp shoulder jabs into my chest, but I ignore it. I couldn't remember the last time Maritza was this affectionate with me.

"That was crazy." I laugh as we watch Maritza saunter away, walking so gracefully she looks as if she's floating.

"Looks like your speech may have inspired even the least likely people. It seems like everyone prefers the real Isabella too, huh?"

"I guess so." I smile.

I spot Silvana slowly approaching me, looking awkward. She crosses her arms and glances over her shoulder, clearly uncomfortable.

"Okay, so...look, I'm supposed to apologize or whatever," she says, barely able to make eye contact. She glances around as if she's checking for an escape route. "For threatening you. And kissing Val. Apparently, Maria told my mom, and now she's on my case, so here I am. Apologizing. Happy?"

I cross my arms and blink at her. "Wow, Silvana. I'm really feeling the sincerity here. You're practically oozing remorse."

"Hey, this is as good as it gets. Take it or leave it. My mom said if I didn't apologize, she's cutting my allowance. So…sorry. There. I said it," she huffs, rolling her eyes as if she's doing me a massive favor.

I hold back a laugh. "Well, when you put it like that, I'm completely overwhelmed with emotion. Your apology is just… breathtaking."

She scowls but there's a hint of amusement in her eyes. "Yeah, yeah. Whatever. Just don't expect a repeat performance. Apologizing isn't really my thing."

"Shocker," I deadpan, patting her on the back. "Don't worry, Silvie. We're good. You can run along now."

She looks around one more time as if she's checking to make sure she's fulfilled her duty, then quickly turns on her heel. "Cool. Later," she says, practically sprinting away.

As we mingle with the other guests, I sample some of the delicious hors d'oeuvres being passed around. There are miniature quiches filled with savory vegetables, delicate phyllo cups stuffed with shrimp and herbs, and skewers of juicy grilled chicken with a tangy dipping sauce. Each bite is more delicious than the last, and I can't help but go back for seconds and thirds. I catch Maria stuffing a few into her clutch.

More guests have approached me to tell me some secrets they've been holding in. Alessandro admits he doesn't live in the condos he posts on social media but in a small studio apartment across the street with his cat. Ramon and Rafael, the twins, admit their father hasn't appointed them to VP positions of his company—they work in cubicles and actually don't mind it. Araceli tells us her parents have been divorced for nine years and lying to everyone about it. Each of them praises me for my bravery and tell me they don't care about my financial status. Some even promise to make plans with me when we all return home. It seems like everyone has secrets they're keeping from others out of fear of judgment. I'm not as alone as I thought I was.

I see Abuelita sitting in the reception area from a distance, peacefully watching the crowd mingle and the servers scurry by.

"I'll be right back," I whisper to Valentina and head toward Abuelita.

I walk under the canopy of lights and sit down next to her. She continues looking at the crowd, or at least it seems like it, through her almost-closed eyes.

"Mijita." She smiles softly as if she's just acknowledging my presence.

"Hola, Abuelita." I kiss her on the head. "How are you?"

"Muy bien, mijita. There's so much love here tonight, verdad?"

"Si, there is," I say, putting my hand on hers.

We sit in silence for a moment, watching the guests laugh, drink, and tell each other stories.

"What's on your mind, Isabellita?" She turns slowly toward me.

"I just wanted to thank you. You were the first to push me to fight for someone, even if it meant doing the same thing my mother did."

"What do you mean, mija?"

"You know, I basically stole Valentina from Silvana. She loved her."

"Oh no, Isabellita. You are nothing like your mother. Valentina didn't love Silvana. Roberto loved Rosita, and Rosita loved Roberto. You're not like Mariposa. You're like Roberto."

"I am? How?"

"You're strong. Loving. Resilient. He was brave enough to try and tell you the truth, even when he was losing his strength. You were so brave today, telling everyone who the real Isabellita is. I am so proud of you, mijita."

I reach over and give Abuelita a big hug.

"I'm just happy I could live long enough to see you return to the family. We missed you, Isabellita. You're so special to us. To me. And Rosita. Te quiero, mijita."

She plants a light kiss on my cheek.

"Is that my Isabellita?" a voice bellows, startling me.

I look up to see Rosita standing a few feet away. She wears a floor-length gown in a rich, deep shade of grey that catches the light with every movement. The fabric is soft and flowing, draping beautifully over her curves. The dress is adorned with delicate, intricate beading that sparkles in the fairy lights, adding a touch of glamour to the already stunning piece. As Rosita moves toward us, the dress skirt sways gracefully, revealing a hint of her strappy, metallic heels. She has accessorized with a simple yet elegant clutch in a matching shade of grey, and her hair is swept back into an elegant updo, revealing sparkling drop earrings that perfectly complement the dress.

"Hola, Tía!" I rush over and embrace her in my arms.

"Isabella, I am so proud of you. You did the thing that so many of us have been too scared to do. I'm so sorry I never told you."

"You don't have to apologize. I understand, I promise. I'm not mad at you. Is Sofia?"

"No." She shakes her head. "She's surprisingly taking it well. That, or she's good at hiding how she really feels."

"It'll get easier, Tía. I promise."

"Come, mija. I want to show you something," Rosita says, leading me toward a random table to sit down.

Rosita reaches into her purse, pulls out a folded photograph, and slowly hands it to me. I open it to see Rosita and Roberto standing next to each other. Roberto is kissing Rosita on the cheek, and she's smiling at the camera. It's very clearly a couple's portrait. I look closer and notice that Rosita is wearing a red shade of lipstick. One that looks nearly identical to the one on the note Valentina and I found in the journal but couldn't match.

"I have to admit," she begins, "that I've been avoiding you a bit all week."

"You have? I guess I haven't seen you much, now that I think about it. I was also super busy trying to discover the truth." I laugh.

"I was. It's been tough for me to see you here. It brought back a lot of sad memories of Roberto and me. All I wanted was for him to dance with Sofia at your quince, but Mari refused because people would know something was up. Or they'd start rumors, and she couldn't have that."

"I'm so sorry, Rosita. That must have been so hard," I say, placing my hand on hers.

"All I wanted was for Sofia to grow up with her father, and she couldn't. I lost my best friend, the love of my life, and my daughter's father all in one night. Seeing you here reminded me of that night. But you've changed them for me. I'm finally at peace now, knowing Sofia knows the truth. I wish I could have done it differently, but I wasn't brave enough. You were, mija, and I will forever be thankful for that."

"I wouldn't have been able to do it without my father's help. His journal revealed everything. It especially revealed just how much you loved him. I only wish you could have had the life you wanted with him. You both deserved that. I love you so much, Tía."

She pulls me in for a hug, her arms trembling slightly as she holds me close.

As she pulls back, she looks at me, her eyes heavy with regret. "I want you to know something, Isa. I never wanted to pretend to be your mother's sister. That was Mari's doing. She was the one who insisted I play along, that it was the only way to keep things quiet. Roberto agreed because he thought it would protect Sofia. It was Mari's idea to tell everyone I was just another sister in the family. That way, no one would ask why I was always around, and no one would suspect Sofia was his daughter. She didn't want anyone to question her marriage to Roberto, not even for a second."

I blink, absorbing the revelation. "So you did it to protect Sofia—and to protect him?"

She nods. "I didn't want to, but I had no choice. Mari threatened to cut me out of your lives entirely if I didn't go along with it. She said I wouldn't be allowed to see you or your father. I couldn't bear the thought of losing both of you. So I went along with it, even though I still barely got to see you. And for years, I lived with that lie. I hate that it kept me from being honest with Sofia, but at least now she knows. Now, we can all move forward."

"I can't believe Mari had that much control over everything," I whisper, my voice filled with a mix of anger and sadness.

"She did," Rosita says, her voice firm but laced with sadness. "But no more. Promise me you will tell Sofia everything you can about Roberto."

"I promise."

The sun has set, and the wedding is bathed in the warm, amber glow emanating from the canopy of string lights above the tables and dance floor.

Sofia and Luciano make their grand entrance, the canopy of string lights twinkling above them. As the band begins to play a soft, romantic melody, Sofia and Luciano make their way to the center of the dance floor, hand in hand. The guests, their eyes fixed on the happy couple, fall silent as the two begin to sway gently to the music.

Sofia is resplendent in her bridal gown, the delicate tulle and flowing train adding to the graceful movements of her dance. In his perfectly tailored suit, Luciano holds her close, his eyes locked on hers as they move together in perfect harmony. As they dance, it's as if they are the only two people in the world.

The rest of the room fades away, and they are lost in the moment's magic. The string lights above them cast a warm, golden glow, highlighting the love and joy radiating from their faces. As the song builds, the tempo increases and Sofia and Luciano's movements become more confident and spirited. They twirl and dip, their laughter ringing across the campsite, and we cheer them on, clapping and whistling in admiration.

Finally, as the song ends, they share a tender, lingering kiss. They pull away, their faces alight with happiness and contentment, and the guests erupt into a standing ovation. It's a moment of pure magic, a celebration of love and joy that will be remembered by all fortunate enough to witness it. As Sofia and Luciano take their seats, their hands still entwined, it's evident that the rest of the night will unfold in a whirlwind of music, dancing, and pure, unadulterated joy.

The tables at the reception area are draped in crisp white linens, and each setting is adorned with delicate silver flatware and shimmering crystal glasses. The centerpieces are an exquisite combination of white roses, baby's breath, and greenery arranged in antique vases that add a touch of vintage charm to the affair. Sitting next to Valentina, I marvel at the beauty of it all, feeling as if I have stumbled into a magical fairy tale and Sofia is the princess.

The reception begins with a sumptuous feast, served individually to each guest by the waitstaff. The menu is a gourmet delight, featuring locally sourced, organic ingredients that have been masterfully crafted by Valentina and her team into an array of mouthwatering dishes. There is roasted salmon, served with a tangy dill sauce and a medley of grilled vegetables; braised short ribs, cooked to perfection and served with creamy mashed potatoes and roasted garlic; and a fragrant mushroom risotto, topped with shavings of aged parmesan cheese. Each dish is a work of Valentina's culinary art, and I savor every bite.

"This has to be your best work yet," I say.

"No, that would be the rice pudding on Monday," she teases.

As we laugh, the sound of a glass clinking silences the room.

"We want to thank you all so much for being here to celebrate our marriage," Luciano begins. "I know it's a lot to ask for an entire week of your time, and we won't ever forget how you all went out of your way to be here for us. I have learned so much about Sofia's family over this week. I have learned they are proud, hardworking, and, most importantly, full of love and care for my wife. I am so proud to be a part of the Perez family, and I hope you all accept my parents and me into yours."

The guests start clapping and cheering.

"So let's raise a toast. To family!"

"To family!" we all yell back and take sips of our champagne.

As the meal ends, the bride and groom take to the dance floor, swaying gently to the strains of a live band that plays a mix of romantic ballads and upbeat classics. The guests begin to join in, their laughter and joy filling the air as they spin and twirl beneath the stars.

"May I have this dance?" Valentina reaches for my hand.

"You absolutely may," I reply, blushing.

As the night wears on, the party only grows more exuberant. The bar flows with top-shelf spirits and local craft beer, and bartenders mix up bespoke cocktails that tantalize the taste buds. Servers bring trays of decadent desserts around the party, but the showstopper is a towering cake adorned with fresh flowers and fruit. There's even a spread of artisanal chocolates and macarons begging to be devoured.

"This has been the best week of my entire life," Valentina says as she sways me from side to side.

"I couldn't agree more," I reply.

"And look. I didn't even rip your dress," she teases.

"There's still plenty of time for that," I say with a grin.

"Promise?" she asks.

I reach up and kiss her gently.

"I promise."

At the stroke of midnight, the newlyweds bid us all farewell, and the party comes to a close. As we make our way back to our cabin, I feel a sense of awe at the beauty and grandeur of the evening and the entire week. It was a week of magic, love, and pure extravagance, and it will be remembered for years.

"Are you ready to spend the night together?" Valentina says.

"Depends. Am I sleeping on the cot or with you on the bed?" I joke.

"I hope to sleep next to you on a soft bed for a very long time, Isa."

"I'd love that," I say, my heart fuller than it's been in ages.

Chapter Twenty-Six

I have mixed feelings about this place. Celebrating Sofia and Luciano in the Berkshires was equally the most stressful and exciting time of my life. Secrets were revealed. A sister was found. A romance blossomed. It's also was where Valentina and I had our first fight, and then where I fought back for our love. Being in a place you'll likely never be in again for the rest of your life is weird. It's like a fleeting moment. Maybe one day, I'll wonder if it was just a dream I made up. If it wasn't for Valentina, I might have believed this was all a dream. But here we are, packing up and preparing to return to reality.

"This was a pretty crazy experience, wasn't it?" Maria chuckles. "I grabbed some extra wedding favors for the road. How's Miss Piggy?"

"You've got that right. I think she'll get us home."

"You think? Oh, God. I'm already dreading this. So did you get the investment at least?"

"I'm not sure, actually. I didn't want to bring it up yesterday, so I've been waiting to see Luc this morning. I have a feeling we didn't. I lied to him. No matter how he feels about the restaurant, who wants to invest in one with so much debt?"

"But didn't you send him the business proposal?"

I bite my lip. "I did…but I think it might've been too late. I rushed to finish it, but honestly, I'm not even sure how good it was. And with everything else? It's hard to imagine it making a difference."

Maria nods, concern etched on her face.

"What about the restaurant? What's going to happen with La Mariposa?"

"I'm not sure," I say, shrugging. "We'll just have to take it one day at a time. If you still want to stick around, that is."

"Until the very end," Maria promises.

We head out of the cabin, and I lock the door behind me, as instructed by Daniel. This is it. The wedding is officially over. I can't believe I feel sad about it. This must be precisely how the kids feel on the last day of summer camp when their parents are coming by to pick them up. They've just made all these new friends, probably from different parts of the country. So many memories were created. Laughs were had. Adventures were taken. To have it all end so abruptly and have to go back to the real world is a lot for an adult. I can only imagine how kids feel. I, too, would cry and throw a temper tantrum. In fact, I feel like throwing one now. Maybe we can stay a week longer. The season is over. Valentina and I can sneak in and live in one of the cabins. We will put on our best lumberjack outfits to gather firewood, and the others will hunt squirrels for food. It'll be cozy and romantic. We'll have to draw straws to see who has to do the murdering-of-little-critters part, but it sure as hell won't be me.

As we head back toward the cars, I see Sofia and Luciano packing their luggage in the trunk of their car. This is the moment.

"Hey! Leaving first, I see. Are you heading straight to your honeymoon?"

"You know it!" Sofia shouts. "Three weeks traveling through Greece, Italy, and France. It's going to be amazing. I'll send you all the pics, of course. You'll get sick of me sooner than you think."

I laugh. "Doubtful."

The idea of having constant contact with my sister makes all of this so worth it. I'll finally have someone I can turn to that isn't just a cousin. Someone who shares something with me. Something deep. We're connected. I can't wait to share my secrets, dreams, and rants with Sofia.

"Hey, Isa. Can I talk to you in private quick?" Luciano pulls me aside.

"Yeah, of course. What's going on?" I say.

"I just want you to know that hearing the truth about the restaurant was a big shock last night. It's not what I expected for my first investment."

"I know, Luc. I'm so sorry for lying to you. I was desperate and scared."

"I'm not saying what you did was okay, but I want you to know I get it."

"You do?"

"Of course I do. Like I told you, I didn't come from money. I know what it's like to struggle. To feel desperate."

I nod slowly.

"I'm very impressed with you, Isabella."

"Me? Why?"

"You may have lied. A lot. But it also takes a lot of bravery and growth to admit to not only yourself but those around you what the truth is. It speaks volumes about who you are as a person. I just wanted you to know that. You would be a great business partner."

"Well, thanks, Luc. That's kind of you to say."

"That's why I want to invest in La Mariposa."

"Excuse me?" I look at him, incredulous.

"You heard me. I want to invest in your business."

"Luciano, you don't have to do that. I lied to you. La Mariposa is in debt. There's no way we'd even be remotely ready to expand—I can barely keep this one location open. I appreciate you doing that, but you don't have to just because we're family now."

"I know, but I want to. We're family. And not just any family. We're Latinos, Isa. We look out for each other."

He hands me a check totaling the amount of the overdue rent.

"What is this?" I blink rapidly, trying to comprehend what is going on.

"I called your landlord, Gabriel, and found out how much La Mariposa owes. Here's the amount you need to get her back to the green. Then, when I get back from our honeymoon, we can get started."

"Luc, I can't accept this," I say.

"Just hold on to it. Think about it. Wait until I come back, and we can talk some more. Promise me you'll at least do that?"

He extends his arm out for a handshake. The handshake will signify that we have a deal. The one motion that could change my life. La Mariposa could stay open. Faye would keep their job. I would keep my job. I'd figure out how to change the business over to me instead of my mother. With this one handshake, I will have done everything I set out to do here. I will have saved La Mariposa, impressed Luciano, and discovered the big family secret.

"All right, I'll think about it," I finally agree, extending my hand.

He reaches in for a hug and lifts me off the ground as a big brother would do. I have a brother now too. I wish I could get a T-shirt in the gift shop that says, "I Went to Camp Hollow Pines for a Wedding, and All I Got Was an Entire Family."

He sets me down and goes back to packing the car. I walk over to Sofia and give her a huge hug.

"I'm going to miss you…sis. It's weird not saying 'prima' anymore, isn't it?" I laugh.

"It is. But we'll get used to it. I'm so happy for you, Isa. I also really can't wait to see what you end up doing. But you better stay in New Jersey! Don't get up and move to California or something. I just got a new sister. I can't have you going on some ten-year-long soul-searching journey, okay?"

"I won't," I say with a chuckle. "I love my home."

"Bueno, you also have Valentina now, too, huh?" She winks. "You two look so cute together! Don't fuck this up, Isa. I'll kill you. I'll come back from Greece and murder you."

"I'll do my absolute best," I promise.

"Good. Don't forget to say bye to my mom before you go. If not, she'll call me and complain about it the entire way to the airport, and I just cannot deal with that. I'm in honeymoon mode. The wedding stress is finally over! Well, ciao, my former prima. I love you!"

I wave as the car drives off, moving farther and farther away from my line of sight. I already know I will be seeing an excessive amount of photos of their vacation for the next three weeks, both on my phone and on social media. I'm excited at the thought. Finally, I get to be a part of my sister's life. The sister I never knew I had. I don't want to miss even a single second of it. I'm already mentally planning the trips we will be going on together to make up for the lost time. Maybe a road trip to Maine? A tropical girls' vacation to Puerto Vallarta? A cross-country train ride to every ghost town in the US? The possibilities are endless.

I continue to walk the campground since I need to drop the key to the main hall at the front desk for Daniel, who has been working tirelessly at getting everyone checked out. Probably to make sure no one is trying to stay behind and live in one of the cabins with their new girlfriend to hunt squirrels and chop firewood. I pass by Rosita's cabin. The door is wide open, and I can see her shuffling inside, gathering the last of her things.

"Hola, Tía!"

"Isabellita! How are you? You know I'm not technically your aunt anymore, verdad?"

"You'll always be Tía Rosita to me," I say, grinning. "You're my family and always will be."

"Ay, mija, Don't make me cry. I cried enough yesterday watching my only daughter get married. Ahora que? Now, what do I do with my life?"

I watch as she zips up her luggage and places it on the ground. She straightens the room a bit before slowly heading out the cabin door.

"You're not alone, Tía. You've got me now. And Sofia isn't going anywhere, trust me. So it's going to feel like nothing has changed. Except now you get an extra sort-of daughter to bother!" I laugh.

"I'm so proud of you, Isabella. You've grown so much, even with the loss of your father and the burden of taking over his restaurant. You persevered. You're a lot stronger than you think you are. I can't wait to continue seeing you grow, but this time not from the sidelines. I want to be up front and center. I want to be in your life, learning all the amazing things you know, seeing the things you create, and being a support system whenever needed. Te quiero tanto, mija. If it weren't for you, I would have never been able to tell you any of these things. Gracias. Por todo."

I embrace Rosita, and my eyes immediately fill with tears. I didn't realize how much I needed this. I swore my entire life that I was okay being an only child. I was okay only living my life with my mother once my father died. I was okay going home to my cat and not having a real social life because it meant I was taking care of my mother and keeping the restaurant afloat. I never realized how badly I wanted a family. A real family. A connection with people, even if they aren't all blood-related. It doesn't matter. Because blood doesn't make a family. How you treat each other, support each other, and love each other makes you a family. To me, Sofia is not my half sister. She's just my sister. Rosita isn't just my half sister's mother. She's known my entire life that we weren't blood-related. But to me, she's always been Tía Rosita, just like many of the other adults I grew up calling Tío or Tía. The difference is, she never made me feel like I didn't belong. She treated me like family in every way that mattered. Maybe that's why none of us ever questioned it—because in our hearts, she was always family, no matter what the biology said. She brought me sweets, attended every big milestone, and even tried to pay for me to come to this very campsite so I could have the same experience as Sofia. She is my family.

Once more, I watch as another family member drives away, back to their everyday lives. It feels as if they're driving away into a different world. Or going back to our home planet. Camp Hollow Pines feels like it's not even in the same galaxy. Stepping outside may even give me a bit of jet lag. I head over to Miss Piggy to check on Maria. She's been sitting in the car, taking selfies and catching up with friends after a week off from social media. I walk over to the back to put my luggage in.

As I lower the door, I feel someone tap my shoulder. I turn around to see Valentina standing there, grinning, but there's sadness in her eyes. She wouldn't admit to anything if I asked, so I choose not to mention it.

"Hey, babe! Are you all packed up?" I ask as I reach in for a soft kiss.

"I am. It looks like you two are ready to leave?"

"Yup. Ready to go back home. How are you doing?"

"Oh, you know. I'm good. Missing you already." She shifts between her feet.

"I know, but we'll see each other soon—I promise." I smile.

"Call me when you get back. Maybe you can schedule a date with me in between work sometime?" Valentina says shyly.

She is entirely different from the girl I remember at the beginning of the week. She was smug, bordering on arrogant, and full of way too much confidence. Now I've seen the real Valentina. The perfect combination of confidence and humility. Witty, silly, caring, and everything I've been looking for. I can't imagine my life without her. I know the second I make it down to New Jersey, I will want to call her and find out exactly what she's doing and where she is so I can rush over and hold her in my arms. Maybe she can come over and meet my cat. Whatever we do, I don't plan on ever letting her go.

"For you? Always," I finally reply and kiss her for the last time today, but not the last time forever.

I get inside Miss Piggy and wave goodbye to Valentina as I watch her get smaller and smaller from the side view mirror.

"So, pendeja, did you get the investment?" Maria asks.

"I did. He gave us a check to cover the rent," I reply.

"Oh *shiiit.* We're saved!"

I shrug. "Yeah."

"Or not? Are you not going to take the money?"

"I'm not sure yet."

"You really are a pendeja," Maria says on a sigh.

I'm not sure what's going to happen when we get back. There's so much that has changed. The future of the restaurant is uncertain. Who knows what will happen between me and my mother and our already-strained relationship? It's scary, not knowing. But I'm excited. Excited about the possibilities.

Miss Piggy sputters a few times before we drive through the gates and leave Camp Hollow Pines.

Epilogue

One Year Later

Come in. We're Open.

I turn the sign to face the street, alerting anyone passing by that we're here and ready. I twist the lock, turn on the neon "OPEN" sign, and pair the Bluetooth speaker with my phone to play the "Chill Music" playlist Valentina made. She says it brings a sense of peace to the restaurant.

It's been a year since we drove through the camp gates to our reality, and I can't believe how much has changed. I look around the restaurant. I take in a deep breath, getting a subtle scent of vanilla. The restaurant has changed so much. I decided not to take Luciano's money, and La Mariposa did end up closing. It just wasn't meant to be. I like to think it was just time for that chapter to end. It was almost like closure for me, letting go of the only memory of my father I thought I had. When I returned, I told my mother the restaurant was closing. She wasn't thrilled. We got into a huge fight about it. She kept blaming Rosita, Roberto, and even me for everything. I'm no longer the perfect daughter in her eyes. I messed everything up. We don't talk much anymore, and I'm no longer plagued with the guilt of calling her every day or trying to keep the restaurant afloat so she doesn't hate me or tell me I'm not good enough. I'm past that now. Maybe our relationship will change one day, but I'm still healing for now.

"Morning!" Faye walks in the front door, causing the bell to ding.

"Morning, Faye! Did you grab the—"

"The marketing materials from the print shop? You know it. And I even stopped by the coffee shop and got a little treat," they say, shaking their iced drink.

They don't have to tell me that it's most certainly a pumpkin spice latte. 'Tis the season, I guess. They hand me the papers, and I look at each one carefully, making sure there aren't any misprints or typos. They don't need to be perfect, I try to remind myself. But when you're running a new restaurant, you want to make a good impression at every opportunity.

I look at the menu flyers. The restaurant's name is on the top in a pale-pink color: La Florecita. The little flower. I smile every time I see the name.

"I'll get started on the arroz con leche for our special this weekend," Faye says as they put their name tag on that reads "Manager."

Once I realized I didn't want to run a restaurant alone, I did the one thing I should have done years ago. I promoted Faye to manager and gave them a hell of a lot of responsibilities, which they handle beautifully. I couldn't have picked a better employee to be a part of my crew.

"Is Valentina coming by later? I wanted her to see the new logo ideas I've marked up."

"Why does she need to when I'm right here?" I joke.

Faye laughs. "Well, I doubt the co-owner would be too happy if she didn't also approve of the logo designs, Isa."

When La Mariposa closed, Valentina and I made a huge decision together. We took out a business loan and bought La

Mariposa from my mother to reopen it. That way, I knew she'd have enough money to live comfortably for the rest of her life, and I could live the life I truly wanted to experience. It was the wisest business decision I have ever made. Valentina completely revamped the restaurant. With my permission, she gave the whole place a paint job. It went from that tacky sponge pattern to a crisp, creamy white. She hung plants from the ceiling near the front window. She claims it gives the impression of "health," which makes me laugh when I think of the arroz con leche Faye is currently making in the kitchen. The fish tank is also gone, so I no longer have to imagine drowning myself in it because of Elvis Crespo. The tables are all lined with tablecloths, and the wood floor got a new stain.

The murals are covered up too, which was a little sad for me initially. Those murals held a lot of memories. I also experienced a serious amount of guilt when we painted over them. After a couple of panic attacks, we could cover them up, and it was as if a weight had been lifted off my chest. Instead, Valentina curated a beautiful collection of photographs to hang up, telling a story. Some were ones she took during her travels when she was younger. One of them was a photograph we took at Camp Hollow Pines. However, my favorite one is photo of my father standing in front of La Mariposa with the words "My dream came true" under it. I thought it was the perfect way to keep his memory alive.

"Hola, mi amor!" Valentina shouts as she walks into the restaurant.

She removes her sunglasses, and I swear it's like watching a supermodel move in slow motion. I'm still so in awe of her. I'm not sure how I got so lucky to say this woman is my girlfriend, but I sure as hell will not question it.

"How's everything going?"

"Great. Faye gave me the flyers to mail out and also created some logo designs that they want to show us. Inventory is stocked, and we're ready to fire it up."

Unsurprisingly, when you go into business with someone who understands marketing and running a business, your business can succeed. Gone are the signs that say "DELICIOUS CUBAN FOOT" on them. We had a booming grand opening six months ago, and we've been going strong since. Each month, our revenue increases. I don't know how she does it. She has been able to get us a promotional spot on the local radio. She's completely revamped our social media channels and hired Maria full-time as our social media manager, which has increased our followers to tens of thousands. The best part about it all is that I'm not alone. I don't feel like I'm juggling ninety things simultaneously, trying to keep the restaurant afloat. I don't have a massive to-do list every day for work that I feel obliged to complete in its entirety to avoid failing. I can delegate work to other people now. Every employee has received more responsibilities. I don't have to stay late at night prepping because I'm worried my employees won't do it correctly. And once I stopped worrying, I realized they do it just fine. No, not just fine. They do it perfectly. Well, as perfect as one can.

I had everything I needed at my disposal, and I refused to see it. I was never alone. I just chose to be alone. I decided to live a lie. Not anymore. Not with Valentina, Maria, Faye, Sofia, and Rosita on my side. It's practically a family business, even if we're not all family.

"All right, Faye. These logos look great, and we'll discuss them more tomorrow. Sound good?" Valentina says.

"You've got it. I've got everything under control here."

"I have no doubt. Here's your to-do list for the night," I say with a stupid grin on my face. Giving someone else a to-do list that would have plagued me all night is probably one of the best feelings I'll ever experience. At least for a while.

Valentina and I are heading out for our weekly date night.

Barring death or a major catastrophe, nothing keeps me at this restaurant. I don't need to be here 24-7. I need to live my life, and my life now involves the most beautiful, unique woman. Not only am I taking her to a nice restaurant to eat a delicious meal, but I'm finally *living.*

As we walk out the door, I touch my pocket to make sure the ring box is still there, ready to change my life forever.

★★★★★